THE

FATE *of*
MERCY
ALBAN

ALSO BY WENDY WEBB
The Tale of the Halcyon Crane

THE FATE *of* MERCY ALBAN

WENDY WEBB

HYPERION
NEW YORK

Library of Congress Cataloging-in-Publication Data

Webb, Wendy.
   The fate of Mercy Alban/Wendy Webb.—1st ed.
      p. cm.
   ISBN 978-1-4013-4193-0
   1. Single mothers—Fiction.   2. Family secrets—
Fiction.   I. Title.
   PS3623.E3926F38 2013
   813'.6—dc23

                              2012027376

Hyperion books are available for special promotions and
premiums. For details contact the HarperCollins Special
Markets Department in the New York office at 212-207-7528,
fax 212-207-7222, or email spsales@harpercollins.com.

FIRST EDITION

Book design by Karen Minster

10 9 8 7 6 5 4 3 2 1

FOR MY
PARENTS,

Joan and Toby
Webb

CHAPTER 1

People were gathering at Alban House for the family's annual summer solstice party—a happy occasion. At least it was supposed to be.

Fate Alban had come running down into the garden that morning wearing the delicate floral print dress she used to like so much, her wispy cornsilk hair fluttering behind her as she ran. She was laughing, a big, throaty laugh that seemed impossible coming out of a girl as small as she. Adele had been sketching on the cool marble bench next to the fountain when Fate flopped down beside her, breathless, and said: "Draw me, why don't you?"

So Adele turned to a new page in her sketchbook and put pencil to paper, amused by the way Fate's hair was framing her face like a halo. The sunlight streamed through the leaves, and Fate blinked against it before placing one hand, wrist as slim as a reed, across her forehead.

Adele looked down at her sketchbook and was surprised to see she hadn't drawn Fate's face, not exactly. It was off somehow. Adele wondered what she had gotten wrong—the angle of Fate's nose? the arch of her brow?—and she squinted to focus more intently on the page.

As she looked closer, the drawing began to move and shimmer, its eyes glowing with life, its mouth contorting from Fate's sweet grin into a wicked smile baring the teeth of a predator. Adele tried to tear her eyes away from the image but found she was caught there, locked into whatever malevolent magic had suddenly taken hold of the page. She could not look away as the image of Fate's beautiful face morphed into that of a hideous demon.

"I'm coming for you," the image hissed.

Adele's eyes shot open and she sat up with a start. She looked around her room, quieting her racing heart by taking in the familiar—yes, there was her desk, the fireplace, the tapestry hanging on the wall—reminding herself she was safe. That terrible day was long in the past. But even after a lifetime filled with love and loss, births and deaths, weddings and funerals, and the glorious minutiae of everyday living, the memory still gnawed at Adele, creeping every so often out of the vault she had constructed inside of her heart to contain it.

A soft rapping at the door brought Adele back to herself, shaking the familiar dream and the ache that always came with it from her mind.

Jane poked her head into the room. "You awake, Mrs. Alban?"

"I'm up, Jane." Adele smiled as she slid her feet into slippers and rested a moment, making sure she was steady enough to stand. "It's a strange sensation, dreaming I'm twenty years old and waking up to seventy. Doesn't seem quite fair, somehow."

"Beats the alternative, so it does." Jane chuckled, crossing the room to draw back the curtains and open the French doors leading out to the patio. "I've got your breakfast all set up out here. Shall I help you?" She came toward Adele, holding her arms wide.

"I can manage, for goodness' sake." Adele wrapped a thick terrycloth robe around her brittle frame. "She's old and rusty, but she still runs."

Jane hovered as Adele made her way out the doors and onto the patio, where coffee, yogurt, croissants, and the morning paper were waiting. Adele braced herself on the back of the chair before sinking down into it. "Another gorgeous morning," she said with a sigh, gazing out over the lake. "I'll tell you, Jane, if I live to be two hundred years old, I'll never tire of this view."

Before her lay a wide expanse of water; steam hovered just above the lake's surface. A rower appeared out of the fog, gliding up the shoreline before vanishing silently into the mist. In another time, Adele would've been out there with him, greeting the early morning with the familiar push-and-pull movements she loved. Not anymore. How many decades had it been since she last rowed?

Jane poured a cup of coffee and Adele added a splash of cream before lifting it to her lips, savoring the heat as it slipped down her throat.

"The journalist called again," Jane sniffed. "He's not going away quietly, that one."

Adele rolled her eyes as she tore off a piece of a croissant and buttered it. "I'm too old for this, Jane."

"Aren't we all?" she said.

"Maybe I shouldn't have opened the house to tours. It's when strangers started coming that all of this was dredged up again."

Adele took another sip of her coffee, the dream still hovering on the edges of her mind.

"You were here that summer," she said, the past closing in around her as she stared out across the hazy lake. "You had come over from the old country with your mother years before, isn't that right? You were learning what it took to run this household, even then, young as you were. Your mother was teaching you the tricks of the trade."

"That's right, ma'am, sure enough." Jane smiled. It was a conversation the two women had had often over the years.

Adele nodded and let out a sigh. "So long ago. You know, Jane, you and I, Mr. Jameson, and Carter are the only ones still alive who were here that summer. When we're gone, nobody will remember what really happened that day."

Jane put a hand on Adele's shoulder. "Aye," she said, "but perhaps that's just how it should be. Let the spirits of the dead rest, I say."

Adele swiveled in her chair to look at the hill in the back of the house. "I'm not so sure about that," she said. "I've been thinking—maybe I will talk to the man, Jane. Maybe it's time the truth comes out. Call him back, will you? Tell him to come this afternoon."

She chewed her croissant as she considered what to do next. "Before he comes, I think I'll go for a walk on the hill," she said finally. "It'll do me good, getting a bit of exercise."

Jane crossed her arms in front of her chest. "Do you think that's wise, ma'am? You've been ill and . . ." She clucked in disapproval.

"Oh, I know it's not wise." Adele chuckled. "But at my age, who cares?"

"Shall I ask Mr. Jameson to accompany you?"

"I'm sure he's got enough to do in the garden." Adele smiled, rising from the table. "I'll be fine on my own."

Jane knew better than to try to talk the woman out of whatever she set her mind to doing. Half an hour later, she watched from the patio as Adele pushed open the side door, waved, and started across the lawn.

The walk took Adele's breath quickly, much more quickly than she had remembered, and at this, she smirked. *The ravages of age.* When she reached the hilltop, she sank down into the soft grass, breathing heavily, and surveyed what was before her.

From this height, she could see all fifteen acres of the property—the house, the extensive gardens, the lawn, and the lakeshore beyond it. If she turned a bit, she could follow the shoreline all the way to downtown, where new shops and restaurants were popping up in the century-old storefronts. She saw the paved path, all four miles of it, snaking along the shoreline, where people were riding their bicycles, walking dogs, or running. A single freighter hovered on the horizon of this Great Lake as gaggles of kayakers paddled their way up the shore. Tourists were waking up in the hotels along the beach, she thought, and marveling at the view. It really was quite magnificent.

That's when she heard the noise, soft and low. A delicate hissing on the wind. Whispers all around her. Adele put a hand to her throat and turned her head this way and that but saw nothing out of the ordinary. Grass bowing low in greeting to the soft breeze. A hummingbird visiting a flower. A caterpillar feasting on a leaf. She exhaled, satisfied she had been imagining things. No whispers here.

But then she heard it again. Louder this time. A voice?

She tried to listen closely—her ears were full of the ringing that came with age—but she couldn't quite make out what the voice was saying. She wasn't even sure of the language. It sounded ancient and guttural, like it was coming from another place, a

more savage and primitive time. And then the memory hit her—
she had heard this voice once before, on a summer night many
years ago. But it couldn't be. Could it?

Adele shuddered and rose to her feet, wanting very much to
be in the company of someone else. Jane, Mr. Jameson, anyone.
She hurried down the hill toward the fountain where she had
found him that night, all those years ago. But the voice was
louder there. It came swiftly nearer until it was right behind her,
whispering in her ear. She swung around and could not believe
her eyes. *What sort of magic is this?* It was the last thought that
ran through her mind before everything went black.

CHAPTER 2

Jane looked at the clock. That journalist would be here in no time, now wouldn't he? Where was Mrs. Alban? Jane rambled from the living room to the library, poked her head into the study—no sign of her employer anywhere. And she certainly wouldn't be in the kitchen, Jane thought with a hint of a smile.

"Mrs. Alban?" she called up the grand staircase. No response. Jane put her hand on the cherry-wood banister and thought about the dusting she'd do tomorrow.

Reaching the second floor, she scurried down the hallway and knocked quickly on the door of the master suite. She pushed open the door and poked her head inside. "Ma'am?"

And then it settled around her like a cloak, the deafening silence. There was no energy, no noise, no signs of life. This enormous house was empty but for her.

Jane hurried down the stairs and out onto the front patio, spotting the gardener kneeling over a rosebush.

"Mr. Jameson!" Jane called out, rushing toward him down the smooth marble patio steps and into the immaculately manicured English garden that he had coaxed to life in this harsh, northern climate for a half century. She was out of breath when she reached him and took a moment to recover before speaking.

"And what can I do for you, Mrs. Jameson?" Her husband, Thomas Jameson, smiled at her.

"It's herself," she said breathlessly, looking into his eyes and putting a hand on his chest. "She went out for a walk on the hill this morning and hasn't come back. That fool journalist is supposed to be here soon, and . . ." She stopped as she watched her husband's expression fade from amusement into worry.

"How long ago, did you say?"

"About an hour. A bit more than that now."

"Did she have any shopping to do?" Mr. Jameson asked, looking across the rose garden toward the carriage house where Carter, the family's driver, lived. "I didn't notice the car pull out, but Carter might have driven her somewhere."

Jane shook her head. "I don't think so. Why would she go anywhere when someone was coming here to meet with her?"

"All the same, I'll check in with him. And I'll get the lads to help us search the grounds." He put down his shears and took his wife's hands into his own. "Don't you worry, dear. I'm sure she's all right. We'll find her. You go back up to the house now and wait."

As Mr. Jameson strode off in search of Carter and the two young men he had hired earlier that spring to help with the gardens, Jane hurried back up the steps to the house. *Where was the old girl?* She rushed from one room to another, one floor to another. Forty rooms later, Jane was officially panicked.

She wound up in the green-and-black-tiled solarium, a room full of leafy plants, gurgling fountains, and plush sofas and chairs, where Mrs. Alban always took her tea in the afternoons.

Breathing heavily after all that rushing around, Jane sank down onto one of the wicker chairs and fished a tissue out of the pocket of her apron, dabbing at her brow. But she couldn't sit still. The feeling, the same one that had taken hold of her moments before when she was upstairs, was stronger now. No-body else was alive in this house.

"Mrs. Jameson!" Her husband's muffled voice startled Jane, and she pushed herself up to her feet and rushed out the doors onto the patio where he and Carter were climbing the steps to-ward the house.

"Well?" Jane asked, knowing the answer by the look on her husband's face.

"Nary a trace," he said. "We've searched the entire grounds. More than once. Even the cemetery beyond, thinking she might have been visiting the relatives, so to speak."

Carter shook his head. "I don't like this."

"I don't like it, either," Jane said, her voice a low whisper. "Something just doesn't feel right."

"Aye," her husband said, pulling the blue felt fisherman's cap from his head and twisting it in his hands. "Aye."

"Tell the lads to search the grounds again," she said. "I'll get us some iced tea while we wait. But if they don't find her soon, it might be time to call the police."

A few moments later, Jane joined her husband and Carter on the patio with a pitcher of iced tea and three glasses on a tray.

As she was pouring, Jane's gaze drifted toward the main garden in front of the house, the one with the fountain and the manicured hedges. Her shriek pierced the afternoon's silence as the pitcher tumbled out of her hand and shattered on the cool cement floor, the dark tea pooling in the crevices like blood.

After a restless flight from Seattle to Minneapolis, my daughter and I rented a car and drove northward, watching the landscape change from city to suburb to farm fields to pine forests. Cresting the top of the hill near Spirit Mountain, I took a quick breath in as I saw the expansive view before me—the bay between the cities of Duluth and Superior, the iconic Aerial Lift Bridge, rising and falling to accommodate the massive ships that needed to get into the port, and the flood of city on either side of the bay that seemed to have crested in my absence. Beyond all that, the vastness and ferocity of Lake Superior shimmered. Taking it in for the first time in two decades, I felt my stomach twist itself into knots.

I had come home to bury my mother, an event that seemed as surreal to me as the circumstances of her passing. As I drove down the hill toward town, it felt like time itself was ticking backward, the years folding in on top of themselves as though I were leafing through a book, back to the page when my mother was a vibrant fifty-year-old who still rowed on this greatest of lakes every summer morning. It simply didn't seem possible that death could find her or, if it did, that she couldn't persuade it to come back another day.

I wondered if it all hadn't been a mistake, if I would arrive at the house to find her on the patio sipping a glass of lemonade or a gin and tonic, as she liked to do in the summer months.

Looking back on it now, it wouldn't surprise me if my mother's spirit had indeed been hovering as I drove toward the house that day. Not to welcome me home but to warn me of what was awaiting me there—memories that would unearth themselves from the graves I had dug to contain them, and things much stranger than that, monstrous things that would creep and lurk and hide. I've always known that old houses are full of such things, Alban House most of all.

As I turned into our driveway, I gasped aloud when I saw a ticket booth at the end of what was now a parking lot. I knew the croquet lawn had been paved over, but it still gave me a jolt to see dark asphalt where the grass my father tended so carefully—obsessively, my mother always teased—used to be.

Visions of our annual summer parties crept into my mind—girls in cotton dresses, boys in seersucker suits, lemonade we'd secretly spike with vodka. A croquet tournament in the afternoon; a bonfire on the lakeshore at night. I could see the shadows of my brothers, the twins Jake and Jimmy, running their ridiculous victory lap around the croquet lawn, mallets held high over their heads. The sound of their laughter floated around me before diminishing little by little until it was gone, as if it were buoyed downstream on a river of memory that flowed through this place and through me.

My daughter's voice pulled me back from those visions of the past. "What's that?" she asked, pointing toward the booth and pulling the earbuds out of her ears for the first time in the nearly three hours it took to drive here from the Minneapolis airport.

"The house is, well . . . it's sort of a museum now, remember?" I reminded her.

Amity's face didn't betray any hint of recognition. She furrowed her brows. "What do you mean, a museum?"

"We talked about this, honey."

She opened her eyes wide and shrugged with the particular type of silent sarcasm that only teenage girls seemed to possess. I sighed and tried again. "The university asked us if it could conduct public tours of the first floor of the house and the garden because of their historic value. I told you all of this last year."

"I don't get it. It's just an old house."

"Oh, Amity, for goodness' sake." I pulled through the parking lot and into our driveway. "Why don't you read a history book or, better yet, listen when your family talks to you? In any case, it couldn't matter less right now."

Instantly, I regretted my shortness with her and put my hand on her arm. "Sorry, honey," I started, but she had already slumped back into her seat and put the earbuds back into her ears. Another fantastic mother-daughter moment.

As I climbed out of the car, I noticed a woman poke her head out the ticket booth's door, eye us suspiciously, and then skitter across the parking lot toward us, her high heels clicking all the way. "Excuse me!" she chirped, wagging a finger at me. "Excuse me! You can't park there!"

I ignored her and opened the rental car's tailgate as Amity unfolded herself from the passenger seat.

"This driveway isn't for visitors, and besides, the house is closed," the woman huffed, finally reaching us. "I'm sorry, but there are no tours today or for the foreseeable future. And we don't want people wandering around the gardens on their own. That's not allowed."

"I'm not here for a tour," I said, managing a smile. "I'm Grace Alban." I watched as the woman's scowl melted into confusion and then recognition.

Then a breathless stream of backpedaling. "Oh! Miss Alban! I'm so sorry! I should have recognized you right away!"

"That's okay," I said with a nod. "I haven't been here in quite a while. Thanks for being so vigilant, keeping people out. We appreciate it, especially now."

"I'm Susan Johnson," she said quickly, still staring wide-eyed at me. "I'm with the university. I'm just here gathering some things. We're not sure how long the house will be closed or if we'll be able to open it up again." She squinted at me. "I suppose that's up to you now."

I supposed it was.

She clutched her clipboard tighter to her chest. "I'm so sorry about your mother. We all are. What a wonderful lady."

Tears were stinging at my eyes, so I grabbed my bag from the back of the car and nodded to Amity to do the same. "Thank you," I said to the woman as I popped the suitcase's handle up into place, grateful for something to distract me from her concerned face. "We'll be in touch with you about reopening, but don't plan on it for a while."

"Of course. And, Miss Alban, this goes without saying, but if there's anything the university can do . . ."

"Thank you," I said to her again, eyeing her name tag. "Susan."

I turned and let myself look at my home, Alban House, for the first time in twenty years. The redbrick façade rising three stories tall, the parapets jutting out from the roof, the enormous stone patio running the entire length of the house facing the lake, the stairs down to the gardens that framed the property—none of it had changed at all.

Growing up in Alban House, I felt I was a princess living in an enchanted castle, and indeed, the house was designed to look like one, patterned after the Jacobean estates European kings built for themselves in centuries past. But I soon learned people who lived in castles—the ones I read about in my storybook fairy tales—didn't necessarily live enchanted lives. Not sweetly enchanted, anyway. Strange and otherworldly things swirled around them, threatening, no, *wanting* their happiness. At least that's how the stories I read went. I held my breath as I realized I was walking right back into mine.

As I climbed the patio steps, I could almost see my mother standing there, her arms open wide. Jane ran right through the very spot, dissipating the image into wispy shards that fluttered away on the wind. "Oh, my girl," Jane whispered into my hair as she threw her arms around me and hugged me tight. "Finally back where you belong."

I relaxed into her embrace and felt the stress of the past few days begin to melt away. I put my head onto her shoulder and wanted nothing more than to stay there for a good long while—safe and comforted by the woman who had always handled everything for my family for as long as I could remember.

"And Amity, dear," Jane said, cupping a hand to my daughter's cheek. "Haven't you grown since the last time you were here! You're taller than your mother already. What grade will you be starting in the fall? Eleventh, is it?"

Amity smiled at this. "That's right. I'll be a junior. Nice to see you, too, Jane." She gave me a sideways glance. "Should I take this stuff up to my room?"

I nodded, knowing my daughter wanted nothing more than to escape adult company, flop onto her bed, and start texting her friends. "Sure, honey. Go and get settled. I need to talk to Jane. Then I'll be up and we'll see about dinner."

Amity lugged her suitcase across the patio, pulled open one of the massive wooden front doors, and disappeared inside.

"It meant the world to your mother that you sent the girl here every summer, once she was old enough," Jane said to me, fishing a balled-up tissue out of her sleeve and dabbing her eyes with it. "Mrs. Alban doted on Amity, so she did."

I cleared the sadness and shame from my throat. "Now I wish I had come with her. I wish . . ."

"I know, child. I know."

Jane hooked her arm into mine and I let her lead me to the patio table. The sight of it, after all these years, gave me a pang of melancholy that reverberated through my whole body. The huge wooden table, with seating for fourteen, had always reminded me of something out of an ancient Celtic legend. My great-grandfather had imported it, and much of the materials used to build the house, from Ireland when he broke ground on this place in the late 1800s—at least that was how the story went.

We used to have meals on the patio during the warm summer months and even into the fall, Mother, Daddy, Jake, Jimmy, and me, along with whatever friends were circulating in our orbit at the time.

I thought of those days, and there it was again—the twins' laughter, low, musical, infectious. I wished it would engulf me and carry me along whatever river their giggling was floating on, back to another time in this same place, back to evenings when my family debated our way through mealtimes, talking about art and politics and literature and even celebrity scandals of the moment; carrying me back further still to the days when our mother would wrestle with the cook for the kitchen so she could bake for us herself, greeting us with love and good humor and a plate of warm chocolate chip cookies as we came through the door after a long day of school; and back further to lazy summer afternoons when my brothers and I would lie on the lakeshore counting the sailboats as they passed.

And now they were all gone. Only I remained.

Jane's voice dissolved these memories. "I thought you might like a bite of something after your journey," she said, patting my hand. I saw she had set one end of the table with a bottle of wine, a basket of bread, some sliced cheeses.

I couldn't remember the last meal I had eaten. Lunch yesterday? Or was it dinner the night before? Time was a blur ever since I got Jane's call. I pulled out one of the heavy wrought-iron chairs and sank into it with a sigh. "This is just what I needed. Thank you."

She hovered beside me, waiting. "Please, Jane, join me," I said, gesturing to the chair next to mine. Even after more than fifty years of running this house, she still stood on ceremony.

I poured some wine for us both and took a big bite of the crusty bread and cheese, Gouda with caraway, which she knew was my favorite. With all she had been through in the past few days, Jane still took the time to attend to the little things to make me feel welcome.

She peered into her wineglass, a bit scandalized. She smiled, and I saw a devilish glint in her eye. "I suppose I could have a wee nip."

Dear Jane. I had missed her gentle, good humor, the brogue making music of her words. I smiled at her for a moment but could feel my smile fade as quickly as it came. I had been dreading this conversation, yet I knew now was the time. I took a deep breath, let it out in a long sigh, and said: "You said on the phone you didn't want to tell me the whole story until we could sit face-to-face. So here we are. What exactly happened, Jane?"

Jane shook her head. "I still don't rightly know."

I waited as Jane smoothed the apron in her lap. Finally, she began. "Your mother had her breakfast on the second-floor patio, right outside her bedroom, as usual. I told her that journalist called again, the man interested in writing the book about Alban House, and—"

I held up a hand to stop her story and squinted at her. "Wait a minute. What book?"

She sighed. "They're always poking around here, the writers, especially after Mrs. Alban opened the house up to tours. They're wanting to know about *that night*. Some want to know about the supposed Alban *curse*." She spat out this last word as though it was tart on her tongue.

I rolled my eyes. "Not that again. You know, Jane, people die in other families and nobody thinks it's a curse. Why can't they just leave it alone? She told him to shove off, right?"

"Not this time." Jane lowered her voice, narrowed her eyes, and looked back and forth, as though checking to make sure no one was listening. "She asked me to tell him to come that afternoon. She was going to talk to him."

I nearly choked on the sip of wine I had just taken. "You're kidding me."

"No. She said she thought it was time. It was then she went out. Walked out the back door, waved good-bye, and that was the last time I saw her." Jane's gaze dropped to her lap, where she clutched a tissue. "Alive," she added.

I reached over and took her hands, dry and red from years of working in the kitchen. "I can't imagine how hard it must've been for you."

"Aye," Jane sniffed. As she dabbed at her eyes, I could see the years had settled into their corners, creating deep grooves where her faint laugh lines had been the last time I had seen her.

Jane cleared her throat and went on. "An hour or so passed, and then I started to get worried. The journalist would be on his way, and there was no sign of your mother. That's when I sent Mr. Jameson and Carter out to look for her."

"But you found her in the study, right? That's what the police said."

She shook her head. "No. That's what I told the police, and it's what they in turn told the reporters, but . . ."

"What, Jane?"

"Your mother disappeared. Vanished. Carter, Mr. Jameson, and his two assistants—those lads he's got helping in the garden for the summer—they searched the entire grounds. I searched this house. She was nowhere to be found. She was not in the study."

"But—"

"I know how it sounds. But I'm telling you, child. She was gone. We searched for more than an hour."

Dread hung in the air, surrounding me. I wanted her to continue, but I couldn't formulate the words to ask.

"Just when I was about to phone the police, we found her." She lowered her voice to a whisper. "Not in the study. In the main garden. She was . . ." Jane stopped, took a deep breath in, and continued, her next words rushing forth like a waterfall. "She was laid out there, with her hands folded across her chest, on the bench by the fountain. As though she were in repose."

I snapped my head around and looked toward the front of the house. "But you said they looked for her outside. You can see the fountain from right here. If she—"

"That's what I'm telling you, girl. They had gone through that garden a thousand times, looking for her. She wasn't there. And then, suddenly, she was."

I held Jane's gaze, shaking my head from side to side. The urge to get up and run away from this whole situation was overwhelming. As if she could see what I was thinking, Jane grabbed my hands and held them, and me, tight.

"I couldn't have the police finding her like that, now, could I? In the same spot, the very same spot, where they found *him* all those years ago. The newspapers would have had a field day. We didn't need that; you didn't need that. So I had Mr. Jameson and Carter carry her into the study. Then we made the call to the police."

I exhaled, not realizing I had been holding my breath the entire time. "You're right, Jane. That kind of publicity is the last thing we need right now."

I poured another glass of wine and gulped it down, thinking it might help quiet the violent shivering that was coursing through my body. It didn't. I set the glass down on the table so I wouldn't drop it.

"What are you saying, Jane? Do you think my mother was—" I had trouble formulating the word. "Murdered?"

Jane shook her head. "It doesn't seem possible. Who would do something like that? And why? Your mother was the salt of the earth."

I let her remark sink in. She was right; there was nobody who would want to hurt my mother. And yet . . . "What do the police say?" I asked finally.

"When the medical examiner was here, she said it was likely natural causes. Your mother was in her seventies, she had been ill and had a heart condition. But they're doing an autopsy so we'll know for sure."

I slumped against the back of my chair.

"So the police say it was natural causes. What do you think?"

Jane looked me in the eye. "You don't want to know what I'm thinking, my girl."

O h, Jane, don't be silly," I said to her as I pushed my chair away from the table. "You know as well as I do . . ." I turned and my gaze fell upon the brick façade of the house.

I was going to say that there was no "Alban curse" despite legends to the contrary that had circulated around my family for generations. But as I looked at the house, the words caught in my throat and hung there.

Finally, I said: "Let's not dwell on those old legends. They'll only scare Amity."

She nodded her head and stood up. "Whatever you say, miss."

I crossed the patio to the front door and pulled it open, peering into the foyer, seeing the grand staircase, the deep Oriental rugs, the sitting room beyond. It seemed to be a snapshot from my childhood, the same as it always was, as though time had never passed. But when I opened the door farther and walked hesitantly through it, I found that everything wasn't the same, not really. The familiar rugs were a little more worn in spots, the patterns on the window seat's pillows badly faded by two decades of sunshine. The cherry-wood paneling on the walls looked dull, like it could use a good polishing, and the curtains in the sitting room hung wearily, as though they had had enough already.

Age had taken root and was weaving its wickedness through

the very foundation here, making the house that had once been so solid, so formidable, so much a fortress, seem vulnerable and even a little bit fragile. I shook that thought out of my head and walked farther into my home, dragging my suitcase behind me.

A small wooden desk stood in the corner of the foyer—this was new. I ran my hand along its surface and picked up one of the flyers stacked neatly in the center.

Alban House, built in 1898, is one of this country's finest examples of turn-of-the-century technology, craftsmanship, and architecture. Built by shipping, mining, and railway magnate John James Alban . . .

A handout from the university's tours. I stuffed one into my pocket for Amity. She seemed uninterested in family history now, but she really ought to have known more about where she came from, who her ancestors were and what they did.

Jane followed behind me. "Let Mr. Jameson take your bag up to your room, child," she said to me, fussing with her apron. "I'll just call him."

"No need." I smiled quickly at her. "I can manage it." I peered up the steps, wondering whether to make my way through the kitchen to the elevator in the butler's pantry or just lug the huge bag up the stairs. "I'm going to get settled and then I suppose—I don't know, Jane. Should I start thinking about the arrangements for the funeral?"

Jane shook her head. "You needn't worry about forging ahead with any planning right now," she said, laying a hand on my shoulder. "Your mother wrote up her wishes years ago, even paid for the arrangements in advance, so you wouldn't have to wonder and fuss when this time came. I'm sure you'll find it all in her desk."

I exhaled, relieved, at least, not to be starting at square one. I wouldn't have known how to begin or whom to call—the minister, the coroner? Funeral director? It seemed inconceivable to me that I was the one who was supposed to handle all these things. When I had left Alban House twenty years earlier, I was only a few years older than my daughter was now. And suddenly I was the head of the family? The one who had to decide on, well, everything? It seemed wrong, somehow. I sighed, not quite sure of what I was supposed to do next.

As if Jane could hear my thoughts, she said: "You go upstairs and unpack. Your room is all made up with fresh linens. I'll have supper ready at six o'clock."

"Unpacking and dinner." I smiled at her. "Sounds like a plan."

I dragged my suitcase up the stairs to the second floor and set off down the long hallway toward my room. The family's bedrooms were clustered in the second floor's east wing in an effort by my parents to make the enormous house seem smaller and more intimate. In generations past, children always slept on the third floor. But when my mother married my father and they moved into Alban House with his aging parents, she made it clear she didn't like that arrangement. She wanted her family all around her, close. No nannies required.

As I walked down the hallway, I was remembering winter days when the boys and I would run down its length. The image of Jimmy, wearing those ratty old blue sneakers he loved so much, whooshed through me and down the hall, where, at the end of the west wing, we had set up a chalkboard to tally how many times we had made it back and forth. The sensation was so real—I could feel the breeze as he ran past me—that I turned to look down the hallway to see if the chalkboard was there, too, jagged tally marks in white and all. But the image faded as quickly as it came, and I was alone again in the hall.

I poked my head into the boys' old room, now used by Amity when she visited, and found my daughter flopped onto her stomach on one of the beds, her iPod so loud that I could hear its tinny music from where I stood at the door. A phone was in her hand and she was texting at rapid speed. I walked over and tapped her foot. She snapped her head around, her eyes wide.

"Don't sneak up on me like that," she said, furrowing her eyebrows at me and pulling the earbuds out of her ears. "I didn't know you were there."

"You need to turn the music down, honey," I told her. "Then you'll hear people. Besides, that's ruining your ears."

She shot me a look and went back to her texting. Why did I always do that? I knew better than to think that kind of motherly badgering did any good with my headstrong daughter.

Trying again, I sat down on the bed next to her. "Jane said dinner is at six," I said, rubbing her back. "Tomorrow's going to be busy, but we could take a walk along the lakeshore tonight. Or we could go to the malt shop. Or shopping . . . ?"

"Nah," she said, sitting up and shrugging off my touch.

Defeated, I stood up and began to walk out of the room. "Maybe we'll watch a movie later?"

"Yeah, maybe," she said, dissolving back into her texting.

I closed the door behind me. Where was the cheerful little girl who had hung on my every word not so long ago? Who was this sullen, moody changeling?

I shook my head as I made my way down the hall to my old room. Opening the door, I saw that the same white linens were on the bed, the same sheer white curtains framed the windows. The room was largely unchanged from the day I left it.

But a certain strangeness hung in the air here, too, something I couldn't quite put my finger on. And then it hit me. Emptiness. When my mother was here, even after what happened with the boys and my dad, every room in this house felt alive, warm, and loving. Now it was as cold as a tomb.

I unpacked my clothes and stuffed my empty suitcase into the back of the closet, then slid my feet into the decades-old slippers that had stood sentinel, waiting for me all this time.

"Here I am again," I whispered into the air. The walls seemed to sigh a tired welcome in response.

Back out in the hallway, I padded down to the master suite and stood outside the door. I knew I'd have to go inside—my mother kept all of her important papers in the study just off her bedroom, and I needed to find the instructions for her funeral, at the very least. But I was having trouble summoning up the courage to face the memories I knew were waiting for me there.

As I stood there leaning against the door, I felt a surge of warmth swirling around me, a soft tickling on my skin. A scent wafted through the air—lake water mixed with morning rain and the minty aroma of the type of bath soap we used as kids.

"Jake? Jimmy?" I said aloud, turning around in a circle, almost expecting to see them standing behind me, their quirky, impish grins firmly plastered on their freckled faces. "Are you here?"

I felt it then: Water. Icy cold. As though it was rising, first around my feet, then calves, then thighs—

"Who are you talking to?" Amity's voice startled me out of whatever was happening.

"Oh, honey." I scrambled, holding her wide-eyed gaze and trying to think of something plausible to say as she made her way down the hall toward me.

In the end, I admitted: "I guess I was talking to my brothers. I know it's silly, but being back here, in the house where we all grew up, and now having to go into Grandma's room . . ." My eyes began stinging with tears. I tried to brush them away, but Amity grabbed my hand and squeezed it.

"It's okay, Mom," she said to me, taking my hand, her face radiating the maturity and serenity of an old soul. "I get that this is really hard for you."

Teenagers, I thought. *Hellions one minute, angels the next.*

I wrapped her in my arms and held her tight. "Oh, Amity," I said into her hair. "I'm the one who should be comforting you. I'm the grown-up here, and you're grieving for Grandma, too."

"Nonsense. It couldn't matter less who comforts whom. What's important is that we're standing together as family," she said in a voice not quite her own . . . or maybe I thought she said it? *Nonsense? Whom?* Amity's teenage vernacular didn't typically include those words. As I stood there holding my daughter, a chill shot through me. Was it my mother speaking?

I broke our hug and looked her in the face. She smiled, back to the teenage girl that she had been moments before. "I used to like sitting with Grandma in her study," she said to me, putting her hand on the knob. "There's nothing so scary in there."

With that, she pushed open the door.

CHAPTER 5

The faint scent of my mother's perfume still hung in the air, her cardigan still lay on the end of the bed, a collection of mail sat next to the letter opener, waiting to be read. Mom had touched all these things just days ago, left her imprint. Her energy still radiated there. But it was fading, and soon everything would be cold.

"I should probably go through this mail to see if there's anything important, but . . ." My words disintegrated into a sigh.

"I know," Amity said, picking up a letter and putting it down again. "It feels weird. Like you're snooping or something."

I leafed through the stack of envelopes—a few bills, several solicitations from charities, a thick envelope from what looked to be her financial adviser.

"Honey, will you run back to my room and get my purse?" I asked my daughter. "I might as well just get these bills paid right now. We don't want the lights or water turned off."

"Sure," she said as she shrugged and walked out the door.

I continued to go through my mother's desk, opening drawers, fingering the pens and sheets of monogrammed stationery. The bottom drawer was filled with hanging file folders, mostly bill and investment related, and I touched each one in turn until my hand came upon what I had been hunting for: a folder labeled FUNERAL ARRANGEMENTS.

I lifted it from its place and opened it on the desk, finding contact information for the funeral director, the caterer, the venue for the service—our longtime family church, a hundred-year-old stone structure that stood on the lakeshore just a mile down from the house—and even the hymns she wanted to be played and the people she'd like to speak.

Both the service and the reception afterward were to be open to the public, but there was also a list of people she wanted to make sure were personally invited—the mayor, the governor, two senators, local businesspeople, university professors, artists whose careers I knew she had championed and supported. I gave silent thanks that she had left such specific instructions.

I folded that sheet and slipped it into the pocket of my cardigan, making a mental note to talk it over with Jane. Then it would be time to call the reporters, many of whom had already left messages for me. The death of an Alban in this town was big news. My head began to pound, wondering how I'd deal with their questions. That had always been my mother's job. And before that, my father's. Now there was nobody but me.

While I was sitting at the desk going through all this information, Amity had returned with my purse and was rummaging around in my mother's closet.

"All this stuff still smells like Grandma," she said, poking her head out the door. She held my gaze for a moment and went on. "It's weird to be here without her."

I closed the file. "I know, honey. It is for me, too."

She shook her head and brushed away tears from her eyes.

"You're a big help to me here, Amity." I smiled at her, not wanting to let on how much trepidation I felt. "This isn't easy, but I promise you, we'll get through it."

I went on: "And if we don't, there's Jane to scold us and pick up the pieces."

This lightened her mood a bit. "All the things you have to do after somebody dies, they're just really bizarre," she said, flopping down on the chaise by the window and wiping her eyes on her sleeve.

I understood what she meant. "In a way, though, honey, those rituals are good things. You want to just shut everything out, but you can't, because you've got to call the funeral director and make arrangements and then you've got to get dressed and go to the funeral and greet people and all of that. The rituals force you to put one foot in front of the other during the first horrible days after someone dies."

I was thinking about how I walked around like a zombie after the accident with Jake and Jimmy, how my dad didn't come out of his room for days, and how my mother somehow handled it all, arranged for everything, even attended a special candle-light memorial service put on by the boys' school.

My mother soldiered on, with a permanent tinge of melancholy in her eyes, yes, but she went on nonetheless. Where she got that strength after the deaths of two children, I'll never know, but wherever it came from, I needed to tap into some of it. I needed to be that pillar of strength for my daughter now.

"Why don't you head down to the lakeshore?" I said to her. "Or take one of the bikes out of the garage and ride on the path to downtown? I'll finish up in here and then we'll have dinner out on the patio. How does that sound?"

She nodded and unfolded herself from her slump on the chaise. "I guess I'll go down to the lake."

She opened the door but turned around before going through it. "What are you going to do now?" she asked me.

"I might as well lay out something for Grandma to wear so it will be done. Her list of instructions says she wants to wear"—I quickly unfolded the sheet and glanced at it—"a blue Chanel dress, so I guess I'll hunt around for that. I've also got to call the funeral director. Oh, and the florist." I sat down with a thud. "Lots to do."

"I'll look for the dress," Amity offered. "I know the one she means. I went shopping with her last summer when she bought it. You make those calls and then we'll both go down to the lake."

"You're some kid." I smiled at her. "You've got a deal."

As I was looking for the funeral director's number, Amity emerged from the closet, carrying the dress. She laid it on the bed, carefully smoothing out the wrinkles. "Does she want the hat, too? She wore this with a hat."

"I'm not sure—" I started, rising from my chair just in time to see her turn back to the closet and reach up onto a high shelf, where several hatboxes stood in a row. Not quite tall enough to grasp them from her tiptoes, she jumped and grabbed, and the whole shelf of boxes came down in a clatter, a shower of hats tumbling onto the floor. Amity looked at me, wide-eyed, holding up the blue hat.

I chuckled. "Well, I guess you found it." We both began to gather up the wayward hats, returning them to their boxes, careful not to rip the fragile tissue paper within.

"What's this?" she asked, scowling at something on the floor. She picked it up and held it out for me to see. It was a worn leather satchel, a little bigger than a clutch purse.

"I'm not sure," I said. "A purse to go with the hats, maybe?"

She handed it over to me. As I took it from her, I felt a tingling, a slight tremor. This wasn't a purse, not one my mother would carry, anyway. I opened its outer flap and peered inside.

"It looks like . . . letters," I murmured, and drew out a stack of two dozen or so envelopes, tied together with a faded pink silk ribbon. I flipped through them. "They're addressed to Grandma." To her maiden name, I noticed. These letters were written to my mother before she had married my father.

Amity's eyes were sparkling. "Who are they from?"

"There's no return address," I said, quickly tucking them back into the satchel. "But anyway, these are Grandma's private letters, so I really don't think we should be reading them. Do you?"

"Probably not," she said, rising to her feet, her interest waning as quickly as it had been piqued. "Is it okay if I go down to the lakeshore now?"

"Sure, honey." I nodded, and she flounced toward the door. "I'll join you in a little while."

But I stayed right where I was, sitting on the floor of my mother's closet, still holding the satchel, until Amity had closed the door behind her. I hadn't been truthful with my daughter and I didn't quite understand why. There *was* a return address on those letters.

Well, not a return *address* exactly. The initials *D.C.* were written in the corner of each envelope. When I saw them, I felt a shiver down my spine. Something about those initials gnawed at me— who was D.C.? Certainly not my dad. They sounded vaguely familiar somehow, but I couldn't quite put my finger on it.

I drew the stack of letters out of the satchel and slowly untied the worn silk ribbon around them. I knew I shouldn't be reading my mother's private correspondence, but I couldn't stop myself. This felt important somehow. I opened the first envelope and began to read.

> *September 1955*
> *My dearest Adele,*
> *I can't believe it has been only a week since I returned to*
> *Boston from Alban House. It seems like a lifetime since*
> *I held you in my arms.*

My eyes grew wide. A love letter? I knew very little about my mother's life before she married my father, and certainly nothing about her romantic life. I had always thought my dad was her first love.

I knew my mother had grown up in a middle-class family that lived a few miles down the road from Alban House and she had been the childhood best friend of my father's sister, Fate. I just assumed she and my dad knew each other as children, and he basically married the girl next door. Theirs was a lifetime romance—at least that's how they told the story to us.

So who was this charmer writing to young Adele Mitchell—I looked back at the date on the letter—just a year before she and my father were married?

She kept the letters all these years, so obviously he was very special to her, somebody whose memory she didn't quite want to let fade. It seemed romantic and lovely, and I smiled at the thought of it. "You can still surprise me, Mom," I said.

I turned to the last page of the letter to read the signature.

All my love,
D

There it was again, that gnaw of familiarity. I could feel my thoughts reaching back through all of my memory banks, searching for the information that hung just out of reach. I knew who D was, I just *knew* it.

I turned back to the first page of the letter and began to read.

September 1955
My dearest Adele,

I can't believe it has been only a week since I returned to Boston from Alban House. It seems like a lifetime since I held you in my arms.

Falling in love with you was not something I had planned—it was a whirlwind! One that I hope will encircle us for the rest of our lives. I pray that you feel the same.

I have passed the time by readying materials for my next lecture series at the university, which will begin very shortly. It seems strange—not so long ago, I was walking these hallowed halls as a student, and here I am, preparing to teach this year. To be honest with you, I still don't quite understand why my thoughts on writing are of value. But I will do the best I can and hope the students get something out of it.

I let the letter drop to the ground and stared blankly at it, my heart beating hard and fast in my chest.

I didn't need to read the rest of it to know the man who wrote these letters was David Coleville, my father's best friend when they were in college.

Before settling in at Harvard, where he met my father, Coleville was a celebrated war correspondent whose stories about the lives of ordinary people in Europe during World War II for magazines like *Life* and the *Saturday Evening Post* had won him the Pulitzer Prize three years in a row. After the war, he began to focus his writing on the home front, illuminating the zeitgeist of a generation coming of age in the early 1950s. His work has been required reading in English classes at colleges nationwide ever since.

Amid considerable buzz in the country's literary circles that he was working on his first novel, David Coleville's spectacular career ended when he shot himself to death at Alban House during a party in the summer of 1956, the same night my aunt Fate disappeared without a trace.

CHAPTER 6

David Coleville and my mother, in love with each other the year before he killed himself right here at Alban House? I can't explain exactly why, but I felt as though the entire world had shifted on its axis because of what I now knew.

That summer night in 1956, when Coleville took his own life and my aunt disappeared, had always been shrouded in a kind of mystery that was hard to define, like a shameful family secret better buried than aired. My mother had never said a word about it, never hinted that she even knew Coleville, much less loved him.

When I was in school, Coleville's work was part of the English class curriculum. The fact that he committed suicide *at my home* always came up, with the other students and even the professors looking to me for additional insight into what was generally believed to be a tragedy for modern literature. But I had no insight to give.

I had asked my parents about it when I was younger but was always rebuffed in the sternest of tones. My brothers and I whispered about it—did the writer kill Aunt Fate and then kill himself? Did she run off when she found his body? We, and all of history, knew what had happened to Coleville, but nobody knew what had happened to my aunt. It was as though the family closed ranks around that night in a secret agreement to keep silent about whatever had gone on.

That's why Jane's revelation that my mother had intended to talk to a journalist about it the day she died was so stunning to me.

"What were you going to say to him, Mom?" I whispered into the air.

And then I took a quick breath in as an icy thread crept its way through my veins. My mother died the very day she was planning to talk about something the family had kept hidden for decades. I shook my head, trying to shake off the thoughts that were taking hold. Were the two connected somehow? It just couldn't be. *Could it?*

I tried to reason it out. What possible relevance could a decades-old tragedy have today? I hadn't even thought about Coleville's suicide and my aunt's disappearance for many years. Decades. By the time I was an adult and had a family of my own, it had simply become part of the past, and not even my direct past. It was just one more scandalous tragedy at Alban House, and frankly, after my brothers' deaths, I didn't even care about it anymore. Theirs was the Alban House tragedy that haunted me, not something that had happened before I was even born.

But now, as I sat cross-legged on the floor of my mother's closet, I let my mind drift back to what I knew about that night: He was found in the main garden in front of the house during a summer solstice party, the same night my aunt Fate disappeared. That was the standard family line about the incident. But it certainly didn't say much, did it?

There would have been a police investigation into the suicide as well as into my aunt's disappearance. I can't believe my grandparents wouldn't have launched a massive search for her, paid anything, done anything to find their daughter. I know I would have. Did they? I didn't know.

I looked at the letters spread out before me, hoping that I could find some answers within them. The first letter was dated September 1955 and referenced my mother's and Coleville's recent time together at Alban House. That told me Coleville visited here the summer *before* his suicide. That's when he and my mother must have met.

I began reading the other letters, one by one. No major bombshells there—they were newsy, romantic letters from a man obviously besotted with my mother. He wrote about his lectures at the university and some of his more outrageous students. He mentioned my father often, outlining in detail their exploits during my father's last year of college. And he wrote of blossoming love, starlit walks along the shoreline, quiet afternoons in the garden. The letters were funny, tender, literate. The more I read, the more I came to know this man who loved my mother, and I began to feel a crushing sadness at the knowledge of what became of him, that he took his life right here in this house.

What drove him to do it? From these letters, written during the year before his death, it was clear to me that he wasn't suffering from the kind of depression that plagued so many writers and artists. There was no angst in his words, only hope, humor, and love.

I wondered, did my mother spurn him? She had married my father very soon after that summer. Did Coleville choose to die because she chose my dad?

I didn't have the benefit of reading her letters to him, but from what he wrote to her ("I miss you, too, darling," and "I read your wonderful letter over and over again, marveling at the fact that someone like you could love me"), it was pretty clear to me that she did indeed love him. So what happened? How did it all go so wrong?

I was nearly ready to pack up the letters when something in the last one, dated May 1956, caught my eye.

> *I'm finally finished with my novel, and as we discussed on the phone last night, I'm sending a copy of the manuscript to you before I send it to my publisher. It's going out today, parcel post, so please look for it to arrive in the next week or so.*

This didn't sound right to me. He had written this letter shortly before his death. I had studied his work in college and I knew there was talk he was working on a book, but I was sure he didn't have one published before or after he died. I read on.

> *I really do want your opinion on it. I haven't told you too much about it because I wanted to see if I truly could finish it before eliciting your thoughts. A novel is quite a different animal from a magazine article, I've found! But it's important that you, of all people, read it before it goes to press.*
>
> *You know that I began this work last summer at Alban House and that I've been secretive about it, but I'll (finally!) reveal to you now that it's about a rich and powerful family, told through the eyes of a young visitor who stays with the family for the summer and falls in love with a beautiful girl he meets there. A thinly veiled version of the events of last summer, I'll admit it. I changed the names, of course—the Albans have become the Brennans, Johnny is now Flynn, I am Michael, and you, my dear, are Lily.*

Why did I choose this subject? Aside from the built-in conflicts and characters involved in a story about a rather poor and common fellow (myself!) suddenly immersed in the world of a wealthy and powerful family, and the love story we lived, which would have been story enough, it was the rather strange experiences I had, and the supposed "Alban curse," that really drew me in. The novel is an old-fashioned ghost story, my dear, reminiscent of the works of du Maurier.

I learned much talking with Johnny, his parents, Fate, and even the staff about the family's history (did they forget they were talking to a writer?) and I've learned even more here at the university's library. What the family didn't tell me speaks volumes.

What of this supposed curse? Here's what I learned, in brief: John James (Senior) came to this country as an immigrant child when his family fled the Potato Famine in Ireland in the mid-1800s. His family was dirt poor, of course—they all were—but young J.J., as he was known, was a hardworking boy who started earning a living gathering coal that had fallen off trains in the rail yards. When he was still a young man, he bought what everyone thought was desolate land in the northern part of the state. Where he got the money for this is questionable; some sources say he won it in a poker game, others allege he killed a man for it. When iron ore was discovered on the land, he was a millionaire almost overnight and eventually became one of the richest men in the country.

When it came time for J.J. to marry, he went home to Ireland to find a bride, wanting to show everyone there what a success he had made with his life. He also wanted to build a fitting house for his bride, and while they were in Ireland he decided to import some materials from his homeland to build his castle in his new land.

We know the patio table at Alban House is an ancient Celtic relic, but maybe you didn't know that much of the wood in the house—the paneling, the floors, the beams on the ceiling in the drawing room—comes from an old-growth forest in the heart of Ireland, near where the Alban family lived way back when. J.J. had played there as a child. He paid off whomever was necessary, and much of that forest was cut down and the lumber sent to Minnesota to build Alban House.

Here's where the tale veers into the otherworldly. You know how the Celtic people love their folktales of magic, witchcraft, and fairies. As the story goes, that forest was a witch's wood. She had been imprisoned in an old oak hundreds of years earlier by a rival. And when Alban felled the trees and brought them to this country, he got her spirit in the bargain. Legend has it that her spirit has been bedeviling the Alban family ever since. Of course, that's all foolish nonsense, but that's the way the story goes in Ireland. They do love their tall tales.

Curse or not, Fate was right in what she said that first evening in the drawing room—accidents, death, scandal, and even murder have taken place in the house over the years. J.J.'s son, John Jr. (Johnny's father), reportedly grew the family's fortune exponentially during the Prohibition era running liquor over the border from Canada—it was a nasty, cutthroat business, and he was the kingpin in the area, from what I have found. We both know the man well—he's so

affable!—but I shudder to think about what he is capable of.
The blood of many stains his hands.

Anyway, that's the story in a nutshell. As I said, it's a
fictionalized version, but I'm going to rely on you, darling, to
tell me if I've skimmed too closely to the truth. The last thing
I want to do is offend Johnny and his family, all of whom
have been so good to me.

I'll see you next week, darling!
All my love,
David

So he finished the manuscript after all? That didn't jibe with
what I knew of history. I opened my mother's laptop computer
and typed "David Coleville" into the search field and watched
hundreds of hits come up.

I clicked on an encyclopedia page to read a quick biography
of the man and saw what I already knew—war correspondent,
multiple Pulitzer Prizes, a lecture series at Harvard, an impend-
ing first novel that had the literary world abuzz, career cut short
by suicide.

According to his letter, he had indeed finished his "impend-
ing first novel," and it was a ghost story about my family, no less.
But it never saw the light of day. Why?

I gathered up the letters and slipped them back into their
satchel, wondering where Coleville had unearthed that otherworldly tale about the witch's wood. I knew about the supposed
Alban curse, of course, but I had certainly never heard this witch
business before. The thought of it crept inside me like the chill on
a foggy autumn morning as I gazed around the room at the
wood paneling on the walls. I tried to shake it off, but it kept

nagging at me. I had to admit it to myself—there was something about this house. I'd always felt it. It was as though Alban House had a presence of its own that wrapped itself around us, my mother most of all.

But that was just nonsense. This was my home, not some chamber of horrors. I stood up and stretched, intending to put the satchel of letters back where I had found it. Then I thought better of it. Those letters contained information that the entire literary world would be stunned to learn. I wanted to keep it to myself, at least for now.

I hurried to my room and slipped the letters into a zipped compartment in my suitcase, remembering that I had told Amity I'd meet her on the lakeshore. I peered out my window and saw her there, talking to a young man. Jane had said they'd hired a couple of kids to help on the grounds this summer; he was one of them, no doubt. I'd just go and make sure this kid knew Amity had a mother who was close by and watching.

About halfway down the stairs, I stopped. My mother had kept Coleville's letters for fifty years; might she have kept the manuscript, too? A chill shot through me again when I thought of what the lost manuscript of David Coleville might be worth today. I wondered where it might be. I turned my head and looked back up toward the second floor—in her study? in the wall safe?—but then I shook the thought out of my mind. I had a funeral to plan, arrangements to make. I'd deal with the manuscript, if it even existed, when all of that was finished.

After dinner on the patio and a movie with Amity, I turned in early, exhausted by everything I had learned that day. During dinner, the coroner had called with the autopsy results. My mother died of a massive heart attack. There would be no further police investigation, and we could go ahead with the business of laying her to rest.

So that was all there was to it, then. The day she died, she was probably feeling tired from her walk and simply laid down to rest on the bench by the fountain and passed away right there. It was nothing sinister, nothing untoward. No Alban family curse was to blame. I chuckled lightly at the thought of it. How ridiculous.

As to why the boys didn't see her on that bench in the garden when they were searching for her—I had no explanation for that. I punched my pillow and turned onto my side.

When I did finally drift off to sleep, I dreamed strange, convoluted dreams. My brothers and my mother surrounded me, trying to speak but not able to get the words out, trying to reach me but not able to get past an invisible barrier. Jake and Jimmy were knocking on what seemed to be a plate of glass separating us, and the sound of it—*bang, bang, bang*—startled me awake. I sat up fast and looked around my room. Was it real knocking I heard?

And then I saw it, a dark figure standing at the foot of my bed. I rubbed my eyes and gasped aloud when I realized who it was.

"Dad?" I said, my voice a harsh whisper.

He was dressed in the same khaki shorts and striped polo shirt he had worn into the lake when he took his own life that horrible day after the boys died, and was drenched from head to foot, water streaming off his blond hair, down his shirt, and puddling onto the floor, covering his Top-Siders until he was ankle deep in dark, angry water.

He opened his mouth to speak, but instead of words, he put forth a spray of water filled with tiny, glistening fish. He coughed and choked until they all fell to the floor in a heap. That's when I noticed his entire body was alive with the silvery swimmers, wriggling through his hair, nestling behind his ears, poking their noses from beneath his shirt, spilling out of his pockets.

I was frozen in terror, staring at this impossible figure standing before me.

"Listen to me, Grace, I don't have much time," my father's ghost said, his voice watery and thick and distorted as though he were speaking from under the surface of the lake. "She's here, Grace. She killed your mother and she's coming for you."

"Who, Dad?" I croaked out. "Who's here?"

"I didn't think she could hurt us anymore, but she can," he went on, talking over my question as though he hadn't even heard me. "It's all true. Be on your guard, Grace."

"But, Dad!" I cried. "Who? I don't know—"

"I have to go now," he said, looking over his shoulder with a shudder. "This isn't allowed. Especially not for the likes of me. I broke the rules to get to you, to warn you."

And then he smiled, releasing another torrent of tiny fish from his mouth. "One last thing, Gracie-bird. You're the best daughter a man could ever have. I love you, sweetheart, and always did. I'm sorry for what happened, for what I said. I wasn't in my right mind, you must know that. You look after that beautiful girl of yours, now, and tell her about me. Remember that sailing trip we all took to Madeline Island? Tell her about that. Pity I never got to know her. It's one of the many crosses I bear, over here."

And then he was gone, dissolving into a million shimmering water droplets and splashing to the ground.

I opened my eyes with a start. *What had just happened?* I sat up and leaned back against the headboard. My dad had been there, and then . . . what? Had I fallen asleep? That didn't seem possible. I didn't remember closing my eyes or laying back down. Had it all been a dream?

"Mom!"

It was Amity's voice, coming from her room next door.

"Mom!"

I flew out of bed and down the hall, throwing her door open so hard it thudded on the opposite wall. I found my daughter huddled in her bed, her arms wrapped around her knees. I was at her side in an instant.

"What is it, honey?" I said, stroking her hair.

"I had a really bad dream," she said, and I could feel her limbs shivering with the force of it.

"Shh, it's okay," I whispered. "Do you want to talk about it?"

"It was a man," she said, looking back and forth in her room as though she was scanning for an intruder. "It was so strange, Mom, but he was all wet. Dripping wet. He was just standing at the foot of my bed, looking at me. Smiling."

My nerves were already on fire, and at this, they went ice cold.

"It was only a dream," I said to her, not quite believing it myself. "First night in this house. Different surroundings. I had weird dreams, too."

"You did?"

I nodded. "Do you want to come sleep with me?"

Amity took a deep breath and leaned back. "I don't think so," she said, settling down under the covers and yawning deeply, the way she used to when she was a baby. "I guess you're right," she said. "It was only a dream." She closed her eyes and then opened them again. "Will you stay with me for a while?"

"Sure." I smiled and continued to stroke her hair. I sat with her until her deep, rhythmic breathing told me she was asleep and then tiptoed out of her room and back down the hallway toward mine, my heart beating hard and fast as I did. What had just happened here? Did my daughter and I both dream the same dream, or . . . I didn't want to think about it.

I crossed the room to the window and looked out into the night. Nothing odd there. Just the garden and the lake beyond, glistening with moonlight across its surface.

Before crawling back into bed, I made it a point to check for water on the floor where my father had been standing. Nothing. Dry as a bone. It had been a dream, then.

Lying there, I listened to the sounds of the night—steam hissing in the radiators that had come to life because of the chill, wind rustling in the trees outside, the clock ticking on my desk. As I breathed in and out trying to calm myself back into sleep, it almost seemed as though the house itself—the very walls—were breathing in time with me.

I remembered feeling comforted by these sounds long ago,

and I settled back down and listened. "Shh," the house seemed to be saying.

I must've fallen asleep because the next thing I knew, the light that had finally begun filtering back into the sky awakened me. I slipped out of bed and into the shower, standing under the stream until the water ran cold, washing the previous night's "visitation" from my mind.

"THE MINISTER CALLED EARLY THIS MORNING," Jane informed me at breakfast. "He wants to go over the service with you."

I sipped my coffee. "I guess I'll need to decide on a date for the funeral. I'm thinking Friday, if nothing else is scheduled in the church for that day."

She nodded. "Would you like me to get him on the phone for you?"

I stretched and looked outside. It was a bright blue day, not a cloud in the sky, and the water was shimmering like diamonds. I had an urge to get out of the house and into the world. "I think I'll walk over to the church to talk with him," I told Jane, and then turned to my daughter. "Do you want to come with me?"

Amity finished the last of her eggs and shook her head. "I'm meeting Cody in the garden in a few minutes. Mr. Jameson said I could help them with the weeding."

Jane and I shared a grin. My daughter had never pulled a weed in her life. As Amity ran upstairs to brush her teeth, Jane whispered: "It's the young man."

"I met him yesterday," I confided when I was sure my daughter was out of earshot. "He's harmless enough. And anything to get her away from that phone and out into the fresh air is a welcome change. But ask Mr. Jameson to keep an eye on her, will you?"

Jane nodded, chuckling. "Don't you worry. He won't let the lass out of his sight."

A short while later, I had grabbed a light cardigan and was headed down the patio stairs through the gardens to the lakeshore, where a path snaked its way from our property through the woods and the cemetery beyond to the church, about a mile away. The walk would do me good.

The church was an enormous stone building, much older than Alban House, where my family had been attending services for generations. My brothers and I had been baptized there; my parents were married there. My brothers and father, along with generations of Albans before them, had had their funerals there. Now it was my mother's turn. It was truly a place of life and death for my family.

I reached the church's red wooden front door just as a man, whom I didn't recognize, pushed it open from the inside.

"Oh," I said, jumping back a bit, not expecting to see anyone except our longtime minister.

He smiled at me and leaned against the doorframe. "May I help you?"

"I-I'm here to—" I stammered, oddly tongue-tied around this man. Then, trying again: "I'm looking for Pastor Olsen."

"You're a bit late for that, I'm afraid." The man grinned. "Chip retired five years ago."

I could feel my face heating up. "Sorry. I haven't been here in a while, I guess."

"Not a problem," he said, extending his hand. "I'm Matthew Parker, the new guy. What can I do for you?"

I squinted at him as I took his hand. He was the minister? This man, who was about my age and wearing jeans, a denim shirt over a faded T-shirt, and running shoes, didn't exactly look the part.

"I'm Grace Alban," I said to him finally. "Our housekeeper told me you called. I'm here to talk about my mother's funeral."

He smiled, the recognition evident in his face as he put his other hand over our clasped pair. "Of course," he said. "Your mother has shown me so many photos of you, I should have known who you were right away. I'm so sorry about Adele. What a great lady. She made me feel so welcome here when I took over for Chip. I'm really going to miss her. I got rather used to seeing her in the front pew every Sunday."

"Thank you," I croaked out, my throat filling up with sorrow. The grief that I had been trying to hold back ever since I heard the news of her death began to claw at me. I couldn't say anything further to him without unleashing it, so I just stood there, holding his gaze.

He put his hand on my shoulder. "I was just headed down to the lake," he said gently. "Why don't you come with me and we can talk there?"

As we walked in silence down the path to a pair of red Adirondack chairs on the rocky shore, I tried to compose myself, breathing in and out, taking strength from the power of the lake itself. It was something I'd done since childhood. Long ago, the native people in this area believed that the lake was a living thing, creating myths about the Great Spirit that embodied the water. Many people still believed in its otherworldly power and its wrath. I know I did. I had seen it firsthand. It was as close to religion or faith as I got.

"I spend a lot of time down here," he said, sinking into one of the chairs. "It's a great place to think and get centered. I write a lot of my sermons right here."

I let out a deep sigh, finding my voice again. "I thought I never wanted to see this lake again, but the truth is, I hadn't realized how much I missed it until now."

"You've been away a long time," he said.

I stared out over the water. "Almost twenty years."

"Why did you leave, if you don't mind my asking?"

This man got to the heart of things, didn't he? No typical Minnesotan small talk about the weather, no chitchat. Right to the real stuff.

"There were a lot of reasons," I deflected.

He was quiet, waiting for me to go on. But I couldn't stomach that conversation, not right then. I saw it all—the dark, angry water, the stark white of the boat's keel against the gray sky, the blue jacket Jimmy was wearing.

"I'd rather—" I began, meaning to say that I'd rather just talk about the funeral, *this* funeral, thanks, but the words wouldn't come without a torrent of tears behind them. So I just sat in silence, looking out over the water, so calm now, so gentle, so comforting.

"Grace," he said, "whatever it was that kept you away from here, you need to know your mother loved you very much. She was so proud of you—she talked about you all the time."

I managed a smile. "Mom and I made our peace a while ago. After Amity was born. She came out to visit me; we talked on the phone. I sent Amity here for a few weeks each summer when she was old enough. I just haven't come back myself. I couldn't. Not until now."

He nodded and leaned forward, putting his hands on his knees. "Are you doing okay? The grief of your mother's death paired with being back home for the first time in a couple of decades—it's a lot to shoulder. A lot of memories here, and not all of them pleasant. I know about your brothers and your dad."

I thought about the troubling dream I had had the night before, but as I sat with this man on the sunny lakeshore, it didn't seem out of the realm of possibility that I could have simply conjured up the image of my dad out of grief on my first night back at the house in two decades.

"I'm fine." I managed a smile. "I'm fairly certain there's enough wine in the cellar to get me through the next few days."

"Regardless, anytime you need to talk, I'm here," he said. "Night or day. It's what I do."

He held my gaze for a moment. As I looked into his eyes, it occurred to me that I had never seen eyes that were quite so deeply turquoise, with rings of indigo at the edges. I fidgeted in my chair and cleared my throat.

"Well, I'm muddling through the arrangements," I said a little too loudly. "The caterer and funeral director and all of that."

"We can get one thing off your list right now," he said. "Do you have any thoughts about what you'd like to include in the service—hymns, readings?"

I fished my mother's list out of my pocket and handed it to him. "She left some instructions."

As he read, a smile grew across his face and he chuckled. "That's Adele, all right. She has the whole thing planned."

"We should decide on a date, too," I said. "I was thinking about Friday. Does that work?"

He pulled a phone out of his pocket and checked his calendar. "That works. How does eleven o'clock strike you?"

I nodded. "Perfect."

He perused my mother's list again and grinned. "I see she didn't want a reception in the church basement after the service. 'No ham sandwiches!' she wrote. Funny."

I felt myself smiling back at him. "I guess she couldn't imagine the governor sitting in one of those little metal folding chairs eating potluck provided by the church ladies. We'll have a reception at the house, just like she requested."

Still looking at the list, he asked: "She's going to be cremated, then?"

I nodded, even though he wasn't looking at me. I couldn't get the words out to respond. He lifted his eyes from the sheet. "It says here she wants part of her ashes scattered in the main garden by the fountain and the rest put in an urn in the family crypt."

"That's right," I croaked out. "Part of them in the garden she loved, the rest with my dad and all the Albans."

He smiled at me, a sad smile of understanding and empathy. "She gave this a lot of thought. It's nice you don't have to wonder about her last wishes. I've seen a lot of families at loose ends when this time comes."

"I'm glad of that, at least," I said, blinking the tears back from my eyes. "So, Friday, eleven o'clock it is."

He nodded. "I'll call the funeral director and make the arrangements so you won't have to deal with that. Then you and I can go through a rundown of the service so you'll know exactly what to expect."

He stood up, offering me a hand. I took it and he pulled me to my feet. "I'd love to get the particulars of the service nailed down right now, but I really should get going," he said, and for some reason, I found myself wishing he hadn't. I'd have liked to sit there on the lakeshore with him for the rest of the afternoon. But he went on: "I'm visiting parishioners at the hospital today. I don't like to go there too near to mealtimes—the smell of that food . . ."

"That's fine," I said. "We could go over the particulars of the service tonight, if you'd like to come to the house for dinner? I'm sure Jane will make something that's a bit better than hospital food."

Why did I blurt that out? I quickly did damage control. "And bring your wife, of course."

"I don't have a wife, and I'd love to come."

"An unmarried minister?" I teased as we walked back up toward the church. "I'll bet the ladies of the congregation are in a frenzy trying to marry you off."

He laughed. "You have no idea."

We reached his car, an old green Volvo, in the parking lot. "Six o'clock, then?" I said.

"Six it is."

I headed toward the path back home, feeling oddly lightened.

CHAPTER 8

W hen I told Jane about our dinner guest, she flew into high gear, calling in Candy and Michelle to help with the cleaning, laying a fire in both the parlor and the dining room fireplaces, polishing the silverware, baking bread, and preparing a chicken to roast.

"It's not a *state* dinner, you know," I said to her, walking into the kitchen just as she plunged her hands into the bread dough. "It's just dinner."

"Nonsense," Jane clucked as she kneaded. "When people are invited to this house, they have expectations."

As she buzzed around, she spread joy in her wake. She clearly loved what she was doing. A visitor was coming to Alban House and Jane was in her element, there was no doubt about that. All at once, I wondered what she was going to do when the funeral was over, when Amity and I went home and this house was empty, for good this time.

I sighed and leaned my chin on my hands, looking out the window and wishing my brothers were around to help me make some of these decisions.

LATER, I SAT WITH A BOOK in one of the oversized leather arm-chairs in the library, my legs curled up under me. It had turned from a beautiful, sunny morning into a gray, wet afternoon, and I watched as the rain hit the windows in bursts. I had nearly forgotten what a chilly, sodden mess June could be in this part of the country. Jane had laid a fire in the fireplace earlier in the day, and now it was blazing, just the thing to take the dampness out of the air.

I caught sight of Amity stomping through the hallway, a pall of negative energy radiating from her. "Hey!" I called out, and she stopped under the library's archway. "What's the matter, honey?"

"Nothing," she groaned. "It's just that I was having fun helping Mr. Jameson and Cody in the gardens all morning, but now this." She flailed an arm toward the rain hitting the window.

"Why don't you come in here with me and grab a book?" I suggested. "The library's full of interesting stuff."

"Right," she sniffed. "I don't think so." She started to walk away, but then a thought came to me, as clearly as if it had been whispered into my ear.

"If you don't feel like reading, we could explore the secret passageways instead," I said as nonchalantly as I could manage, pretending to go back to my book.

This stopped her in her tracks, just as I knew it would. I tried to stifle a smile as she turned back toward me, a scowl on her face. "What are you talking about?"

"Didn't Grandma ever tell you?" I said, leaning forward in my chair. "This house is full of hidden doors, secret passageways, rooms within the walls. There are tunnels to the lake and the gardens and even to the cemetery."

She raised her eyebrows and crossed her arms over her chest, jutting one hip out to the side. "Seriously?"

"Seriously," I said, closing my book and setting it on the end table nearest me. "My brothers—your uncles—and I discovered them when we were kids, and we used to play in them all the time."

"Why would old John James Alban the First have built this house with secret passageways?" she wanted to know, taking a few cautious steps into the room. I held my breath. It was as though I was coaxing an elusive wild animal to come near.

"The same reason castles have them, I'd expect," I told her. "Quick getaways, clandestine operations, evading people. Do you want me to show you?"

"Yes!" she cried, her eyes shining. A minor miracle: I could still impress my daughter and I was going to get to spend some time with her. As I unfolded myself from my armchair, I gave silent thanks for the rain.

"Come on," I said, putting a hand on her back and steering her toward the kitchen. The passageways had electricity, but I had no idea if it was still working. "We should get a couple of flashlights just in case."

A few minutes later, flashlights in hand, we were climbing the stairs. "This is so cool," Amity murmured, her face aglow as she scanned the walls with new eyes, wondering what secrets lay hidden within them.

"All the bedrooms have hidden doors that lead to the passage-ways," I explained. "It really is quite an extensive network of tunnels."

I opened the door to the master suite and led Amity through the study to the bedroom and pointed toward the wall, where an enormous tapestry, a medieval-looking image of a girl sitting in a garden surrounded by animals, stretched from the ceiling all the way to the floor.

"Pretty much anytime you see a tapestry hanging in a bedroom in this house, you'll find a hidden door behind it," I told her, remembering now. My mind drifted to the long-forgotten rainy days of my childhood, when my brothers and I would sneak through these secret doors into, we thought, magical worlds where anything might happen. Our imaginations in overdrive, we pretended we were going back in time to the days when Alban House was first built, when Minnesota itself was fairly new. We believed we just might encounter our grandfather as a boy, playing in the same passageways. I felt that way now.

I lifted the tapestry's edge and ran my hand on the wall behind it, stepping sideways toward the rug's center. Amity followed. "See this panel?" I showed her. "It's spring-loaded. All you have to do is press on it like this—" I put both hands in the center of the panel and pushed. It sprung back open toward me.

"Awesome," Amity whispered, her eyes wide.

I pulled the door open farther to reveal the dark, dusty passageway behind it. I felt around for the light switch and flipped it a couple of times. Nothing.

"I'm sure these bulbs must've burned out long ago," I said to my daughter. "I can't imagine Grandma used these passageways very much."

"No," she murmured, peering around me into the darkness.

"You're sure you're up for this?" I asked her, teasing a bit. "You never know what we'll find in here." I knew there was nothing to be afraid of, nothing more terrifying than the odd spider or bat, but it was fun to give my daughter an adrenaline rush.

She nodded. "Let's go," she said, nudging me a little.

I pressed the button on my flashlight and watched as the shaft of light illuminated the passageway beyond, where the years hung in the air, clung to the wood-paneled walls, and blanketed the dark floorboards. Spiderwebs were stitched in intricate patterns, their weavers at work undisturbed for decades. It smelled of the past, of countless childhood afternoons when my brothers and I would explore here. Our footsteps echoed in the emptiness as we walked along, and I could hear Amity's shallow breathing soft and low in my ears.

"This leads to your room," I told her, pointing to a door that was nearly indistinguishable from the wall on either side of it. It groaned as we pushed on it, voicing its displeasure at being awakened after such a long rest.

"I didn't even know this door was here," Amity whispered as she pushed aside a tapestry and peered into her room, its light and color and brightness contrasting sharply with the dingy, shadowy passageway in which we stood.

"Come on," I told her, gently shutting the door and leading her farther down the hallway. "You won't believe what's down here. It's almost like a house within a house."

And then I noticed it, what seemed to be a darkness within the light-colored dust on the wall. I shone my flashlight beam in its direction and saw, for lack of a better description, a trail along the passageway's wall, roughly at hand height. I squinted at it. Had someone been walking there recently, absently trailing one finger through the dust as they went? That just couldn't be. It wasn't like my mother would've been creeping around these passageways, and Jane certainly wouldn't, either. A workman, perhaps? One of Mr. Jameson's lads?

I shone the light to the floor looking for footprints but didn't see anything out of the ordinary there. Just my imagination, then.

We reached the end of the hall, where narrow spiral stairs led either up to the third floor or down to the first floor and basement beyond it.

I started up the stairs but then thought better of it. There was always an air of taboo about the house's third floor. Even as kids, my brothers and I didn't play up there. We knew that generations of Albans had grown up on the third floor in the nursery, and it felt as though something—one of them, perhaps?—didn't want us up there. It felt that same way now, as though walking up those stairs was unwise and going down was the safer path. I didn't think too long before heading down.

The stairway was even more narrow than I remembered—barely wide enough for a person to fit through. "Careful," I told Amity, pointing at a broken step.

On the first floor, the passageways ran around each of the main rooms and were lined with peepholes, each with its own cover that could be slid on or off, so undetected lurkers could easily spy on the people who happened to be in our parlor, salon, library, living room, and dining room. My brothers and I used to haunt these halls when my parents had dinner parties. We loved listening in on the hushed conversations of those who thought they were speaking in private. With our ears to the walls, we heard about all manner of affairs and alliances, secrets and scandals. We were privy to political intrigue and upsets, business strategies and tactics, even the odd criminal alibi or two.

I took a quick breath in when I saw it: the same slim trail along the dusty wall. What could it possibly be?

I motioned toward one of the peepholes and slid open the cover. Amity brushed off the dust on the wall around it and then put her eye to the hole.

"It's Jane!" she whispered, her face a mix of delight and dev-ilishness. "She's setting out the crystal glasses and wine decanter. What for?"

"The minister is coming to dinner," I whispered back to her.

"Groan," she mouthed, with a mock grimace. I squeezed her arm and we walked on.

At the far end of the passageway that ran behind the grand living room walls, we came upon another stairway that led, I knew, down to a false basement room. This hidden room was ad-jacent to the main basement that held the furnace and other equipment needed to run the house and the grounds, along with a dark-paneled studio that contained leather armchairs, a long bar, a fireplace, a billiard table, and a dart board.

This main basement room had always been called Scotch and Cigars, because generations of Alban men would retire down there after dinner for those two indulgences and to discuss poli-tics or the day's events, or to simply play billiards or darts in the company of friends while the women took tea in the parlor.

Amity might or might not have seen this main room in ear-lier visits to the house—it was accessible via the main stairway—but the false basement room would be the one I knew would interest my daughter.

A mirror image of Scotch and Cigars, it was a hidden, se-cluded lair for those same generations of Albans who needed to evade the law or other pursuers, or to conceal all manner of il-legal substances—liquor during Prohibition, I suspected, think-ing back to David Coleville's letter—or to otherwise hide what they didn't want seen in the light of day. There was even a day-bed, a refrigerator, and a bathroom for those who needed to hide out for an extended period of time. When Jane discovered my brothers and me playing there one afternoon, she gave us strict orders to stay out of the room on pain of the severest punishments.

Just a bit farther down the passageway from the false basement room was a series of tunnels leading outside—one went directly to the lakeshore (for speedy getaways by boat, we always thought), one into the gardens, another led toward the back of the house, and still another found its way toward the cemetery beyond. It was as though John James Alban had wanted the ability to flee in any direction if necessary, and I had no doubt that in a family as wealthy and potentially scandalous as mine, it had been necessary often.

"Wait until you see this," I said to Amity as we reached the door to this secret room. I put my hand on its center and pushed the groaning door open into the darkness.

The beams of both of our flashlights illuminated the room's interior, resting on leather armchairs and sofas, alighting on walls and floorboards.

I noticed she was squinting, trying to make out something in the darkness. "Mom," she said in a harsh whisper, grabbing my arm. "Look."

As I stood there straining to see what she was seeing, a feeling of tangible dread seeped out of the room and surrounded me, settling on my skin and taking hold. Something was not right here.

I felt along the wall for the light switch and flipped it, illuminating the room in a yellowish glow. And I saw it then, the thing that had caught my daughter's eye. On the daybed, a pillow and a blanket were strewn on top of the quilt, not so unusual for a daybed, but it looked mussed, as though somebody had been sitting or lying there . . . recently. On the end table, a glass of water. Out of the corner of my eye, I saw, or thought I saw, movement in the doorway to the bathroom. A dark shape shifting.

I grabbed my daughter's arm and pulled her back into the passageway, slamming the door shut behind us.

"Move, honey, move!" I shouted as I pushed her along the corridor to the narrow staircase leading upstairs. We pounded upward, my heart racing, until we reached the hidden doorway to the living room. I popped it open and pushed Amity inside, through the hanging tapestry, slamming the door shut behind us and finally leaning on it to catch my breath.

"Mom, was that . . . ?" Amity's words stopped short, her eyes imploring mine for answers.

"I don't know," I said to her, grasping her arm again and hurrying us out of the room and into the foyer. "You just stay close." I called out for Jane, who came scurrying out of the kitchen carrying a silver candlestick. Her smile faded when she saw the look on my face. "What is it, miss? What's happened?"

"Jane, we might have an intruder in the house," I said. "There was somebody in the false basement room."

Jane squinted at me. "Whatever are you talking about, child?"

I tried again, slower this time. "I was showing Amity the passageways."

She clucked and shook her head. "Not that again. Why all the children in this house gravitate toward those infernal passageways, I'll never know."

"Just listen." I put my hand up. "We went down to the false basement, turned on the light, and . . . Somebody had been in there, Jane. Slept there, maybe. We saw a pillow and a blanket, even a glass of water."

"I thought I saw something, or someone, move in the darkness," Amity said, her voice cracking.

"I did, too, honey," I said, draping an arm across her shoulders and pulling her close.

Jane crossed her arms in front of her chest as her mouth straightened into a thin line. "That's simply impossible," she said. "Nobody apart from family even knows that room exists."

I looked from Jane to Amity and back again. "I think we should call the police."

"It just can't be, lass." Jane shook her head. "There's no way anyone could've gotten into the house, much less stumbled upon that hidden room. There's a reason it's hidden—your family didn't want anyone to know it was there."

"I know, Jane. I know it sounds ridiculous, but the fact is, Amity and I both saw evidence that somebody had been there. Recently." I turned around and marched toward the door to the passageways. "Come on. We'll show you."

"Seriously?" Amity stood right where she was. "We're going back down there?"

I hesitated for a moment and then smiled at my daughter. "I want to know if we really saw what I thought we saw. If somebody is down there, what's he going to do against three strong women?"

With Jane brandishing the heavy candlestick and Amity and I wielding our flashlights, we made our way through the hidden door, down the rickety staircase, and through the door leading into the false basement room. I flipped on the light, and Amity gasped, her hands flying to her mouth, at what we all saw: Nothing. No blanket. No pillow. No water glass. It was all gone.

"Mom," Amity said to me, her eyes wide. "I know we saw what we saw down here."

I nodded, staring into the room, as though, if I looked closer, I would be able to discern what happened to the items we had seen there just moments before.

"It's just your eyes playing tricks on you," Jane said, patting me on the shoulder. "Not to worry. You were all worked up with your secret passageways and false rooms and . . ."

"No!" Amity interrupted, walking farther into the room and holding her arms wide. "I know what we saw. It was here, and now it's gone."

I approached my daughter and took her by the hand. "Let's go upstairs," I said, slowly pulling her toward the door. "I don't like this."

Jane and Amity crouched through the doorway, but I stayed where I was for a moment, looking at the table where the glass of water had been. The other furniture in the room was covered by a thin layer of dust, but that table was wiped clean.

CHAPTER 9

Back in the main part of the house, Amity curled up in an overstuffed chair with her arms wrapped around her bent knees, while I paced, my mind racing in several directions at once. I knew what we had seen. It had been there, and then it wasn't. But how . . . ?

A thought hit me, one I didn't have any intention of sharing with my daughter. Did whoever was in the false basement room hear us when we told Jane about what we had seen? Was he in the passageways spying on us when we were here in the living room?

I looked at my daughter, who suddenly seemed very much a child, curled up as she was, and I felt a sense of utter vulnerability, a barrage of questions running through my mind. Why would someone hole up in our basement? How did whomever it was learn of the existence of the passageways? And, worse, how long had he been there? With access to those passageways, he had access to the house and very easily might have entered our rooms while we were sleeping. That thought made me shudder.

"I'm calling the police," I announced, crossing the room to the telephone sitting on one of the end tables.

"Are you sure that's wise?" Jane asked, smoothing her apron and slightly shaking her head. "I didn't see—"

"I know you didn't, but we did," I interrupted, irritated by this household's age-old tendency to close ranks. As I held the receiver in my hand, I continued: "The fact that the evidence disappeared so quickly is even more troubling, frankly. That tells me someone not only *was* here but *is* here, and heard what we were saying."

"He could be watching us right now," Amity added, wrapping her arms tighter around her knees.

That did it. "Jane, ring for Mr. Jameson and the lads. I want all the secret doors in this house locked from the inside, every one of them. And all the peepholes need to be covered, too. It has to be done right now. If anyone is or has been in the passageways, I don't want him getting into the interior of the house or spying on us."

And just as quick as that, the indecision and paralysis I'd been feeling since I'd been back at Alban House vanished. I was the head of the household, like it or not, and as uncomfortable as I had been in that role since I arrived, it now seemed to slip over me like a second skin. It was up to me to make sure this house and the people in it were safe and secure.

Jane gave a quick nod and rushed off into the kitchen, where the somewhat complicated buzzer system was located. Each room in the house and the buildings on the grounds had been wired with a buzzer, which would ring in the kitchen, illuminating the location on a map grid. That way, family could summon staff from wherever they were in the house. And it worked both ways; the kitchen could buzz the rest of the house as well. It was revolutionary technology more than a century ago when the house was built, and it still functioned today.

As Jane was ringing for her husband, I dialed the police station. But before blurting out the nature of my call to just any officer who answered the phone, a bit of Jane's—and this household's—tradition of privacy and discretion seeped into my thinking.

"Chief Bellamy, please," I heard myself saying. "This is Grace Alban."

A moment later, my mother's old, dear friend was on the line.

"Gracie!" he said, his mellow, fluid voice erasing the years since I had last heard it. "It's so good to talk to you. I'm sorry it isn't under more pleasant circumstances."

"It's good to talk to you, Chief."

"I suppose you're calling to go over security for the funeral," he said. "It's a damned shame, Gracie. A damned shame."

"Thank you, " I said, clearing my throat. "Actually, we probably will need security for the funeral, but that isn't what I'm calling about."

"Oh?" he said, the concern reverberating from his end of the line to mine.

And I told him the whole story, how we had seen evidence of someone staying in the basement (I didn't say "false basement") and how, when we went back a few moments later, it was gone.

I heard Chief Bellamy let out a long sigh. "For God's sake, Grace, that's the last thing you need. Now of all times. I told your mother last year I didn't think it was a good idea to open the house for those goddamned tours. But she didn't listen to me. She never did." I could hear the slight chuckle in his voice as he remembered his old friend.

I hesitated a moment before responding. But then I thought I might as well say it. "Chief, this might not mean anything, but there's something else you should know."

He waited for me to continue, and I said it all quickly, in one long stream. "My mother died on the very day she was going to talk to a reporter who was planning to write a book about my family. I know she died of natural causes—it was a heart attack—but now with this happening, I thought I should mention it."

He was silent for a moment and then said: "Don't worry, Grace. Just as you said, it's probably nothing, and I don't want you to make too much out of this, but I'm going to send a squad over immediately. They'll check the whole place out."

I wondered how effective that would be. If someone was lurking here, the place was big enough to get lost in. Especially since the intruder knew about the secret passageways, he could stay one, or several, steps ahead of whoever was looking. Hide and seek was an impossible game within these walls, I knew. Those hiding would always win. Still, I'd feel safer if I knew the police had secured the house. Their very presence might be enough to scare whomever it was away.

"Thank you," I said, and then, thinking out loud, continued. "And what I'd also like is for a squad to patrol the grounds tonight. I'm worried that, if we do indeed have an intruder, he has found a way to come and go."

"Oh?"

The words I was about to say to the chief caught in my throat. Spilling secrets just wasn't done in my family, but I knew I had no choice. My daughter's welfare was more important to me than the almighty Alban traditions.

"I'm sure you're not aware of this," I began, "but this house is filled with passageways behind the walls, and some lead to the outside. I think the intruder might have been in those passageways."

"Passageways?" the chief said, a slight lilt in his voice. "Why am I not surprised? You Albans have always had a flair for the dramatic."

He had no idea how right he was. "The doors to the outside can be locked, of course, but I'd feel better with a police presence. My daughter's safety is my main concern."

"Consider it done," he said. "Twenty-four-hour guard, until further notice. Grace, your mother—" His words stopped in midair. I heard him clearing his throat.

"I know, Chief. She loved you, too. The service is Friday morning. I look forward to seeing you there."

"Anything you need, Grace. Anything. The entire force is at your disposal."

"Thanks, Chief Bellamy. It means a lot, it really does." I intended to hang up then, but a thought crept in. "I do have one more thing to ask of you, if I may."

"What's that?"

"Your discretion and that of your officers. I don't want it getting out that there was an intruder at Alban House. You know what a field day the press would have with that."

"Of course."

I put the phone down and turned to see Mr. Jameson and his two young men coming out of the kitchen through the swinging doors.

"We're on the job, Miss Grace," he called to me over his shoulder as the three of them began to ascend the stairs. "All the doors and those infernal peepholes will be secured in a jiffy. Don't you worry now."

"Wait a second," I said, hurrying toward the bottom of the staircase. "Cody, you and—" I looked at the second young man. "What's your name?"

"Jason, ma'am."

"Cody and Jason. You two are living in the groundskeeper's quarters for the summer, isn't that right?"

They nodded, exchanging a quick glance. That was the usual practice, the outdoor help stayed in a small two-bedroom cottage located between the gardens and the lake, which had originally been intended for the head of the groundskeeping staff. But Mr. Jameson, of course, lived with his wife in her large suite of rooms off the kitchen, so the cottage was vacant unless he hired outdoor staff.

"I'd like you both to move into the main house, effective immediately," I said. "I'm sorry about this and I know it's a bit of an upheaval for you, but I'd really feel better with you guys in the house. Is that all right? You'll have the west wing on the second floor all to yourselves. There are bedrooms and bathrooms, a library, a media room, and even a small kitchen. I think you'll find it much larger than the groundskeeper's cottage. Come and go as you wish, and don't worry about using the back stairs. You're perfectly welcome to use this main staircase."

It was strength in numbers I was going for. If there was an intruder and he was still here, I felt a bit safer knowing that two strapping young men were going to be in the house with us overnight rather than just me, Amity, and an elderly couple.

Cody and Jason exchanged a quick glance and tried to hide their smiles. "Sure, Miss Alban," Cody said. "Anything you want."

"Okay, then," I said, turning to Jane. "Will you make up rooms for these boys?"

"I'll also make up the master suite for you and Amity," Jane said, nodding her head toward my daughter. "There's a big daybed in the study that she can use."

That hadn't occurred to me, but of course she was right. Mr. Jameson had hired these kids and I trusted his judgment completely, but how much did we really know about them? I might have spoken too soon by inviting them to stay in the house. Best to have Amity safe with me, behind my locked door.

And the master suite was the only one on the second floor with its own exit to the outdoors. I liked the idea that we could get out quickly if necessary. To my great surprise, Amity didn't balk at the suggestion.

Jane had started up the stairs with the men and Amity and I were headed back into the living room, but all of us stopped dead when we heard a knock at the front door. The police? Already here with information? I exhaled in the hopes that they had found whomever it was and we could all go back to normal.

But it wasn't the police. Jane opened the door to reveal the minister, Matthew Parker, standing there, holding a bottle of wine.

Our stunned expressions must've been rather overt, because he said: "We said six o'clock, right?"

CHAPTER 10

O f course, Reverend Parker." Jane smiled, instantly regaining her composure and slipping right back into her role. "Please do come in. Miss Alban has been expecting you."

As she ushered him inside, Jane shot a look at her husband, who then hurried the lads up the stairs and out of sight.

Before I took Amity on our ill-fated tour of the passageways, I'd been planning to shower and change before the reverend arrived, but with everything that had happened, it had flown out of my mind. And now here I stood, fresh out of the dusty, musty tunnels, not knowing the last time I had run a brush through my hair. Was I even wearing makeup? I wasn't sure.

I pushed a stray strand of hair behind my ear and smiled my best smile, hoping my face wasn't as grimy as it felt. "Hi!" I chirped a little too loudly. "Welcome! You brought wine! How lovely."

Jane took the bottle from him with a nod and disappeared into the kitchen as he walked hesitantly into the foyer, looking up at the stained-glass window and chandelier.

"Wow," he said. "This is the first time I've been inside this house. It really is quite something."

"Home, sweet home." I grinned, holding my arms wide. "Let's go into the parlor, shall we? We'll have drinks there before dinner. An Alban tradition."

Amity sidled up to me, then.

"Reverend Parker, this is my daughter, Amity," I said, putting an arm around her shoulders and brushing the dust off them at the same time.

"Amity, what a pretty name." He smiled at her. "It's a pleasure to meet you."

"Nice to meet you." Amity nodded quickly, then turned to me. "Mom, I thought I'd go upstairs and watch a movie. Is that okay?"

I wasn't sure how I felt about Amity going off by herself given all that had just happened. But with the police on their way, with Mr. Jameson and the boys securing the house, and with us downstairs, I guessed she'd be okay. "Just make sure you sit next to the buzzer." I squinted at her.

"May I take my dinner up there, too?"

The reverend grinned. "Oh, you're not going to be joining us? Are you sure? We're going to be talking about funeral arrangements! Come on, what teenager wouldn't love that?"

Amity giggled—a real, genuine giggle. This man actually amused her. She volleyed back: "Only if you tell me that my math teacher will be there, too, and we can do a few equations between deciding on readings and hymns."

He let out a laugh, and I patted my daughter on the back. "Go ahead, then," I said to her, shooing her up the stairs. "I'll have Jane bring up your dinner. But listen, keep that buzzer next to you at all times."

She and I exchanged a glance, and then she ran up a few steps. Turning back to Reverend Parker, she sang out, "It was nice meeting you!" and was gone.

"Nice girl," he said to me as we walked into the parlor, where the fire was now blazing.

"She has her moments." I smirked. "You know teenagers."

On the sideboard, I saw uncorked bottles of red and white wine and sherry; crystal decanters of scotch, gin, and vodka; tonic water; an ice bucket; and various glasses—the usual bar setup, just as my father and probably his father before him had preferred it. Jane had also lit candles around the room, making it seem welcoming and homey.

It occurred to me that this was the first time I had entertained here at Alban House as an adult. I'd had birthday parties as a kid, of course, and attended my parents' various functions and events, but I was never the hostess in the house where generations of Albans had welcomed friends, businesspeople, and even dignitaries. Five U.S. presidents had taken drinks in this room before dinner, most famously Franklin Roosevelt on the eve of this country's entry into World War II. It was said that he and my grandfather talked about steel and iron ore production.

I could feel the mantle of that tradition, passed from one generation to the next, now wrapping itself around my shoulders as I walked over to the sideboard and said, for the first time in my life, what I had heard my parents and grandparents say countless times over the years: "What's your pleasure? If you don't see it here, just ask. We've got it all at Alban House."

"Wine would be great," Matthew Parker said, and the evening had begun.

I poured both of us some wine and gestured to a pair of leather armchairs by the fire. "Shall we sit, Reverend?" I said, handing him a glass.

He reached out to take it. "Please, call me Matthew." He smiled. "Your mother never would. She was uncomfortable with the informality, I think, even though I prefer it."

"Matthew it is," I said, settling into my chair. I looked down and noticed I was wearing my ratty old slippers. Lovely. A quick glance at my dusty jeans and I was fully chagrined. It occurred to me that I was now the perfect picture of the eccentric lady of the manor. What a cliché. I put a palm to my cheek in a futile attempt to fend off the reddening I could feel seeping out of my pores.

"I'm sorry about my appearance," I said quickly, brushing the hair out of my eyes. "We had a bit of a situation here just before you arrived and I didn't get the chance to change my clothes. Usually I'd be, at least, clean when a guest showed up."

Reverend Parker—Matthew—chuckled. "You look lovely, so you've got no worries there. But—a situation? Nothing serious, I hope."

Contrary to what Jane, and generations of Albans, might have done, I made the decision right then and there to confide in this man. I relished the idea of having somebody to talk to, another adult who might help me navigate my way through what had just happened. Not that Jane and her husband weren't a help to me, but they always seemed to have their own agenda in matters of Alban House, dispensing information on a need-to-know basis, always weighing their actions against public opinion of the great Alban family if whatever it was "got out." Always prefacing everything with the question, spoken or unspoken: "How will it look if we . . . ?"

And, it occurred to me, listening to parishioners was part of this man's job. That's why he was here, after all.

"I think somebody might have broken into the house," I blurted out. "And may have even been living here."

Matthew furrowed his brow. "Really? You're kidding."

I took a sip of my wine and nodded. "The police are on their way, actually." And I told him the whole story—taking Amity through the passageways, finding the blanket and pillow in the false basement, all of it.

He leaned back in his chair, shaking his head. "Hidden tunnels, secret doors, mysterious intruders. It would be the most intriguing story I'd heard in a long while if it didn't involve your safety. And Amity's."

"That's exactly what I was thinking—the safety part, I mean," I said. "I'm most worried about whomever it is getting into the interior of the house at night while we're sleeping."

Matthew held my gaze for a long moment. "Grace, if you'd rather just sort this out with the police, we don't have to do this now." He put his wineglass on the end table next to him. "We've got a few days before the funeral, so I can come back another time. You've really got your hands full and—"

"Don't be silly!" I interrupted a bit too forcefully. "I'd really like to go over the service now so that's off my plate. And, this just occurred to me, I think it's good to have some activity going on. I'm hoping that our intrepid intruder is gone, scared off by us stumbling upon his hiding place, but if he isn't—the more people around, the better."

Just then, I noticed lights outside the window and unfolded myself from my chair, moving across the room to get a better look. I pushed the curtains aside and peered into the twilight. "There's the police now." Matthew joined me at the window and we watched two squad cars pull into the drive.

A few moments later, the doorbell sounded. I started to answer it but saw Jane scurrying from the kitchen and stopped in my tracks. I had to remember that answering the door was Jane's job. I watched her wipe her hands on her apron before she pulled the door open and ushered a man inside.

Stepping into the parlor, she said: "The police to see you, miss."

As Matthew and I walked into the foyer, I smiled at two uniformed officers, extending my hand to one of them. "I'm Grace Alban and this is the Reverend Matthew Parker. Thank you for coming so quickly."

And then it was time to repeat the whole story, yet again. As I finished, one of the officers nodded. "The chief has asked us to patrol the house and grounds, securing any exits. I'm assuming you've got all the doors and windows in the house locked?"

Of course! I had been so worried about securing the interior passageway doors and peepholes that I didn't even think of locking the outer ones, too. When I lived here, it was one of the household staff's last duties of the evening, locking everything up tight. But with only Jane and her husband here with my mother for all these years, I wasn't sure if that was still the case.

"If they aren't all locked, they should be," I said. "Jane, will you ask Mr. Jameson and the boys to tend to that, please? All the doors and windows on the first and second floors."

"Right away, miss," she said, adding a quick aside to me, "We'll be ready for dinner in just a few minutes." With that, she headed back toward her kitchen lair.

"Chief Bellamy said he was arranging for a twenty-four-hour guard," I said to the officers. "Is that right?"

"We'll be here overnight, Miss Alban," one of them confirmed. "When we've given the house a look, you'll have two men in the front, two in the back. Nobody's getting into this house on our watch."

"Thank you." I exhaled. "I've got my young daughter here and it's good to know you'll be on guard."

"Just doing our jobs, ma'am." He smiled. "Protect and serve."

"Well, then. Do you have everything you need?" I crossed my arms in front of my chest. "You'll be warm enough outside?"

"Don't you worry about us," he said as he took a walkie-talkie from his belt and held it out to me. "And if you need us, if you hear or see anything, just holler. Press the red button to talk."

Jane and her husband floated back into the room so silently I didn't even realize they were there until Mr. Jameson spoke. "I'll take you and your men through the house," he said to the officers, who followed as he ascended the stairs.

"So that's what police protection feels like," I said to Matthew, exhaling again.

"You can't be too careful," he said, watching the officers until they turned out of sight on the second floor. "I'm glad they're here."

"I am, too," I said, picking up my wineglass and taking a sip. "Once they finish going through the passageways and are patrolling the grounds, I'll have Jane bring them out some supper. And ours is probably just about ready, too, so we should migrate to the dining room. I hope you like chicken!"

As we took our places at the table—me hesitantly taking the head and Matthew next to me on the right—Jane brought out our first course, French onion soup with crusty bread with butter, and we got down to business, talking about how the service would go, this reading followed by that hymn.

Discussing my mother's final wishes at our dining room table, where my family had eaten countless dinners together, conjured her spirit in a powerful way. Matthew was sitting in her usual spot. As I looked at him, I could also see my mother's image superimposed over his own, there in her blue Chanel dress and hat, a strand of pearls around her neck. She smiled and nodded, and I heard her voice, soft and low, in my ear. "Thank you, darling. You're doing everything right." I felt a whoosh of cool air, buoying along the faint scent her favorite perfume, and then it was gone.

I sopped up a little of the soup with the last of my bread. "It's so strange to be in this house without her," I said. "It's not just that it feels empty to me; it's almost like the house itself feels her absence somehow. As though the walls and floorboards and banisters are grieving with me over the loss of her. Does that make any sense?"

"In a way," he said slowly, "I can understand that. There's so much family history here, it's as though the house is infused with their spirits."

But that's not what it was, not really. Certainly, I felt the spirits of my family keenly, but that's not what I was talking about. He didn't get it, and I didn't blame him. He didn't know what it was like to live in this house and feel whatever it was that radiated from its very foundations. I thought about the letter from David Coleville to my mother that I had read the day before. I could see the words in my mind as though they were right in front of me.

As the story goes, that forest was a witch's wood. She had been imprisoned in an old oak hundreds of years earlier by a

rival. And when Alban felled the trees and brought them to
this country, he got her spirit in the bargain. Legend has it
that her spirit has been bedeviling the Alban family ever since.

It was complete nonsense and I knew it. And yet . . . when I really thought about it . . . I shuddered and took another sip of wine.

"And I know it can't be easy for you," Matthew continued, his voice snapping me back to the present. "You're dealing with your mother's death on top of being home for the first time in so many years. The emotion that surrounds those two rather monumental things would be overwhelming for anyone. And now you've got to worry about a possible intruder? You're shouldering it all very well—the name 'Grace' fits you, it really does—but it's a lot to deal with."

He was looking into my eyes with such genuine concern, just like he had earlier in the day. This man really did seem to care, and it occurred to me that he was in the perfect occupation.

"It does seem like it's been one thing after another, doesn't it?" I managed a smile. "But it's fine. I'm okay."

"I know you are." He smiled back. "From what I've seen of you, I have gotten the impression that you're a strong woman. Your mother's daughter through and through. But—" he hesitated a bit and then continued. "Something you said this morning, or rather didn't say, has been on my mind."

"What's that?" I wanted to know. I put my elbow on the table and rested my chin in my hand.

"You never did tell me what kept you away from here all these years," he said, his voice softening. "It's clear to me that you feel a certain reverence for this house and your family history, and yet you stayed away for decades. You evaded the question when I asked it this morning, and I've been wondering if you just thought it was none of my business, that I had no right to ask, or if it was something else. Whatever it was, I just want you to know that I care and that you can talk to me about it—or anything else—if you ever decide that you want to. It's a big part of my job, listening."

I looked at Matthew Parker and, for reasons I can't quite explain, I felt that he was safe harbor, somehow. He was right—it was his job to listen, to counsel. Maybe I could get it off my chest, once and for all.

I hadn't intended to talk about this to anyone, ever. But it was as though being back here, and especially my father's "visit" the night before, had unearthed the box where I had put these memories and buried them, and now they were screaming to get out. Before I knew it, the words were spilling forth.

"When I was twenty and my brothers were eighteen, we decided to go sailing one November afternoon," I began, the images of that day swirling in front of me. "We had been sailing our whole lives—it was a passion of my father's and he brought us out on the water when we were very young. Some of my earliest memories are of skimming across our bay in one of the several sailboats our family had back then."

Matthew leaned forward. Now it was his turn to put his elbow on the table and rest his chin upon his palm.

"It was an unseasonably warm day, so we thought nothing of it when the wind picked up a bit." My voice broke, remembering my brothers' laughing faces as we zipped along. "We sailed out of our protected bay and into the main body of the lake. We went farther out than we should have. But it was just so much fun, we were going so fast."

My hands were shaking as I picked up my wineglass. I took a long sip and continued.

"But as it turned out, it was one of those deceptive, sly November days here on Lake Superior. The weather changed. Lake Superior is like that, you know. Murderous when it wants to be. It wouldn't have blown up a storm when we were safe in our own bay, not then. It waited until we were far away from shore. We should have known better. I should have known better. But we hadn't noticed the clouds building up, or if we did—kids that age. They think they're invincible. We certainly did. But when the wind shifted and the rain started, we realized we were in a lot of trouble out there."

My eyes were unfocused, staring back into a moment in the past that I had all but blocked out of my mind. I could feel the spray on my face, the stiff wind tangling my hair.

"We sailed for hours against that wind, trying to get back to shore. The waves were so huge and the rain was just beating down on us. The boys were expert sailors, but this was too much. If we had just taken the larger of our boats, we might have been all right. But we weren't. And it was my fault. I was the eldest, I should have gotten us to shore sooner."

I saw his lips moving: "It wasn't your fault," but I could barely hear him, so deeply was I caught in the story that was unraveling.

"The boat capsized," I went on. "All of us tumbled into the water and then it was a frenzy—grasping for the side of the boat, flailing around in the water. I saw a huge wave—to me it looked three stories tall—bearing down on us. And everything went an icy black. I was clinging on to the side of the boat, but my brothers . . . they were gone. Just gone. Taken by the lake, both of them."

Matthew shook his head and closed his eyes.

"I hung on to the boat until the Coast Guard arrived. I never saw my brothers again."

I could see the image of my father watching the Coast Guard vessel, with me on it, pull up to our dock. His eyes were bright, his face expectant—his children were saved!—but then he saw me alone coming toward him, still wearing my life vest, wrapped in a blanket. He ran past me and onto the boat, looking everywhere, calling the boys' names. "Where are they? Where are my sons?" And when the reality hit him, he staggered onto the dock and collapsed onto our beach where he let out a wail that seemed to have no end—an ancient primal keening that pierced my soul with its power.

Jane led me into the house, into my mother's open arms, where we, too, collapsed onto the floor and wept for those impish, devilish boys whom we loved more than anything.

I swallowed hard and continued. "My father sent out a fleet of boats to look for the boys, but their bodies were never found. He was never the same after that. His grief for them, it consumed him. The man he had been, the father I had known, was gone—his humor, his wit, the sparkle in his eyes—taken just as swiftly as the boys were taken by the lake."

I could see him, then, standing in the pounding rain, raging at the lake itself. He was in the water up to his waist when

Mr. Jameson and some of his groundskeeping staff reached him and pulled him back onto land. Jane called our family doctor, who hurried to the house and sedated him, and my mother and me, too.

"After that day, my dad started drinking heavily and just withdrew. He was angry, despondent, and crushingly sad all at once. I never heard him speak another civil word, not to anyone. And he never looked at me the same way. Before that day, I had been his little princess. But I could tell he blamed me. Losing Jake and Jimmy—it killed him. Literally. Not long after they drowned, he took his own life. He walked out into the lake to be with them, forever."

"Oh, Grace," Matthew said, his eyes brimming with tears. "I'm so sorry. I . . ." He let out a long sigh. "There are no words."

And then I told him what I had never told another living soul, not my mother, not my husband, not anyone. "The last words he spoke to me were: 'Why couldn't it have been you?'"

I had finally said it out loud, I had told a man I'd just met hours before what I had been too ashamed to reveal to anyone for more than twenty years.

"You know he didn't mean that," he said, fishing a handkerchief out of his pocket and handing it to me. "It was the grief talking. Not your dad."

As I dabbed at my nose and eyes, the minister did what he does best. "Lord, please grant this woman peace." Looking toward the ceiling, he added, "Right now would be good."

This brought a slight smile to my face. "A little demanding, aren't we?"

He smiled back. "I wanted Him to know I was serious. No fooling around, God. Peace for Grace Alban. Now."

I tried to hold on to that smile but it faded as quickly as it came. I was shivering deep inside my core. I was as cold as I had been in the middle of the lake that day.

"I felt like my mother blamed me for all of it—she never said as much, but I know she did," I said. "I blamed myself. Her husband and sons were dead because of me."

He shook his head. "Not because of you. None of it was your fault. You must know that, Grace."

"I could never get away from it here in this town," I told him. "Everywhere I went, people knew I was the Alban daughter who had been on the boat that day. The stares, the whispers. Their pitying faces—or it might have been scorn, I really wasn't sure. Everyone knew what had happened. Another in a long line of Alban tragedies. I couldn't stand being at the center of it."

"I'm sure it wasn't scorn," Matthew said, his face earnest. "I think you know that, too. People don't know how to react to tragedies like the one you experienced. It's their worst fear come to life. They don't know what to say, what to do. They can be awkward and even cruel without really meaning to."

Somewhere deep down, I knew he was right. But when I was young, I just couldn't see it that way. I took a long sip of wine and continued. "A few months passed, and I had turned twenty-one and was in college at the time, and I began thinking of transferring to a school out west. Somewhere, anywhere away from here. When my mother had no objections to the idea, I did it. I moved out to Seattle. And slowly, in that environment of anonymity, I began to heal. Nobody had any idea or, for that matter, cared about who the Albans were or who I was. Nobody knew I was on a sailboat that day with my brothers. They didn't even know I'd ever had any brothers. Or a father who killed himself because of me. Even now, most of my friends out there don't know. It was liberating, in a way. I loved that people didn't know anything about Grace Alban, because it meant I could pretend I didn't, either. I could pretend I was a different person. And eventually, I became that person."

Just then, Jane came into the dining room with our main course, a platter of roasted chicken and vegetables. She set it down and cleared our soup dishes, eyeing me darkly. I had no doubt that she heard and objected to my airing our family's dirty laundry, but I didn't care. It felt good to talk about it.

"I can understand how you felt," Matthew said when Jane had left the room after serving us each some sliced chicken and roasted tomatoes, onions, and asparagus. "You went to a place where the slate was wiped clean."

"That's right. And then I met Andrew, who grew up out there, and before I knew it, we were married and Amity was on the way. I never really made a conscious decision to stay away from Alban House, but the more time that passed, the less reason I found to come back. I had built a life elsewhere, a life I loved. I was happy for a long time. I really was."

He chewed a bite of chicken and considered this. "You said 'was.' You were happy. What happened?"

"Another woman." I sighed. "I guess my husband got tired of the person I was pretending to be."

"You're divorced, then?"

I nodded. "It's been nearly a year. He's remarried and has another child already. He hasn't seen much of Amity since."

Matthew and I locked eyes. "It's not my place to criticize Amity's father, I'm sure he's a fine man"—he shook his head slightly—"but he's also a blind son of a bitch."

I let out a laugh. "Such language, Reverend!"

"Just calling it the way I see it." He grinned and took another bite of his chicken. "If you have a daughter like that girl upstairs and a wife like you, you thank God every day for your good fortune."

We smiled at each other and I felt a sizzle, an electricity wrapping around us and charging the air. I shook my head and pushed away the feeling—that was the last thing I needed right now.

"So," he said, breaking the silence, "what's it like finally being back here after all this time?"

I looked around the room. "I was dreading it. I knew it was going to dredge up memories that I had tried very hard to forget. But just being here, I know it's going to sound a little crazy, but I feel so close to my brothers, and to my mom and dad for that matter. I've heard the boys' laughter and smelled my mom's perfume. I really feel their presence in this house. It makes me realize how much I've missed them."

My eyes brimmed with tears.

"That doesn't sound so crazy to me," Matthew said. "I deal with the supernatural on a daily basis, you know. I have no doubt that you can feel the spirits of your family here."

He took a sip of wine and continued. "So what's next for you? What happens after the funeral?"

"I really don't know," I admitted to him as I bit the top off an asparagus spear. "Amity and I had a great life out in Washington—our house is on Whidbey Island, which really is quite beautiful. But I'll be honest. Ever since her father left us last year, things have gone downhill and it has been pretty lonely for me out there. That's his hometown and all of our friends were his friends first, and they basically got him in the divorce, if you know what I mean. I'm off the dinner party list. He's got a new wife and baby now and we're completely out of the picture. And it doesn't help that everything about the place reminds me of our life together. He introduced me to it all."

For the first time, this occurred to me: "I really wouldn't mind leaving there for good."

"And Amity? What does she think?"

I thought out loud about how a move might affect my daughter. "She doesn't see her dad very much as it is, so moving across the country wouldn't change that. Actually, it would provide an excuse for why she doesn't see him, other than the fact that he's an ass and much too busy with his new family to care about his old one."

The more I talked about it, the more it seemed to make sense. "Amity has been coming here during the summers for years," I went on. "She loves it almost as much as I did at her age. And back on Whidbey, this next school year she's got to change schools—redistricting, it's quite annoying—and she's going to have very few friends at her new school. If we were going to make a change, now is a good time."

He smiled a broad smile, his eyes shining. "So are you saying that you'd consider moving back here to Alban House?"

"I'm not sure," I said. "It's funny. This house and my family's legacy haven't meant much to me for a couple of decades, but now that my mom's gone and I'm basically the head of the Alban family, I do feel a certain—I don't know. A sense of responsibility, I guess. I feel it especially strongly when I'm here inside the house. Albans have been leaders in this town for a hundred and fifty years. Without me here, what will happen to that legacy? And what will happen to this house? I hate to think of it withering and dying or becoming a museum. This is my family's home and a part of this town's history. It's important to me to uphold it."

At that, I distinctly heard a loud exhale. I didn't know if it was Jane in the butler's pantry eavesdropping on our conversation or the house itself breathing a sigh of relief.

CHAPTER 11

After Reverend Parker had gone home, I sat in the parlor until the fire settled into embers and then I retreated to the master suite, where I found Amity already asleep on the daybed in my mother's study. I locked the door behind me and stole over to her bed, tucking the covers up around her neck and giving her a soft kiss on the cheek. She'd be perfectly safe here with me, intruder in the house or not.

I felt my way behind the tapestry and checked the hidden door—locked tight. A quick look in the closets turned up nobody lurking. I peered out the window and saw two uniformed officers sitting on folding chairs near the side door, a small flame burning in a fire ring between them. I hoped they weren't too terribly cold out there as I slipped into my mother's bed and pulled the quilts around me.

Jane had lit a fire in the fireplace and, as I burrowed under the covers, I watched it burn in the darkness, its flames casting wild shadows that looked like trees with gnarled and leafless limbs, witches reaching out from behind them toward me. That image sounds rather macabre but it felt just the opposite—I was content and comforted there among my mother's mountain of pillows and down quilts, listening to the crackling fire and watching the shadow play on the walls.

. . .

SEVERAL DAYS PASSED with the police turning up nothing in the way of an intruder—perhaps Jane was right and it was my imagination working overtime—and finally Friday arrived. I awoke to rain on the day of my mother's funeral. Not a delicate, whisper of a rain like I had been used to in Washington but a good, old-fashioned Minnesota downpour with electricity crackling through the sky. As Amity and I walked hand in hand down the main staircase, a booming clap of thunder shook the house so hard that the stained-glass window quaked and rattled its displeasure.

I had been moving through a dense fog for most of the morning, relying on my familiar routine—showering, drying my hair, applying makeup, pulling my dress over my head—to guide me. I smiled at Amity, who was looking so grown-up in her black skirt and blouse. I squeezed her hand, trying to put on a strong façade for her. But the truth was, I was splintering inside.

My mind drifted back to the day of my brothers' funeral, when my mom and I walked down these stairs hand in hand, just as I was now doing with my own daughter. Mom had turned to me as we stood on the second-floor landing, her face a mask of grief and pain, and managed a smile. "We'll get through this together," she said, her voice wavering. She was always a tower of strength, even on what was undoubtedly one of the worst days of her life. I hoped I could be half as strong for Amity.

Jane stood at the front door, her mouth in a tight line, her eyes reddened. I could feel the tension radiating from her. I wanted to run to her and throw my arms around her, tell her how much she had meant to my mother over the years, how completely my family had relied on her, and how grateful my mother had been for her steadfast presence in this house. But I knew that if I said anything of the kind, her false display of strength would crumble to the ground right along with mine.

So instead, I was all business: "You'll be one of the first ones out after the service, and you'll be back here before anyone else to supervise the catering, right?"

"That's right, miss." She nodded tightly, her gaze fixed on the wall behind me. "Mr. Jameson and I will sit in the back and slip out during the last hymn. The car's waiting for you now."

"Okay, then," I said, putting my arm around Amity's shoulders and trying to smile at her. "It's time to go."

Jane had arranged for Carter to bring the car around to the front of the house to take Amity and me to the funeral—she wouldn't hear of riding with us herself, stickler for protocol that she was—and although the church wasn't more than a mile away, my stomach tightened as I saw the thundering downpour outside. I wondered if old Carter could keep the car on the road.

Jane opened the door onto the patio, where Mr. Jameson stood in the deluge holding an enormous black umbrella. He ushered Amity and me down to the waiting silver-and-black Bentley, the same car, I thought with a pang in the pit of my stomach, that had brought David Coleville to this house all those years ago. He opened the back door for us and we slid in.

"Miss Grace." Carter smiled at me from the driver's seat, the years evident on his impossibly kind face. He looked the picture of a driver—black suit, white shirt, black tie and hat. I had never seen him wear anything else. "So good to have you back at Alban House."

I smiled back at him and nodded, holding his gaze for a moment before my eyes began stinging. Amity handed me a tissue and I held it to my face, trying to hold back the flood of grief.

He cleared his throat and pulled away, and I watched as the rain distorted Jane, her husband, and the house behind them into an Impressionist painting.

Just a turn here and a turn there down the road and we would soon arrive. But we were crawling at a snail's pace as the rain beat down onto the windshield and the wipers flew back and forth in a frantic attempt to clear the way.

As we inched along, I thought about how I'd always loved this tree-lined street. Maples and elms arched over the roadway on either side as though they were trying to grasp one another's hands. It made for a beautiful scene in the fall when their leaves were ablaze, but on this day, with their branches shaking violently in the wind and lightning crackling through the dark sky, it seemed sinister and foreboding, as though we were creeping through a haunted wood.

We were nearly at the church. I turned to smooth a stray curl off Amity's forehead when I felt the car jerk to a stop, my head hitting the back of my seat with a thud. Carter gasped aloud and I looked out the front window to see a woman standing in the roadway. She was wearing a long black dress and a black hat with an extremely wide brim, and was holding a large black umbrella. Obviously, she was there to attend the funeral. She had been looking down at the car, but then she raised her head and stared right in at us, and a slow smile crept across her face.

"Oh my God," Amity gasped, her mouth in a grimace. This woman was made up like something out of *What Ever Happened to Baby Jane?* Heavy black eyeliner and mascara, bright red lips with the lipstick applied rather . . . haphazardly. A wrinkled, ghostly white face with violent streaks of blush on her cheeks. She was elderly, but I couldn't quite tell whether she was my mother's age or much older.

I was about to ask Carter to offer her a ride to the door—peculiar though she was, it was raining heavily—but before I could get the words out he veered around her and sped the rest of the way so aggressively that I thought he might hit the building's stone foundation. He jerked to a stop and hurried out of the car, unfurling an umbrella as he did so.

Opening the back door, he leaned in to us and said: "Ladies?" He was smiling but his eyes had a hint of fear behind them, and I noticed beads of perspiration on his brow.

I looked out the rear window at the woman, who had been joined under her umbrella by a young man, who was leading her away. I turned back to Carter. "Is everything okay?"

"Fine, miss. Fine."

Reverend Parker stood to welcome us at the church door. In the midst of that storm, he seemed to me to be an oasis of serenity, smiling that warm smile, his blue eyes shining. Upon seeing him, all the tension I had felt during the morning pooled onto the ground in front of me and I stepped over it, just like one of so many puddles.

He held out his hands and I slid mine into his.

"I'm going to get you through this day, Grace," he said. "I'll be right here, next to you, with the widest shoulder you've ever seen. You are not doing this alone. I'm asking you to do me the favor of leaning on me."

I managed a smile.

We had timed our arrival so that most of the people coming

to the funeral would have been seated before us. Avoiding the throng, that was the goal. I saw that the parking lot was full and cars were snaking out onto the side streets. Fleets of official-looking limos lined one side of the lot—the vehicles of the governor, senators, and various congressmen. Satellite-laden vans from the three local news stations stood just past the limos. Adele Alban's funeral would be the lead story on tonight's news. I had asked reporters to stay away from the reception following the service—I had no wish for my grief to be on display—but there wasn't anything preventing them from filming here in the parking lot. It was a public place, after all. Cameramen and dark-suited reporters with microphones had jumped from the vans as we arrived, but I knew the rain would hamper their ability to get a clear shot. Good, I thought. Still, they called out to me.

"Grace! What's it like to be home after all this time?"

"Any comment about your mother, Miss Alban?"

"Amity! Over here!"

I ignored them and turned to the minister. "Is everyone in place?" I asked.

"They are," he said, scowling across the lot at the newscasters. "The beginning hymns have started, so you're right on time. When you're ready, the three of us will walk up the aisle together. You'll take your seats in the front pew, I'll go up to the pulpit, and we'll get this started. Then, after the service is over, I'll lead you back down the aisle. Your driver will be waiting right here to take you back to the house so you don't get caught in a line of well-wishers."

"Got it," I said.

"Grace! What's it like—"

We stepped inside, leaving the reporters and their questions behind. As we stood in the vestibule, I pushed that same stray curl from Amity's forehead, my palm lingering on her cheek. I saw that the church was packed, every seat filled, with even more people spilling out into the side aisles and standing in the back.

"Are you ready, honey?" I asked my daughter. She looked into my eyes and nodded. I put my arm around her shoulders and we followed Reverend Parker up the center aisle as every head turned to see the last two surviving Albans.

CHAPTER 12

I sang the hymns, listened to the readings, cried at the eulogies delivered by the governor, the mayor, and an old friend of my mother's, and was utterly grateful I had decided not to get up and speak myself. I knew I'd never be able to get the words out. I felt as though I were seeing it all from a distance, that I wasn't really sitting there, that I was removed somehow. Before I quite knew what was happening, Reverend Parker was standing at the side of our pew. *Oh,* I thought. *It's over? It's time to go?*

As I stood up and turned around, I glanced at the people sitting in the pews behind us. Their features seemed hazy and distorted, as if I were outside peering in at all of them through an old and weathered pane of glass. As we walked down the aisle, I could see a second set of mourners overlapping the first: wispy, spectral figures dressed in black. Long dresses, high collars, top hats. They were nodding at me, smiling sad smiles, holding out their hands toward me. I gasped and clutched at Matthew's arm to keep from stumbling when I recognized the faces of my ancestors—John James Alban, his wife, Emmaline, his children, and others, all there to pay their respects to my mother. I stopped and looked around wildly—*Jake? Jimmy? Dad?* Where were they? They had to be here!

"Grace?" Matthew's soft voice brought me back to reality.

I shook my head and looked around me—there were no

ghostly mourners after all. No dead ancestors. Only a church filled with people staring at me. It must have been some sort of hallucination brought on by the history of this place, each stone, each pew, each stained-glass window steeped in the lives and deaths of my family. I held Matthew's gaze and nodded—*I'm okay now, really*—and started down the aisle once again. I wanted nothing more than to get out of this church and into the light of day.

BACK AT THE HOUSE, I rushed up to bathroom of the master suite and splashed water on my face. I'd have to reapply my makeup, but I didn't care. I just wanted to feel something cold and wet and real.

"Mom?"

I snapped my head around to find Amity hovering in the bathroom doorway. I hadn't known she had followed me upstairs. "Are you okay?" she asked.

I blotted my face dry with a fluffy towel and smiled at her. "I'm fine, sweetie," I said, trying to quiet my racing heart. "It's just—I'm sorry. It was hard getting through the service, but everything's fine now."

Amity put her arms around me and held me tight. "I don't want to go back downstairs to the reception," she said. "Do I have to?"

I stroked her hair the way I used to when she was a child and needed comforting. "People are expecting to see you, honey," I said. "They want to pay their respects. The governor is coming. So are our two senators. And the mayor. The chief of police. So many others."

She pulled back and leaned against the doorframe. "I don't care," she said, sighing. "They're just a bunch of strangers."

I didn't blame her for that. Truth be told, I felt the same way.

"Listen, I'll make you a deal," I said as I fished my foundation out of my travel kit, squeezed a bit onto my fingertips, and began smoothing it over my face. "We'll wait up here until most everyone has arrived, and then we'll walk down the stairs together. I'm going to ask you to stick around for a half hour. Make an appearance. Let people pay their respects to you. Eat something if you want. And then if you'd like to slink off and come back up here or go outside if it ever stops raining, fine. Maybe you can find Cody and watch a movie or something with him."

Then another thought occurred to me. "Just let me know what you're doing, where you'll be," I went on. "I don't want to lose track of you today. Okay?"

She considered this as I stared into the mirror and rubbed some cream blush onto my cheeks. "Okay," she agreed. "I saw Heather and her parents in the church, so maybe they'll be here."

"Heather? Is she the girl you met when you were here last summer?"

Amity nodded. "Grandma signed me up for tennis lessons. Heather was on my team."

"Well, good," I said, silently hoping Amity would cement a friendship with this girl. If I was going to seriously consider moving back to Alban House, it would be nice if my daughter had a friend waiting for her in this town.

I peered out the window and saw row upon row of cars lining the parking lot where the ticket booth stood. The house was filling up. I smiled when I saw Matthew's old green Volvo parked next to a sparkling new Mercedes.

Staring at my reflection in the mirror, I said: "How do I look?"

"As good as can be expected for an old lady," Amity teased, smiling at me in the mirror.

I put my arm around her shoulders and took a deep breath. "I guess now's as good a time as any to head downstairs. The sooner we start, the sooner we'll be finished."

And we walked down the long hallway, listening to the amalgam of voices wafting up from the living room below, and descended the grand staircase into the fray.

I steered Amity through the sea of faces, stopping to speak with this one and that one, accepting sympathies and sad smiles. The caterers had laid a spread of hors d'oeuvres on the dining room table; several bottles of wine were open on the sideboard. Servers in black-and-white uniforms were circulating throughout the rooms, refilling glasses, scooping up used plates and silverware, offering trays of canapés and cheese and finger sandwiches to the attendees.

Flowers were everywhere, orchids and lilies and complicated arrangements of pink and white and lavender blooms. An enormous bouquet of fiery-colored tulips, red and orange and yellow, stood in the center of the dining room table. Next to sunflowers, tulips were my mother's favorite flower. Fires were burning in the living room, dining room, library, and parlor; candles flickered on the tabletops. Everything seemed to be humming along as it should.

I saw the governor and the two senators huddled with their heads together in the parlor. The image made me smile, knowing how many political campaigns were forged and funded in that very room.

As I mingled, I noticed a couple of uniformed officers standing at the bottom of the grand staircase, where a velvet rope had
been draped across the stairs after Amity and I had descended.
Apparently Jane had positioned them there to prevent any curious
guests from venturing up to the second and third floors. That
hadn't occurred to me, but I was glad she thought of it. I wondered, not for the first time, what sort of pandemonium would
overtake us if not for her steadfast presence in this house.

I spied Reverend Parker across the room talking to a group
of ladies from the church and made a beeline for him through
the crowd, smiling and patting people on the back as I went. He
excused himself from the brood of hens and steered me toward
the sideboard, pouring a glass of wine for both of us.

"I'd like to say the service was lovely, but truthfully it was a
blur," I said, taking a sip of wine.

"Understandable," he said. "Are you getting through this okay?"

"I am." I exhaled, seemingly for the first time that day. We
chatted for a few moments about nothing in particular until the
mayor pulled me away, wanting to pay her respects.

And so the afternoon went on. More hugs and reminiscences,
more condolences and well wishes, each of them melting into the
others until I couldn't distinguish between them. I would never
remember anyone's name or whose story about my mother was
whose. But the one thing I did take away from the reception was
the knowledge that my mother was well and truly loved and re-
spected by the people of this town, and for that I was grateful. As
much as I hadn't wanted to come downstairs after the funeral
and face this crowd, I was glad that I had.

As the reception was winding down and the throng was
thinning out, I caught sight of Amity across the room. She was

talking to a woman whose back was to me, and I saw one of her arthritic hands clamped around Amity's upper arm. I locked eyes with my daughter and saw a look of panic, a pleading sort of expression that I had never before seen on her face.

She opened her eyes wide and mouthed: "Mom!" I excused myself from whomever I was talking to and hurried across the room toward her, but before I could get there, the woman turned around to face me. It was the same woman we had nearly run down on our way to the church, bright red lipstick, heavily made-up eyes, and all.

"What a lovely party, isn't it, Adele?" she said to me, smoothing the front of her black dress, which I saw was worn and threadbare in spots. "Will we be playing croquet later? You know how I love croquet."

Adele? This woman thought I was my mother? I held out my hand to Amity and she slipped away from her and in behind me.

"Hello," I said slowly. "I'm Grace Alban."

"Grace Alban?" The woman's ashen face cracked into a wide smile. "But there's no such person! Unless you're some long-lost cousin I didn't know about. People are always coming out of the woodwork here at Alban House. Out of the woodwork!" She winked at me.

I was at a loss. I saw Matthew crossing the room toward me—bless him, coming to the rescue again—and I also saw the uniformed officers move closer.

"I'm the Reverend Matthew Parker," he said to the woman, moving slowly toward her as though she were a wild animal he was trying to snare. "May I get you some punch?"

She dropped her chin and batted her obviously false eyelashes at him. "Punch? How lovely, Reverend. I adore punch!"

He held out an arm to her and she slipped hers through his. "My, aren't you handsome!" she chattered away. "Adele always has the most handsome men around her. Don't you, Adele? The most handsome men."

I thought I detected a faraway fire behind her cloudy, weepy eyes. Matthew began to lead her away when Jane appeared in the room carrying a tray of wineglasses.

"Jane, will you bring us some punch?" the woman called to her, waving her arm in a wide arc. "I'm in the mood for punch, Jane. And then we're going to play croquet."

Jane took one look at her and cried out as the tray she was carrying clattered to the ground, glasses shattering everywhere. A stunned silence fell over the room.

"My goodness, Jane, whatever has come over you?" the woman wanted to know. "You're looking at me like you've seen a ghost."

CHAPTER 13

As the servers scurried into the room with mops, brooms, and dustpans to clean up the tray of glasses Jane had dropped, a man whom I had never seen before—midfifties, tall, wearing a black suit—slipped into the room and held out his hand to the woman.

"Now, now," he cooed. "Didn't I tell you to stay in the wing chair in the parlor until I could talk to our hostess?"

The woman huffed and pouted. "I didn't want to stay in the wing chair. I wanted to find Adele." Then, looking to me, her eyes brightened and she said: "Let's go upstairs and change out of these ridiculous black clothes. This party is dreadfully dull, don't you think? Maybe we could go for a swim!"

Jane had regained her composure and was helping guests with their coats and umbrellas, trying, it seemed, to usher the stragglers who remained at the reception out the door. I agreed with her. Everybody out. As she held the door, I saw that her face was gray and lifeless, a mask of confusion and questions.

A chill ran through me as I looked from the obviously old woman to her younger companion, who stood ramrod straight, chin jutted out, a slight smile on his face. Cockiness, that's what he projected. I shot a glance toward the officers, who were slowly approaching.

"I'm Grace Alban," I said to the man. "And you are . . ."

He held out his hand to me. I hesitated a moment before crossing my arms over my chest.

"I'm Harris Peters," he said, smiling broadly. But there was no warmth in his smile or behind his steel-gray eyes. "I'm here to pay my respects. I had an appointment to meet your mother the day she died."

"You're the journalist." I narrowed my eyes at him.

"That's right," he said, brushing a bit of lint from his lapel. "I'm writing a book about your family. I was so looking forward to meeting your mother."

"I specifically didn't invite any journalists to this reception, Mr. Peters," I told him. "I didn't want the press intruding on our grief today. So I'm afraid I'm going to have to ask you to leave."

"I thought you might say something like that," he said, still smiling that broad smile. "So I brought along a guest. I think she'll change your mind about my being here." He gestured toward the woman, who was now batting her eyelashes at him.

"Miss Alban," he said to her. "Isn't it lovely to be back home?"

"Miss Alban?" I furrowed my brow. "There is no Miss Alban other than myself."

"Yourself?" The woman laughed, a gurgling, throaty sound. "Adele, have you gone mad? You're no Alban, although you're certainly around here enough to be part of the family." She smiled up at Matthew and sniffed, "Herself. Who does she think she is, claiming to be an Alban?"

Harris crossed the room and put his arm around the woman's shoulder, leading her slowly away from Matthew. A proprietary gesture. "Of course she's a little confused," he said to me in a stage whisper. "Being in an institution for fifty years will do that to a person."

Time slowed to a crawl, groaned, and stopped. I looked around to the fire crackling in the fireplace, the candles burning low on the table. I noticed the hors d'oeuvres were nearly gone; several wine bottles were emptied. The heavy, deep red curtains in the parlor swayed ever so slightly, as if they were being blown by an unseen breeze. I could hear the rain still pounding away outside, and I smelled the particular spicy scent of my mother's perfume. And then, overpowering that, the fresh aroma of lake water that had accompanied my father's visit a few days earlier.

I locked eyes with Jane and there was something about her expression that told me, in that instant, who this woman was. I took a few steps toward her and held out my hands.

"You're Fate Alban, isn't that right?" I said to her. "I'm Grace, Adele and Johnny's daughter."

She shook her head. "Grace? I don't understand." She put one age-spotted hand, rings on every finger, up to my face and stroked my cheek. "Why are you acting like this? Whatever is the matter with you, my darling Adele? And where's my mother? I can't imagine where my mother has gone."

I grasped for Matthew's eyes with mine, silently pleading for help.

He understood immediately. "It's been a long day and you must be very tired, Miss Alban," Matthew said to her.

She smiled up at him, and as she did so, the years seemed to disappear from her face. Beneath all that garish makeup, I could see the beauty she had once been.

"During Daddy's summer solstice parties, we girls always take naps in the afternoons," she said, turning in a slow circle to address all of us. "That way, we're fresh for the nighttime activities. We'll have a bonfire! Down by the lakeshore. And we'll dance and dance and dance to the ancient songs. Mama likes that, don't you know. I'm quite light on my feet, that's what they say. All the fellows want to dance with me." She had turned full circle and held out her hands toward Matthew. "I'll save you a dance if you're lucky."

As she was speaking, a shroud of chill wrapped itself around me. It was clear—this woman was time traveling, perhaps even back to the party, fifty years earlier, when David Coleville took his own life. To the night she herself disappeared. I wondered if she had ever left that night or whether she was stuck there, reliving whatever happened to her, year after year after year.

Jane must've realized the same thing because she sprung into action, hooking an arm around Fate's waist and leading her away. "You're right, it's time for your nap now, Miss Fate," she said. "You want to be fresh for dinner and the evening's festivities. Your mother and the rest of the girls are already sleeping. I'll make up the chaise in the library for you. That's where you like to rest. Come on now."

Fate sighed and rolled her eyes dramatically for the benefit of all of us. "All right, Jane. If you say so." And she waved at us over her shoulder as she let Jane lead her out of the room. What a character she must've been in her youth, I thought.

When they had gone, I whirled around to face Harris Peters, the grief I had been keeping at bay for the past several days finally and completely catching fire.

"What is the meaning of this?" I demanded, my voice louder than I had intended, gesturing my arm toward the room where Jane had led my newly found aunt. "You burst in here on the day of my mother's funeral using a poor, confused old woman as a prop? I don't know what you think you're doing or what you're trying to accomplish with this stunt, but you're not making any friends here. Today of all days!" I stomped toward the window determined to hold back the tears that were threatening to erupt. "What kind of person are you?"

He just stood there, cool and collected. "I should be asking you that question," he said. "You're the head of a family that kept this 'poor woman,' as you called her, a prisoner in an institution for fifty years."

"That's not true," I spat back. "We had no idea where my aunt was. Nobody knew what had happened to her. She *disappeared* from this house fifty years ago. We all thought she was dead."

But even as I said the words, they rang hollow in my ears. Hadn't I been wondering, just the other day, about her disappearance and whether my grandparents had launched a search for her? The old family story just hadn't seemed right to me, it never had. This, at least, explained where she had been all this time.

Harris walked over to the sideboard and poured himself a drink. "You Albans might have controlled the press and the police generations ago, but not anymore. I knew something didn't add up about her disappearance. I knew she was out there somewhere, and I just couldn't stop wondering about it. Why send her away and cover it up?" He took a sip and continued. "I've spent years trying to find out what really happened."

He reached into his pocket, fished out a folded sheet of paper, and handed it to me.

"What's this?" I asked, but as I looked at it, I answered my own question. My college French told me it was the address of a hospital in Switzerland.

"Go ahead, call them," he went on. "You'll be told that Miss Alban has been living there since 1956. When I started this investigation, I figured she was in hiding somewhere. A plush villa in Italy. An estate in Ireland. After years of turning up nothing, I finally got the idea to check the best mental institutions worldwide. I don't know what made me think of that. Just a sixth sense, I guess."

While he was talking, my mind was racing in different directions at once. On the one hand, I should've been thanking this man for finding my long-lost aunt and bringing her home. I had no idea why she was institutionalized, but even if she needed around-the-clock care, we could certainly afford to hire a live-in nurse for her so she could stay at Alban House or, barring that, place her in the best care facility in town. But his demeanor made it impossible to be grateful. He stood there so proudly, so defiantly, as though he had unearthed a dirty family secret that we had intentionally kept hidden. I had no doubt that was the slant his book was going to take and I wanted to squash it here and now.

"She was in a mental institution and my family didn't feel the need to tell the world about it," I said, trying to steady my voice. "So what? Back in those days, mental illness *was* covered up. There's no bombshell here."

"Are you kidding?" Harris laughed at me. "I've solved the mystery of the Alban daughter who vanished the night of David Coleville's suicide! It's like finding the Lindbergh baby. Only her disappearance wasn't at the hands of a servant wanting ransom, it was the work of the family itself. Again, Grace, you have to ask yourself: Why?"

"You have no idea how or why she ended up in that institution, only that she was there," I said slowly, choosing my words carefully. "She might have run away from this house on her own. Others have. She certainly had the means."

"Do you really think I haven't asked her about it?" Harris chuckled. "What do you think we chatted about during that long plane ride across the Atlantic? And boy, does she like to talk."

"You went over there to get her," I said.

"I did indeed. Apparently her father had an entire wing at the hospital built just for her. It really is quite beautiful. That's how I found her, you see. One of my sources told me about how this hospital in Switzerland was a replica of a famous mansion in the United States, and it got me thinking. I pushed further, paid off a few people, and found her. And my source was right. It's a dead ringer for this place."

He took another sip of his drink and then continued. "She's all the way across the ocean imprisoned in a psychiatric hospital, and it's like she never left home. Maybe that's why she remembers the past so well. Especially when it comes to your mother. She's quite fixated on her."

I could feel the hair on the back of my neck bristle. I didn't know what he was implying, but I didn't like his tone.

"Of course she remembers her." I shrugged. "My mother was Fate's best friend when they were growing up. Again, that's some 'bombshell' you've got there, Harris."

But even as I said it, I realized I was feeling my way blind. I was trying to downplay an event in my family history that I knew nothing about. But then a thought occurred to me and I ran with it.

"If she told you so much, why are you here?" I asked him. "Why aren't you holed up someplace writing that book of yours or trying to convince a literary agent that it's worth publishing? I'll answer my own questions, Harris. It's because she hasn't told you anything you can use, or enough, at any rate. And you're here to get me to fill in the blanks for you. Isn't that right?"

He swirled the scotch in his glass. "I'm here because after learning what I did from your aunt, I wanted to talk to your mother—"

"You're a bit late for that, I'm afraid," I interrupted him, my voice disintegrating into a rasp.

"I realize that. Just before I was to meet your mother, your housekeeper called to tell me she had passed away. It was quite a shock."

"I'll bet it was," I spat back at him. "Imagine, spending all those years solving the mystery of the vanished Alban girl, only to lose the last remaining eyewitness just minutes before she might have told you all you needed to know. And now here you are, with a crazy old lady on your hands, and nobody to make sense of what she's saying."

"As I said, that's why I'm here."

"Now you're the one who's not making sense," I said. "Knowing my mother had passed away, why didn't you just get in touch with me? I've been here for more than a week. Why pull this stunt now, showing up like this at her funeral?"

"I tried to contact you," he told me. "Your housekeeper wouldn't put me through. I came in person; your police guards did their job. Talk about a stone wall. But I kept trying because, after all, I had your aunt and I needed to bring her here, whether you were going to talk to me or not."

I had heard enough. "Well, you've done that. Now it's time for you to leave." I shot a look at the officers, who were at his side in an instant.

"But we still have so much to say to each other," he said.

I crossed my arms in front of my chest. "I don't think so."

As the police escorted him to the door, he turned. "You need to know that this book is going to come out whether you talk to me or not. I had my tape recorder turned on during the entire flight and your aunt talked of nothing but the past. I don't have to write the book so much as transcribe it. And I promise you, Grace, much of what she said is going to rock the literary world. Scholars have been speculating for fifty years about the night Coleville killed himself. Now they'll have a firsthand account."

"And I promise *you*, Harris, if you slander my family in any way, you will know what it feels like to be on the wrong side of one of the most powerful families in this country."

"I'd think twice about making threats in public if I were you, Grace." He smiled.

"Think about this, Harris: You set one foot back on this property or try to contact me and I'll be delighted to have you arrested."

"Arrested?" He laughed. "On what charge?"

"I'm an Alban." I walked up to him, locked my eyes with his, and lowered my voice to a hiss, feeling the presence of my mother, father, and brothers behind me and invoking the spirits of that very house as I spoke. "If you know anything about my family, you know there doesn't need to be a charge."

I turned to the officers. "Gentlemen, please escort Mr. Peters from this property. Far from it."

As they led Harris Peters out of Alban House, I hurried to the window to see them put him into the back of their squad car. He saw me and waved, the cocky bastard. I watched as they pulled out of the drive, satisfied that he was really gone.

I turned around to find Matthew and Amity staring at me, openmouthed. "Anyone else thirsty?" I asked, making my way over to the sideboard and pouring myself a large glass of wine.

"I'll have one," Matthew said, grinning at me. "Whoa. I knew you were a strong lady, Grace. But I didn't know how strong."

I handed Matthew a glass and we stood in silence for a moment, my heart pounding so hard that I was sure the others could hear it. And then Amity said something that made it nearly stop. "Mom," she began. "Do you think he was the one in the false basement?"

This hadn't occurred to me, but it made perfect sense. "Aunt Fate could've told him all about the secret passageways when they were on the airplane coming from Switzerland! What a great way for him to dig up information from a family that he knew wouldn't talk to him."

"Unbelievable," Matthew murmured, staring down into his glass. Then he looked up at me, his brows furrowed. "You know, you threatened to have him arrested, but I wonder—do you think you could file kidnapping charges against him? He did walk out of a hospital with a patient."

That hadn't occurred to me, either, but it, too, made perfect sense. "I'll check into it. And I'm going to have the police put a trace on him, to make sure he doesn't worm his way back into the tunnels."

I crossed the room and sank into one of the armchairs by the fireplace, weighed down by what I had just learned. Fate Alban, suddenly alive, and sleeping on the chaise in the library.

My aunt had been, apparently, institutionalized since the night of David Coleville's suicide. I didn't want to admit it, to myself or to anyone else in the room, but a deep sense of dread was wrapping around me. I knew Harris Peters was right, that my grandfather, most likely, had put Fate away and covered it up, not even telling the family where she was. But why? Was whatever happened here that night horrible enough to drive her insane?

"Grace," Matthew began, his words pulling me back into the room. "How, do you think, did Peters get your aunt out of the hospital? I mean, you can't just waltz out of a locked ward with a longtime patient. If she suddenly turned up missing, why wouldn't the doctors there have called you?"

"They did." It was Jane, leaning against the doorframe.

CHAPTER 14

Nobody said anything as Jane slowly entered the room, exhaled, and sank into a chair. She fished a tissue out of her sleeve and dabbed at her brow.

"You knew about this?" I asked her finally.

She shook her head. "No. But I did take a call. The day before your mother died."

I exchanged glances with Matthew and then rose from my own seat and pulled up a chair next to her. "Go on, Jane. What did they say?"

"There was a call from a hospital in Switzerland," she confirmed. "I couldn't make heads nor tails of what they were saying at first, but finally it became clear that they were talking about a Miss Alban, that she had gone missing from their facility. I nearly had a heart attack myself when I realized what it all meant."

"Did you know she had been living there all this time?" I asked. "What I'd always been told—"

"No!" Jane shook her head violently. "You were told the truth, as we all knew it. Miss Fate disappeared from Alban House that night. We in the household were asked never to speak of it again, that Mr. Alban's grief at losing his daughter was too great. We did as we were told!"

By this time, Mr. Jameson had crept into the room and was

standing at his wife's side, patting her shoulder and cooing comforting words, his voice nearly a whisper.

Her expression, the look in her eyes, was wrapped in guilt and shame. I got the impression that she was feeling somehow responsible for this situation, that she had let the household and, worse, my mother down. For Jane, there could be no greater failing.

"Of course, Jane," I said, smiling slightly and patting her hand. "Of course you'd do what my grandfather asked. You didn't do anything wrong. Let's just back up for a second. What did they say on the phone, the people from the hospital?"

She cleared her throat. "They were calling to report that Miss Alban had gone missing from their facility," she repeated, her face ashen.

"And that's all?" I asked. "Nothing about how long she had been there or why she was there in the first place or how—"

Jane let out another long sigh and twisted the apron in her lap. "I know I should've asked all those questions, Miss Grace, but I was so stunned—struck down, almost—when I realized what they were saying. Miss Fate, alive! I didn't think to ask anything else."

I could understand that. "You said the call came just before my mother passed away. Did you tell her about the call?"

Jane held my gaze for a long time, and in her reddened, pained eyes, I saw the answer. She shook her head just the slightest bit before confirming what I knew. "I did not," she whispered, her voice breaking apart like shattered glass.

I wasn't sure what to say to Jane—I didn't know if telling my mother would have been the right thing to do or not—but I didn't have to respond, because Jane went on.

"Your mother hadn't been feeling well off and on for a couple of weeks," she explained. "It was one of those spring colds she always used to get. The horrible coughing. She was on the mend and just starting to get her strength back when the call came in. I wasn't quite sure what to do. I talked to Mr. Jameson about it and we decided to wait a few days to tell her, until she was feeling strong and well and more of herself."

"Aye," Jane's husband piped up, nodding his head. "We didn't want to give the lady too much of a start, not until she was up to it. We were"—his voice broke—"worried about her heart."

"But the journalist," I said. "When he called, didn't you think—"

"That we did," Jane confirmed. "He had been calling for weeks. When I took the call from the hospital, I put two and two together. I suspected he had been the one who had found Miss Fate. Too much of a coincidence, it was. I don't believe in coincidences."

Jane dabbed at her nose with the tissue. "Because your mother agreed to talk to him—it surprised me, sure it did—I was planning to tell her about it before he got here. When she came in from her walk. I thought that, if she was feeling up to going outside, well, she could handle the news that Miss Fate was alive and that I suspected this journalist was the one who had found her. And maybe it would convince her not to talk to him. That's what I was hoping. Never in the world did I think he would bring her here. Like this. Today of all days."

I took Jane's hands in mine. It was time to come clean, for both of us. High time. "I want to hear exactly what you know about that night, Jane. The night David Coleville killed himself here at Alban House. And I have something to tell you in return. I found some letters—"

But I didn't get a chance to tell her about the letters, and she didn't get the chance to tell me what she knew about that night, not just then. Before either of us could get any more words out, I heard my daughter's voice, distant and small, hesitant at first. "Mom?" And then more urgent. "Mom!"

I turned in the direction of her voice, the grand staircase, and saw her on the second-floor landing. I hadn't realized that she had slipped out of the room. "Mom, you need to come up here."

"What is it, honey?" I asked, almost afraid to approach her.

"Somebody has been in our rooms," she said, her voice a harsh whisper.

A chill fell around me, and in an instant I was flying up the stairs, grasping at Amity and running with her toward the master suite, Matthew, Jane, and Mr. Jameson following close behind. The door was ajar, and I pushed through it to find a scene of utter disarray—clothes and hats strewn everywhere, the desk overturned, its contents littered all over the floor. The computer was lying sadly on its side and half of the books on my mother's bookshelf were thrown this way and that. I could see that the tapestry was drawn back, the hidden door wide open like a gaping maw.

My hands flew to my mouth. Amity was clutching me and I put an arm around her.

"Honey," I began, "you said somebody had been in our rooms. Plural. Just this suite of rooms, or—?"

She shook her head tightly. "Yours, too."

I flew back out the door and down the hallway. The door to my old room was open, my suitcase splayed out in the center of the floor, clothes from the closet tossed about, the dresser drawers open, their contents rifled through.

And then I saw them—the letters David Coleville had written to my mother, strewn about on the floor like so many fallen leaves. I gathered them up and held them close to my heart. My mother's private letters, a love she had kept hidden for decades, so violated and exposed. On the day of her funeral, no less. This felt like an attack on her. My eyes stung with tears.

"How could this happen?" Amity's voice wavered, vulnerability seeping through her words. "Guards were here the whole time. They've been here for days."

"Not the whole time," I said, glancing at the window. "They took Peters away in their squad car just now. No guards are here."

Matthew shook his head. "There wouldn't have been enough time for whoever did this to do so much damage," he said. "The guards left just a few minutes ago. This scene took a while to create, I'm afraid."

"They were standing by the stairs most of the afternoon," Amity said. "There was another pair outside."

"That's right!" I said, remembering seeing the velvet rope across the staircase. "Whoever did this must've used the passageways. It very well could have been Harris Peters, before he made his grand entrance."

By this time, Jane had made it to the second floor and was peering into the room. "Jesus, Mary, and Joseph," she whispered.

I bent down to retrieve a jacket from the floor, but Matthew grasped my hand before it made contact with the fleece. "I think you should leave everything just as it is, for now," he said, his eyes scanning the room. "The police are going to want to see this untouched. Maybe whoever did this left fingerprints."

He was right. I put my arm around Amity and led her out of the room and into the hallway, shuddering to think that, had

I not insisted she make an appearance at the reception, she might have been up here when the thief burst in.

Jane looked at me, and as if she could read my thoughts, she said: "I'll make the call to police, miss." And she hurried off toward the telephone in my mother's study.

Matthew, Amity, and I walked the other way, down the hall toward the stairs, but before we descended, he stopped and turned back toward the master suite. "What I don't get is, why?" he said, narrowing his eyes and shaking his head. "Why would anybody do this? What did they think they were going to find? Something valuable—jewelry, maybe?"

The realization washed down around me like a cold rain. Scenes flashed in my mind, me talking with Amity in my mother's study the first day we arrived, me sitting alone on the floor of her closet reading the letters my mother had kept hidden all these years, me hurrying into my room and tucking the letters inside my own suitcase. Someone had been in the passageways watching us, *watching me*, all the while. It was the only way anyone would have known those letters were in my suitcase.

I was still clutching the letters in one hand, and I quickly scanned the envelopes. The last one, the one describing Coleville's unpublished manuscript, was gone.

"I know what they were looking for," I said, my voice dropping to a low whisper as I scanned the walls, wondering if whoever did this was still lurking behind them. "It was something very valuable, but not jewelry. Let's go into the solarium." Holding Matthew's gaze and putting an arm around my daughter's shoulders, I explained: "It's the only room in the house that doesn't have hidden passageways running through the walls. I've got something to tell you."

CHAPTER 15

The rain was still coming down, hitting the windows and roof of the solarium in bursts, creating a sheen of opaqueness through which the gardens and the lake beyond seemed distorted and strange, a world of illusion and fantasy. Amity and I settled onto the sofa farthest away from the door, Matthew took the armchair next to us. They both were looking at me with the same expression of expectancy—waiting for whatever it was I had to say.

Jane had made her way downstairs and had followed us into the solarium, carrying a tray of teacups and a pot. As she began to pour, I said to her: "You should hear this, too. Why don't you pour yourself a cup and join us?" It was then I noticed she had indeed brought four cups.

I unfolded the first letter and smoothed it onto the coffee table between us, a stalling gesture while I thought about exactly how to say what I had to say.

"We all know that the writer David Coleville was a good friend of my father's and that he killed himself here at Alban House during a summer party in 1956. What some of you may not know, and what I just found out a few days ago, is that he also visited here the summer before, in 1955."

The room was oddly silent but for the patter of the rain, as though everyone was holding their breath.

"I found these letters—*we* found these letters, Amity and I, in my mother's closet the first day we arrived," I went on, looking at my daughter. "I told you, honey, that I didn't know who they were from, but I found out. They were from David Coleville."

Amity and Matthew exchanged puzzled glances. "We read some of his stories in journalism class," Amity said. "He wrote to Grandma?" I smiled at her then, noticing how much she suddenly resembled my mother and her familiar worried expression.

"He did. He wrote to Grandma. They met, here at Alban House, the summer before he killed himself. They wrote letters to each other that whole year while he was in Boston and she was here. The letters don't say much, they're newsy accounts of his life, the classes he taught that year, his writing. But they did say one thing loud and clear. David Coleville and my mother were very much in love."

"Are you saying that you think these old letters have to do with the break-ins?" Matthew asked.

"I do," I said. "One of them was what was stolen. And it's not just the letters themselves but what they contain that's valuable— worth stealing, in other words. But there's something else, too. I just have a feeling, deep down, that it's all connected."

Matthew, Amity, and Jane were looking at me with quizzical looks on their faces.

I tried to clarify. "Look at what has happened: my mom's death on the *very day* she was going to talk to a reporter about the night David Coleville killed himself and Aunt Fate disappeared, a night that has been shrouded in family secrecy for fifty years. Then we found letters from Coleville just a few days after that. Then our house was broken into, multiple times, and one of those letters was stolen. And now this reporter—who just happens to be the very person Mom was going to talk to on the day she died—shows up with Aunt Fate, the very person who disappeared on the night Coleville died. The same thread is running through all of it. It just has to be."

I noticed Jane's hand shaking as she lifted the teacup to her lips. Her face was pale, her eyes red with grief.

"In order to get to the bottom of what's happening now, we have to understand what happened that night," I concluded.

Jane set her teacup down with a clatter and cleared her throat.

I turned to her. "You were here that summer, Jane, isn't that right?" I asked her.

She nodded. "Aye," she said, a faraway look in her eyes. "I was here. I was a young girl, about the same age as your mother and your aunt Fate. Already married to my Mr. Jameson. My mother ran this house in those days."

"Did you know, Jane? Did you know that my mother and David Coleville were in love before she married my father?"

Jane held my gaze, her eyes steeled. "Aye." She looked out the window into another place and time. "It was no secret. Your mother practically lived here at this house when she was a girl, growing up. She was like a daughter to mister and missus, so she was. And wee Fate, she doted upon her. Those two girls were thick as thieves. Fate loved her like a sister, so she did. And lucky for it. After Miss Mercy passed on, Adele was the only sister Miss Fate had."

I squinted at Jane. I had never heard of a Mercy. "Who did you say passed on?"

Jane's eyes opened wide and she stared at me, taking in a

silent gasp and holding it. She raised a hand to her cheek. I got the impression she was backpedaling, trying to think of a way to take back the words that had just come out of her mouth.

"Jane?"

She sighed and sat back, resting her head on the back of the chair and raising her eyes to the ceiling. A lone tear trickled down her cheek.

"Mercy was the sister," she said finally. "Fate and Johnny's sister. It's time you knew."

My mouth dropped open. How many more bombshells were going to burst over my head today?

"My parents never spoke of her, not even once," I said.

"Mercy left this earth as a very young child," Jane said, clearing her throat and straightening the apron in her lap. "That's one reason your mother was so welcome here. She brought life and laughter back into this house when it was sorely needed. Mrs. Alban, your grandmother Charity, nearly went mad with grief for her daughter. Miss Adele helped her heal, so she did. She helped all of us."

So my father had a sister who had died young. Another Alban mystery, another Alban body unearthed. I wondered what else I would dig up under the shroud of secrecy that surrounded my family's history.

I'd ask Jane all about my doomed aunt Mercy some other time. It wasn't important to what was happening at that moment and I didn't want to get sidetracked. I wanted to talk about the question at hand—my mother and David Coleville and the night he died.

"I know Mom and Fate were the best of friends," I pressed on, drawing Jane back into the present. "But what I was asking

was, did you know Mom and David Coleville were in love, and—"
I stopped and looked from Matthew to Amity, who, for once,
was rapt by what I was saying. "Did you know they planned to
marry? Was that common knowledge back then?"

"Wait a minute," Amity interrupted, leaning forward and putting her hand on my arm. "Grandma was going to *marry* David
Coleville?"

I nodded. "That's what it said in the letters. He was coming
back here that summer of 1956 to marry her."

Matthew whistled, long and low, and pushed his back against
his chair with a thud.

I looked to Jane and continued. "But she married my father
shortly after that summer. In October of that year, if I'm remembering their anniversary right. Is that why Coleville killed himself? Because she spurned him when he had come back here to
marry her? She had obviously fallen in love with my dad, and—"

Jane's lips formed into a tight line. "No, child. No. Everybody
knew how much Miss Adele loved David Coleville, and how much
he loved her. Why, she and Missus Charity were chattering about
it all that year, how the wedding would be held right here at Alban House. It was like Charity was her own mother. And Mr.
Alban, don't you know, he was going to pay for the whole thing.
Plans were already in the works. The dress was bought, the menu
decided on. The staff was buzzing about it the day Mr. Coleville
arrived that summer. We knew we'd have a wedding to throw by
the time August rolled around."

"But why?" I shot back. "Given all that, why would he have
killed himself? It doesn't make any sense."

Jane held my gaze for a long time. "Suicide never makes any
sense, it's simply a tragedy through and through," she said.

And then she stood up, clattering the tray in front of her. "I'm afraid it's time I checked on Miss Fate."

Of course. In all the commotion, I had nearly forgotten that I had an ancient aunt sleeping on the chaise in the library. Whatever was I going to do with her?

"Jane, will you make a note to call the hospital tomorrow morning?" I asked her. "I want to speak with her doctors about any medication she should be taking. We also need to get her seen here, so please call Dr. Johnson's office and make that happen sooner rather than later."

I closed my eyes for a moment, suddenly feeling the weight of the world. If this was what it was like to be the head of Alban House, maybe I didn't want to stay here after all.

"So what happened?" Amity picked up the thread of our conversation after Jane slipped out of the room. "Grandma was going to marry this guy, he winds up dead, and she gets married to Grandpa instead? That's just too weird."

I shook my head. "I know. I was thinking the same thing. What possible reason would Coleville have had to take his own life?"

Matthew leaned forward, his voice dropping low. "What if he didn't?"

I held his gaze, and I could feel a tingling working its way up my spine. "What do you mean?"

"Well, suicide on the eve of his wedding doesn't make any sense, right? What if he didn't kill himself?"

"You mean . . . murder? Who would want to kill him? Why?" But even as I said the words, I knew.

"Oh my God," I whispered. "He really might have been murdered. There's something else about those letters, something you don't know." I paused for a moment before continuing. "And it could explain a lot of things. It's what our thief—whoever broke into the house and rifled through our rooms—was looking for. And it could also be the reason David Coleville is dead."

Both of them leaned in toward me. "Our thief stole the last letter Coleville wrote to Mom before coming here that summer. It had some pretty explosive things to say about the Alban family."

Amity squinted at me. "Like what?"

"Criminal things," I said, my voice dropping low. "Things that I'm sure the Albans wouldn't have wanted to come to light. Illegal activities during Prohibition, that sort of stuff. Apparently David Coleville had done some research into the family's past."

"Wait a minute," Matthew interjected. "Why would your thief have wanted that information? I mean, it's not like anybody is concerned now about people running liquor during Prohibition. It was so long ago that it's almost romantic when you think about it. Nobody cares about that stuff now."

"No," I said, shaking my head and leaning forward. "The letter said that during the first summer he spent here at Alban House, David Coleville started writing a novel. It was a thinly veiled account of that first summer he spent here, and it dredged up all sorts of unsavory information about the family. The letter also said he sent my mother a copy of the manuscript! I'm sure that's ultimately what our thief is looking for."

"Are you saying he might have been killed because of what was in that book?" Matthew said.

I didn't much like that idea because it pointed to a member of my own family. But it certainly made sense. "A book by Coleville would've been a bestseller, and if it was full of dirt about this family, it's certainly possible he was killed because of it."

Matthew and Amity were silent for a moment. "I think I get what you're saying," my daughter said finally. "It's like two generations, two crimes, one reason."

I nodded. "We don't know for sure that he was murdered. But he might have been. And that manuscript is as good a reason as any. He was messing with a very powerful family."

"Right," Amity said. "But what I don't get is, what's so important about it now? Why would someone have broken in here now to get it?"

Matthew answered her question. "A half century after Coleville's death, finding the novel everyone was anticipating before he died and bringing it to the world—I can't imagine how much that manuscript would be worth today."

"Millions?" Amity said.

"I'm not sure about millions, honey," I said. "But at any rate, it would be worth a lot."

Amity opened her eyes wide. "Whoa."

"Whoa is right." I smiled at her. "I'd been planning to look for it after the funeral. He sent it to Grandma, and considering the fact that she kept his letters, it still could be among her things."

"If your thief didn't get to it first," Matthew said, his eyes narrowing. "Actually, Grace, I've been wondering if you and Amity should move into a hotel. It's sort of a romantic notion, looking for an undiscovered manuscript by a literary giant, but we can't forget that someone else is looking for it, too. And he's already broken into this house more than once."

I let his remark sink in for a moment before responding.

"No," I said. "I was away from this house for too long. I'm not going to let some thief run me out of it again. This is my home, and if I've got to have an armed guard in every one of its forty rooms to be safe, then that's what I'm going to do. But I'm not leaving."

Amity nodded in agreement and I squeezed her hand. "There's another reason I want to find that manuscript," I went on. "Other than the value it will have to the literary world, that is. If Harris Peters is really going to write some tell-all book about this family based on the reminiscences of my crazy aunt, the news of a previously unpublished, unknown work by David Coleville that just happens to be about my family will absolutely bury it. Nobody's going to care about his little book in the face of that."

"You're absolutely right." Matthew smiled back at me. "So where are you going to begin looking?"

"I really have no idea where it might be, but I'm thinking that my mother's safety deposit box at the bank might be a good place to start."

Amity settled into the back of the sofa, pulled up her legs, and crossed her arms around her knees. Her eyes were narrowed.

"What is it, honey?" I asked her.

"There's one big thing about all of this that I just don't get," she said.

"What's that?"

"If Grandma was so much in love with David Coleville, why did she get married to someone else so soon after he died? You said it was just a few months after his death, right? That seems really weird to me."

As Amity's words hung in the air, a cold wind wrapped itself around me. There could be only one reason for a rushed wedding so soon after a planned one had fallen apart because of a tragedy, and the look I exchanged with Matthew told me we both knew what it was.

CHAPTER 16

The math just didn't add up, not by a long shot. I was my parents' eldest child, and I was born years after their wedding day. There was no way I was David Coleville's child.

Still, my father's last words to me were knocking at my brain as I quickly ticked off the months between my parents' marriage and my birth. If I hadn't been his child, it certainly would've explained why he was so utterly despondent that Jimmy and Jake had perished that day in the lake instead of me.

I didn't want to say any of this out loud, didn't want to let on to Amity what I had been thinking. But I knew Matthew had been thinking the same thing, and I wanted him to know it wasn't the case. I held his gaze and shook my head slightly, silently saying "No" in my own head, and by the way his features relaxed, I knew that he got the message.

As it was, we were left with a snarl of questions and no definitive answers. I knew only one thing for sure. All of it, every last thread, was running through one terrible night here at Alban House more than fifty years ago.

I took the last sip of my tea and placed my cup back on its saucer, wishing I could somehow time-travel back to a summer solstice party in 1956 to see for myself what really happened there.

"Miss?" Jane's voice broke my concentration. "The police

have arrived and Mr. Jameson has taken them up to the master suite. I've told them what I know, and they'll be wanting to talk with the three of you next."

Matthew, Amity, and I stood up, and I saw him stretch his arms above his head and yawn. I wasn't the only one who was tired.

"Every time you're here, the police come." I smiled at him. "Coincidence? I'm not so sure."

He chuckled and raised his eyebrows. "The sinister minister. It has a nice ring to it."

"You're not going to want to visit me anymore," I went on. "It gets a little tedious, crime after crime after crime."

"Ah, the monotony of constant danger and intrigue. You really should try to liven things up around here."

Despite our attempt to lighten the mood, a shroud of exhaustion was wrapping itself around me and pulling in tight. I had dealt with enough today—the last thing I wanted to do was to talk to the police yet again. What I wouldn't give for a long, hot bath and a good book. But if we were ever going to get to the bottom of who was lurking within the walls of this house, I knew it had to be done.

We briefed the police on the latest developments, and as they began another sweep of the passageways and the grounds, I walked Reverend Parker out.

"Thank you for today," I said as we neared the big double doors in the front of the house. "I appreciate everything you've done, truly."

He smiled and shook his head. "It's what we clergy do. I know it's not easy for you, Grace, especially not now with all of this going on." He gestured toward the window, where we both could see three squad cars parked in the driveway.

He grasped the doorknob but then hesitated a moment. "This is where you grew up, but you haven't been back here in a couple of decades," he said, his eyes reaching for mine. "I'm not sure how many people you know in town anymore. I guess what I'm trying to say is, anytime you'd like somebody to talk to, or even just take a walk with, please know you can call me."

I leaned against the doorframe and managed a smile. "Thanks. Maybe I will."

"I hope so," he said, and walked out into the night, closing the door behind him.

As I turned to climb the stairs, despite how tired I was, I found myself wishing he had stayed awhile.

CHAPTER 17

When I left the house for my appointment with our family's lawyer the next morning, I found that the rain that had drenched the funeral had dissipated during the night, and it was a bright and blue day. The sun shone on my face as I made my way up the stairs to the old stone office building downtown, so I peeled off the cardigan I had thrown on over my cotton dress. I was grateful that our lawyer had made an exception for me and agreed to meet on a Saturday. I was eager to dispense with this formality—the reading of my mother's will—and get on to the next phase of things.

I sat across the enormous wooden desk from Bob Robinson, who had handled my family's affairs for as long as I could remember.

"The reception was nice," he said as he assembled the paperwork. "Adele would've loved it."

"Thank you." I nodded, twisting my cardigan in my lap. As he looked up at me over his bifocals, he held my gaze a bit longer than I would've liked, a stern expression on his face. I got the feeling he was getting ready to tell me something unexpected and strange, and it made my stomach do a quick flip.

He cleared his throat. "First things first," he began, handing me checks my mother had designated for Jane, Mr. Jameson, and Carter. Generous sums, as I knew she would give our family's most trusted employees.

"They could retire on this," I said, flipping through them.

He still held my gaze. "That's up to you," he said. "It depends on what you want to do with the house, of course. I know you've made your life out on the West Coast, but your mother has left you a suggestion that I think might change things in that regard."

I squinted at him. "What kind of suggestion?"

He pushed a piece of paper across the desk toward me. It was written in my mother's delicate handwriting.

> *In conjunction with the university that is already conducting tours of Alban House, I propose, each summer, to turn the house and the grounds into a monthlong retreat for writers and artists who either:*
>
> - *Intend to write or are writing works of fiction of a gothic nature.*
> - *Intend to paint or sketch a series of landscapes and wish to use the Alban property as inspiration.*
>
> *The program, to be deemed the David Coleville Retreat, will house up to three artists and three writers during the month of June.*
>
> *The writers and artists will be expected to work full time on their projects, emerging at the end of the month with, if not finished work, then good, solid progress.*
>
> *The writers and artists in attendance will be chosen by a panel of writing and fine arts professors at the university, with the final decision being made by Grace Alban, who will also administer and host the program.*

I sat there staring at the page and the potentially new future it held for me. A purpose. Something to dedicate my life to, other than raising my child, who was already beginning to become more and more independent. In just a couple of years, she'd be in college, and then what would I do with myself? It seemed that my mother had provided an answer to that question.

"I think it's an excellent idea," the lawyer said. "Your mother was a great patron of the arts, as you know, and this is a wonderful way to honor her. But it's up to you. She spoke about this with me and was going to bring this up to you within the next year or so. Specifically, she didn't want to force you into anything, so she didn't tie your inheritance, which is the bulk of the estate, to this. Take some time, process the idea, and know that you can put it into motion anytime you wish."

I nodded, and a pang of melancholy went through me when I realized how much she must have loved the man to create a retreat in his honor.

"For now," he said, shuffling more papers on his desk, "we should finish the business at hand. I've got a noon tee time."

There were no more surprises in her will. A generous trust for Amity, which she could access only after she had finished college and embarked on a meaningful career of her own. Everything else went to me. So that was it, then.

On the way home in the back of the car, something about this proposed retreat gnawed at me. If I was going to take on this project, dedicate my life to running a retreat in the name of this man, I really needed to know, more than ever before, how and why he died.

After Carter dropped me off at the front of the house, I headed toward the kitchen to find Jane.

Pushing open the door, I asked: "Do you have a minute?"

She looked down at the vegetables she was chopping and looked back at me. "Of course," she said, "but—"

"You don't need to stop what you're doing," I said quickly. "I just have a few questions about the night that David Coleville died."

She eyed me darkly. I could see full well that she wasn't happy about this topic of conversation. But I leaned my elbows on the counter and continued. "It's just—everything happening around here lately seems to be tied to that night, and I was hoping, since you were here, you could shed some light on it."

She wiped her hands on her apron. "Miss Grace, you're searching for answers that don't exist. It's best you leave it be."

"But you were here," I pressed on. "What is it that I don't know?"

She shook her head. "I wish I had the answers for you," she said. "It's true, I was here. But you have to understand, that night was your grandfather's annual summer solstice party. This was the social event of the season. Hundreds of people were here. Politicians, artists, professors, dignitaries of all kinds. I was busy making sure the whole thing went off without a hitch."

I squinted at her. "So as far as you knew, nothing out of the ordinary was going on that night? Nothing to explain what happened?"

"Aye. That's what I'm telling you. The first I heard of it—his death, I mean—your father had already called the ambulance."

"My dad found him, then?"

Jane shook her head. "The way it was told to me, your mother came upon his body in the garden. It was her screams that brought Johnny running. Always looking after her, he was. Ach, such a scene. I wasn't sure she'd ever come out of the shock of it."

"And when did you realize Aunt Fate was missing?" I asked her.

Jane thought for a moment. "Hours later. It was pandemonium—the ambulance arriving, guests leaving. Mr. Alban wanted everyone to leave immediately, and I was rushing to get their coats and hats."

That didn't sound quite right to me. "But didn't the police want to question everyone who was here?"

"Child"—she smiled—"this was Alban House fifty years ago. Your grandfather and the chief of police . . . Let's just say they had a rather special relationship."

I nodded. Of course they did. Just like my mother and Chief Bellamy.

"Your grandfather called the police—actually made the call himself—and told them what had happened here," she said, holding my gaze. "And that was all there was to it. There was no investigation."

"And when you realized Fate was missing . . . ?"

"Mr. Alban said he was handling it, that he had dispatched people to find her and we, the staff, were told not to worry about it. We did what we were told, Miss Grace."

"And that's all you know?"

Jane nodded. "That's all I know, child. As I said, I was just a girl myself. If anyone in the household had known anything else, it would have been your grandfather's man, Hamilton. He handled everything for Mr. Alban back in those days."

And he was long dead, I knew. I had never met the man.

Changing the subject, Jane said: "The doctor from the hospital in Switzerland returned your call while you were out."

"On a Saturday?" I wondered if Swiss doctors kept different hours from their counterparts in the States.

"He said he'll call back," Jane said. "He's not going to be available tomorrow, so it'll have to be Monday."

"Damn it!" I whispered under my breath. Another whole day would go by without my talking to him, and I needed information about my aunt's condition, sooner rather than later. I was worried my aunt was supposed to be on medications that she wasn't taking, and that her care was being compromised because of Harris Peters's rash action of taking her out of the facility and bringing her here. I thought about Matthew's suggestion that I sue him or make it a police matter—a kidnapping charge certainly wasn't out of the realm of possibility—but my first action needed to be to secure her care. Then I'd deal with Harris.

I made a mental note to wake up early Monday morning (or stay up very late) in order to call the doctor during his workday, some seven hours earlier than it was here in the Midwest.

"How has Aunt Fate been doing today, Jane?" I asked. "I haven't been to see her myself, I have to admit. I know I should just go and talk to her but I . . ." I didn't quite know how to explain the fact that I'd been avoiding my aunt. Jane must've seen the guilt on my face because she did her best to absolve it.

"With all that you've got on your shoulders right now, miss, you don't also have to be dealing with a sick, old woman," she said. "I am taking care of her. It's my place, not yours. I've known her since she was a girl, remember, and I can deal with her care now until things get sorted out with her doctor. Miss Fate is tired and confused—the journey alone must've taken it out of her—and she needs her rest. When she's back on her feet, then you can have a nice long chat with her." Jane cast her gaze up to the ceiling. "I must confess that I've been keeping her suite locked on the third floor."

I bristled at the thought of it—it sounded rather Dickensian to me. I didn't know if I liked the idea of keeping the woman locked up. "But—" I started to protest, but Jane cut me off.

"It's for her own safety," she said, straightening her apron. "I can't be watching her all the time, not with everything I have to do. Until we get a care nurse for her full time, or whatever we do with her, she needs to be where she's safe. I don't want her wandering outside and getting lost or hurting herself on the stairs."

She took a deep breath in and let it out. "Not that there's much chance of that," she continued. "Miss Fate seems more than content to stay in her childhood rooms on the third floor. She looks out the window, reads some of her old books, and even watches a little television. It's where she's always felt the most safe, so it is."

"Still, I don't relish the idea of keeping her locked up," I said. "Use your discretion, Jane, but maybe we could just lock the doors at night?"

My head began to pound at the weight of everything I was dealing with.

"Do you ever wish for the bliss of being bored with nothing to do?" I managed a weak smile and ran a hand through my hair. "I'm not sure I even remember that feeling."

"Aye." Jane nodded. "That's what it is to be the head of Alban House. Always has been."

I supposed she was right.

"Your mother took things one at a time," Jane went on. "Got one crisis off her plate, then on to the next. It's the only way."

I smiled at her. "Good advice."

As I made my way up the steps to the second floor, I looked around and thought of the proposed retreat that I very well could be running here the following year. I imagined artists painting outside in the garden and writers with their heads bent over their manuscripts . . . just as my mother and Coleville had done all those years ago. And then it hit me—she not only wanted to honor the man, she wanted to re-create what they did here together, making the house a sort of shrine to their relationship. How she must have loved him.

My heart began to ache for her, for what she lost that night at a summer party fifty years earlier.

"What happened that night, Mom?" I said aloud. "If the Albans killed the man you loved, how in the world did you end up here, with them?"

WITH JANE BEING A STONE WALL, I realized that if I wanted more information about what had happened, there was only one place I was going to find it: Coleville's lost manuscript. It wouldn't tell me about the night he died, obviously, but it would provide the background for his death and, if it was as inflammatory toward my family as he said it was, perhaps even the reason for it. It also wouldn't tell me how and why my mother had married my dad, but at least it was a start.

My mother had kept his letters. I couldn't imagine her not keeping the manuscript, too. It had to be here in the house.

But where?

I opened the door to her bedroom and put the packet of papers from the lawyer's office into her desk. Then I began rummaging around—the desk, the nightstand, the armoire. I scoured her bookshelf, riffled through the closet, and peered under the bed. I opened her wall safe. Nothing. And then I remembered there was another wall safe downstairs in the library.

My mind flipped back into the past as I hurried down the stairs, and I gave a small, internal cheer when it hit on the crucial bit of information I was trying to remember: the combination. My mother had changed it years before to my brothers' birthday—01-27-19-73—and had told me about it at the time.

In the library, I carefully took one of her paintings off the wall, the one I knew concealed the safe, and, with shaking hands, dialed in the combination. The safe opened with a *chock*. It was as easy as that! But as I drew out its contents—cases of old jewelry that I knew belonged to my great-grandmother, legal papers, even an ancient-looking pistol (loaded, I noticed)—I realized the manuscript wasn't among them.

"Where did you stash it, Mom?" I said to her, my mind running in several directions at once. But as I sank into one of the armchairs, I wondered if anyone could ever find something that was deliberately hidden in this house of secrets.

I spent the rest of the day scouring every place I could think of where my mother might have hidden that manuscript for safekeeping—I riffled through bookshelves in the library, opened dresser drawers, peered under beds and in the backs of closets. I even sifted through the attic, picking through relics from my family's past. Nothing.

Defeated, I tramped back down to the main floor, wandering into the library and realizing my search was at its end.

Just then, the phone rang, and I snatched it before Jane could pick it up, hoping it was the doctor in Switzerland calling back.

"Hello?" I said. "This is Grace Alban."

"Hello, Grace Alban," said a familiar voice. "This is Matthew Parker."

CHAPTER 18

Hi," I said, a little startled to hear his voice on the other end of the line.

"I know we left it that you were going to call me if you needed to talk to somebody," he began, and I could hear him clearing his throat. "But even though we extend the offer, people don't always follow it up. So I thought I'd just give you a quick call to see how you were doing."

I smiled. "I had a meeting with my mother's lawyer today," I told him, crossing the room and settling into an armchair. "She wants me to turn Alban House into a retreat for writers and artists during the month of June every year. She wants it to be named for David Coleville."

He was silent for a moment. "What a marvelous idea. What do you think about it?"

"I'm not quite sure," I admitted. "It will be up to me to administer it—to run the program, in other words. I'm to choose the participants from a pool sent to me by the university."

I could almost see him nodding. "Is it something you'd want to do?"

"The more I think about it, the more I like it," I said, looking around the room, imagining a group of artists and writers gathering for drinks before dinner.

"It's fraught with meaning, all of it," he said, and I could hear him pouring something into a cup. Coffee? "In terms of the timing, I mean."

"How so?"

"She wants it named for Coleville, and June is the month in which he died, at the very house where this retreat is to take place. She wants her one remaining child to spend at least part of her life dedicated to honoring his memory."

I shifted in my seat. "I hadn't thought of it that way." I hesitated before continuing. "Obviously, she loved the man. The more I think of it—his death, I mean—the more I don't like the conclusions I'm coming to. I really don't think there was any way it was suicide."

"You're thinking that whatever is in that manuscript . . ."

"I turned the house upside down this afternoon looking for it," I admitted.

"And you didn't find it, I'm assuming."

"No. I looked everywhere I could think of—safes, secret drawers, under beds, in the attic. It's not here, unless my mother had another secret hiding place, which, when you think about my family, isn't out of the realm of possibility."

Matthew was quiet for a moment. "Oh, Grace. I can't believe I didn't think of this before."

"Think of what?"

"What you said just now, about another secret hiding place?" he said. "This might turn out to be nothing, but I think I might know of one."

"You think you know where the manuscript might be?"

"I'm not sure, but I've got an idea. Are you busy right now?"

I looked around. Amity was off in the gardens; dinner wasn't quite ready. "I guess not."

"I'll pick you up at Alban House in ten minutes."

CHAPTER 19

I jumped into the passenger side of the green Volvo, and Matthew pulled out of our driveway. He surprised me, just a short ways down the road, by turning into the church parking lot.

He raised his eyebrows at me, his face lit up with a grin, and he hopped out of the car. By the time I climbed out of the passenger seat, he was already fumbling with his keys at the side door of the church. He opened the door and held it wide, beckoning me inside.

"Is this a ploy to get me into the church for some kind of secret ritual?"

"As delightful as that sounds, no." He smiled and closed the door behind us. "I know something you don't know, and I can't believe I haven't thought about it before now."

His eyes were shining so brightly that I couldn't help getting caught up in his enthusiasm. "And what do you know that I don't know?"

"This church has an archive vault," he explained, leading me down the dark hallway, our footsteps echoing in the emptiness. "Generations of parishioners, especially people who lived through the Great Depression and didn't trust banks or safety deposit boxes, have stored important items there for safekeeping."

He opened the door to the basement and flipped on the light.

"Maybe your mother came to Chip Olsen, who was the minister back then, with the manuscript—"

"To avoid having it destroyed!" I finished his thought. "If my grandfather had thought it was inflammatory enough to have killed for it, he certainly would have wanted to get rid of it."

"And since she loved Coleville, your mother definitely would have wanted it saved," Matthew said as we descended the stairs toward the basement. I noticed the air was getting colder and colder, the smell of stale earth stronger and stronger.

"Chip would have absolutely kept her confidence about it," he went on. "She could've brought it here with nobody else knowing where it was."

I could imagine my mother doing just that, saving the last work of the man she loved.

When we reached the bottom, Matthew flicked on the light, bathing the room in a yellowish hue. I gasped when I saw several stone sarcophagi, worn white with age, lined up in a row. This wasn't just a church basement—it was a crypt.

I took a quick breath in, delicately touching one of them. "Who are they? What is this?"

"Freaky, huh?" Matthew smiled broadly. "I was stunned the first time I saw them, too. Church elders, mostly, from two centuries ago, and some even older than that. There's even a Native American chief and his wife—a testament to how closely the settlers and the natives lived together at that time."

He led me to a massive metal door on the far side of the room and quickly worked the combination lock, which responded with a loud *click*. "The church archives," he said with a flourish, opening the door and ushering me inside.

Matthew flipped the light switch and I saw a cavernous room

containing shelf upon shelf of items, almost like the stacks in a library. "This is where we keep old church records of births, deaths, baptisms, marriages, that sort of thing, along with valuable items parishioners want stored," he explained.

"Lots of these things look really old," I said, noticing a dusty felt box.

"Most of it is old. People don't so much use church vaults nowadays. Frankly, lots of these items are forgotten, their owners having passed away without telling anyone they've stored something here."

"And you don't keep records?"

He nodded. "We do, but some parishioners didn't want to leave a paper trail, especially if they were hiding something."

A chill shot through me at that thought. That's exactly what my mother was doing with the manuscript—hiding it. "How are we ever going to find it amid all of this?" I asked, looking around at the shelves. "There's an awful lot of stuff in here."

"Look here," Matthew said, running a finger along the side of one of the shelves. "The shelves have dates on them. What year did this all go down again?"

"Nineteen fifty-six," I said, moving from shelf to shelf, counting my way back in time as I went. He started at the other side of the room and did the same.

A few moments later, he called out. "I found something!"

I flew to his side and saw a box just big enough to contain a ream of paper. It was marked ADELE MITCHELL, 1956.

"I can't believe it," I whispered, taking the box gingerly in my hands. "This has got to be it."

Just then, I heard a loud *click*. Matthew snapped his head around and ran toward the door.

"Damn it!"

I poked my head around the shelf to face him. "What's the matter?"

He didn't have to respond. I saw him standing against the closed door.

CHAPTER 20

P lease tell me this door opens from the inside," I said, rattling the handle.

He shook his head. "It's a vault. It locks from the outside when the door is closed."

I looked at him, openmouthed. "You mean we're locked in?"

Matthew fished a cell phone out of his pocket. "I'm afraid so. I'll just call my secretary and she can come . . ." He stared at the display on the face of his phone and then looked up at me with a sheepish grin. "No bars. I guess the stone of this subbasement is blocking the signal."

My stomach did a quick flip. "Now what?"

"I guess we wait," he said, shrugging his shoulders with an ease I found disarming, considering we were locked in an ancient stone room adjacent to a basement crypt. I looked around at the generations of dust on the shelves and I wondered just how much air there was in there. The vault certainly didn't have a vent to the outdoors.

"Don't worry," he said. "We won't be here long. The janitorial crew will be here soon. They'll see my car, they'll see the lights on leading to the basement, and they'll put two and two to-gether."

"What if they don't?"

"We'll bang on the door and the ceiling," he offered. "They'll hear us. Worst-case scenario, we'll have to wait until morning. Martha will be here at the crack of dawn and will figure out we're down here. It's Sunday tomorrow, remember? The whole church will fill up before eight thirty, and when I'm nowhere to be found, she'll track me down, believe me. The woman is like a bloodhound."

"All night?" I squeaked, a sense of unease growing inside of me.

He took my hands in his. "Listen, Grace," he said. "Everything's going to be okay. I promise. We'll be out of here before you know it."

"Do you really think so?"

"I do." He smiled. "I'm just hoping it's not one of the ladies from the church who finds us, or the scandal of us being alone together in this vault will spread faster than a swarm of locusts."

I could see that he was trying to lighten the mood, so I tried to follow his lead. "What I want to know is why, every time I'm with you, something dramatic happens."

"It's just business as usual for an average Lutheran minister," he said. "Sermons, marriages, funerals, and the odd life-threatening incident or two."

I chuckled. "There are worse people to be locked in a vault with. I mean, if we have to start praying to be rescued, you've got a direct pipeline to the man upstairs."

"The man upstairs that I'm most interested in reaching at this moment is the janitor," he said, staring at his dead phone.

I sighed, looking around the room, dust hanging in the air like fog. I wrapped my arms around my chest and shivered.

Matthew's eyes met mine. "Are you cold?"

I nodded. "A little. It really is dank down here, isn't it?"

He peeled off the jean jacket he was wearing and held it open for me.

"Are you sure you don't need it?" I asked.

He shook his head. "Not at all. Please."

I slipped my arms inside and felt his warmth wrap around me. The jacket smelled like him—a hint of spiciness from his soap mixed with fresh air. I turned to thank him, and our eyes locked for a moment that seemed to go on forever. I could feel my face heating up and was grateful for the dim light in the room.

We stood like that for a while, neither saying anything, each holding the other's gaze, and then he reached toward me and pushed a stray tendril of hair off my forehead. I knew exactly what this moment was and exactly what was about to happen if I let it, and I stepped back a few paces. The attraction between us was undeniable, but getting involved with him, or anyone, was the last thing I needed.

"Thank you for the jacket," I coughed, clearing my throat.

His eyes still held mine for a few seconds. "You're welcome," he whispered.

I turned and walked down one of the aisles. "What shall we do with ourselves, then, while we wait?" I asked a little louder than I intended.

"You could open the box, for starters."

"You're right!" I smiled at him. "I could." I made my way over to the shelf where it had been sitting for decades. The box was wrapped in heavy brown paper that had begun to yellow and fray around the edges.

I slipped my finger under one end of the paper and ran it down the length of the box, the wrapping crackling easily with age. I tore the rest away and then lifted the lid, conscious that the last person to touch it had been my mother before she married my dad.

Inside was a large manila envelope containing what seemed to be a ream of paper. On the front of the envelope, my mother's address, in the now-familiar handwriting of David Coleville.

I looked up at Matthew. "We found it."

He nodded, his eyes shining. I opened the envelope and drew out the final work of David Coleville, a book the literary world had anticipated but never received; wondered and speculated about, but never got to read. Only we knew it existed.

My hands were shaking as I held the pages.

I had no idea what this manuscript might have been worth in monetary value, but as I sat there in the dusty, dank vault, I knew that its real value to me wasn't in dollars and cents.

My mother wasn't here to tell me about what happened all those years ago. I couldn't simply ask her about her secret romance with one of this country's most talented writers, but his unpublished novel, the ream of paper I held in my hands, would bring that summer to life for me in vivid detail—Coleville's version of it, anyway.

Reading this story would be as close as I would ever get to time traveling. The words would transport me back to another time at Alban House, to a time before I was born, when my mother and father, David Coleville, and my aunt Fate were much younger than I was now, when my grandparents were vibrant and energetic and commanding. Through Coleville's words, I could immerse myself in the world of my parents and grand-parents in a way few children have ever had the opportunity to do.

I knew Coleville had changed the names of people and places, but I was sure I'd be able to discern who was whom. I stood there for a few minutes with the manuscript in my hands, an odd mix of excitement and trepidation bubbling up in my stomach. I had been dying to know more about their relationship, how they fell in love and why it all went wrong, but now that I had at least some of the answers at my fingertips, something was holding me back from turning that first page.

A voice then, soft in my ear. *Be careful what you wish for, Gracie. Once you learn the truth, you can't unlearn it.*

I stared down at the first page and read the title aloud to Matthew.

"*The Haunting of Whitehall Manor* by David Coleville." A tingling traveled through the page and into my hands as I said it. "Shall I read it aloud to you?"

"Let's just take a moment to realize that you and I are the first people in fifty years to be reading this work," he said, his eyes glowing. "This is a real gift, Grace. Months and years from now, when the whole world knows about it, when this very manuscript has been sold at auction, when you have been interviewed on the *Today* show talking about how you found it, we can look back on this moment and remember that it was just the two of us, here in this vault."

He sank down onto the cement floor and motioned for me to join him, which I did. "That said"—he smiled—"I'm ready to hear it."

I took a deep breath and began to read, the words immediately transporting us out of that damp church basement and into the glittering showplace that was Alban House, fifty years earlier.

Chapter One

The first time I laid eyes on Whitehall Manor, it was a cold, dreary June evening. I was squinting to see anything out of the fogged-up window in the back of the car that my companion's father had sent for us, but the world seemed dull and hazy around the edges, as though it was formulating itself, working to make itself whole out of the mists in preparation for our arrival, as Avalon did for Arthur. I let my mind drift to mystical kings and knights and wizards as we bumped along the road toward our destination. I didn't know it then, but looking back on it now, it is an apt analogy, for just as Avalon was home to sorceresses and magic, so, too, was Whitehall, containing secrets and mystery and enchantment, like the island that is steeped in Celtic lore.

As we rounded the corner of the driveway, the house appeared, solid now, sturdy and whole, shrouded in the fog that had crept on land from its birthplace on the lake and lay heavy around the place. The house was not a castle, not exactly, but an enormous, imposing structure all the same, a full city block long at least. It reminded me of an old manor house in the windswept British countryside, the moors. It was an ancient and formidable place that had stood against the ravages of Lake Superior's icy winds for generations.

As we got out of the car, I strained my neck to take it in, all three stories, with turrets and a tower, brick and stucco, several chimneys—I quickly counted fourteen, but there might have been more—and a patio

running the entire length of the house overlooking ten-
derly manicured English gardens and the lake beyond.
The staff stood at attention, at least a dozen of them,
in a line snaking from the massive wooden front door
onto the patio, in position to welcome their returning
son home.

"We're here!" announced Flynn, my traveling companion, otherwise known as Donald Flynn Brennan IV, the
grandson of the man who had come to this country as the
child of a poor Irishman escaping the Potato Famine and
had made his fortune when this country was new, thriv-
ing, and growing.

I met Flynn at Harvard, where we were roommates anticipating our senior year, although I was older than he,
having worked for several years to save up the funds to
attend. I was lucky enough to have also received a small
scholarship, being the ancestor not of a long line
of well-heeled businessmen as was Flynn, but of the
working-class stock from Boston who had built (and,
yes, cleaned) the venerable institution so long ago. While
my relatives were toiling with bricks and mortar and
dust mops, Flynn's were acquiring railroads and giant
tracts of virgin forests and iron ore mines.

But despite his great wealth and lineage, Flynn
wasn't anything like the other "children of privilege"
who haunted Harvard's hallowed halls. We had lived
together since we were freshmen, and I found him to be
humble, curious, and, above all, a good laugh. He swept
through life with a smile on his face, a joke on his

lips, and a sense of ease that, I suppose, is the providence of the very rich.

Flynn had invited me home with him every summer and I had always refused, making up some excuse or another. But not this year. I felt that, as a man who would soon graduate from one of the most formidable educational institutions in the world, I had something respectable to offer.

Climbing out of the car, Flynn pushed the thick blond hair out of his blue eyes as he flashed me a wide grin. He looked the picture of a typical Ivy Leaguer, wearing a cream-colored cable-knit sweater with navy-blue trim around its V-neck; a blue button-down shirt underneath, tails untucked and hanging below his sweater; khaki pants; and loafers without stockings. This boy was to the manor born, no doubt about it, but the way he was laughing and shaking hands with the staff, he didn't show it.

"Mary-Ruth!" He grinned, pulling a formidable-looking woman into his arms. "Give us a hug, lassie!"

"Welcome home, my boy. We've missed you, so we have."

"It's good to be home," he said, resting his head on the old woman's shoulder for a moment.

Flynn turned to me, then. "Mickey, meet one of the best women on this or any other planet, Mary-Ruth Mc-Bride. She runs things, and I do mean everything, here at Whitehall. Mary, here's my much ballyhoo-ed roommate, Michael Connolly."

"Ma'am, it's a pleasure to meet you," I said, bowing low.

But the woman had eyes only for Flynn, placing one hand, red and worn from a lifetime of working in the kitchen, delicately on his cheek. A moment of tenderness between herself and the boy, now a man, that she had obviously raised since childhood.

Just then, the two massive front doors burst open and the family appeared, right on cue.

"Darling!" Flynn's mother held her arms wide for her son, and he flew into them as his father beamed and patted Flynn on the back. Hugs and laughter all around. I thought back to the chilly relationship I had with my own parents, especially my father, and I was, not for the first time, envious of Flynn. Wealth, privilege, and happiness, too. It didn't seem quite fair, somehow.

"Mom, Dad, this is Michael Connolly—soon-to-be world-famous novelist, currently crew captain and pool shark." Flynn smiled, winking at me. "Mickey boy, my parents, Donny and Honor Brennan."

"We're delighted you could join us for the summer, Michael," Honor cooed, taking my hands in hers and giving them a squeeze. "We do so enjoy having the children's friends here. Life, laughter, love, that's what we're about here at Whitehall. The more, the merrier!"

I can't explain why, but I felt an odd tingle in my hands when she touched them. A slight jolt of electricity passed between us and she shot me a look with her steel-gray eyes that made me decidedly uncomfortable. Those eyes did not evoke life, laughter, and love. Just the opposite.

"Thank you so much for having me," I said quickly, pulling my hands from hers and brushing my hair out of my eyes. "I'm starting my first novel, and I'm hoping to get some good writing done over the summer before the fall term puts an end to all that. Flynn convinced me this was just the place to do it."

Flynn's father patted me on the back as we all walked through the doorway and into the house. "Writing, you say?" he said. "A novel, is it?"

I suppose I should've responded with more than a grunt and a smile, but my words sifted down into a gasp when I stepped through the threshold and took in this place my roommate called home. It was like nothing I'd ever seen. Towering ceilings, a grand staircase, an enormous stained-glass window, one full story tall, overlooking the gardens and grounds. I had hoped to hide my rather pedestrian awe, but I'm afraid I stood there like a lump, mouth agape, eyes wide.

"What a beautiful home you have, Mr. Brennan," I murmured.

"It'll do, son." Flynn's father smiled. "It'll do. And please call me Donny. Mr. Brennan was my grandfather."

He led me into the drawing room next to the foyer, a decidedly masculine, dark-paneled room with a floor-to-ceiling bookshelf on one wall and a wood-burning fireplace on another with leather armchairs, couches, a scattering of end tables and ottomans grouped around it. The staff had laid the fire earlier and now it was blazing, just the thing to take the chill out of an early June night here on the shore of Lake Superior.

Donny walked over to the sideboard, where decanters of scotch, chilled white wine, a bucket of ice, and various glasses had been arranged. As he began pouring drinks, I heard laughter, and looked up to see two girls come running down the grand stairway, arm in arm. I knew one of them from the family photographs that Flynn displayed in our dormitory—she was his younger sister, Prudence. Pru, he called her. The other girl, an auburn-haired beauty, I had never seen.

The girls swept into the room, bringing an air of fun and vitality with them that caused everyone to smile.

"Well, look what the cat dragged in," Pru sniped at Flynn while flashing me a big smile. "This whole house has been in an uproar for *days* about your arrival. You'd think the pope himself was making an appearance."

"I thought I smelled something foul when I walked in, and here you are!" Flynn retorted, making a show of sniffing her hair and wincing.

"Welcome home, I suppose." She sighed, her eyes settling on me. "At least you brought someone interesting with you this time."

"He's quite interesting, my dear sister. He intends to write novels. Those are books with big words in them." Flynn shot Prudence a look and turned to her friend. "Now the lovely Lily here reads all the time, so she knows what I'm talking about."

He wasn't kidding about the lovely part. Lily was delicate and had a soft way about her that contrasted with Pru's boldness. She blushed, glancing shyly at me.

"With all this talk of books, I hope we're not going to be sitting around reading all summer long," Pru said. "What a bore."

I laughed out loud, bowing slightly to the girls. "Perish the thought, Miss Brennan. Flynn tells me you ladies play a mean game of croquet."

"That's right." Pru brushed the wispy blond hair out of her eyes and flashed a smile. Then she hooked her arm into Lily's and began leading her out of the room, giving me a backward glance. "We play for money here, Mr. Connolly. Are you up to it?"

"I think I can hold my own."

The girls giggled and disappeared under the archway. "They really are good fun, if we can't find anything else to do with ourselves," Flynn said. "Pru's a horrible flirt, though, so watch out for her."

"What's Lily's story?" I asked as Honor and her husband joined us, handing us each a glass of scotch. I took a sip of the amber-hued drink—it was spicy and smooth on the way down, and from the first taste, I could tell it was a damn sight better than the swill we students bought back home.

"She's Prudence's friend," Honor said. "The girl is with us so much, she's like family now. She loves nothing more than to sit in the garden and sketch. So we'll have an artist and a writer in the house this summer. How grand!"

"Tell me, Michael." Donny cleared his throat. "You say you intend to write here at Whitehall. What's the novel about, if I may ask?"

I grinned and looked down into my glass. "I don't have the slightest idea," I confessed. "I've had a horrible case of writer's block for months now."

Flynn sank into a leather wing chair by the fireplace, swirling the ice in his lowball glass of scotch and propping his feet on the nearby ottoman. "Dad, I told Mickey that if it's inspiration he's after, there's no better place to find it than Whitehall."

Donny slung an arm over the back of his son's chair and nodded. "Indeed. 'If these walls could talk,' as they say."

"Lots of history here, I imagine?" I asked, raising my eyebrows.

"History, scandal, suspicious deaths, ghosts around every corner," Prudence said, reentering the drawing room with Lily by her side. "Haven't you heard, Mr. Connolly? Whitehall is cursed."

As I read those words, I shuddered and put the papers down in my lap. I had goose bumps.

"So that's what David Coleville thought of his first experience at Alban House," Matthew mused.

"I can see the real-life people easily corresponding with the characters in his story," I said, looking down at the page. "Flynn is obviously my dad, Johnny Alban. The characters Donny and Honor are my grandparents John James and Charity Alban. Lily is my mother."

"And Prudence is your aunt Fate," Matthew finished my thought, leaning his head back against the door. "The character seems so vivacious and feisty and full of life. Even on paper, her character took over the scenes, commanding attention. She reminded me a little of Scarlett O'Hara from *Gone with the Wind* or Lady Brett Ashley in *The Sun Also Rises*. A stark contrast to the woman we met yesterday at Alban House, isn't it?"

I thought of my poor, bewildered aunt Fate, who had spent her life in a mental hospital and was now locked away on the third floor of Alban House.

"Makes you wonder what happened that she ended up in an institution, doesn't it?" I said. "More now than ever before."

"Read on." He smiled. "Maybe we'll find out."

Chapter Two

A shaft of moonlight illuminated my darkened bedroom, so bright that it woke me from a fitful sleep. I stretched and rubbed my eyes, repositioning the pillows that surrounded me on the king-sized bed. I had remarked on its massive, intricately carved wooden headboard and footboard earlier in the evening when one of the staff had shown me to this third-floor room.

"It's the kind of bed I'd imagine King Henry the Eighth sleeping in," I had said, running my hand over its deep red bedspread.

"Fit for a king, indeed," the girl had replied. "It may well have belonged to royalty, now that you mention it. Old Mr. Brennan, the man who built this house, imported it from Britain around the turn of the century."

I noticed that my suitcases had been brought up and

were standing near a cherry-wood armoire. "Is much of the furniture in the house antique?" I asked the girl.

"It is," she said, chattering away as she opened the shutters to reveal a sweeping view of the lake, which was choppy and tumultuous on this windy night. "I'm charged with polishing it, all the furniture on the second and third floors. I tend to the tapestries as well. Some are said to have come from ancient castles in Britain, so there's your royalty for you."

The girl finished opening the shutters, turned to me, smoothed her white apron, and asked, "Shall I get you unpacked, then, sir?"

I frowned at her.

"Unpacked, sir," she said again. "Shall I put your clothes away?"

"I think I can manage, thank you." I smiled, and she took her leave. As I hung up my shirts and put my socks into a drawer, I thought about how living in a household with servants was going to take some getting used to. Put my clothes away indeed.

I rolled over and punched my pillows a bit and closed my eyes, but sleep wouldn't come. I kept thinking about the curse Prudence spoke about earlier that evening—what could she have meant? From where I stood, the Brennans had the world by the tail—great wealth, success, a happy and healthy family. The only curse I could see was what to do with it all.

I lay there for a while, staring at the ceiling as the glow of the moon lit up the room. It was too bright, I thought, so I pushed off the covers and padded over to the window, intending to close the shutters. But instead I stood transfixed by what I saw on the lakeshore below.

Flames crackled in a fire ring on the beach. A girl wearing a white nightgown—or was it a dress?—was dancing around the fire, turning in circles with her arms held wide. I squinted through the distance and darkness to make out who it was. Lily? No, her hair was longer than this girl's. Was it Prudence? One of the servant girls, perhaps? I wasn't sure. I couldn't see clearly—reality seemed to be hazy, as though the window itself was warped. But I was mesmerized by the girl's movements, slow and wavy, as though she was moving her arms and legs through water. Or a dream.

Then I heard her voice, soft and low, through the open window. I could make out faint strains of a verse but couldn't understand the words. They were strange, guttural sounds, like an ancient language from a different time.

I stood at my window until the girl stopped and snapped her head in the direction of the house. Did she see me? I jumped away from the window, my heart beating hard and fast in my chest. I smiled to myself, feeling like a little boy who'd been caught spying on girls through a peephole.

I peered out the window again, but . . . it couldn't be. The girl was gone. The fire was out, the lakeshore was empty, and there was no sign of anyone, anywhere. What had just happened here?

I crawled back into bed and pulled the covers around

me, but the gnawing in my stomach chased sleep away. Little by little as the hours passed, the reality of what I saw eroded in my mind. When the sun finally came up again, I wasn't at all sure that the whole thing hadn't been a dream.

I shivered and was suddenly aware of my dark and dusty surroundings. I was about to turn the page to the next chapter when I heard a loud rapping at the door.

"Reverend Parker! Are you in there?"

"Yes!" Matthew shouted. And we exchanged a look of relief.

We both jumped up, and he rattled off the combination to the janitor as I placed the manuscript back into the box and stood up, hurrying to smooth my dress just as I heard the lock click. The door popped open, and there stood one of the janitors looking slightly bewildered.

"Oh, thank goodness," Matthew said, brushing the dust off his jeans. "We were in here retrieving a family heirloom of Miss Alban's, and the door latched shut. I tried to call someone to get us out of here but my phone didn't have any service."

The janitor eyed the two of us. "I got suspicious when I saw your car in the lot and the lights on leading down here," he said.

"Thank God you did, Pat," Matthew put a hand on the man's shoulder and gave it a squeeze. "Heaven knows how long we might have been trapped in here if not for you. I was beginning to get more than a little claustrophobic."

We hurried out the door, and he leaned onto it, shutting it with a thud. Twirling the combination lock a few times, he said, "Let's get back upstairs."

We made our way through the crypt and were halfway up the

stone stairs when Matthew and I both stopped short. He turned to look at me and said aloud what we were both thinking.

"How in the world did that heavy door shut behind us?"

"That's what I was wondering, boss," the janitor said.

"Did you see anyone?" I asked.

He shook his head. "I sure didn't. But when I got here I noticed the side door of the church was ajar, as if someone had left in a hurry and didn't pull it closed."

CHAPTER 21

D o you think someone could have been following us?" I asked Matthew as we climbed into his Volvo.

He grimaced. "I don't much like that idea . . . but somebody had to have closed that door."

I rested my head against the back of the seat and stared at the ceiling. "You know what I think? I think it was Harris Peters."

"Me, too," Matthew said, nodding.

"I know I can't prove it, but I'm sure he's the one who was rifling around my room that night and very likely the one who was in the basement room, too," I said, narrowing my eyes. "He was creeping around in the passageways trying to dig up more dirt on my family and he saw me find the letters. Now he's read them, so he knows about the manuscript. He's looking for it, too."

"But that's where it gets odd," Matthew said. "If it was Harris, as you said, he's looking for the manuscript just like we are, right? And we just found it. So—what? He closed us in the vault with the thing we were all looking for? That just doesn't make any sense."

I turned to look at him. "You're right. It's a rather—" The next word stuck in my throat, and I stared at Matthew, open-mouthed.

"A rather what?" he said, his eyes on the road.

"A rather insane thing to do," I said, my voice lowering to a whisper, as though someone were lurking and could hear us. "And I only know of one insane person in my life at the moment."

Matthew pulled the car over to the side of the road and stopped. "You don't suppose . . ." He didn't finish his sentence, but I knew full well what he was thinking.

I shook my head. "It can't be," I said. "There's no way my aunt could have done it. Jane has her locked on the third floor of Alban House." As soon as the words escaped my lips, I regretted them.

His eyes grew wide, just as I suspected they would. "Did you just tell me that you've got that poor woman locked—?"

I held up a hand. "I know, I know, that's how I felt at first, too," I said quickly. "But Jane said she can't watch her all the time, and she's afraid she'll get into something or fall down the stairs or get lost. Jane says she's perfectly happy in her rooms on the third floor. That's where she's been living, or thinks she's been living, for the past fifty years." I let out a sigh. "I know it's not ideal, but it's just until we can talk to her doctor and get her back on her medications. I'm not sure what else to do with her."

He put the car back into drive and edged back out onto the roadway. "Your life isn't exactly the average church social, Grace Alban," he said, eyeing me with a smile.

"There are some nights when I just order a pizza and watch a movie," I said. "Really."

He pulled into our driveway and hopped out of the car with me, walking me up to the patio. We lingered at the railing awhile and I was glad of it. Something was scratching at the edges of my emotions when it came to this man. I had to admit it—I liked being in his company. I wondered if there was anything more to it than that.

"I don't suppose you'd like to come in for a drink?" I offered.

He shook his head. "I'd love to, but I've got an early day tomorrow. Robes, rituals, hymns, all that stuff."

Of course. I had lost track of the days. Tomorrow was Sunday. "What time is the service?" I asked.

"In the summer, we've just got one." He grinned, leaning against the patio railing. "Nine thirty."

"Well, you never know, Reverend Parker." I smiled back at him. "I might just slink through the forest to see you in action."

"I can offer you weak church coffee and homemade lemon bars after the service," he said. "I don't know how you could possibly pass that up."

After Matthew got into his car and left, I climbed the patio steps, clutching the manuscript to my chest. Once inside, I hurried upstairs to the master suite, where I tucked it into the wall safe in my mother's study. It would be secure there for the time being.

THE NEXT MORNING, I showered and dressed early while Amity was still sleeping. I thought about waking her to ask her to come to church with me, but we were not normally a churchgoing family. I suspected she'd figure out immediately that the only reason I was going was to see Matthew, and I decided that was one can of worms I definitely wanted to leave closed. So I just let her sleep. I gave her a quick kiss on the cheek and made my way downstairs, where the aroma of coffee perfumed the air.

I pushed open the kitchen's swinging door and saw Jane with

her head in the refrigerator. I crossed the room and poured my-self a cup from the pot.

"Oh, Miss Grace!" Jane swung around, a hand to her throat. "I didn't see you there!"

I smiled. "Sorry, Jane. I was just grabbing some coffee before I head off to church."

She squinted at me, a peculiar look on her face. "Church is it now? This is something new. After you went through your con-firmation classes, you rarely went back, as I recall."

"Well, then it's high time I did." I winked at her, pouring a splash of milk into my coffee and heading out to the patio from the kitchen door.

It was another bright morning, the air clean and crisp, a slight breeze tickling the surface of the lake. As I pulled out one of the wrought-iron chairs at the patio table and sank into it, I wondered if my mother's old rowing shell was still in the boat-house. Just then, Jane came up behind me carrying a muffin on a small plate.

"I haven't yet got the eggs and sausage cooking, but here's something to tide you over." She smiled at me.

"Thanks, Jane," I said, tearing the top off the muffin.

"A couple of meetings with a minister and he's got her going to church," I heard her mutter as she walked back into the kitchen. "Truly a miracle, so it is."

I arrived just as the service started, and Matthew's face broke into a wide grin when he saw me slip into a pew in the back of the church. "For those of you who are new here, the hymn num-bers are on the wall there"—he pointed to a series of numbers on the side wall—"and the order of the service is in the bulletin." And then, turning to his congregation, he said, "Welcome, everybody. I'm truly glad you're all here this fine morning. Let's get this party started, shall we?"

I fumbled through the first part of the service, scrambling to follow along, but when it came time for Matthew's sermon, I settled in. His passion as he talked about the most important thing in his life was infectious and—I had to admit it to myself—more than a little bit sexy. He talked about things lost and found, weaving it into biblical tales, but I knew he was referring to finding the letters and the manuscript, and how those two things would bring me closer to my mother. When it was all over, I was glad I had come.

I leaned over the back of the pew while the other parishioners made their way through the receiving line to shake Matthew's hand, watching how he smiled so warmly, exchanging personal words with each of them, even putting a hand on top of the children's heads in blessing. He truly was in his element, and it warmed me from the inside in a way I hadn't expected. When they had all gone, he joined me in my pew.

"It's nice to see you here." He smiled. "I wasn't sure you'd show."

"I came to extend an invitation," I said. "That, and to save my eternal soul."

He chuckled. "Right. We got the soul-saving part handled. What about the invitation?"

"Come to the house when you're done for the day? I'm dying to read more of the manuscript, but since we started it together, I thought we could finish together. If you're interested, that is."

His eyes lit up. "You've got a deal, Miss Alban," he said. "It won't be until later this afternoon, though. I've got some business to finish up between now and then."

"Just prior to dinnertime, perhaps?" I offered.

"I'll be there." He stood up and extended his hand, a grin spreading across his face. "And now, can I interest you in a lemon bar?"

After a polite grilling by various ladies of the church about my future plans for Alban House, I extricated myself from their web and made my way down the path toward home, hoping Amity would be receptive to the plan I was hatching in my mind.

I found her on the patio diving into the eggs and sausage that Jane had prepared. Slipping into a chair next to her, I said: "Honey, I've got something really exciting to tell you."

Amity's smile morphed into a scowl. "You do?"

"Reverend Parker and I found the manuscript last night," I told her, lowering my voice. "The manuscript David Coleville sent to Grandma."

Her eyes grew wide as she held her fork aloft.

"I've got it in Grandma's wall safe in her study," I said, leaning forward and squeezing her hand. "Reverend Parker and I read the first two chapters of it last night—"

Her scowl intensified. "You started without me?"

I brushed her off. "Don't worry about that, Amity. Listen. It's really good so far. Why don't you read those first two chapters sometime today. He's going to come over later on, around dinnertime, and I thought the three of us could read it aloud together. What do you think?"

"He sure is hanging around a lot," she said. "Are you dating this guy or something?"

"Dating?" I recoiled. "No! That's ridiculous. We're just friends." But as I said it, I wondered what, exactly, was happening between me and the good reverend. Amity was right; he certainly was hanging around a lot.

I shook those thoughts from my mind. "Besides," I deflected, "don't you want to know what's in that manuscript?"

I watched as her scowl faded and a smile threatened to break free. I held my breath as she popped another bite of eggs into her mouth. "I suppose," she said. "I'm going to help Mr. Jameson and Cody in the garden, but after that we could read it."

"Okay, then!" I said, and left her to finish her brunch, wondering what I was going to do with my day until Matthew arrived.

LATER, WE SAT IN THE PARLOR, Matthew, Amity, and me, the manuscript out of its box and in my lap. With Amity curled up on one of the leather sofas, her arms wrapped around her knees, and Matthew seated in the leather wing chair next to mine, I leafed through the manuscript's pages until I came to the third chapter.

"Ready to dive in?" I asked, looking up to see my daughter's shining eyes.

I began to read.

Chapter Three

At breakfast the next morning, I mentioned that I had seen—or thought I had seen—a girl in white doing a midnight dance by the fire ring, but my hosts brushed it off, first with Flynn laughing about the imagination of a novelist doing strange things at Whitehall, and then Pru settling on the idea that I'd simply had a dream.

"If I were to dance by the lakeshore in the moonlight, I certainly wouldn't do so alone." She giggled, a musical sound that reminded me of a delicately rushing stream. "But I don't blame you for conjuring up a dream about me, Mr. Connolly. You're not the first man who has."

Donny cleared his throat, his wife, Honor, smiling shyly over her coffee cup. Looking back on it now, I think I glimpsed something in their eyes then, a flash passing between them and vanishing as swiftly as it came. But hindsight plays funny tricks with memory. There may have been nothing at all.

"Oh, for goodness' sake, Pru, you're incorrigible. Can't you go five minutes without flirting?" Flynn tossed a piece of breakfast sausage at his sister. It landed near her plate and she speared it with her fork, popping it into her mouth with a flourish.

"I flirt, therefore I am," she purred, batting her eyelashes at me.

I didn't meet her gaze, instead turning my attention to the scrambled eggs on my plate. I had no wish to be cast as Prudence's love interest this summer and needed to nip this flirting business in the bud. Although Prudence was a beautiful and vivacious girl, I found myself longing for the quiet company of her friend.

"And where is Lily this morning?" I asked her. "Don't tell me she's still sleeping . . . ?"

"Of course not, silly," Prudence sniffed, as Mrs. McBride, who had been hovering all throughout breakfast, refilled the girl's coffee cup with shaking hands.

I smiled at the old woman, thinking of how the ravages of age were taking their toll.

"Lily lives down the lane, on the other side of the church," Prudence went on. "She doesn't stay here at Whitehall—not all the time, anyway."

"She'll be here soon enough," Flynn offered, taking another helping of hashed brown potatoes. And then, looking across the table at his sister, he asked: "What do you girls have planned for the afternoon? Anything? I thought we'd play a round of croquet and then maybe go for a sail. Are you game?"

Now it was Prudence's turn to shrug. "If nothing more interesting comes along," she said, standing up from the table and dropping her napkin on her plate. But the dramatic wink she shot in my direction let me know that I would indeed be seeing the girls that afternoon.

"Perhaps I'll get some writing in this morning, if nobody minds," I said a bit hesitantly. I was unsure of how much time I was expected to spend with my hosts, but I had promised myself that I'd at least come away from this summer with an outline of a new book, a skeleton that I could fill in at a later date.

"To inspiration!" Donny said, holding his coffee cup aloft. "You go shutter yourself away, son, and let your imagination take flight. It's what you're here for."

"My, yes," Honor said, her steely eyes gentle now, as big and round as a doe's. "Don't feel like you need to stand on ceremony with us."

Flynn pushed his chair away from the table and stood

up, stretching. "I think I'll head down to the garden and pester Brinkman," he said, turning to me. "What say you toil away for a few hours, we meet back here at noon for a spot of lunch, and then we'll play with the girls for the rest of the day. How does that sound?"

"A fine plan," I said, hurrying to my feet and patting Flynn on the back as we walked together out of the room.

He went one way, toward the front door, as I headed toward the grand staircase. He grasped the door's handle and turned back to me, staring at me for a moment before he spoke. "Hey, old man," he said, glancing this way and that as if making sure we were alone. "A word."

He nodded his head toward the parlor and beckoned me to follow.

Flynn put his hand on my shoulder and said, his voice almost as low as a whisper, "I'd advise you not to mention anything more about seeing girls in white out by the lakeshore."

"Whyever not?" I asked, surprised.

Flynn sighed deeply. "You know how Pru was saying Whitehall is cursed?"

I nodded, a gnawing developing in the pit of my stomach.

"That's what she's talking about."

I stared at him. "I'm afraid you've lost me, Flynn."

He held a finger to his lips and motioned for me to follow him to the sofa, which I did. After we had sunk onto its soft leather seat, he continued.

"Prudence and I had a sister," Flynn explained. "Her name was Felicity. She was Pru's twin."

I squinted at him. "You've never mentioned—"

He cut me off, shaking his head. "I know. She died years ago, when we were just kids. It nearly destroyed my parents, and Pru has never been the same since it happened. It's something we don't talk about often in this family." He hesitated for a moment. "Actually, we don't ever talk about it."

My thoughts were swimming. What did that have to do with what I saw down by the lake the night before? I remained quiet, waiting for him to continue.

"I know how this is going to sound, Mickey, but for years afterward, my mother was sure Felicity was still here, with us, at Whitehall."

"What do you mean, still here? Are you talking about"—the word felt strange and a bit silly as it rolled off my tongue—"a ghost?"

He nodded. "Her spirit. Mother would tell us she had seen her down by the lakeshore. Wearing a white gown."

I finished his thought: "Dancing around a fire?" My blood ran cold as I pictured the girl I saw with my own eyes, just a few hours before.

"It wasn't just my mother who saw her," Flynn continued, his voice a harsh whisper. "Prudence would tell us that she saw her all the time. My father and I were quite worried about the two of them, back then. But the whole business sort of dissipated when I went away to college, and to tell you the truth, I haven't thought much about it in recent years. But now—"

I stared at my friend, openmouthed. "Good Lord," I murmured, leaning back against the sofa.

"I'm just asking you not to mention it again because it upsets my mother and Pru so much," Flynn said, putting his hand on my knee and giving it a quick pat.

"I'm so sorry," I began. "I didn't mean . . ." I thought of the jocularity at the table just moments before, Prudence's flirting, Honor's shy smile.

"Flynn," I began again. "I don't quite know how to say this, but they didn't *seem* upset by what I said. Not in the least."

He smiled at me. "It's the Brennan way," he said, shaking his head. "Smile when your heart is breaking. Isn't that how the old song goes? It's what we do here at Whitehall."

"Well, I do apologize," I said. "Had I known my comments would offend—"

"You couldn't have known. I only brought it up because I didn't want you walking into another minefield. I thought you'd appreciate the warning."

"I do," I told him. "And you have my word, I won't mention it to them again. Even if I see her dancing in my room."

We both chuckled a bit at this. But as we stood to leave, another thought shook me. "Flynn, do you mind if I ask you one final question?"

"Not at all," he said, straightening his cardigan.

"You said Felicity died when you were small," I began hesitantly. "But this girl, the girl I saw last night, she wasn't a child. She looked to be about Prudence's age. I thought she *was* Prudence at first."

Flynn held my gaze for a moment before responding. "That's the truly horrifying thing about this, Mickey. That's why Prudence insisted on calling it a curse. Pru believes—I know this is going to sound mad—but my sister believes her dead twin is, in fact, the image she sees reflected back to her in any mirror here in Whitehall, and that Felicity's spirit is aging along with her."

I stared at Flynn, trying to make some kind of sense of what he had just said to me.

"Is it some kind of psychosis, then?" I whispered, shaking my head. "Brought on by the trauma of her twin's death? Surely . . . ?"

"To tell you the truth, Mickey, right now I don't know what to believe," Flynn said. "As I said, my mother and Prudence are the only ones who have ever claimed to have seen Felicity." He looked off into the distance and seemed to be struggling with his words. "I've always thought, or rather, my father and I have always thought, they were, well, for lack of a better term, manifesting it in their own minds. Not on purpose, you understand, not because they're crazy, but out of their sheer grief at losing Lissy."

"I can completely understand that," I said to him. "It makes perfect sense."

"But now it doesn't make sense, not when you pipe up over eggs and sausage that you—a stranger here with no knowledge of prior events—have seen the very same manifestation my mother and sister have been claiming to see all these years. Right down to the white gown and fire ring."

We sat in silence for a moment, neither knowing, I supposed, what to say next. What *was* there to say?

As we both rose from the couch and began to make our way out of the room, Flynn put a hand on my shoulder. "If you see her again," he said, his voice low, "don't mention it to the others. But let me know. I'd like to see for myself what this is all about."

"You have my word," I said to him, and watched as he pulled open the door and went through it, outside into the sunshine.

I made my way up to the third floor, thinking about what Flynn had told me. Were Honor and Prudence right? Had I truly seen a ghost? The thought of it shook me to my core.

Back in my room, I fished my leather-bound journal out of my suitcase and sat, pencil in hand, at the desk adjacent to the window where I had seen the vision the night before. I looked through the pane and saw Flynn in the garden, talking and laughing with an older man whom I presumed to be the gardener. This moment of normalcy quieted my racing heart.

Maybe there was nothing to this after all. Maybe there was a rational explanation for this ghost sighting. Maybe, I thought with my fiction writer's mind, Prudence herself was somehow involved in this "apparition," whether a result of some psychosis on her part or, more likely, as a way to play an elaborate trick on a newcomer and her own brother.

Maybe, I thought as I sat gazing out the window, something monstrous and hideous and undead was not lurking at Whitehall.

Oh, what the mind allows us to believe, even contrary to what we have seen with our own eyes.

CHAPTER 22

I looked up from the manuscript and saw Amity staring at me, her eyes as big and round as moons.

"I thought this was supposed to be the love story of David Coleville and Grandma," she said, her voice wavering. "Not a ghost story." She drew her knees closer to her chest and held them with her arms tighter. "It's creepy," she went on, "having it set right here."

Matthew and I exchanged a quick glance. "Honey, it's just a story," I said, smiling a broad smile. "Just a work of fiction. It's not the true story of what happened here that summer. Not at all."

But even as I said the words, I wasn't so sure. Coleville himself had written to my mother that this manuscript was indeed a "thinly veiled account" and had wanted her to read it to make sure it didn't skim too terribly close to the surface.

"Listen," I said to my daughter, "if you were a writer and you came to this house for the first time to get inspiration to write your first novel, wouldn't your imagination go into overdrive?"

Matthew echoed my thoughts. "I agree with your mother. Seeing all this"—he gestured widely with his arms—"the secret passageways, the antique furnishings, the tapestries, I might conjure up a ghost story about it, too. Wouldn't you?"

Amity considered this as her gaze traveled around the room. "I guess," she said tentatively.

Still, I was wondering if asking Amity to listen in on this reading had been a good idea after all. She wasn't a girl who typically was attracted to scary movies or books. Even television shows about police solving particularly violent crimes weren't her speed. But like her, I had hoped that it was going to be primarily a love story, and I hadn't seen the harm in sharing that with her. Now I was hoping she'd lose interest.

I placed my hands on top of the manuscript. "Honey, would you rather not hear the rest of it? You can go back upstairs or outside into the garden if you'd like—"

"No!" she said, cutting me off. "I'm already hooked! I want to know what happens. It's just a little creepy because it's set right here in this house, that's all."

I smiled at her, noticing for the first time that the late afternoon sun was streaming in through the window, shining on her face and warming the room. The sight seemed a little incongruous to me, as though I should be reading this eerie story on a dark and stormy night. "How about we take a quick break and you run into the kitchen to get some lemonade or a soda from Jane?"

Amity shrugged and unfolded herself from her chair. "Okay," she said. "I guess I'm a little thirsty." Heading toward the kitchen, she turned and wagged a finger at me. "Don't start up again without me. I'll be right back."

After she had gone, I lowered my voice and said, "Do you think it's okay that we're reading this to her?"

"It depends on how sensitive she is."

"And how frightening this story gets," I said, quickly flipping ahead a few pages. "The thing is, it's hitting a little close to home.

It's not like this house is without its ghosts. Do you remember the other night at dinner when I told you that I had the feeling my mother and brothers were here?"

"I do remember that," he said. "And it's not so unusual, Grace. Most everyone who has lost someone dear feels their presence from time to time. I think it's comforting, actually. Especially for those who doubt there's an afterlife. It's a way for us to know that our loved ones are okay and happy, and that we'll be okay and happy when it's our time to go."

A ghostly visit sounded rather lovely when he put it like that. But he hadn't heard the full story from me yet.

"There's something I haven't told you," I continued, my eyes on the door, making sure Amity wasn't within earshot. "I had a horrible dream about my dad." I shuddered, remembering. "He drowned, I think you know, and I had a dream . . . at least I think it was a dream, that he was standing at the foot of my bed. He was wearing the outfit he died in, and he was dripping wet. Fish were glistening in his hair and wriggling out of his mouth."

Matthew's smile faded into a look of concern and he squinted his eyes. "That's a little less comforting, I'll grant you."

"You don't know the half of it," I said, lowering my voice and hurrying the story along before Amity came back. "He told me he didn't have much time. He said *she* was here, and that she killed my mother and was coming for me."

Matthew leaned in closer to me. "Who?" he asked.

"He didn't say," I told him, holding his gaze. "The only woman who has come into my life recently is my aunt Fate, and she's so frail, there's no way he could've been talking about her. He said that he didn't think she could hurt us anymore, but she can. He said it was all true, and that I should be on my guard."

Matthew was silent for a moment. And then he said: "I'm sure there's a plausible explanation for all of it. You being home again for the first time, the resurgence of memories about your father. It makes sense, Grace, you having a dream like that, it really does."

I took in that comment, wondering if he made it a practice of telling parishioners that their outlandish or even borderline crazy stories "made sense." He had certainly said that phrase enough times to me.

"Amity had the same dream, just moments later," I informed him, thinking perhaps that this wouldn't make so much "sense" to Matthew. "She woke me up, calling out for me."

Matthew gave me a look of such concern that I wondered what he thought of me—*as crazy as her aunt Fate?*—and hoped I didn't make a mistake by telling him what I just told him. I fidgeted in my seat.

Finally, he said, "Well, I don't—"

But I cut him off, grabbing his hand when I remembered something that hadn't occurred me to until just then.

"I don't mean to change the subject here, but there *was* a twin who died as a child! In real life, I mean. This manuscript talks about a twin who died, and—remember? Jane told us about Fate's twin the other night! Mercy was her name, wasn't it? I hadn't heard anything, not one word about her until Jane told us about it. It's like the family covered it up. And now . . . Coleville's story about the twin. Do you think—you don't think . . . ?"

We sat there a moment looking at each other, and I realized I was holding his hand. Electricity shot through me and I dropped it, as though shocked.

I couldn't discern what the look on his face meant—did the contact make him uncomfortable? Or was he distressed that I had let go? I didn't get a chance to find out because Amity breezed back into the room carrying a big tumbler of lemonade, her sunny energy dissipating the cloud that had fallen around us. She settled back onto the couch and put her glass down on the end table. "Are we ready for the next chapter?" she asked, looking from one of us to the other, a wide smile on her face.

"I don't know, honey," I said, hoping my own face didn't look as ashen as it suddenly felt. "This might be too scary for you."

Her grin got even wider. "Not a chance, Mom. I'll admit I was a little creeped out at first. But I thought about it and what you guys said made sense to me. Anybody, especially a writer who comes here for the first time, would start thinking about ghosts. Alban House is that kind of place." She shot Matthew a look. "Help me out here, Reverend Parker."

Matthew shrugged and held up his hands. "This is your mom's call, kiddo," he said. "I'm just an innocent bystander."

They both turned to me. "I'm not sure—" I started, but my daughter cut me off.

"Mom, I can tell you exactly why I'm not scared by this story," she told me. "I've been coming here in the summer ever since I was little and I've never seen a girl in white. And you grew up here! You lived your *whole life* here before you moved to Seattle. Did you ever see a ghost like that?"

Of course, she was right. "No, I didn't," I admitted. No girls in white, no dancing around the fire ring, no strange and guttural language borne on the wind. I'd lived a lifetime in this house without seeing anything like that. My brothers never saw anything like that, either—they certainly would've taken the opportunity to scare me with it. And what about my mother and Jane? They had lived their whole lives here, too! Despite the admittedly strange dream about my father, the visions I had had of my mother and brothers, and the old legend about the witch in the wood, I knew Amity was right. There were no ghosts here, at least not the malevolent kind.

I exhaled and leaned against the back of my chair, shooting Matthew a glance—chagrin mixed with relief. He winked at me.

"I guess this story got to me," I said. "What a great writer Coleville was, huh? He had us all worked up about ghosts being here at Alban House when we knew better."

"Well, I wouldn't say he had us *all* worked up." Matthew grinned at me. "Some of us kept our heads. I'm just saying."

I shot him a mock scowl and stood up to get us a couple glasses of wine as Matthew and Amity shared a laugh at my expense.

"So can we go on?" Amity asked as I handed Matthew his glass and settled back down in my chair.

"Onward we go." I smiled at her, then opened the manuscript once again.

Chapter Four

I sat at the desk by the window for an hour or so, staring at the page. All I had managed to write was "The girl in white" over and over. I had to admit it to myself: I was preoccupied with the story Flynn had told me.

I closed my eyes and tried to clear my mind of all its racing thoughts about ghosts and fires and dancing, breathing in and out slowly, calming my pounding heart, feeling my cells begin to vibrate in their own internal rhythm, listening to the soft sound within my own ears. It was a technique I often used to combat writer's block, a clearing of the external noise that can conspire to stop creativity from flowing. I exhaled and sat for a moment, savoring the exquisite sense of peace this technique always brought with it.

And then I heard . . . something. A shuffling sound, muted, muffled, but there nonetheless. I listened closer. Scraping? The rhythmic motion of heels on a wooden floor?

Then a paper-thin singsong voice in my ear: "Michael . . . Michael Connolly . . ."

My eyes shot open. "Is somebody there?" I said a bit louder than I had intended. I stood up and whirled around, but all I saw was my empty room. My desk, my bed, the dresser, the closet door. The tapestry hanging on one wall. I was alone.

I rushed to the door and flung it open, believing I'd see one of the maids in the hallway. But no, looking both ways I saw only a long, empty expanse. So it wasn't a maid. Who had said my name?

I closed my eyes and listened again, but heard nothing. After the story Flynn had just told me, my imagination was likely working in overdrive. That had to be it. Nobody had said my name. Of course not. And the footsteps . . . Perhaps it was an animal, a mouse scuttling through the walls? A wayward squirrel that had made a nest in the attic, which was, after all, just above my room?

I picked up my pencil once again, bent my head over my journal, and began to write, not full sentences, but concepts, words. *The girl in white. A death in the family. A mother's grief. A twin's heartbreak. A brother's concern.* It might not have been the stuff of a novel, not yet, but it was getting there. Maybe I had found my germ of an idea after all, in just one morning at Whitehall Manor. I smiled, staring toward the window and tapping the end of my pencil on the page, wondering what kinds of fancy a whole summer here would produce.

I turned my gaze back to my work when I felt a shiver run all the way down my spine. The hair on the back of my neck stood up, and I felt, and then saw, goose bumps form on my forearms. Someone was watching me. I could feel eyes boring into my back. Was someone standing right behind me?

I stood up, whirling around once again and knocking my chair to the floor as I did. "Who's there?" I said again, more forcefully this time. I wondered—was Prudence hiding in the closet? Would the girl really be so bold?

I strode across the room and flung open the closet door. "I found you!" I exclaimed . . . to an empty closet. Apart from my clothes and an extra blanket and pillow, it held nothing. I turned around and surveyed my room, at a loss. Nobody was there, nothing was amiss.

I was obviously gripped in a state of wild imagination, spurred on by my unfortunate experience of last night coupled by Flynn's disturbing news of today.

I shook my head and looked at my reflection in the mirror. "Get ahold of yourself, old boy," I said aloud.

Glancing at the clock, I saw that it was nearly noon already. Time had flown. I needed to get downstairs to meet Flynn and the girls for lunch. I closed my journal and slipped it into the desk drawer. Then I took one long look around my room before shutting the door behind me and making my way downstairs.

In the dining room, I found Lily standing alone by the wall of windows overlooking the garden. Beyond her, I could see the garden's lush plants and flowers, and as she stood there, wearing a delicate floral dress, she seemed part of the garden herself.

"Hello," I said, startling her.

"Oh!" She smiled, shaking her head. "It's you. I didn't hear you come in."

I crossed the room to join her at the window. "And what had you so rapt?" I smiled back at her.

She gestured toward the garden. "I love it this time of year," she said. "The plants so newly green and vibrant, the tulips in full bloom."

Her eyes shone as she spoke and I found myself lost in them for a moment before gathering myself to respond.

"You're an artist, I'm told," I said. "Do you find your inspiration in nature?"

Her face reddened slightly. "I wouldn't call myself an artist," she said. "But I enjoy sketching and painting. I spend much of my time in these gardens. They're so beautiful."

I was about to say they weren't nearly as beautiful

as she, when Prudence and Flynn bounded into the room, breathless, as though they had been chasing each other like two puppies. Flynn pushed his sister and she collapsed onto one of the chairs, laughing.

"You will never beat me," Flynn said to her, picking up a glass of water from the sideboard and drinking it down in a gulp. "You should just admit it now and get on with your life."

"Never!" she replied, waving an arm.

I furrowed my brow at them and shot a glance toward Lily.

"These two have been racing from the lakeshore to the house ever since they learned how to walk," she told me, taking her place next to Prudence at the table. "Everything's a competition with them. Watch out when we play croquet."

"She tries every trick in the book." Flynn laughed. "Today she tripped me, and I still beat her."

"Anything to give me an advantage, brother," Prudence said, lifting her water glass to her lips and taking a long sip.

As I looked at Prudence's expression—amusement with more than a touch of defiance—I wondered about that statement. It wasn't hard to believe this girl would indeed do anything to give her an advantage, and not just against her brother in their childhood games.

Just then, Mrs. McBride entered the room carrying a large tray. One of the younger maids followed behind, carrying an enormous soup tureen.

"Your parents are lunching in town," Mrs. McBride

informed Flynn, setting the tray on the sideboard. "Soup and salad, that's lunch for you today."

She ladled the steaming soup into waiting bowls and the younger maid hurriedly set them in front of us, along with crisp salads and warm bread.

"So," Flynn said, tearing off a bit of his bread and popping it into his mouth, "croquet after lunch?" He looked at each of us in turn, his blond hair falling onto his forehead, before his gaze fell upon Lily. He smiled at her warmly, so warmly that it made me a bit uncomfortable.

"I want Michael on my team," Prudence announced.

"Perfect!" Flynn piped up, still smiling across the table at Lily. "The losing couple has to serve the winners when we go out for a sail. I've had Mrs. McBride bring a basket containing plenty of adult beverages down to the dock, and I'm sure Flaherty has already stowed it."

"But how are you going to serve drinks to us when you've got to be the one sailing the boat, brother?" Prudence asked, shooting me a sly glance.

Flynn grinned. "Exactly. Which is why we're not losing. Right, Lily?"

"I'll do my best, Flynn." She smiled at him. "But I'm not promising anything. You remember what happened during the tournament at the last solstice party."

"Dead last," he said to me in a stage whisper, laughing. "It's a good thing you're so pretty, Lilybelle, because you're all but useless on the croquet lawn."

Laughter all around, then, but I was getting a knot in my stomach as I sat there watching the interplay between Lily and Flynn. It seemed to me that my best friend was a little more than fond of the girl, and it was beginning to trouble me, considering my growing feelings for her. I decided to ask him about it at our earliest convenience. I'd bow out if he confessed to having feelings for her—he was my best friend, after all. I wasn't about to let a girl, even this extraordinary girl, come between us.

That's what I told myself, but as I gazed across the table at the way Lily's auburn hair was falling so delicately around her face, I knew I was already far gone, and I found myself wondering if I'd be able to bow out and remain here at Whitehall.

I set the manuscript in my lap and looked up at my daughter, whose eyes were shining.

"Now here comes the romance!" She smiled. "Mom, do you think that's how it really happened?"

"I'm not sure, honey." I smiled back at her. "They definitely fell in love here that summer, but we'll never be sure exactly how it happened. I think we have to take everything we read in this book with a grain of salt—the stuff about ghosts and the love story, too."

I sat up a bit straighter in my chair and stretched before reaching for my water glass. I had been reading aloud for a long time, longer than I had in many years, since Amity was small and we'd huddle together reading book after book at bedtime.

I glanced at the clock—it was already nearly six. "How about we take a break until after dinner?" Then, looking at Matthew: "Can you stay? I'm sure Jane has cooked enough for a state dinner."

"I'd love to," he said.

Amity shrugged. "I'd like to hear more, but I guess that's fine with me, too," she said, unfolding herself from her spot on the couch. "I'm supposed to text Heather, anyway. Is it okay if she sleeps over?"

I blinked a few times. "I really don't think it's a good idea."

"Mom!" Amity protested, crossing her arms and jutting out one hip.

"Honey, it's just that with all that's happened here lately, the break-ins and Aunt Fate being upstairs and everything, I'm a little uneasy about somebody else coming into the house," I explained. "It could be dangerous and I don't want to be responsible—"

"With half of the town's police force here at any given moment?" she argued, gesturing wildly toward the window. She looked at Matthew, and for the second time that day, she enlisted his aid. "Come on, Reverend Parker, help me out here!"

He folded his arms across his chest and smiled broadly at her, shaking his head. "Nice try, kiddo, but this is your mom's decision." He grinned at me. "But, if I were to be asked, I'd say I didn't see the harm in it."

Amity's eyes brightened, and she ran with it. "See? He thinks it's okay! Mom, we'll hang around outside for a while after dinner, and then we'll stay in the media room on the second floor and watch movies, I swear. You can assign a police detail to us if you want."

I was torn. I loved that my daughter was making a friend

here. It would certainly ease the transition if I decided to relocate to Alban House permanently, which was becoming more and more attractive to me with every passing day. But on the other hand, considering the recent break-ins, I didn't like the idea of being responsible for someone else's child as well as my own.

And yet her face was so hopeful. She was bouncing up and down on her toes, her eyes wide. I shrugged at Matthew and he nodded back at me.

"Do you promise you'll stay out of the passageways?" I asked her.

"I promise!" She flew to my side, throwing her arms around me.

"Now, listen," I said, pulling back, "I mean it. I'm going to lay down some rules here, and if you break any one of them, Heather is going home and you'll be grounded, do you understand?"

Amity nodded her head, serious now. "I understand. What are the rules?"

"No going into the passageways. They absolutely need to stay locked."

"Okay."

"Don't even mention them to her. Until now, nobody but family even knew about the passageways, and that's how I want it to stay. It's a family secret. Got it?"

"Got it. I won't tell."

"Do you swear?" I pushed it, wagging a finger at her.

"I swear."

"And no going up to the third floor. That's where your great-aunt Fate is, and I don't want her disturbed."

"That's fine. We don't want to hang around her, anyway."

"And one more thing, Amity," I said to her. "If Heather comes over tonight, there'll be no more talk of this manuscript." I shot a quick look at Matthew. "The two of us might finish it tonight, but if we do, I'll read it with you some other time."

"Aww," she protested loudly.

"Not negotiable," I said, shaking my head. "Nobody apart from the three of us is to know this manuscript even exists. It's extraordinarily valuable, and until I decide what to do with it, it's still lost to history. You've never heard of it. I know this is a strong word, honey, but I absolutely forbid you to mention it to Heather. Not a peep. Do you understand?"

"I get it," she said.

"It's important, Amity," I pressed. "If the wrong people knew about this . . ."

"I *get* it," she repeated, her tone bordering on annoyance.

But I still had more to say. "And come to think about it, don't talk at all about David Coleville."

"Oka-a-ay," she said, rolling her eyes and drawing the word out into several syllables, fidgeting where she stood.

I guessed I had set enough ground rules for a simple sleepover—they seemed a little rigid, even to me. I quickly looked at Matthew. He nodded his head, shrugging his shoulders slightly.

"All right," I said. "She can come. But I want to talk to her parents first."

Beaming, Amity fished her cell phone out of her jeans pocket, dialed, and thrust it at me.

Approximately thirty minutes after talking with Heather's mother—who sounded more than a little excited about having her daughter spend the night at Alban House despite the fact there had been a recent break-in—I watched from the window as their car pulled into the driveway.

"I won't be a moment," I said over my shoulder to Matthew as Amity and I went outside to greet her friend.

"Hello again!" I called out, walking down the patio steps toward the driveway. "We're so glad to have Heather with us tonight."

"She was thrilled you called," Heather's mother said as the girls ran off toward the south lawn.

"I want you to know the house is 100 percent secure despite the recent break in," I said, trying to remember the woman's name. I knew I had met her at the funeral, but there were so many people that day, I couldn't quite place her.

"I'm sure it is." She smiled warmly. "Thanks so much for having her."

"Reverend Parker is here," I said. "Would you like to come in and have a drink with us? Or stay for dinner?"

"I'd love to, but can we do it another time?" she asked, looking wistfully up toward the house. "We've got dinner reservations. We sprung into action when we learned we'd have a free evening. You know how it is."

I chuckled. "Yes, I do. Another time, then."

After she had left and I had gone back up to the house, Matthew and I watched out the window as Amity and Heather explored the gardens. I snuck a glance in his direction. I wondered—

The intercom interrupted my thoughts. "Miss Grace?" Jane's voice sounded scratchy and far away. "Dinner is served."

CHAPTER 23

As we ate, Matthew and I talked of everything and nothing—college experiences, friends we had in childhood, even things as mundane as our favorite movies.

"So why did you become a minister?" I asked him.

Chewing a bite of his fillet, he considered this. "Rebellion."

I took a sip of wine and eyed him. "Most kids rebel by doing drugs or stealing cars or getting tattoos."

"I know." He laughed. "It sounds pretty strange. But . . ." He hesitated for a moment. "I don't tell this to many people."

"I won't tell the church ladies." I smiled at him. "Or the press." I almost teased him further about it, but a seriousness descended around us, and I knew this wasn't a joking matter.

He cleared his throat. "I didn't have the most idyllic upbringing imaginable."

I looked at him, not knowing quite what to say, suddenly feeling a bit ashamed of all the opulence around us.

"My father," he began, and then was silent for a moment before continuing. "Let's just say he wasn't the world's best role model."

I wanted to reach across the table and take his hand, but I didn't know if I should.

"I'm so sorry, Matthew," I said to him.

"He was a drug addict and an alcoholic," he said, and sighed deeply. "But even when he wasn't using, he was a bully. An abuser. The whole nine yards. I know I'm supposed to try to see the good in everyone, but Grace, the truth is, he was a monster. My mother was working three jobs to try to support the family, while he came home every night and . . ." I saw tears glisten in the corners of his eyes.

"One night when I was sixteen, I had enough," he went on. "I had seen enough, had experienced enough, and had heard enough. He was all jacked up on something, and he started threatening her, as he always did. I knew he wouldn't stop. Every night, it was either her or me. So I stopped it."

My fork hovered in midair. "Stopped it, how?"

He held my gaze. "I beat him within an inch of his life, literally. All those years of helpless rage . . ." He shook his head. "My mother was terrified I was going to kill him—not terrified for him, you understand, but for me. She didn't want me to spend my life in jail because of that man. So she called the police. They had to drag me off him."

A chill ran through me. I couldn't imagine this gentle, good-humored man in that kind of a rage.

"I spent two years in juvenile hall," he said. "I was sinking fast, Grace. People talk about standing at a crossroads, and that time in my life was definitely mine. There were a lot of messed-up kids in there with me, and I might have easily chosen another path, their path. I might have ended up just like my father."

"Why didn't you?"

He smiled. "One of the ministers who counseled juvenile offenders took a liking to me for some reason. Somehow, he saw the good kid hiding behind the anger and rage. He took me in, made sure I got my high school diploma, and gave me a job at the church. I had never been to church a day in my life, and to me, it was a whole new world. A world where kindness and love existed. I never looked back. It was my—" He stopped, and a grin spread across his face.

"Your what?"

"My saving grace."

I could feel my face start to redden. "I'm glad he was there for you. Just when you needed him."

"Heaven-sent, some would say."

"Don't you think—" I started. But Amity's voice on the intercom stopped me midsentence.

"Mom?" Her voice had a tremor I didn't like.

I hurried across the room and pressed the button. "What is it, honey?"

"Mom, will you come up here?" She sounded small and very far away.

What was this about? "We're just in the middle of dinner, honey. What do you need?"

"Um . . ." she began, and then I heard another voice, a paper-thin, singsong voice, in the background.

"*The witch in the wood comes out to play / By the light of the solstice moon . . .*"

CHAPTER 24

W e'll be right there, honey," I said into the intercom. Matthew and I raced out of the dining room and toward the stairs.

"Jane!" I called, and she popped her head out of the kitchen. "I think Fate is upstairs with the girls." She was at our side in an instant, and we climbed the stairs together, hurrying toward the media room where I knew Amity and Heather had been watching a movie.

I opened the door to find both girls huddled together on one of the leather sofas. Fate, dressed in a tattered, old gown, was twirling in slow circles in the middle of the room. She didn't seem to realize anyone else was there. Her eyes were closed, and she was chanting, over and over:

> *The witch in the wood comes out to play*
> *By the light of the solstice moon*
> *To sing and sway and conjure and pray*
> *Awakening them with her tune!*
> *Come devil, come imp, come monstrous thing*
> *That hides underground in the day*
> *Come alive this night and give them a fright*
> *When the wood witch comes out to play.*

I stared at Amity, openmouthed.

"She just came in here and started . . . chanting," Amity said, her eyes darting from Heather to me to Fate, her voice a harsh whisper. "We tried to come downstairs to get you, but she grabbed us every time we tried to get out of the room. That's when I thought of the intercom."

Thank goodness for Jane, who stepped into the room, marched right up to Fate, and shook her by the shoulders.

"Now, now, Miss Fate," she said as though she were talking to a child. "That's enough dancing for today."

Fate opened her eyes wide, startled by the sound of her own name. She looked at each of us in turn and only then seemed to realize we were there.

"What are you doing here, Miss Fate?" Jane asked her, patting her hand. "You should be in your own room. You know that."

Fate broke free of Jane's grasp and twirled again, her arms out wide. "I heard the girls talking and laughing and it sounded like so much fun, I wanted to join in," she said, frowning at Jane. "I was all alone and didn't have anyone to play with."

Jane grabbed Fate by the arm to stop her twirling. "It's time for bed, Miss Fate," she said, her tone as firm as a schoolteacher's.

"But they get to stay up." Fate pouted, pointing at the girls.

Jane eyed her. "Yes, they get to stay up. But it's your bedtime now. Be a good girl and come along."

"It's not fair," Fate complained, stamping one foot and sighing loudly. But she let Jane lead her out of the room, even as she continued to protest.

"You're not going to be alone," I heard Jane say to Fate as they were making their way down the hall. "I'll stay with you until you fall asleep, just like I always do. How about a story?"

I turned to the girls, who were still huddled together on one of the couches. "I'm sorry about that," I said to them. "Heather, that was Amity's great-aunt, who recently arrived here from the hospital. She is a little..." I searched for the right word. "...confused."

Heather nodded. "That's okay. My grandma has Alzheimer's. She lived with us for a while."

"That was really creepy," Amity said, pulling her knees into her chest and hugging them with her arms. "I know this is bad to say, but I wish she wasn't here. Where did she even get that dress?"

I sat down next to her and put an arm across her shoulders. "It was probably in her old room or tucked away in a trunk somewhere. But either way, don't worry about her. She's harmless. Jane's going to make sure she's down for the night. Her room is locked so she won't bother you girls again, and I've also got a call in to her doctor at the hospital. I'll get some answers when I talk to him, and then we'll decide what the right thing to do is. It could be that she goes back there or into a nursing home here. We'll do what's best for her and it'll all be taken care of within the next few days."

Amity's frown told me she wasn't buying it. I wasn't sure I was, either.

"Do you want us to hang out with you up here and watch a movie?" I asked her, shooting Matthew a look, and he nodded. "Or you could come downstairs. There's a TV in the parlor."

Amity and Heather shared a look, and I could tell some wordless communication had passed between them.

"We'll stay up here, and you don't have to babysit us," Amity said. "But if she comes in here again—"

I cut her off. "She won't."

"If she does," Amity insisted, "I'll call you right away. And we're locking the door in my room when we go to sleep."

Turning to Heather, I said: "Are you cool with all of this?"

She nodded, smiling. "I'm cool with it."

"Okay, then," I told them. "We're going back downstairs. If you need us, just call on the intercom. After we finish our dinner, we'll be in the parlor."

As we were walking down the stairs toward the dining room, Matthew stopped midway and turned to me. "How did Fate hear them?" he asked.

I frowned at him. "What do you mean?"

"She said she heard the girls playing and it sounded like such fun," he said. "If she was in her rooms on the third floor, she couldn't have heard them—right? And didn't you say she was locked in?"

Had she remembered the passageways from her childhood? A sense of dread seeped its way into my skin. I knew she was just a harmless, confused old lady, but I didn't like the idea of Fate creeping around the house, listening to my daughter.

CHAPTER 25

Since Jane was busy tending to Fate, I headed to the kitchen to retrieve our dessert (crème brûlée) and coffee, put it all on a tray, and brought it into the living room, where Matthew was sitting in front of the fire.

"Never a dull moment around here," I said, setting the tray on one of the sideboards and handing him a cup.

"Have you decided what you're going to do about her?" Matthew asked. "It's obvious she can't—shouldn't—stay here. She needs full-time care."

"I'm not sure what to do," I admitted, sinking into a chair. "As soon as I've talked to her doctor in Switzerland—first thing tomorrow morning, I hope—I'll make the decision."

"There are lots of resources here in town, of course, and I could certainly help you find the right facility for her, but it might be best that she goes back there," he said. "It has been her home for a half century, after all."

"That's what I've been thinking," I said. "I may have to take her back myself. That way, I can check out the place and make sure it's of the best quality."

We made small talk while we finished our desserts, but after he put down his spoon, he locked his eyes with mine. "Grace, can I ask you something?"

The energy between us began to swim and bubble, and I got

the feeling that whatever he was about to say was important in a way nothing else had been. "Of course."

He took a deep breath. "What is this?"

I looked around the room. "What is what?"

"This." He gestured from himself to me. "Us having dinner. Reading the manuscript together. Talking on the phone."

I smiled, but a sense of dread was wrapping itself around me. I didn't want to define what was going on—I didn't know enough to define it—and I had the sense that calling it out, saying its name, might make whatever was happening, if anything was, vanish.

"Well, Amity says you've been hanging around a lot lately," I said finally, bringing my coffee cup to my lips with shaking hands.

"I have indeed been hanging around lately." He leaned in toward me. "About that, I've got something to confess."

"I thought people were supposed to confess to you," I deflected.

"Those are the other guys, the ones with the head man in Rome." He grinned. "We don't do much confessing in our church. We leave that between each person and God. Thank goodness. I really don't want to hear that the ladies who run the church social are lusting in their hearts. That I can do without."

I chuckled. "So what is it you have to confess to me?"

He cleared his throat. "It could easily be assumed that I've been hanging around because I'm simply tending to the needs of a parishioner who just lost her mother. And in one way, I'm certainly doing that. It's my job. But if I'm going to be honest with you—and that's also in my job description—that's not why I'm here. At least, that's not the whole reason."

A tingle ran up my spine. "It isn't?"

He shook his head. "No. The truth is, I'm here because I'm finding it very difficult to stay away."

I wasn't sure what to say to that. I couldn't deny that I had felt something the moment I had met this man, and those feelings were growing with every encounter we had. But—a minister?

"I'm finding it difficult to stay away, too," I admitted, but in the same breath, I glossed it over. "You're the first friend I've had in this town in twenty years. I consider you a friend, Matthew. I hope you consider me one, too."

"Friends," he said, nodding and taking a sip of his coffee. "Is that what you're thinking we are?"

Since he was being honest, I should've been, too. But I couldn't bring myself to say the words. The truth was, I wasn't crazy about the idea of getting involved with somebody who had the kinds of very public responsibilities a minister had. After all, I had left this town two decades ago because I couldn't stand the scrutiny of people after my father died. That would be nothing compared to the kind of grilling I'd receive if I were dating the minister of a large church. Why couldn't he have been a lawyer or a doctor or a car mechanic?

But I didn't say any of those things. Instead, I said: "I don't know. What do you think?"

He held my gaze. "I don't know."

"Friends is good."

"Friends is good." He nodded.

What had I just done?

The whole conversation was making my skin itch, so I got up and walked to the window. It only took a moment for me to realize what I was seeing.

"Matthew. Look."

He joined me at the open window. "Is that . . . ?"

And there she was, white dress and all. Somehow, she had made her way out of her rooms and down to the lakeshore, and built a fire inside a ring of stones. And she was dancing around and around, her spidery, singsong voice carried by the wind into my ears.

> *The witch in the wood comes out to play*
> *By the light of the solstice moon*
> *To sing and sway and conjure and pray*
> *Awakening them with her tune!*
> *Come devil, come imp, come monstrous thing*
> *That hides underground in the day*
> *Come alive this night and give them a fright*
> *When the wood witch comes out to play.*

She was repeating it, over and over, louder and louder, until her voice, at first so hesitant and shaky, was strong and booming and firm.

"Matthew," I whispered, locking my eyes with his and grasping at his arm. "She's supposed to be upstairs with Jane."

"She's just a confused old lady, Grace," he said, but the look on his face betrayed his words.

I hurried to the buzzer. "Jane? Jane! It's Fate. She's outside, down on the lakeshore."

Jane was in the living room in an instant, and together the three of us opened the French doors and walked out into the night.

"*Come devil, come imp, come monstrous thing!*" Fate screamed, snapping her head toward us, a look of wild abandon in her eyes.

Jane rushed at her and took her by the arms. "You have been very naughty, Miss Fate," she scolded, her words bringing Fate back into the present moment from wherever she had gone. "You know you were supposed to stay in your rooms. How did you get out?"

"It's the solstice," she whispered, her voice a harsh rasp.

And then, turning to Matthew and me. "*Friends is good*," she sang. "*Difficult to stay away! Friends is good!*"

Caught in Fate's gaze, a coldness seemed to take hold of me from the inside. A seeping, slithering sense of foreboding was working its way through my body, curling around my heart, slipping up my throat, and finally wrapping itself around my neck like a noose. It was fear and terror and insanity and anger all at once, all of it seemingly passing from Fate into me. Like a spell. Devils and monstrous things?

I felt Matthew slip an arm around my shoulders. I looked up at him. "I thought those passageways were locked," I whispered.

"All right now," Jane said, her voice stern. "Enough is enough. We're going back upstairs. And let this be the end of it."

She took Fate's hand, and as she led her toward the house, Jane looked back over her shoulder. "Your mother had some sedatives prescribed during her illness," she said softly. "I think it's time we used them."

I nodded, not knowing what else to do.

"Mr. Jameson and I will stay in her rooms with her tonight to watch her," Jane continued, over her shoulder. "And you should position a policeman outside her door. She'll not be getting out again, by God."

CHAPTER 26

The next morning, I awoke to Jane's gentle nudging. "Miss Grace," she said, her voice low. "Miss Grace, the doctor from Switzerland is on the line."

I shot up, fumbling for my robe.

"I'm sorry to wake you so early, but I knew you'd want to take this call," she said.

I saw it was seven o'clock. I hurried across the room to the phone, which was on the desk in my mother's study.

"Hello?" I said, clearing my throat as Jane handed me a cup of coffee and set a glass of water on the desk. "Hello, this is Grace Alban."

"Miss Alban," said a heavily accented voice on the other end of the line. "I'm Dr. Baptiste. I've been in charge of your aunt's care for nearly thirty years."

"Hello, Doctor," I said, taking a sip of my coffee. "As I think you probably know, my aunt was taken out of your facility by a person with no connection to this family and without the knowledge of this family. She showed up here as a complete surprise to us. I'd like to know exactly how that happened."

He was silent for a moment. "Miss Alban, your family has been very good to us over the years, and I can assure you that your aunt was given the highest quality of care here and will be for the rest of her life. Please accept my sincere apologies for this situation and know that I launched a full investigation into this the moment we realized she was missing. I've been trying to contact your family for days."

"I know," I said. "That's our fault, I'm afraid. It's been a very hectic time. My mother passed away and we've had a lot to deal with here, not the least of which is my aunt's arrival."

"I'm so sorry," he said. "But please rest assured I will find out who is to blame for this situation. Frankly, Miss Alban, I'm afraid that in order for her to have left this facility, someone here on the inside must have been involved, and when I find the guilty party, corrective action will be taken. You can be sure of that."

"I'm not calling with recriminations or to cast blame. It happened, I'm satisfied that you're looking into it, but now we need to move forward."

"Thank you, Miss Alban," he said. "Your aunt is on several medications. I'll transfer those to your local pharmacy immediately. She needs these medications, and I'm quite worried she has been off them for so long already."

I looked at Jane and mouthed: "Pharmacy number." She hurried off to find it.

"What are the medications?" I asked him. "I guess what I'm really asking is, what exactly is her condition?"

"Your aunt is on antipsychotics."

"She's psychotic?" I coughed into the phone.

"A form of schizophrenia, yes," he said. "I'm sorry, I assumed you knew and were taking the proper precautions. She hasn't had any medication for, what has it been, a week's time?"

"At least that. Maybe more."

He was silent for a moment. "And you say she's at home with you?"

"Yes." A tingling sensation crept up my spine, and I wondered exactly where this conversation was headed.

"Miss Alban," the doctor said, "I don't know how much you know about your aunt's history, but you very well could have a dangerous situation on your hands."

"What do you mean, dangerous?" I said louder than I had intended. "You're right in that we don't know much about my aunt's condition. My family didn't know where she was living all these years. All I know is she came to you some fifty years ago and has been there ever since."

"Your grandfather was a large benefactor of ours," he began. "You may know that he built a wing of this hospital to simulate his own home, the home where your aunt grew up."

"I do know that now," I said.

"What you might not know is that he built it in the 1940s, when your aunt was still a child," he went on. "It was all very hush-hush, but I don't believe in keeping secrets, even long-standing ones, when it comes to a patient's health and well-being."

A chill began to wrap its way around me and I had the urge to hang up the phone, to not hear what the doctor had to say. But I knew I had to hear it, no matter how unpleasant. "I agree," I said, my voice a rasp. "Please go on."

"As I said, he built the wing for her when she was just a child, because he suspected she'd be coming here someday," he continued.

"I don't understand," I said, shaking my head and trying to focus on what he was saying, but I just wasn't grasping it. "I had never met my aunt before she arrived here unannounced just a few days ago, but by all accounts, she was fine—perfectly normal—

until something happened here at Alban House during a summer party in 1956, and the stress or trauma of it apparently drove her into a kind of madness and she ended up with you. So . . . what you're saying doesn't make any sense to me. Why would my grandfather have gone to the trouble to build an entire wing on a psychiatric hospital for her a decade earlier?"

"A psychiatric hospital?" asked Dr. Baptiste. "Is that what you think we are?"

"Well . . ." My mind was reeling. "Aren't you?"

"In a manner of speaking, yes," he said. "But not strictly. Miss Alban, we are a private facility for the criminally insane."

I PULLED OUT THE DESK CHAIR and sat down hard.

"All of our patients, Miss Alban, have been the perpetrators of violent crime," the doctor went on. "That's who we serve here. As I said, we're a private facility. Families turn to us to care for their loved ones who simply cannot function in society."

My thoughts were going in several directions at once. "I'm sorry to keep repeating this, Dr. Baptiste, but I don't understand. A private facility . . ."

"We are located in Switzerland, as you know, where the extradition laws for various countries are rather ambiguous. When a family brings a patient here . . ."

His words trailed off, but I was beginning to see his point. "Do you mean to tell me that people—rich people—arrange somehow to have their family members who have committed violent crimes—"

"Exactly," he said. "I'm only telling you this because you are an Alban, and your family has been one of our most trusted benefactors throughout the years. Sometimes circumstances arise . . . situations happen, shall we say . . . and families don't want their loved ones spending time behind bars or in one of the ghastly institutions you have in the States. Or they don't want the whole scene to be played out in the newspapers. So they come to us. Their loved ones 'disappear'; they are no longer a danger to the family or to society at large, and the family is spared the embarrassment of dealing with the situation in a public way."

"Spared a trial?" I managed to squeak out.

"Exactly," he said quickly. "We provide their loved ones with the highest quality of care, while making sure they are no longer a danger to society, themselves, or their families. Our facility is quite secure."

"And yet a reporter waltzed right out of there with my aunt."

"And that," said Dr. Baptiste, "is under serious investigation, as I have said."

Just then, Jane came back into the room and held my gaze, a concerned look on her face.

"This must be coming as quite a shock to you," the doctor said, his voice taking on a gentle, yet forceful tone. "Let me suggest this. You get her back on her medication today. I can put a nurse on a plane this afternoon so she can be returned to us and simply bill you for the cost. This is the best place for your aunt, Miss Alban. This is her home. It's what she has known for fifty years and she is happy here. It's a safe place for her to live out the rest of her days—her father saw to that, leaving us a trust for her care. We will correct the security breach that allowed her to leave, believe me."

What he was saying made sense. I held Jane's gaze and mouthed: "Send her back?" She gave me a quick nod.

"Make the arrangements and let us know when the nurse will get here," I said to him. "You can feel free to talk with Jane Jameson, who works for me. Let her know the specifics. I'll give her to you now and she'll relay the information about where to send my aunt's prescriptions."

I held out the phone to Jane, but then heard the doctor's voice, small and far away, from the receiver. "Miss Alban?" I put it back to my ear. "Until our nurse gets there, I ask you to keep your aunt sequestered, if possible. I cannot say this strongly enough. You need to watch her."

Another chill ran up my spine. "Why do you say that?"

"She is fixated on your family," he explained. "You may have already learned that she is firmly planted in the past, believing it's still 1956, the year she came to us. She is reliving it, day after day."

"There was a death here at Alban House," I told him. "It was a suicide."

He was silent for a moment. "Miss Alban, you need to take precautions and protect yourself. Without her medication, I'm afraid her hallucinations will return. She will begin to hear voices and—"

But I didn't let him finish. I thrust the phone at Jane and raced out of the room and down the hallway, knocking on the door of Amity's room until she opened it.

"Mom?" she said, rubbing her eyes, still in the throes of sleep. "What's the matter?"

"Do you think you could sleep at Heather's tonight?" I said, my voice low.

She yawned. "I don't know. Why?"

"I just talked to Aunt Fate's doctor, and because of several things he said, I want you away from here. The hospital is sending a nurse to come and pick her up and take her back there. But I don't want you around here until she's safely gone."

"But why? You said she's harmless."

"Honey, for once, just don't ask questions," I whispered. "Just trust me."

Heather stirred and blinked at me. I turned my gaze to her. "Heather, do you think Amity could spend the night at your house tonight?" I asked her. "I'll call your parents to make sure it's okay."

Heather nodded. "Sure." She shot Amity a sleepy smile.

"Great," I said. "I'd like you both to go right after breakfast. Pack an overnight bag before you leave this room—both of you, pack up. And take those bags with you when you go down for breakfast. I don't want you coming back up here."

"Wow, you're really trying to get rid of us," Amity said with a long stretch.

"That's the idea." I smiled. "Now do as I say and head down to the dining room. I'll have Jane get something for you for breakfast." I winked at the girls and closed the door behind me as I left the room.

Back in the master suite, I saw Jane sitting at the desk, holding the phone's receiver, writing information down on a note pad.

"We'll pick up those medications today," she said, nodding her head. Looking up, she saw me. "And now here's Miss Alban again." She handed the phone to me.

"Dr. Baptiste, please forgive my abrupt departure, but I have my daughter here in the house with me, and when you told me about my aunt Fate's condition, I felt the need to get her out of the house until my aunt is safely back in your care."

"That's wise," he said. "She's especially fixated on—" and then he stopped short and was quiet for a moment. "What did you just say, Miss Alban?"

"I was talking about my daughter and getting her out of the house until my aunt is safely back with you."

"I believe you also said your aunt *Fate*," he said.

"Yes, that's right."

He was silent for another moment. "Why did you call her that?"

I wasn't quite getting the point of his question. "Because that's her name . . . ?"

"I think we're having some sort of misunderstanding," he said slowly. "You must know—I believe you know—that the woman who has lived here since 1956, the patient whose care we have been discussing, is Mercy Alban."

CHAPTER 27

I stared at Jane, holding the phone in one hand and shaking my head. After a few false starts, I finally said: "I'm really at a loss here, Doctor. The woman who arrived here a few days ago has identified herself as Fate Alban."

"I'm not surprised about that. Mercy is fixated on her sister and, at certain times, insists that she *is* her sister. It's one of the things we have been working on over the years in terms of her care. Without her medication—"

I interrupted him. "But Mercy died when she was a young child."

Hearing me say the name "Mercy," Jane sat down hard on the bed, her face ashen, her mouth agape.

"No, Miss Alban," he said. "Mercy has been living here with us since 1956. Mercy is the reason your grandfather built the entire wing onto this hospital. Did you not notice the name of our facility? It was changed to Mercy House when she came to us."

The room felt cold, as though an arctic chill had suddenly blown through it. "So what you're saying is that Fate Alban has not been in your facility, not at any time?"

"No," he said. "Our patient, the patient who has lived here for five decades and who left here unsupervised more than a week ago, is *Mercy* Alban."

"But—" I started, but didn't quite know where I was going with the thought.

"Miss Alban, I hate to cut this conversation short, but I have patients to see," Dr. Baptiste said. "I'll be in touch with Mrs. Jameson about when to expect the nurse to pick up Mercy. Tomorrow, the next day at the latest, depending on flight schedules. And do make sure she gets her medication between now and then. It's vital. I'll prescribe a sedative also. Please call me if you need anything. I want to be in closer touch with you as we move forward."

"Yes," I said, staring out the window into the garden. "Yes, I will."

And he hung up. I sat, cradling the phone in my hands.

"What was that about?" Jane asked, her eyes watery, her voice cracking.

I just looked at her for a moment. "Jane, it's the oddest thing," I began, the words sounding strange and otherworldly as they slipped from my tongue. "The doctor told me that the woman upstairs on the third floor is Mercy Alban."

She shook her head, smiling slightly, a chuckle on her lips. "That's impossible."

"That's what the doctor said."

"But Miss Grace, that's *impossible*," Jane repeated, still smiling. "Mercy died, right here in Alban House, when she was ten years old."

"I don't understand this any more than you do, but apparently, she didn't die back then," I said, finally hanging up the phone. "That's Mercy up there, Jane. The doctor said my grandfather built a *wing* on that hospital for Mercy when she was a child, and she came to live there a decade or so later. Why would a father build a wing on a hospital *for the criminally insane* for his daughter—who was a child? Why would someone do something like that, Jane?"

Her mouth was a tight line, her spine rigid. "But it's Fate Alban who disappeared that night."

"How can you insist that when the doctor tells us different?" I shot back.

"The doctor wasn't here all those years ago," she cried. "I was!"

"But you weren't there at the hospital for the past fifty years," I said. "They even named the facility after her, because my grandfather gave so much money for her care. It's called Mercy House."

Jane shook her head slowly. Her eyes were focused on me, but I knew she was looking into the past, back to a rather chaotic night a half century earlier.

"And, here's the other thing, Jane," I went on. "Say the woman upstairs right now, the woman who lived in that hospital for the past five decades, is indeed Fate Alban. Why would her father have built a whole wing on that hospital to mimic this very house *ten years or more before* the night she disappeared? Fate wasn't insane as a child. Was she?"

Jane shook her head. "Ach, no. Never more a sunny girl than your aunt Fate. Sweet and dear and funny until the day she disappeared."

"So why then would her father, my grandfather, have built a wing at a hospital for the criminally insane for her, thinking she'd end up there someday? It doesn't make any sense, Jane. It just doesn't."

"He wouldn't."

I watched Jane's face morph from defiant to ashen to stone as something, a realization, took hold of her. She leaned across the desk between us and, uncharacteristically, took my hand.

"Miss, I want you to listen to me carefully," she said slowly, holding my gaze with her steel-gray eyes. "If it's truly Mercy up there, I think it's best that you and the girls don't spend another night under the same roof with her."

"I've already arranged for Amity to stay over with her friend," I said, pulling free of Jane's grasp and walking across the room toward the window. "And it's no problem for the lads to move back into the gardener's house. But Jane, you and I have been here for days with Fate—*Mercy*—whomever. You're going to the pharmacy to get her meds today. The doctor said he's going to prescribe a sedative as well, so I think she'll be pretty harmless. Don't you? I certainly don't want to leave."

"Can't you stay with your pastor friend?" she asked, her eyes earnest.

I leaned against the window frame. "No, that's out of the question. I could just stay in a hotel . . . but Jane, aren't you over-reacting? Getting the girls out of here is one thing, but me? You sound afraid, Jane. But she's just a sick, old lady. Isn't she?"

"Miss Grace," she said, her voice low and guttural, her old accent more pronounced than I had heard it in years. "You need to understand. Listen to me, and hear this now. It may be true that it's not Fate Alban upstairs in her old suite of rooms. It may be true that, like the doctor said, it is indeed Mercy Alban." She took a long breath and shook her head. "But it is also true that Mercy Alban died, right here at Alban House, when she was ten years old. I buried her myself."

CHAPTER 28

I blinked at Jane and then closed my eyes, draping a hand across my forehead. I was having a hard time processing everything that had come at me in the past few minutes, especially considering the fact that I had had only one cup of coffee to kickstart my brain.

"So Mercy died," I said, my voice dropping to a whisper. "You buried her. Then . . . I don't get it. Why are you even entertaining the thought that it might be Mercy upstairs?"

Jane twisted her apron in her lap and shifted her eyes from side to side. Obviously, there was something she wasn't telling me.

"What is it, Jane?" I prodded.

Jane leaned in close to me, her voice gravelly and rough. "She didn't stay dead."

I squinted at her, shaking my head. "That's . . . well, forgive me, Jane, but that's just crazy."

"I know how it sounds," she said to me. "But it's the honest truth."

I waited another moment for her to go on, but she stayed quiet, twisting her apron and looking down.

"You'll have to do better than that," I told her. "You're telling me a girl died and then came back to life. You've got to know that's impossible, right?"

Even as I grilled Jane about this, an idea was formulating in the outer reaches of my brain. Coleville's story about the dead twin still haunting Whitehall Manor was becoming all too real.

Jane shook her head and closed her eyes, and, as though she could read my thoughts, I saw a shudder pass through her.

"Listen, maybe Mercy slipped into a coma and came out of it?" I offered. "Couldn't that be what it was? Back then, medicine certainly wasn't as advanced as it is now. It might have seemed—"

Jane's eyes shot open. "Medicine had nothing to do with this. What I'm telling you is Mercy was dead and gone. Died in the very rooms where she is right now. We laid her to rest in the family crypt."

"And then?"

"You have to understand a mother's grief, child." Jane's voice was barely audible now.

As she met my gaze, I thought again of Coleville's manuscript and the description of the ghostly girl in white, whom Mickey—Coleville—saw out of his bedroom window the first night he stayed here. Was it just artistic license, or could it be . . . ?

I also thought of my father's warning, and an icy chill ran through me.

Jane stood up in a hurry. "I can't talk about this anymore, Miss Grace," she said. "Not right now. I'll tell you everything, but time is of the essence. The nurse from the hospital is on her way here, but she won't arrive for more than twelve hours. The girls are leaving—"

I interrupted her. "After breakfast, yes. They're going to bring their bags downstairs with them."

"Then I had better get to the kitchen to make sure they get

something to eat," Jane said, moving toward the door. "Once they're off, I'll head to the pharmacy. I'll take *her* with me. I don't want her in the house alone."

"Are you sure, Jane? If she's as dangerous as you say—" I began, but was greeted with her shaking head, stopping my words.

"She's been as cooperative as a child up to now," Jane said. "And we've got things to do. You need to get your daughter safely out of this house. When that's done, and when you're packed to leave for the night, I'll tell you the truth about Mercy Alban. It's a story you're not going to want to hear, child, but it has to be told."

And with that, she flew out the door, presumably down to the kitchen. I turned around in a slow circle in my room and wondered what had just happened.

I found myself with my hand on the phone receiver and hesitated for a moment before picking it up to dial. What I said to Matthew the night before was true—he was my only friend here in town and I desperately needed to talk to somebody. But after the awkwardness that passed between us—friends? more than friends?—I wasn't sure it was right to make contact again so soon.

Oh, what the hell, I thought and dialed his number.

"Hello?" Matthew said, coughing slightly on the other end of the line.

"Sorry for calling so early," I said. "You probably haven't had your coffee yet."

"Oh, I'm an early riser," he said. "I've had my run on the lakeshore already. What's up?"

Now that I had him on the line, I didn't know quite what to say. How could I tell him the ghost story we had read the night before was becoming all too real. Finally, I said: "I'm getting Heather and Amity out of the house this morning."

"Did something else happen last night? She didn't find her way out of her rooms again, did she?"

"No," I said, sitting down in the chair by the desk. "It happened this morning. I don't want to get into it until I get the girls out of the house, but . . ." I stopped short.

"But what?"

Good question. What is it that I wanted of this man who I was determined to keep as just a friend? "I'm hoping we can meet for coffee and I'll tell you all about it," I said finally.

"How's the Breakwater Café in an hour?"

I looked at my watch. It was only eight o'clock—yet it felt like I had been up forever. "Sounds perfect," I said. "I'll see you there."

I hung up and buzzed Jane in the kitchen. "Are the girls downstairs?" I asked her.

"Aye. I'm just ready to serve their breakfast, and Mr. Jameson is with Miss Mercy. Do you want some eggs?"

"No thanks," I said. "I'm going to hop in the shower and leave for a bit when I take the girls to Heather's house. Then I'll come back and we can finish our talk."

AN HOUR LATER, I was standing on the doorstep of Heather's house, the girls and their bags in tow. I didn't intend to tell her parents the whole story, obviously, but I also didn't want them to think I was a flake for dropping the girls off so early and then asking if my daughter could spend the night with them.

"I'm sorry to throw this onto you so abruptly"—I smiled

broadly at Heather's mother, whose name I still couldn't remember—"but it has to do with Amity's great-aunt, who is decidedly unwell. Frankly . . ."—I lowered my voice, taking her into my confidence—". . . and please keep this between us, but I'm not quite sure about her mental state. I'm afraid she gave the girls a start last night."

"It's like Grandma," Heather piped up.

Her mother nodded. "I understand," she said with a genuine smile. "It's not easy, dealing with a relative with Alzheimer's."

If she only knew. "We've got a nurse on the way to take my aunt back to the hospital," I explained. "She should be here later today or tomorrow. But until that happens, I think it's best that the girls be out of the house. For their sakes as well as for my aunt's."

"Not a problem," Heather's mother said, grasping my hand. "I know how trying this type of thing can be." She radiated warmth. "More than trying."

"Thank you," I said to her, and I could feel the stress seeping from my shoulders. Trying, indeed. "It has been quite a lot to deal with."

"Grace, I'm sorry I couldn't join you last night for a drink. Would you like to come in for a cup of coffee now?" Heather's mother asked.

I squeezed her hand. "Thank you, but now I'm the one who has to get going." Her face dropped. "I've got an appointment," I quickly added. "But I'd love a rain check, after all of this gets settled. Next week?"

"You've got it." She smiled. "We'll have you over for dinner."

I held her gaze and thankfully, her name popped into my

mind. "Sarah, that would be lovely," I said, meaning it. "And I really appreciate you taking Amity for the night. I don't have many friends here in town anymore. I've been away for so long and it feels good—really good—to be able to rely on someone."

"Not a problem. Amity is welcome here anytime. She's a lovely girl."

I started off down the steps and then turned back. "Next week, then?"

Sarah nodded. "If not dinner, maybe the two of us could sneak off for a glass of wine. There's a new wine bar downtown I've been wanting to try."

I liked her better and better with every passing minute. "Sounds great!" I called over my shoulder, giving her a quick wave. "I'll be in touch. And thanks!"

I PULLED INTO THE PARKING LOT at the old Breakwater Café, glad to see Matthew's green Volvo. I found him sitting at a booth by the window, cradling a cup of steaming coffee in both hands.

"Hi." He smiled at me as I slid into the seat opposite him.

I held his gaze for a moment and then put my head down on the table, gently knocking my forehead on the Formica a few times. "You are not going to believe this," I mumbled.

"What can I get you, honey?"

I looked up to see the waitress, holding a pot of coffee.

"Some of that," I gestured toward the pot. "With cream. And do you still have the Trail Breakfast?" I remembered coming to this place when I was a kid and ordering their sinfully enormous concoction of crispy hash browns topped with onion, sausage, and eggs, all smothered with cheese. I hadn't eaten anything like that in years, but if ever I had a need for comfort food, it was right then.

"We sure do." She smiled, her free hand on her hip.

She turned to Matthew. "Make it two," he said, and she was off.

"I've been eating low-carb, low-fat, egg white omelets for so long that my heart may actually stop when I take my first bite," I said. "Get me directly to a hospital if that happens, will you?"

"With their menu, I think they're required by law to have a defib machine in the back." He took a sip of his coffee. "So what's up, Grace? You sounded fairly upset on the phone."

The waitress set a ceramic mug in front of me, along with a small silver pitcher of cream. I poured a splash into my coffee and stirred.

"The crazy lady at Alban House right now isn't my aunt Fate," I said, taking a sip.

Matthew wrinkled his nose. "Okay," he said, drawing out the word into several syllables. "Who is it?"

"I finally connected with her doctor in Switzerland this morning," I continued. "The woman at the house right now is my aunt Mercy, Fate's twin. The place where she's been living all these years is called Mercy House because of the enormous sum of money my grandfather donated for her care."

Matthew shook his head. "But didn't Jane tell us that Mercy—"

I cut him off. "Died? Yup." I took another sip of my coffee, and as I looked at his utterly confused face, I began to laugh, my shoulders shaking and eyes watering with the force of it.

"I'm sorry," I choked out after the wave had passed, dabbing at my eyes with a napkin. "I shouldn't be laughing. None of this is funny in the least. But I am completely overwhelmed right now and the absurdity of my life has just hit a new high."

Matthew reached over the table, took my hand, and squeezed it. The simple, kind act nudged my borderline-hysterical laughter over to tears. My eyes welled up and I covered them with my napkin, shaking my head. "I've officially gone off the deep end," I squeaked out.

"This is what I've been saying for days, Grace, you've got a lot to deal with right now," he said as the waitress returned to our table with our heaping plates. "I'm surprised you've held it together as well as you have."

"Oh, you don't know the half of it." I shook my head. "It's not just that her name is different. The place where she's been living all this time? Mercy House? Not a psychiatric hospital."

He furrowed his brow. "What is it, then?"

"A private facility for the criminally insane." I couldn't believe I was even saying the words, and Matthew's expression told me he couldn't believe he was hearing them.

"And that's . . . what, exactly?"

I sank my fork into the pile of hash browns, eggs, and cheese and took a huge bite, savoring the decadence of this forbidden food before continuing. "It's a place where ultrarich people put their family members who are crazy and violent. *Criminally insane*, it's a perfect term. They're nuts and they've hurt somebody or worse. Instead of delivering them to the police, the families hide them away in facilities like Mercy House, so they're locked up, out of society, but without the embarrassment and scandal of a public trial."

As I said it, I knew that's exactly the sort of thing my Alban ancestors would have done with one of their own who they realized was a danger to herself or others.

"Mercy was taken to this facility that night in 1956, not Fate?" Matthew asked.

"Exactly."

"So where's Fate?"

"Whereabouts unknown." I took another bite.

"But, Grace, can we go back a little bit? Jane told us Mercy died when she was a child, right?"

"That's right."

"So obviously that didn't happen."

My fork hung in the air just over my ever-shrinking plate of breakfast. "Oh, but it did," I said. "That's what I'm telling you. I know how this sounds, Matthew, but Jane insists Mercy *did* die. It was a fever or something. She was buried in the family crypt on our property."

Matthew put his fork on the table and turned both of his palms upward, shrugging his shoulders. "Meaning . . . what?"

"Jane said Mercy was dead and buried. And then she wasn't."

He was silent for a moment before continuing. "Grace, there's only one human being that I know of who was dead and buried and then he wasn't. His name was Lazarus, and a guy from Nazareth had a little something to do with his improved situation. I'm assuming the Lord Himself didn't pay a visit to Alban House way back when."

A chill ran through me. "From what Jane said this morning, I got the impression that this situation is on the other end of the spectrum from holy."

Matthew shook his head. "What exactly are you getting at, Grace?"

I took a deep breath and the words poured forth. "The truth is, when Jane learned that it was Mercy, not Fate, upstairs, she seemed . . . afraid. She insisted the girls get out of the house immediately, and had Mr. Jameson's helpers move back to the cottage. If Mercy isn't gone by tonight—and I don't see how she could be—Jane wants me out of the house, too."

"So she thinks Mercy is dangerous."

"Yes. Mercy's doctor agrees, because she's been off her medications now for several days. He says she's psychotic and her hallucinations will likely return. And from what we saw last night, I think both of us know that they have."

We looked at each other for a moment, both remembering the strange scene on the lakeshore the night before, neither one knowing quite what to say next.

Matthew shook his head and ran a hand through his hair, grimacing. "You realize you just told me that an undead, hallucinating psychotic is living in your house."

I couldn't stop a chuckle from escaping my lips. The absurdity of it was too much. "Correction. An undead, hallucinating, *criminally insane* psychotic."

Matthew took a gulp of his coffee. "I think we can both agree that this undead business is ridiculous. I mean, seriously, Grace. This is real life here, not Coleville's story. Do you think she was—I don't know—in a coma or something like it, they pronounced her dead and then she was . . ."

"Do not say 'buried alive.' I saw that Vincent Price movie when I was a kid and I'm still not over it."

"Well, what other explanation could there be?"

Finally, the first hint of rationality in regard to this whole situation was whispering in my ear. "That really could be it, actually," I said. "If she did slip into a coma, or something like it, and was placed into the family crypt and then came out of it somehow . . ."

Matthew grinned and slapped a hand on the table. "You've got it! That would do a huge number on anyone's psyche, let alone a child's. You just wouldn't be the same after that."

"That would really damage a child, you're right." I exhaled and then lifted my coffee cup to my lips, feeling saner than I had in several hours. "Not to mention do a number on everyone else who thought she was dead. It would explain a lot. Family lore tells us that Fate disappeared the night of Coleville's suicide at Alban House. Now we know it was really Mercy."

"So, then, what happened to Fate?" he asked. "You said her whereabouts were unknown."

I put my elbows on the table and leaned my head into my hands. "I'm really confused. Fate disappeared that night, but Mercy wound up in the facility in Switzerland. So we still have no idea what happened to Fate."

"That's right." Matthew nodded. "That night was when the twins were somewhere between eighteen and twenty years old, give or take a few years, right?"

"Right. The summer of 1956."

"That leads me to yet another question: Where was Mercy from the time everyone thought she died until then? From all you know about your family history, there was no Mercy during that time."

He was right. My family had all but erased her from our lineage. "Maybe she was in an institution here in the States?" I offered, but then another, darker thought floated into my mind. "Or maybe she was at Alban House the whole time."

Matthew took a big bite of his eggs. "Do you know what this is sounding like to me?"

I held his gaze. "I was thinking the same thing. The manuscript. The girl in white."

"Exactly. Except that in the story, the girl in white is a ghost. The twin did actually die and was haunting the place. But the lady on your third floor right now is very real."

The waitress breezed by with the check, which Matthew quickly paid as I was reaching for my purse.

"Jane said she'd tell me the whole story about Mercy once the girls were out of the house and she picked up Mercy's prescriptions," I said. "Care to come home with me to hear it?"

"I thought you'd never ask."

CHAPTER 29

An eerie silence hung in the air as we walked from room to room. Jane was still out, likely driven by Carter to the pharmacy. Mercy had apparently gone with them, as Jane had mentioned. The boys were nowhere to be seen. Mr. Jameson wasn't in the garden. I didn't see either of the guards I knew would be, or should be, patrolling. The house was still and empty; our footsteps echoed on the wood floor.

"You know, I don't think I've ever been in the house without Jane," I said to Matthew. "It's a little weird, to tell you the truth."

He sank into one of the armchairs and crossed his legs as I paced from window to window.

"I wish she'd get back here," I said, peering out at the empty driveway. "I'm dying to hear what she has to say."

"I've got an idea," Matthew began, his eyes bright. "Jane's not here right now to tell us what went down all those years ago, but we do have another window into the past, don't we?"

"Oh!" I said, realizing what he was getting at. "I've got it in the safe upstairs. Maybe it will shed some light on things."

A few minutes later, we were settled in my mother's study, the manuscript in my lap.

"It's part love story and part ghost story," I said, flipping ahead a few pages from where we had stopped reading. "In the next chapter he's talking about the croquet match." I turned more pages. "And here they're going sailing. We don't really need to read the love story part of it now, do we? We can come back and read it later, but I'm more interested in what he's going to say next about the girl in white, aren't you?"

"Absolutely," Matthew agreed. "When all of this is said and done, when Mercy is back in the hospital and we've got a boring, completely normal afternoon on our hands without any break-ins or funerals or long-ago mysteries to solve, we can come back to the rest of it."

I noticed he said "we" and smiled at him. "That sounds lovely, doesn't it? Just a normal day without a new crisis to deal with."

"It's out there, Grace, I promise you."

"Okay," I said, turning back to the manuscript, "let me flip through this until I find more of the ghost story." I kept turning pages. "Here!"

Chapter Six

I flew up the stairs to my room, dripping wet from Flynn's prank. What a goof! I chuckled to myself. He wasn't kidding when he told me how cold Lake Superior was—I could still feel the sting, like a thousand icy knife blades, from when I plunged beneath the surface.

Wondering if Arctic waters could possibly be as frigid, I peeled off my sodden clothes and eyed the clock on my bedside table. I'd have just enough time to clean up and get downstairs for dinner. I turned on the shower, grateful for the stream of hot water bringing life back into my shivering limbs, and thought about how the sunlight had danced on Lily's hair as we sailed.

I chose a crisp striped shirt and khaki slacks from

the closet—this seemed to be the uniform of choice for the Brennan men here at Whitehall—and as I stepped into my pants, my eyes fell upon the desk by the window. The drawer was open, just a hair. But I was sure I had closed it completely when I went downstairs earlier. Hadn't I? Buttoning my pants, I crossed the room to investigate. Everything was still as I had left it—my writing pad and pen, my typewriter. And yet something seemed amiss somehow, as though someone had been in my room and riffled through my papers, and then carefully put them back—but not exactly as they had been.

I picked up my writing pad and then dropped it again quickly, as though it stung me.

There, on the top sheet where I had written my thoughts that morning, was something else. *The girl in white,* I had written. And next to it, in a spidery scrawl: *loves you.*

The girl in white loves you. Did Flynn write this? Was it another of his pranks? Or was Prudence to blame? I picked up the pad and stood there, staring at the words on the page, and the more I thought of it, the more I knew it couldn't have been Flynn or Pru, because they had been with me the whole afternoon. And when we returned from our sail, there was no way either of them could have made it up to my room before me.

As I stared at the page, another thought hit me: I had been in the shower for several minutes. Either of them could have crept in and out of the room during that time. But why? I understood their penchant for pranks, but this seemed . . . I don't know. Unnecessary? Unfunny? And more than that, anonymous. Flynn loved nothing better than to have the first laugh at one of his victims, like me today, the rube he had tricked into slipping over the side of the boat. Doing something like this just wasn't his style.

I remembered our conversation of that morning and decided not to mention it to anyone at dinner. I'd pull Flynn aside to talk to him about it or, better yet, simply bring him up here to my room as the night drew to a close. If he did do this, he wouldn't be able to contain his laughter upon being confronted. And if he didn't do it . . . ?

I looked around the room and felt, not for the first time, eyes watching me. Just a reaction to finding the note, perhaps? I wasn't sure. A shudder passed through me as I caught my own face in the mirror and found that I had no wish to see, reflected in the glass, whatever was behind me. But I forced myself to stop and look. Nothing, thankfully, was there.

I put those thoughts out of my head as I hurried down the stairs toward the dining room, where I knew I would find jocularity, laughter, good friends, and—dare I say it?—maybe even love, just the thing to scare away the chill that had encircled me.

Later, after an evening filled with good food, good conversation, and good drinks, I pulled Flynn aside.

"About the matter we talked of this morning?" I started, my voice low. "I'd like to show you something in my room, if I may."

All the good humor drained from his face, and he gave

me a curt nod. "You go up now, making a show about being tired from all the fresh air today," he whispered to me. "I'll come up in a few minutes. That way, Pru won't think we're up to something and insist on joining us."

I stole up the stairs and waited. Nearly a half hour later, there was a soft rap at my door.

Without a word, I showed him the writing pad.

"I don't know what to make of it," he said after studying the scrawled message. He held my gaze and I saw it in his face—he wasn't behind this and didn't know who was.

"You don't think Prudence could have come into the room while I was taking a shower and written on the pad . . . do you?" I offered. "Is this the sort of thing she'd do?"

"Absolutely not," he said, setting the pad back down on the desk and gazing out the window. "And besides, Pru was downstairs with me the whole time. We had a game of backgammon while you were cleaning up."

"And Lily?"

"She was in the parlor as well, sketching."

I sat down on the bed, shaking my head. "Well, what is it, then? Surely not one of the maids?"

He turned to face me and leaned against the window frame. "I don't know. But if you see anything else—if you see *her*, I mean, come to my room and wake me immediately. That is, if you feel comfortable remaining here. I wouldn't blame you if—"

I cut him off. "I'm fine, Flynn. I'm sure there's a reasonable explanation for this."

But as he bid me good night and closed the door behind him, leaving me alone, I wasn't so sure.

I tossed and turned for hours, my eyes shooting open at every night noise—every rustle of wings, every soft scurry of feet, every breeze whispering through the cedar branches.

When I finally did drift off to sleep, I dreamed I was standing at the window, entranced by the sight of the girl in white dancing around a small fire on the lakeshore. She was so beautiful, so enchanting, that I couldn't look away. Her singing drifted up to my room and surrounded me, a strange Celtic tune that sounded ancient and magical, as though it had the power to evoke the spirits of the night. I was so enraptured by the sight and sound of her that I didn't notice I was rising from the floorboards, held aloft by her tune. I reached down to open the window and then flew through it toward the lakeshore, landing gently in front of her. She smiled at me and took my hand, but I couldn't quite see her face, obscured as it was by the harsh light of the fire. We began to dance, slowly at first, and then faster and faster still, engulfed by strange and beautiful music that seemed to be emanating from the rocks and water and soil around us.

When the music finally stopped, she turned to me, and only then did I see her face—a hideous mask of death, worm-eaten and dirty, as though she had just risen from the grave. She smiled and floated toward me, saying the words "My love, my true love, has come for me," though her lips did not move.

I opened my mouth to scream and was awakened by the very force of it, never so happy to find myself in my bed between sweat-soaked sheets. My heart beating furiously, I padded to the bathroom and turned on the tap with shaking hands, trying to steady the glass I held under the stream. I took one gulp after another and then splashed water on my face in an effort, I suppose, to banish the dream back to whatever dark and evil place it had come from. I dried my face on a towel and shook my head—*enough nonsense, it was only a dream.*

It was only then I noticed the footprints on the white tile floor. My footprints. The bottoms of my feet were caked in dirt. *How in the world . . . ?* When the answer passed through me, I slumped to the floor, wrapped my arms around my knees, and began to shake, unable to get the dance, and her monstrous visage, out of my mind.

I stayed there like that until the first rays of sun streamed through my window, and during the hours that passed, I had all but convinced myself it had been a case of sleepwalking or some other decidedly real-world event that led me outside in the dead of night. What other explanation could there possibly be? Even so, I had had enough of girls in white and midnight dances. I vowed to leave Whitehall that very day.

But I should have known better. When one has been caught up in a dance with the very face of evil, there is no running away.

CHAPTER 30

I looked up from the manuscript and shivered. "That was rather intense, wasn't it?"

"It's a perfect ghost story," Matthew said. "But I think it also tells us something about what really went on that summer, don't you?" He smiled a broad smile and gestured toward the walls.

"Exactly what I was thinking," I said. "The passageways."

"Without knowing about them, the story reads just a like an old-fashioned ghost tale," he said. "But with what we know about the way this house is laid out . . ."

I nodded. "I'll bet my father and his sister didn't tell Coleville about the passageways. My brothers and I were always forbidden to talk about them with outsiders and I'm sure they were, too. I think it's clear that Coleville sensed he was being watched that summer, even heard whomever it was shuffling around in the passageways. Add a writer's imagination to that—"

"And you've got a ghost story!" Matthew finished my thought.

"I think we both know who was creeping around in those passageways scaring the life out of Coleville," I said.

He leaned forward in his chair. "If Mercy had developed some sort of mental illness because of her ordeal in the crypt, maybe she was kept away from visitors. Her parents simply didn't introduce her to Coleville. It's a big enough house to have pulled that off."

"It's exactly the type of thing my family would do, keep a sick relative hidden away. Very *Secret Garden*."

"And let's say Mercy didn't much like that, being away from all the fun," Matthew went on. "What would she do?"

My eyes opened wide. "She'd do what my brothers and I would do when we didn't want to stay in our rooms . . . but also didn't want our parents to know we were watching them."

We sat in silence for a moment. We might never know what really happened all those years ago, but this explanation was sounding more and more plausible to me. But then another thought floated through my mind.

"You know," I began, "something else is bothering me. We suspected that my family was upset about what Coleville wrote and killed him because of it. But this isn't some sort of exposé of my family's dirty laundry. This is just an old-fashioned, gothic ghost story. Who would be upset enough about that to kill him because of it?"

Matthew leaned back and crossed his legs. "What if it wasn't the manuscript that got Coleville killed?"

And there and then, the explanation for Coleville's ill-timed death seemed to simply lay itself out before me. "In Coleville's story, he found on his writing pad: 'The girl in white loves you,'" I said. "What if that really happened? What if Mercy, creeping around in the passageways spying on him, really did fall in love with him?"

Matthew picked up my train of thought. "And what if she found out he was coming back the next summer to marry Lily—er, your mother?"

"People have killed for a lot less," I said, the certainty of it wrapping itself around me. "If she killed Coleville, that would explain why my grandfather put her in Mercy House. Mystery solved! I'll bet you anything that's what happened."

But Matthew began shaking his head. "Nope," he said. "It still doesn't explain what happened to Fate. I'm wondering—"

The crackling of the intercom interrupted his thought.

"Miss Grace, are you up there?" It was a man's voice.

I crossed the room and pushed the button on the desk. "I'm here. Who's this?"

"It's Carter, miss," he said, his voice harsh and full. "You need to get down here to the main floor immediately. I've rung the police and the ambulance, but—"

"Ambulance? Police?"

"It's Jane, miss. She's been hurt. We're in the kitchen."

CHAPTER 31

M atthew and I flew out of the study and raced down the hallway, taking two stairs at a time on the way down. We reached the main floor just as the ambulance was pulling into the driveway, lights blazing, and I gave a quick thanks for living in a small town where ambulance response times can typically be counted in the seconds.

I burst through the kitchen door to find Carter standing against the wall of cabinets, his face ashen, and Mr. Jameson crouched over Jane, who was lying on the floor, a small pool of blood from her midsection seeping into the tile.

"You're going to be just fine, dear," her husband was whispering to her, his voice shredded to bits. "You rest now. You're going to be just fine."

My hands flew to my mouth. "What happened?" But even as I croaked out the words, a feeling was creeping its way up my spine. I exchanged glances with Matthew and could tell that he was thinking the same thing I was.

Mr. Jameson didn't seem to hear me or register that I was there. Carter met my gaze and shook his head. Just then, the ambulance drivers were rapping on the kitchen door.

"We found her like this, just a few moments ago," Carter told them after opening the door and standing to the side so they could rush in with their stretcher. "I had been waiting to take her into town. Mr. Jameson was with me in the carriage house playing cards. When she didn't come—"

"We thought you all were in town when we got here," I said, glancing at Matthew. "The house was so quiet."

"How long ago was that?" one of the ambulance drivers asked as they worked to get Jane on a stretcher.

I searched Matthew's eyes. "A half hour? Maybe a little more."

I hurried to Jane's side and grasped her hand, which was limp but still warm. "Jane," I said to her. "Jane, what happened? Who did this to you?" But she didn't even open her eyes. And then the ambulance drivers were ready to take her away. "I love you, Jane," I choked out. She didn't respond, but I felt her, ever so slightly, squeeze my hand.

"St. Mark's?" I said to the driver, who nodded as they were wheeling Jane out the door, Mr. Jameson following close behind.

"I'll get the car," Carter said, his voice wavering.

"No," I said to him over my shoulder as I locked the kitchen door. "This time, we'll drive you."

THE ER WAITING ROOM was full of people, some slumped in their chairs, others staring out into space, and still others pacing back and forth.

"*J-a-m-e-s-o-n*," I said to the woman behind the reception desk. "She was just brought in, for goodness' sake."

"Are you family?" she asked, snapping her gum and barely looking up from her computer screen.

"Yes," I said to her louder than I had intended. "Where is she? How is she?"

"I'll find out," she said, rising from her chair a little more slowly than I would have liked and disappearing through an automatic door that led, I assumed, to the emergency room.

Several minutes later, she reappeared. "She's in surgery," she informed us as Carter blew his nose loudly into his handkerchief. "I'll take you to a family room, where you can wait for the doctor to come and talk to you."

Carter, Matthew, and I followed her to a small room where Mr. Jameson was slumped in a chair.

I didn't even have to ask the question. "Collapsed lung," he said, shaking his head. "Multiple stab wounds."

I held my breath, not wanting to hear more.

"The doctor said she's lucky," Mr. Jameson went on. "He said it could have been much worse. He'll know more when she's out of surgery, of course."

I sank into the chair beside him and squeezed his hand. "Jane's one tough gal. If anyone could get through this, it's her."

He let out a deep sigh and pushed himself to his feet. "I can't just sit in this blasted room. Does anyone want coffee?"

I glanced at Carter, who was staring off into space, his lips moving slightly, seemingly having a conversation that none of us could hear.

"I think we could all use some coffee," I said, fishing a few bills out of my purse and handing them to him. "Do you want me to go with you?"

Mr. Jameson shook his head, his eyes brimming with tears. "I'll get it. I need a walk on my own."

When he had gone, Matthew sank down onto the sofa, where I joined him. But I couldn't take my eyes off Carter. He seemed elsewhere, as though his present was hazy and unfocused, and he was instead immersed in the past.

"What happened, Carter?" I asked him, trying to prod him out of his funk. "When we got home, we assumed you all were out at the pharmacy because the house was so quiet. Jane was going to pick up the prescriptions Mercy's doctor—"

Carter snapped his head in my direction. "What did you just say?"

Obviously, he hadn't been told the identity of our houseguest. "Mercy, Carter," I said with as much gentleness in my voice as I could muster. "I talked to her doctor in Switzerland early this morning." It seemed like a lifetime ago. "We all thought the woman who showed up at my mother's funeral was my aunt Fate, but the doctor let me know she's really Mercy."

Carter put his face in his hands and leaned forward, his elbows resting on his knees. "Oh, dear God, no," he murmured. "No."

"Carter?" I said, a chill running through me.

He lifted his head from his hands to look at me. "You don't know," he said. "You don't understand."

"I think I'm beginning to," I said, "but you're right, I really don't quite understand. Can you tell me—"

"We all thought she was gone," he said, shaking his head. I wasn't quite sure he had heard me. "We thought she was back with whatever had made her. I put her in the crypt myself."

"I know," I said to him. "Jane told me she was ill when she was a little girl, but—"

"For fifty years we thought we were safe. Jane, Thomas, your mother, God rest her soul, and I."

"Carter—" I tried again, but he seemed to be caught once again in the web of his own thoughts. He turned his gaze back to a spot on the wall opposite us, but I knew he was looking at something else, something I couldn't see.

"I think Carter is in shock," I said, my voice low. "Will you get a nurse? I think he needs something. A sedative, maybe?"

Matthew nodded and slipped from the sofa and out of the room. A few minutes later, he returned with a nurse in tow.

"Mr. Carter?" she tried. "Mr. Carter? Are you all right?"

But Carter just shook his head. "She cannot stay at Alban House, not another day."

The nurse nodded at Matthew and me. "Please come with me, Mr. Carter," she said, gently taking his arm. And then to me, over her shoulder, "We'll take his vitals and give him something."

Carter looked back at me, his eyes seeming very far away. "We'll be here waiting for you," I said to him, squeezing his hand. "We'll be right here."

I slumped back onto the couch next to Matthew. "I really don't know how I could have possibly handled this—any of this—without you."

"I think you would've handled things just fine, with or without me. But I'm glad it was with me."

I sighed. "You don't think there's any doubt that Mercy did this, do you?"

"I'm afraid not, Grace," Matthew said. "Who else? Maybe Jane told her that the nurse from the hospital in Switzerland was coming to get her. Maybe that's what set her off."

My daughter's face floated through my mind just then, and an ache reverberated through my core. "Do you think I should call Amity and let her know what's going on?"

Matthew shook his head. "She's safe at Heather's, right?"

"For the night, yes."

"And there's no reason they might head back to Alban House?"

I had given Amity strict orders to stay away from the house. I didn't believe she would go against my wishes on this. "None that I can think of."

"Then I wouldn't call her, not until we know what's going on with Jane," he said, leaning back and resting his head on the sofa. "When you have something to tell her, some news that presumably Jane's going to be okay, then you can call."

I opened my mouth to respond, but I didn't have a chance because Chief Bellamy poked his head through the door of our waiting room, rapping slightly as he did. He held four paper cups in a cardboard tray.

Mr. Jameson followed him into the room and slumped back down into his chair as the chief handed the cups all around. "I understand Jane's in surgery, the victim of a stabbing," he said.

"That's right," I said, sitting up a little straighter and taking a sip of the coffee. It was bitter and harsh.

"Start from the top," the chief said, taking a seat and turning to Mr. Jameson.

"I was in the carriage house with Carter," he began, his voice wavering. "We were playing cards. Jane had let him know she was going out, and there we were, waiting for her. She didn't come and she didn't come, so I called up to the house. When she didn't answer . . ." He sighed. "If only I had been in the kitchen with her."

"Then what happened?" the chief prodded.

"It's not like Jane to keep us waiting so long without a word, and it's certainly not like her to not answer when I call," her husband went on, a mix of guilt and shame radiating from his face. "Carter and I rushed up to the house, thinking something must be wrong. We found her in the kitchen." His eyes were brimming with tears. "Carter called 911 and then called Miss Alban."

"And where were you, Grace?" the chief said, turning to me.

"Matthew and I had met for breakfast at the Breakwater, and when we got back to the house—" I turned to Matthew. "What time was it? Around ten thirty? Eleven?" He nodded. "We thought the house was empty. Jane was supposed to be going to the pharmacy, so I assumed that's what she was doing when she didn't come to greet me."

"She usually did that?"

"Yes," I said, my voice cracking. "Every time I've walked through the door at Alban House, Jane has been there to welcome me home."

Mr. Jameson blew his nose and coughed into his handkerchief.

"But not today," I went on. "That's why we thought she was out. We were in my study when Carter called us to come down to the kitchen, and that's where we saw Jane."

Chief Bellamy held up one palm. "Let's back up just a minute," he said. "You've had a police presence at the house since you called about the break-in several days ago. Do you believe this is related to that break-in?"

Matthew and I exchanged a look. I wasn't sure what I believed. "Chief," I said finally, "there's a lot you don't know."

He leaned back in his chair and crossed one leg over the other. "I've got nothing but time, Grace. Start from the beginning."

And so I told him about Harris Peters showing up on the day

of my mother's funeral in an effort to dig up dirt about my family for the exposé he was writing.

"He's the journalist who was supposed to meet with my mother the day she died," I said. "You had already left the reception, but two of your men were there. I think your guys questioned him after the second break-in, the day of the funeral when we found our rooms had been rifled through."

And then I told him about my aunt, whom Peters had found in Switzerland, and how he brought her to the house after my mother's funeral.

"Let me stop you for a second, Grace," Chief Bellamy said, his intense eyes boring into mine. "As far as I know, and I've known your mother for thirty years, you don't have an aunt on either side of the family. Can you connect the dots for me?"

I took a deep breath in. "There is a lot of backstory here, but suffice it to say that she basically disappeared fifty years ago, hadn't been heard from since, and the entire family thought she was dead."

Chief Bellamy blinked several times. "Oh, *that* aunt? Alive? I remember the story about her. Wasn't Fate her name? "

"Yes, but it's a little more complicated than that, I'm afraid. We initially thought she was Fate Alban, but as it turns out, she is Fate's twin sister, Mercy, who, as far as anyone in the family knew, had died when she was a child. You might imagine it was quite a shock to learn she was alive and kicking."

"On the day of your mother's funeral, no less," the chief said.

"Exactly," I went on. "But that shock wasn't anything compared to the one when I found out where she had been for the past half century. I talked to her doctor this morning."

I paused for a moment before continuing. I knew if I went

on, I'd be opening a can of worms that I could never close. But I felt I had no choice. "She'd been in Switzerland, in a hospital for the criminally insane that my grandfather basically built for her."

"Dear God," he said, shaking his head.

"And there's more," I said, sensing a floodgate somewhere inside of me had been opened. The information kept pouring out; I was powerless to stop it. "She's supposed to be on medication, antipsychotics or something, and the doctor has been quite worried about her since she turned up missing. That's why Jane was headed to the pharmacy today, to pick up those medications. She was taking my aunt with her because she didn't want to leave her alone in the house."

"So you've got someone who has been in a lockup for the *criminally insane* for fifty years. She's here now and off her medications. And you believe she might be the one who did this to Mrs. Jameson. Is that what you're telling me, Grace?"

"That's exactly what I'm telling you."

The chief stood up, fished his cell phone out of his pocket, and dialed. "There's an older lady who has been staying at Alban House. An Alban relative, yes. She's probably about"—he shot me a look—"seventy?" I nodded. "Have you seen anyone like that at the house? Well, find her, Johnson. She is psychotic and off her medication, and—have you found the weapon? In that case, she might still have it with her. I know she's seventy but you're to consider her armed and dangerous. I want the house searched from top to bottom, and I want her taken into custody."

He hung up. "Grace, you need to know that the house is now a crime scene. Until my people finish up there, I'm going to have to ask that you stay away."

"Understood." I nodded. From years of watching police dramas on television, I had expected as much. "For how long?"

"They'll be gathering evidence, fingerprinting, that sort of thing. It could take from a few hours to overnight."

I certainly could go to a hotel for the night, but looking down at my jeans and flats, I realized I had no pajamas, no change of clothes. And then the image of the manuscript, sitting on an ottoman in the study, flashed into my mind. With it, an icy tendril of dread overcame me. The precious manuscript was so exposed, so vulnerable. Why hadn't I remembered to lock it up?

"Can I go into the house to get some things?" I tried. "I don't have so much as a toothbrush with me."

The chief looked at me long and hard. "No, Grace. Let us do our work. I'm sure you can find what you need at the drugstore."

I shrugged at him and smiled, but inside my stomach was turning. "Any excuse to go shopping, I guess," I joked.

The chief got to his feet, his work here done, and was on his way out. I stood to walk him to the door when a thought hit me. Looking from the chief to Matthew and back again, I said: "I just remembered—a nurse from the hospital in Switzerland is on her way here to bring my aunt back there."

"When is she going to arrive?" the chief wanted to know.

"I have no idea," I said. "Jane made the arrangements. It could be a few hours from now. It could be tomorrow. I think she's coming directly to the house."

"I'm on my way over there right now," the chief said. "I'll alert my men. Maybe this nurse can be a help to us when she shows up.

"You know, Grace," he continued, clearing his throat, "if your aunt is the one who attacked Mrs. Jameson, I am going to take her into custody. This is attempted murder we're talking about." He glanced at Mr. Jameson. "If she's guilty, she will be prosecuted to the full extent of the law. This story will come out."

I nodded and felt myself bracing for the onslaught of media that would surely come. "I know."

"And another thing," he said, drawing out his words. "I know I don't have to tell you this, but considering your lineage, I thought I'd bring it up, anyway. You do know she's not getting on a plane with that nurse until she faces these charges."

"I know," I repeated.

He took my hands. "We'll get this handled for you, Gracie. Sooner rather than later. I'll be in touch."

And then he was gone. I slumped back down onto the couch and looked from Matthew to Mr. Jameson and back again, not knowing quite what to say.

A few minutes later, Carter appeared at the door, escorted by a young nurse. "Oh, for heaven's sake, I'm fine," he said, pulling his arm away from her and wavering a bit on his feet. I stood up and took his arm, leading him to one of the chairs.

"Mr. Carter was resting in the ER and he insisted he be allowed to come back here to wait with you," she explained.

"I feel like a bloody fool," he said, sitting down with a thud.

"Not at all," I told him. "You had quite a shock."

"That's exactly what it was," he said, smiling slightly. "Mild shock. They took my vitals and gave me a little happy juice in an IV drip."

Mr. Jameson reached over and patted his knee. "It's not the usual course of events on any given day, is it, old boy?"

The two men exchanged a charged look. "Something's got to be done," Carter said, his voice low. "You know it as well as I do."

I waited for him to say more, but the look that passed between the two men told me that the subject, whatever the subject was, was now closed.

"Carter," I began, "the chief let us know that the house is now a crime scene. I'm putting up Cody and Jason in a hotel, and while you could stay in the carriage house, I'd feel better if you were safe in a hotel, too, until all of this is settled. How does the presidential suite at the Sheraton sound?"

"Oh, Miss Grace, that's certainly not necessary." He shook his head, a slight smile creeping from the corners of his mouth.

"I know it's not necessary, but I want to do it. You deserve it. After we're done here, we'll take you there and you can live in the lap of luxury for a while." I turned to Mr. Jameson. "I'm assuming you're going to stay here at the hospital with Jane?"

"If they'll allow it, aye." His eyes were rimmed in red, his face radiated hope mixed with sadness.

"Allow it?" I managed a smile, leaning over and squeezing his knee. "My great-grandfather built this hospital, my grandfather built the neonatal ward, my father built the cancer wing, and my mother was on the board. You can bet they'll allow it."

THE MINUTES CREPT BY AS I PACED, Mr. Jameson stared at the floor, and Carter chatted softly with Matthew about church business. Finally, a doctor in surgical scrubs and a nurse appeared in the doorway. The doctor pulled off his surgical cap as Mr. Jameson jumped to his feet. I rose and took his hand.

"The news is good," the doctor said. "She came through the surgery just fine, and she's in recovery."

I hugged Mr. Jameson as he murmured, "Oh, thank God." Turning to the doctor, he said: "Can I see her?"

"I'll ask you to wait until she's out of recovery and into her room," the doctor said, nodding. "It won't be long now."

"Please make sure they put Mrs. Jameson in the Alban suite," I said to the nurse, referring to the private set of rooms reserved for my family. "Her husband will be staying with her overnight as well. I hope that's not a problem."

"Not at all, Miss Alban."

Mr. Jameson nodded his thanks to me with a slight smile. "I'll call you later to check on her," I said, squeezing his hand. "And don't make me worry about you, too—make sure you eat something. Not hospital food, either. Call Smith's and order yourself some dinner, and have them send me the bill. Promise?"

"I will, miss," he said over his shoulder to me as the nurse led him away, the relief dripping off him.

I turned to Carter, who looked exhausted. "Let's get you to the hotel," I said to him, eyeing Matthew. "I think you could use a good dinner and a nice long soak in the Jacuzzi."

"That sounds positively decadent," Carter said as we headed off down the hallway toward the door. "Positively decadent indeed."

CHAPTER 32

After talking with Amity, giving her the latest on Jane and making sure she was safely ensconced at Heather's house for the night, I asked Matthew to drop me off with Carter at the hotel.

"Sure you wouldn't like to grab some dinner?" he asked, shooting me a sidelong glance from his spot in the driver's seat. "You haven't eaten anything since breakfast and must be starving by now."

Tempting though it was, I needed some time alone to decompress. After everything that had happened within the past few days, my mind was swirling with thoughts of Coleville, my mother, Mercy, and Jane.

And the manuscript! My stomach twisted as I thought of those sheets of paper, priceless to the literary world, just sitting out in the open on the ottoman in my mother's study, where I had so carelessly left them. I hoped a curious police officer on patrol in the house wouldn't realize what it was.

"To tell you the truth, I'm exhausted," I admitted. "Room service and a soak in the Jacuzzi are about all I can handle at this point."

After a quick trip to the hotel gift shop to pick up the essentials for Carter and me, we headed up to our rooms, leaning against each other as the elevator rose to the hotel's top floor.

"Jane's going to be just fine," I said, my head resting on Carter's shoulder.

"And so will we all," he replied, "as soon as *she* is out of the house."

We stopped at our floor, the electronic key poised in my hand. "You have a good night, Carter," I said. "If you need anything, just call."

"I will, miss. And you, too." I watched him as he trundled off down the hallway toward the presidential suite and could almost see the entire weight of the world, or at least our little corner of it, on his shoulders.

I ordered a rather decadent dinner of a croque-monsieur, French onion soup, and a salad, and devoured it all as I sat on the bed watching mindless television programs. It felt good to be medicated by the luxury of thinking about nothing at all, even as the week's events tried to slither back into my brain. I was just about to pour myself a glass of wine and fill up the tub when my cell phone rang. It was a local number but one I didn't recognize. Thinking it might be the police or the hospital, I answered it.

"Hi, Grace. It's Harris Peters."

I let out an audible groan. "Forgive me, Harris, but you're the last person on earth I'm interested in talking to right now."

"I heard about your housekeeper and I thought—"

I scowled into the phone. "How did you hear about Jane? And for that matter, how did you get this number?"

"I'm a reporter, remember? Anyway, listen. I have some information for you. At least I think I might. I was intending to keep this all close to the vest until the book came out but now . . ." His words dissolved into a sigh.

"Now what?"

"I never intended for anyone to get hurt," he said. "I was horrified when my source at the police station called to tell me what had gone down."

"I'm not sure what I'm supposed to say to that. You're the guy who searched for years for my aunt, you're the guy who marched her out of a locked facility. You could be charged as an accessory to all this, for all I know."

He was silent for a moment. And then: "I'm calling to see if you want to meet. To talk. As I said, I've got some information that I think you'll be interested in. You'll certainly want to know it before I go public with it. If I go public."

"I'm not I'm up for a meeting tonight," I told him. "I've just come from the hospital and—"

"I could come to Alban House," Harris offered.

"I'm not there," I said. "It's a crime scene now. Can't this wait until tomorrow? Or, better yet, never?"

"It won't take long, I promise. Please, Grace?"

There was something in his voice that worked its way under my skin. This wasn't the pompous, arrogant man who had confronted me at my mother's funeral; he was instead pleading with me.

"Where are you?" he continued. "I'll come to wherever you are. I won't take much of your time. An hour, tops. Can't you give me an hour?"

I sighed, gazing at the Jacuzzi in the bathroom. "I'm at the Sheraton."

"I'll meet you in the bar in ten minutes," he said, and the line went dead.

I didn't even bother to put on my shoes. I tucked my feet into the slippers I had purchased at the hotel's gift shop, gave my teeth a quick brush, and padded down the hallway toward the elevator.

I was sitting at a table by the window in the hotel bar, sipping a glass of wine and watching the activity on the busy street outside, when Harris Peters walked in. If I hadn't known he was coming, I might not have recognized him—his designer suit and expensive shoes were replaced by a faded pair of jeans and sneakers. His hair wasn't slicked back as it had been the day of the funeral; instead it was wavy and rumpled, as though he had just gotten out of bed. But the most striking change was in his attitude. It was just as I had picked up on the phone. He had an air of defeat about him, a resignation that seemed to seep from his very pores. He pulled out the chair next to me and sat down with a thud.

"Please, don't get up," he said with a slight smile.

"Harris," I said, holding my wineglass aloft. "I wish I could say it's nice to see you again, but unfortunately . . ."

"I'll have a Belhaven," Harris called out to the server, who disappeared behind the bar and reappeared a moment later with a bubbling glass of amber ale. He took a long swig, set the glass down, and leaned back, running his hands through his hair.

"You said you wanted to talk," I began, taking a sip of wine. "I'm listening."

"You know the expression 'Be careful what you wish for'?" He took another sip. "I now know what it means, in great detail."

I squinted at him. "I'm afraid you've lost me, Harris," I said.

"I'm talking about what I think I've uncovered. The information I've spent years searching for. Maybe it should have stayed buried."

I leaned back and crossed my arms, wondering where he was going with this.

And Harris began to tell me the tale of how he searched for and ultimately found my aunt, a tale of bribery, backdoor payments, hushed meetings with other reporters in European alleyways. I had to admit, I was drawn in. We finished our drinks and ordered a second round as he told of a series of rather unsavory connections, through which he was able to find information on a nurse at Mercy House who suffered from a gambling problem. It was a simple matter for him to confront her and offer her enough money to arrange for my aunt to go missing one afternoon during a walk on the grounds.

I took a sip of wine and eyed him. "That's a fascinating story, Harris, it really is, but I don't see—"

He put a hand up to stop my words. "Let me finish. As I already told you, this whole thing started because I'd been rather obsessed with your family, specifically with the mystery of how and why Fate Alban disappeared."

I can't explain why, but in that moment, the bar seemed to fall away, taking the bustle on the street, the shoreline, and the other patrons with it, leaving only Harris and me. I could feel the air around us begin to thicken with dread, and I wasn't at all sure I wanted to know what this man was about to reveal. But before I could stop him, he began.

"Your aunt said something on the plane that got me thinking," he said finally. "I'm just going to ask you straight out, Grace. Do you know if your father ever had an affair with someone before he married your mother?"

Out of all the possibilities, of all the things Harris might have brought up, this was completely out of left field.

"Absolutely not," I said, sitting a little straighter. "My father adored my mother. He was in love with her his whole life."

But as I said the words, David Coleville's name swirled into my mind. If my mother was in love with another man before marrying my father—

"He may have loved her his whole life," Harris said, interrupting my thoughts. "But that doesn't mean he didn't have an affair."

"Why would you possibly imply that?" I wanted to know, my face reddening. I wasn't sure where he got off, making these kinds of accusations.

Harris put his palms in the air as if to hold back my anger. "It's just something your aunt kept repeating on the plane. She was talking about a baby and wondering what had happened to it. She kept asking if I was taking her to the party, and would we see the baby when we got there.

"And it got me thinking, Grace," he continued, clearing his throat and holding my gaze. "That party was in June of 1956."

We sat there, staring into each other's eyes for a moment, and something unspoken passed between us. That's when I noticed the faint smattering of freckles across the bridge of his nose. The same as Jimmy's.

He took a deep breath. "I was adopted, Grace. My birthday is February 6, 1957. I've suspected this for a while. A good long while. It's the reason I was, well, I guess you could say, obsessed with your family. When your aunt confirmed the existence of a baby, or a pregnancy, back then—"

"You've been obsessed with my family for years and now—what? You think you're actually one of us?" I could feel my face heating up. "Just because you were born within nine months of that party? It's ridiculous, Harris, the whole thing." I pushed my chair back and downed the last of my wine. "I think this meeting is over."

"Wait," he said, leaning toward me, his voice low. "Don't go. Please. There's something else you don't know."

I sighed and settled back down in my chair, knowing I should at least hear the man out. Whatever crazy theories he had come up with, it was better I knew them now rather than later. "I'm going to give you exactly two minutes to tell me what you have to tell me, and then I'm going back up to my room."

"I've been receiving payments since I was a child," he said quickly, gulping air as he did. "Anonymous payments. Didn't you wonder how I could have done all the traveling to Europe, the bribing of sources, even the payoff to the nurse at the hospital on a reporter's salary? I'm here to tell you, Grace, we don't make that much."

I wrinkled my nose at him. In truth, I hadn't even considered where he got the money for it all. "Payments? You mean like . . . child support?"

"Something like that, yes. According to my mother, they started coming when I was about five or six years old. Cash began arriving in the mail in an otherwise unmarked envelope with my name on it."

That sent a chill through me. "And you have no idea who sent it?"

"It's been the great mystery of my life," he said, leaning back and sipping on his ale. "My unknown benefactor. I got the feeling that my mother knew who it was, but she never would tell me. It's what caused me to become an investigative reporter—I grew up with this mystery, so it was natural for me to gravitate toward solving other mysteries."

My thoughts began to tie themselves in knots. What Harris was saying made a kind of sick sense, but something about his theory didn't seem quite right, somehow. Something was off.

"I'm sorry, Harris, but I just don't think—"

"It would explain the anonymous payments, though, wouldn't it? Think about it, Grace. Who else in this town is rich enough to send that kind of money every month for a lifetime, and who else in town would want to cover up an illegitimate child? You have to admit it—this has Alban written all over it."

I shook my head, intending to deny what he was saying. But somehow, I couldn't seem to get the words out. Who else, indeed? He was right—it *did* have Alban written all over it.

"Would you be willing to take a DNA test?" he pressed. "That way we'd know for sure."

That crossed a line. Speculating was one thing, but DNA? I recoiled, pushing my chair away from him and standing up. "Not a chance."

"Grace, this could mean—" Harris started, scrambling to his feet and leaning across the table. "Okay. Let's dial things back a few notches before this friendly conversation gets out of hand. Sit down, please."

"This is really poor timing," I said to him, my words crackling in my throat. "You know Jane's in the hospital. You know I just lost my mother."

I wondered if Harris had laid this on me that very day on purpose, specifically because he knew what had happened to Jane. I'd be off my game, and he knew it.

"I'm sorry about the timing," he said. "I guess—I don't know. I didn't think about how hard of a day you've already had."

I studied his face, which was beginning to seem so familiar. The angle of his jaw, the slope of his nose. Could it be? Could Harris Peters be my father's child?

I shook my head. Something about this whole thing was gnawing at me. There was a disconnect that I couldn't quite get my mind around, a flaw in his theory that was just beyond my reach. An idea began to take shape in my mind.

"You said you're still getting the payments, isn't that right?" I asked Harris.

He nodded. "I am."

"My dad died twenty years ago," I told him. "If he were making clandestine payments to an illegitimate child, the payments would've stopped then."

Harris leaned forward in his chair. "I've already thought of that. He could have made provisions for me in his will."

"Impossible," I said, slapping a hand on the table in front of me. "I was at the reading of his will. I know exactly what was in it, and I can tell you here and now that it didn't include you or any child other than me and my two brothers, both of whom were gone when my dad died."

My voice splintered as I thought of Jake and Jimmy, and what they would do to this interloper who was trying to worm his way into our family. And then, as clearly as if one of them had spoken it in my ear, I heard a whisper that illuminated exactly what was gnawing at me about Harris's theory. In that moment, I knew why it seemed right and yet wrong somehow.

He wasn't my father's child. He was my mother's child. With David Coleville.

CHAPTER 33

It made perfect sense. If my mother had been pregnant the night Coleville died, it would explain why she and my father had married so quickly—a course of events that I had no answer for. My dad did love her his whole life, just as he told me he did, and when his best friend died, he stepped in and married the girl in trouble. But I wasn't about to tell Harris Peters any of that. I needed a moment alone to sort this through and think about what to do next.

I shot Harris a look and pushed my chair back. "I'm sorry, but I've got to go."

"But—" Harris began, hopping to his feet.

I held out my hands, palms toward him. "Listen, you've given me a lot to process here," I said. "We can continue this conversation, but not right now. Can I call you in a day or so?"

He nodded and simply said: "Sure."

I turned to go back up to my room, but then I looked over my shoulder at Harris. He had slumped back down into his seat and was running a hand through his hair, shaking his head slightly. He radiated exhaustion mixed with a hint of despair. I couldn't imagine feeling much—if any—compassion for the man who had so arrogantly interrupted my mother's funeral. But Harris looked so utterly defeated he touched me, just a little.

I sat back down.

"I don't get it, Harris," I said to him, reaching across the table to place my hand over his. "You seem completely wiped out by this. You, who has spent a good many years digging up dirt on my family to write a tell-all exposé. You, who crossed an ocean and bribed unknown numbers of people to bring my aunt here—on the day of my mother's funeral, no less. It's almost like you had a vendetta against us. I'd think you'd be gleeful, uncovering the scandal that an Alban had an illegitimate child—if, indeed, it's true."

Harris took another sip of his ale. "It's funny. You're right, I've spent years on this, all the while suspecting I was your father's son. And now when I've found your aunt and maybe found a thread that leads me to the truth about who has been sending those payments to me my whole life, suddenly now all the drive, all the anger that has been propelling me through this has evaporated. It's like finding the key to the biggest puzzle of my life has done nothing but take the wind out of my sails."

I furrowed my brow. "How so?"

He looked up at me. "Your mother died on the very day I was going to ask her about all of this. And the aunt I unearthed very likely tried to kill someone today. Talk about the Alban curse. I had seen it from afar before, but now I'm caught up in it. More than that, it's like I'm the catalyst for the curse this time around. I caused all this, in a way. It's one hell of a feeling."

And suddenly, I realized what he was saying was familiar to me. All too familiar. I shivered as I remembered being in the epicenter of the curse two decades ago.

"I had three deaths on my hands," I said to Harris, my eyes

filling with tears. "My brothers and my father. I felt then just like you do now, like I was the catalyst for it all. I had to leave town to break the spell."

He and I gazed into each other's eyes for a moment that felt like forever. Something passed between us, I'm still not quite sure what it was—an understanding? A spark of kinship? A whisper from beyond the grave?

"The good news is that now you have all you need for your tell-all exposé," I said, managing a smile.

"Yeah." Harris chuckled. "The only problem is, now I'm sort of afraid to write it."

"Let me ask you a question, Harris. It's time for honesty now. Did you break into Alban House? Were you the one who rifled through my mother's papers and my room?"

Harris shook his head. "The police have already questioned me about that. Why would I break into Alban House? I had already found the aunt—she was the 'bombshell' I had been looking for for years. What possible reason would I have to break in?"

"So you're not the one who went through my room?" I reiterated. "You have no idea what was stolen?"

"No," he said.

I eyed him and sat back, crossing my legs. I had been sure he was our intruder, but now that I thought about it, what he was saying sounded right. What reason did he have to break in? Mercy couldn't possibly have told him about Coleville's letters because my mother didn't live at Alban House when they were written. The letters were addressed to her at her parents' home, so there's no way Mercy could have known about them when she was on the airplane with Harris.

As I sat there, I was becoming more and more confused about what to do. Here was a man who was questioning his parentage, and rightly so. But he was the same man who intended to write a book about my family. He hadn't renounced his intention to do that. If I told him what I suspected, the secret my mother had kept for fifty years might very well be exposed for all the world to know.

I nearly gathered my things, got up, and walked away from Harris in that moment, but I didn't. I heard, or imagined, my mother's voice, soft and low in my ear. "Exposing the secret is exactly what I intended to do the day I died."

And then it hit me—Harris was the very man she was to have met that day. He was the one to whom she was going to tell her deepest secrets. Perhaps her own son. Did she know? And now I sat here with him, newly armed with the very information she was going to tell him that day. Was it a coincidence? Did I find the letters by chance or . . .

Oh, Mom, did you have a hand in all of this?

I needed a moment alone.

"Will you excuse me?" I said, as I stood up and headed toward the restroom. Looking over my shoulder, I said: "I have a story to tell you, Harris, and I have a feeling we're going to be here awhile."

IN THE LADIES' ROOM, I fished my cell phone out of my purse and clicked on the Internet search engine, typing "David Coleville" into the search field. I found the photo I was looking for and an icy thread worked its way up my spine. It was true, then. That's why he had looked so familiar to me. Harris Peters was a dead ringer for David Coleville, with a little of Jake and Jimmy thrown in for fun. He was, without a doubt, a mixture of Coleville and my mother.

Still, even though I saw the resemblance clearly, the gnawing in my stomach was telling me to keep Harris in the dark about this. The Alban silence was wrapping itself around me—keep scandals hidden! Close ranks! But, I told myself, despite what it might mean to the Alban family, this was a man's parentage we were talking about. We could certainly do a DNA test, but this photo told me all I needed to know.

I had no idea how or why my mother would have put the child up for adoption—I couldn't imagine any possible scenario in which she would have given one of her children away, especially the child of the man she loved and intended to marry—but there was Harris, with the truth written all over his face. I had no right to keep this information to myself.

And if Harris told the whole world, well, that's what my mother had intended to do the day she died, anyway.

I took a deep breath and rejoined Harris at our table. "So," I began, "are you familiar with the journalist David Coleville?"

And I told him the story of finding the letters, and how Coleville and my mother had fallen in love. I told him they had planned to marry the summer Coleville died.

"Highly interesting," Harris said finally. "This is something the literary world needs to know. But—"

"But what's it got to do with our topic of conversation?"

He smiled. "Well, that's what I was thinking, yes."

I took the cell phone out of my purse and showed him the photograph of Coleville. "You're a dead ringer for him, Harris."

He leaned forward and squinted at the small image. Then he looked up at me, his eyes wide.

"I knew it didn't add up, your theory about my dad," I said to him. "You're right in that only someone very rich could've made those payments all these years. But my dad died twenty years ago and I knew he didn't have you in his will. Your birthday, along with the payments, got me thinking."

I reached across the table and took his hand before continuing. "My mother was planning to marry David Coleville the summer he died. She married my dad that fall. Ever since I learned about her love affair with Coleville, it struck me as odd that she and my dad would marry so quickly after Coleville's death. I initially thought she must've been pregnant. But I'm the eldest child and I was born years after that summer. And now here you come . . ."

"Whoa," Harris said, wiping his eyes on his napkin. "I don't . . ."

"Listen, we can sort all of this out," I said. "We've got time. We don't know yet if this is true. I suspect it is, but we don't know for sure. So, yes, we can get a DNA test, and in the meantime, I'll run down a paper trail to see if my mother made those payments to you over the years. If it does turn out that you're my mother's son, you need to know right now that I'll welcome you into this family with open arms."

For a moment, Harris stared at me, openmouthed. "How can you be so impossibly kind to me?" he said finally. "After everything I've done?"

I smiled. "I'm only doing what generations of Albans have done before me, Harris. We close ranks. If you're family, you're in the fold."

. . .

BACK UP IN MY ROOM, I drew a bath and stared at my cell phone. I had to admit it: The only person I wanted to talk to at that moment was Matthew Parker.

As much as I had been fighting my attraction to him, I couldn't stop myself from circling back into his orbit. We're just friends, I said to myself. This is what friends do, we tell each other things. Satisfied with that, I dialed his number.

"This is Reverend Matthew Parker, minister of Prince of Peace Lutheran Church. Sorry to have missed you. Please leave your name and number, and I'll call back as soon as possible. God bless you."

I hung up without saying anything. Instead, I grabbed the paperback I had bought in the hotel gift shop and slipped into the tub, hoping to savor the escape into another world that reading always provided me. That night, however, it didn't. The truth of my life at the moment was stranger, and more encompassing, than the fiction on the page. I closed the book and slid down farther into the bubbling water, thinking of my mother and David Coleville and Harris Peters, and what it all might mean to me and to Amity, to have a new member of the family. I wondered how Jane would take to it. Not well, I was imagining.

I was having trouble keeping my eyes open when the phone rang.

I turned off the tub's jets, cleared my throat, and answered. "Hello?"

"Grace, it's Matthew. I saw you called."

"Hi," I said.

"Hi," he said.

I sat up a little straighter in the tub and suddenly felt a little strange, being in the tub and talking to him. "I'm just getting out of the bath," I said to him. "Can I call you back in two minutes?"

"I'll be here."

I hopped out of the tub, quickly dried off, and wrapped a fluffy white robe around me before padding to the bed, cell phone in hand. I dialed.

"Hi," I said again.

"Hi," he said again.

I was silent for a moment, not knowing quite what to say. "Harris Peters came to see me at the hotel," I said finally.

"What did he want?"

"You're not going to believe it," I said.

"Is it a bombshell?"

"I think this qualifies as a bombshell, yes."

"Do you know what I want to know?" he asked me, chuckling. "Why is it every time you call me, you drop a bomb?"

"It's my way." I smiled into the phone and leaned back against the pillows. "I like to keep people interested."

"I don't think you have anything to worry about in that regard, Grace Alban. I'm interested. Despite what we said the other night, I think you know that."

I hesitated, all of my fear—a minister, public scrutiny, responsibilities—curdling in my throat. "I'm interested, too," I finally admitted, and could feel the weight of the words all throughout my body.

"I don't suppose," I continued, "that you're free to talk about this supposed bombshell?"

"I'll be right there."

We might have met in the bar downstairs. But instead, I closed my eyes and jumped off the cliff I had been avoiding for days. "I'm in room 1201."

CHAPTER 34

Rain hit the window in bursts and thunder boomed, waking me from a most pleasant dream. I blinked and looked around, and for a sleepy moment I didn't know where I was. As I drifted further back into consciousness, I remembered. I was in the Sheraton Hotel, with a man by my side.

As I listened to the rainstorm and watched Matthew's chest rise and fall next to me in the slow rhythm of sleep, I wasn't quite sure what to do—get up and order breakfast? Pretend to be asleep until he got up and headed for home? I didn't have much experience handling these sorts of situations and tried to remember my scant dating life before I married Amity's father. In the end, I snuggled back down and gazed at the sleeping face of the man I was sure I could love.

We hadn't talked much the previous night, not at first, anyway. As soon as I opened the door to my room, he pulled me into a kiss that seemed to go on forever. Despite whatever horrors and sadness had befallen me in the past week, my journey back to Alban House had led me straight to him, and for that I let out a grateful sigh.

Within a few moments, he opened his eyes. "I'm Matthew Parker," he said, stretching and putting an arm under his head. "And you are?"

"Just a wayward soul who called you last night when she had no one else to turn to."

"How lucky for me." He smiled, his sleepy eyes bright. "Ensnaring a wayward soul has been on my list for quite some time now."

"I'm happy to oblige," I whispered, and melted into him.

Later, we ordered breakfast from room service. Omelets, sausage, coffee, and croissants. It all felt blissfully ordinary and normal—no decades-old mysteries to solve, no aunts to deal with, no half brothers to think about.

I knew the normalcy was just an illusion—every one of those problems, and more, hung in the air just outside the hotel's front door, waiting to affix themselves to me when I emerged. But for those scant early morning hours, I luxuriated in the simple everydayness of just being a couple eating breakfast together, like millions of other couples around the country were doing at the same time.

We were savoring the last bites of our omelets when the muffled ring of my cell phone pulled me back to my other reality. I groaned. "Can't I let it go to voice mail?"

"I wouldn't do that." Matthew crossed the room to the sofa where I had left my purse. "It could be Amity. Or the police. Or the hospital." He fished the phone out of my purse and handed it to me.

"Miss Alban?" said a soft, accented voice on the other end of the line. "This is Marie Bouchard, your aunt's nurse. I'm at Alban House, and I'm afraid nobody is answering the door. Were you not expecting me?"

I slapped my forehead with the heel of my hand. "I'm so sorry! No, I didn't know what time you were coming. I'm afraid we've had a bit of a situation here and . . ." My words trailed off. No point in explaining everything over the phone. "Just wait right there, Marie," I continued. "You can get out of the rain under the second-floor patio—do you see it? Good. I'll be there in a few minutes. And again, my apologies for not being home when you arrived."

We got dressed, scrambled down to Matthew's car, and drove through the pounding rain with lightning crackling through the sky, thunder growling in the distance. On the way, I checked my phone for voice mail messages and found one from the chief, sent early that morning, telling me it was okay to return to the house.

"But one thing, Grace," he cautioned me, "your aunt is still at large. We've checked the house and the grounds, but we've turned up nothing. I'm sending a squad car back to you later today, but until then, just be careful."

When we reached the house, Matthew handed me an umbrella from the backseat and I unfurled it as I stepped out, waiting for him to run around the car to join me. We hurried up to the patio steps, expecting to find Marie huddled under the second-floor patio's overhang, but the nurse was nowhere to be seen.

Matthew tried the door—it was locked. I fished my house key out of my purse and unlocked the door. We stepped across the threshold and looked this way and that, but the house seemed as empty as it had been the day before. Our footsteps echoed as we walked through the foyer to the living room, parlor, and library, flipping on the lights in each room as we went.

"Do you think she came inside and then locked the door behind her?" Matthew wondered.

"Miss Bouchard?" I called out, but there was no reply. "Marie! Are you here?"

Matthew shrugged his shoulders. "Maybe she went upstairs? Or . . ." He walked toward the kitchen as I grabbed my cell phone out of my purse and hit redial. The nurse's cell rang and rang, eventually landing in voice mail.

"Miss Bouchard, this is Grace Alban," I said. "We're here at the house now. Not sure where you are. Please give me a call when you get this message. And again, I'm sorry for this mix-up." I clicked off and dropped the phone back into my purse.

Matthew came from the direction of the kitchen, shaking his head. "She's not in there, either."

"I'm betting she got into the cab that brought her here from the airport and went to a hotel or something," I said, glancing up and down the main hallway.

"But why would she do that?" Matthew squinted at me. "You told her we were coming right away."

He was right. She wouldn't have gone anywhere. With that realization, a seeping sense of dread began to fall around us, as real and tangible as the rain outside.

"The chief said Mercy is still at large," I said, wrapping my arms around Matthew's waist and eyeing the staircase. We both stood there for a moment, neither knowing quite what to do, before he unwound my arms from around his waist and held my hands. "Let's do a quick check of the upstairs and—"

But his words were cut off by the sound of the buzzer, soft and low and distant. I frowned at Matthew and hurried toward the ringing, pushing open the kitchen door, with him at my heels. I stopped short when I saw the display. Somebody was buzzing from the master suite, over and over and over again. I shot Mat-

thew a look—his face was a mixture of confusion and suspicion—
and I hit the intercom. "Hello? Who's up there?"

The ancient device crackled and sputtered with static, but
behind all that noise, I heard a thin, faraway voice. "*Mama . . . ?*
Mama, is that you . . . ?"

I held Matthew's gaze for an instant, and then we both burst
out of the kitchen and bounded up the stairs, headed down the
hallway toward the master suite in a full-on run. I flew through
the door, Matthew close behind. "Amity!" I shouted, checking the
closet, the study, the bathroom, the patio. But nobody was there.
No Amity, no Mercy, no nurse, nobody.

While Matthew checked the media room and Amity's room,
I dialed my daughter's cell phone.

"Hey, Mom," she answered, and the relief that washed over
me was so strong that I thought it might knock me to the
ground.

"So, you're okay," I said, leaning against the doorframe.

"Sure," she said. "Why?"

"No reason," I said too quickly. "But remember, don't come
back to the house right now. You can stay at Heather's for a while,
right?"

"Yeah, Mom. Not a problem. But . . . is this about Jane?"

"No, honey," I said to her. "Jane's resting in the hospital and
she'll be fine. Just promise me you won't come back to the house
until I call you to tell you it's okay."

"That's fine," she said, and I could almost see her shrugging
her shoulders. "It's raining too hard to go anywhere, anyway."

I told my daughter I loved her and hung up, and the tears I
was holding back began to fall. Matthew was at my side in an
instant and took me into his arms.

"She's okay," he said into my hair. "She's okay." He pulled away and looked me in the face. "But Mercy is obviously here, playing with you."

"Let's find her," I said to him, clearing my throat. "I want this to end. I'm tired of being afraid in my own house."

We headed down the hallway, calling the nurse's name all the while, and found that the guest rooms where Mr. Jameson's lads had been staying were similarly empty, the disarray of unmade beds, half-full water glasses, and clothes strewn on the floor—as the boys had hastily gathered their belongings to move to the hotel—a stark contrast to the neat, untouched silence of rooms unoccupied.

Matthew took my hand. "Come on," he said, leading me to the back stairs. "She's probably on the third floor."

At this, I stopped. "Should we call the police, do you think?"

Matthew pulled his cell phone out of his pocket and dialed. After a few quiet words with the police, he hung up.

"I didn't realize this storm was so bad," he said to me. "They might not be able to get here for a while. Apparently, it's a mess out there. Trees down, roads impassable. There's some flooding downtown. They said to wait for them in the living room."

"But the nurse!" I protested. "We can't just stand here and do nothing until they show up. I've got a bad feeling about this."

"Agreed. If Mercy is still armed, that nurse is in danger. And by the time the police get here, we can have the third floor checked out. I think we can handle her together if we find her before they get here."

She was a seventy-year-old woman, for goodness' sake. Armed, dangerous, yes, but if we found her, Matthew and I could certainly subdue her.

Still, as I climbed those stairs, the gnawing in the pit of my stomach tightened into a hard knot. I hadn't been up to the third floor in years—it was a part of the house my family rarely used. There was the extensive nursery and children's quarters where Mercy was living, along with the children's library and a few guest rooms in one wing. A ballroom, closed off from the rest of the floor, with a set of double doors on one end and an elevator on the other, so party guests would neither be troubled by children nor the prospect of climbing the stairs in high heels.

As we crept hand in hand through the children's quarters—several small, connected rooms—we saw my aunt's clothes hanging neatly in the closet and her bed made with tight corners, just as Jane had always done. If Mercy was here, she hadn't slept in this bed since she'd put Jane in the hospital. I checked the secret doors—locked. The other guest rooms were silent and unused, dust hanging in the air.

"Let's check the ballroom," I whispered to Matthew, leading him down the hallway, turning the lights on as we went.

We pushed open the double doors, and as our eyes adjusted to the darkness, with the rain beating down on the floor-to-ceiling windows on the wall facing the lake, I squinted at the sight of something that shouldn't have been there.

I exchanged a puzzled glance with Matthew and crossed the room to flip on the light to get a better look.

There, in the middle of the ballroom's dance floor, was a ring of stones obviously brought up from the lakeshore. In the middle of that ring, a silver bowl containing the ashes of what had been a small fire. Strewn about outside the ring—photographs. As I looked from one to the next, my throat felt dry as I recognized shots of Amity, myself, Jane, Carter, Mr. Jameson.

Under it all—symbols, thick black lines that looked Celtic in nature. Matthew blanched, gulping in a mouthful of air. "What *is* this?"

That knot in my stomach was working its way through my whole body. "It's for the girl in white," I said, my voice a harsh whisper. "It looks to me like this is where she dances these days. What better place than a ballroom?"

Matthew was staring at the fire ring, his eyes wide and round. "But wouldn't the police have found this when they searched the house earlier? Why—"

I interrupted his thought. "Maybe she came back after they had gone. Or maybe she never left at all." I turned around in a slow circle. "I've always thought it was sort of futile, the police searching this house. It's a game of hide and seek they can't win. There are too many places to hide."

Matthew crossed the room to take my hand. "I think we should go downstairs. Now. We can wait for the police in the library or even in the car."

We pushed through the double doors and made our way down the hall toward the staircase, descending it hand in hand, me squeezing his a bit tighter than I had intended. As we passed the second-floor landing, I heard voices coming from the floor below. Not voices. A voice.

Matthew and I stopped in our tracks to listen, my heart pounding.

"Miss Grace!" I heard. "Reverend Parker! Are you here?"

Matthew and I hurried down the rest of the stairs to find Carter standing near the front door, holding a massive umbrella in one hand.

"Oh, Carter, thank God!" I ran to him and threw my arms around his neck, trying to catch my breath.

"Oh, for goodness' sake, Miss Grace, I'm all wet!" he fussed, pulling away. But I saw the smile on his face and the twinkle in his eyes. "I just returned from my wonderful stay at the hotel—thank you so much for that—and I saw the reverend's car in the driveway."

We got him up to speed—the police were on their way, Mercy was still missing, her nurse was now also missing, and we had checked the entire house and found nothing.

"Nothing, except a very strange sight in the ballroom," I said.

Carter squinted at me. "What do you mean, strange?"

I told him about the fire ring and the photographs and what looked to be Celtic writing scrawled on the floor. He let the umbrella drop from his hand.

"I meant it, Miss Grace, what I said in the hospital waiting room yesterday," he said to me, a frightened look in his eyes. "She cannot stay in Alban House for one more day. She simply cannot."

I shot Matthew a look and said, "Carter, I think it's time you told us everything you know about Mercy."

"Indeed, Miss Grace—" he started. Then there was a massive crack of thunder and lightning, and everything went black.

CHAPTER 35

I fumbled for the long matches on the hearth in the parlor, and soon the kindling I'd laid in the fireplace ignited, bathing the room in a warm, yellowish glow.

"It's terrible outside," Carter said as he slipped off his overcoat and draped it on one of the chairs. "Power is out all over town. The poor taxi driver had quite a job of it getting me home from the hotel. It's like a puzzle trying to drive anywhere because so many trees have fallen onto the roads. They're predicting straight-line winds and hail before it's all said and done."

At this, the whole house shook. I settled onto the sofa and grabbed an afghan. Usually I loved being at Alban House during a thunderstorm—it was such a solid fortress, I knew that even the worst of nature's fury couldn't damage it or hurt me. But this was different somehow. It felt dangerous and confining, as though we were trapped in the house instead of sheltered by it. I wrapped the afghan around me and listened as the wind howled and the waves crashed against the shore.

Matthew joined me on the sofa and draped an arm around my shoulders. "This may sound a little hysterical, but I'm going to say it, anyway," he began, looking at Carter and me in turn. "None of us is going anywhere because of this storm, including Mercy, and it might be a while before the police get here. We don't know where the nurse is, but she may well be with her. Or, I hate to say this, she may well have come to harm."

He paused before continuing. "I guess what I'm saying is, I'm not crazy about this whole situation. Because of that, I think we should all stay right here in this room together. No wandering alone to the kitchen, no going upstairs. And, not to be indelicate, but if one of us has to use the bathroom, we're all going."

Carter nodded gravely. "Agreed," he said. "Neither of you really knows what you're up against. I do. She is not a harmless old lady. Not by a long shot."

Matthew moved closer and held me tighter. "Now seems like a good time to tell us what you know," he said to Carter.

Carter crossed the room, nodding his head, and opened a decanter of scotch that was standing on the sideboard. "I'm sorry to be so bold, Miss Grace, but this calls for a little fortification." He poured us each an ample drink. "What do they say—it's five o'clock somewhere?"

He handed Matthew and me lowball glasses almost half full of scotch and sank into an armchair across from us. I took a sip and felt the spicy liquid warming me from the inside as I curled my legs up onto the sofa and leaned into Matthew.

With the wind roaring outside, the rain punishing the windowpanes, and the fire crackling in the fireplace, Carter took a gulp of his drink and began to speak.

"It was just this same time of year, the early summer of 1947. The war was over, and I was a young man fresh off the boat from England. I served in a regiment with a friend of old Mr. Alban's in the war, that's how I came to work here, you see." He smiled a melancholy smile, his eyes focused on the past. "My fiancée had been killed during one of the bombing raids in London, and when the war was over, I just couldn't go back there. Not without my darling Roz. I desperately needed a new life, away from everything that reminded me of her, and Mr. Alban gave me that."

I looked at him with new eyes. My whole life, he had just been Carter, our impossibly kind driver. I had never realized he was in the war, or had had a fiancée, or . . . well, anything. My face reddened with the shame I felt for not ever asking, or even thinking to ask, about his life before he came to us.

He went on. "The girls, Fate and Mercy, were just children then, no more than ten years old. And what scamps they were! Always playing hide and seek, racing around the place like puppies, tormenting their brother. I wanted a new life, and indeed I got it, coming to a house filled with so much love and laughter." He let out a deep sigh. "But then everything changed."

He took a sip of his drink, and I saw a shudder pass through him.

"That's when Mercy fell ill?" I nudged him to go on.

He nodded. "Influenza. A bad strain was going around that year and both the girls caught it. Fate recovered, but poor little Mercy got weaker and weaker until . . ." He shook his head. "I was in the carriage house when I heard Mrs. Charity's screaming, a wail the likes of which I hope never to hear again."

"Jane said Mercy died, Carter," I said. "But surely that's not the case . . . Right?"

He locked eyes with me, and in his, I saw fear. "It is indeed the case," he said, his voice low and wavering. "The whole household was in mourning. Mr. Alban retreated into his work, Johnny became unusually quiet and withdrawn, and poor little Fate was lost, absolutely lost. But it was Mrs. Charity who scared us the most. She was utterly and completely destroyed. It was as though her own life force had been extinguished when her daughter died. She was but a shadow of the vibrant person she had been."

The image of my father on the horrible day when he realized Jake and Jimmy were dead swirled through my mind. And it hit me how much grief this house had seen over the years. So much suffering, so much death, family mourning loved ones over and over again. I thought about my conversation with Harris the night before, and I could see why people believed my family was cursed. The tableau of grief seemed to play out the same way for every generation. We were all haunted by tragedy.

"We laid poor Mercy to rest in the family crypt," Carter continued. "And life went on. Mr. Alban, especially. Even Charity seemed to be perking up, coming out of it, and we were all so relieved. We had no idea her change in mood was because she had put a plan in place. If we knew about the evil she was preparing to invoke we surely would have stopped it."

As he lifted his glass to his lips, a crack of lightning sizzled across the sky and lit up the room with its flash. I noticed his hands were shaking and his face had gone white.

Matthew shot me a look. "What type of evil are you talking about, Carter?" he asked.

Carter sighed and shook his head, a faraway look in his eyes. "This goes back to Mrs. Charity's family in the old country," he began.

"The family Jane and her mother worked for?" I asked, remembering her history.

"That's the one," Carter said. "I got this straight from Jane, so there's no speculation here when I say that Mrs. Charity came from a long line of women who had . . ."—Carter seemed to be searching for the right words—". . . rather special abilities."

He looked from Matthew to me, as though we would understand. But I was still confused.

"You're saying they were—what? Healers? Medicine women?" I asked.

"Healers, psychics, witches, whatever label you want to attach to them fits," Carter said. "They practiced black magic, the lot of them. They passed the art from mother to daughter, right down the line."

I squinted at him and noticed Matthew was shaking his head, a look of disbelief on his face. I wondered how his strong faith would dovetail with a story like this, and I sensed we both were thinking the same thing: this was veering off into the realm of fairy tale and legend. "That's what Jane told you?" I asked.

"And what her mother told her," Carter said, nodding. "They saw it all when they worked for Charity's mother, I'll tell you. But when Mr. Alban married Charity and brought her here to his home in America, Jane and her mother with them, they believed that was the end of it. Charity hadn't seemed interested in the family ways, so to speak, and was more than happy to move far away. She was more interested in being the lady of this fine manor, being a good wife to the husband she adored and raising the children she doted upon."

"Until . . . ?" I prodded.

"Until she lost one of those children," Carter said, shaking his head and taking another sip of scotch. "Shortly after Mercy died, Charity's mother and grandmother traveled to Alban House for a visit. Charity had summoned them. And when they arrived, they were carrying—I saw it myself—an ancient-looking book."

I snuggled closer to Matthew. He shook his head, a small,

almost imperceptible movement that told me he wasn't buying this fantastic tale.

"Jane's mother was terrified, I don't mind telling you that," Carter continued. "She said it was *the spell book*, and she had seen it before. She knew full well that the three of them were coming together for a dark and evil purpose. She nearly took Jane away from here the night they came, but we all convinced her to stay. She was needed here by the other children and Mr. Alban, and even Mrs. Charity needed her."

I took a moment to let all of this sink in. "Does this have anything to do with the old legend—the one that says my great-grandfather cut down a witch's wood to build this house and that he got her spirit in the bargain?"

Carter smiled. "That silly tale was just that, miss. A tale."

It didn't sound right to me. "But I've felt it myself, Carter," I protested. "I've always felt this house hummed with a life of its own."

"I'm not saying there's no truth to what you've experienced," he went on. "I'm saying the tale about the witch's wood is just a legend. It sprung up, as legends tend to do, from a grain of truth, from the women who have always been ladies of the manor here at Alban House. Until your mother, of course."

My mind felt fuzzy and fluid, as though I couldn't focus on what he was saying. It didn't make any sense to me. "But Carter, my great-grandfather John James Alban the First built this house. He was the son of refugees from the Potato Famine; he made his fortune and went to Ireland to find his bride and—" My words stopped cold when I realized I had just uttered the answer to my own question.

"Exactly, my dear," Carter said. "He went to Ireland to find his bride. Emmaline. She's the witch he brought back to this country, not some silly story about a witch imprisoned in the wood. A real-life, flesh-and-blood witch. I've no doubt that you've felt her presence here, miss. Once they infest a place, they never leave it."

I stared at him. "But you were talking about Charity, my grandmother. Surely—"

"Emmaline sent your grandfather, her son, to the old country to find a bride, just as his father had done," Carter said. "Charity wasn't a relation to Emmaline, but she and her mother were a part of the same coven. Jane can attest to this."

Matthew and I exchanged confused glances. This story was getting more and more outlandish by the minute.

"Okay, Carter—" I began, but he cut me off.

"I know what you're thinking," he said quickly. "But you haven't heard what comes next. I think you'll change your mind when you hear what happened."

"We were talking about Mercy, and I think we got sidetracked," Matthew offered. "So she fell ill—"

"We didn't get sidetracked and she didn't just fall ill," Carter said, slamming his glass down on the table with a thud. "Listen, man, you of all people should understand that there are things in this world beyond our comprehension, beyond our sight, and beyond our ability to believe. Isn't that, essentially, what you spend your life doing? Asking people to believe a fantastic, rather supernatural story that happened two thousand years ago involving a man who could walk on water and turn water into wine?"

Matthew smiled at him. "That I do, Carter," he said. "You've got me there. I'm sorry. I'll tell you this—in my church, we don't put a whole lot of stock in the occult. We think all of that stems from the most evil source there is, so that's where I'm coming from. But I promise you, I'll listen to the rest of your story with an open mind."

"That's good," Carter said. "Because Mercy is creeping around in this house right now, and both of you need to hear this, loud and clear."

"So," I prodded, "Charity's mother and grandmother arrived with a spell book. Then what happened?"

"They were huddled together, poring over that book, for days," Carter said, picking up his glass again and swirling the scotch around. "Until one night. I was in the carriage house and could see it all clearly. The three of them, dressed in flowing white gowns, down by the lakeshore."

A chill ran through me. "Dancing around a fire ring?"

He nodded. "That's exactly what they were doing. Dancing, chanting in a language I didn't recognize. They were reciting an ancient Celtic spell, invoking an evil force."

"How do you know that's what they intended?" I asked him. "Maybe—"

"No maybes about it, dear girl. I know because that very night, Mercy rose from the grave. The women had opened the door of the crypt, and I saw it with my own eyes, little Mercy walking out of there on her two legs in the dress she was buried in, as though she had simply been hiding in the crypt all that time."

Matthew held my gaze and I couldn't tell whether he thought Carter, along with Mercy, was a candidate for a psychiatric hospital or whether he was entertaining the thought that this fantastic story was true.

"Her mother, grandmother, and great-grandmother greeted her with tears and wails and cheers," he said, his eyes looking deeply into the past. "They took her down to the lakeshore, where the four of them danced and chanted and sang until the sun came up. By that time, Mercy was exhausted, and Charity carried her into the house and placed her in her bed, waking Fate so she could see that her sister was home now to stay."

"But," Matthew began, "how could she possibly have explained this to her husband and to all of you? People don't just rise from the dead. It doesn't happen."

"She didn't have to explain," Carter said. "It was the three of them, Charity, her mother, and her grandmother. They stood together and told all of us, Mr. Alban included, to not question these events and, furthermore, to stay silent about them. There was a horrible mistake, they said, a misdiagnosis of death, and Mercy was alive after all. End of story. And we were to leave it at that."

"And you believed them?" I asked.

Carter let out a snort. "Of course not. But you don't understand what kind of force they—three witches together—put out. It was as though we were standing in the very presence of evil. We knew better than to question anything."

Carter took another sip of scotch as the wind and thunder roared outside and the fire flickered. "Fate saw it first," he continued. "A few days later. It was a look in Mercy's eyes that hadn't been there before. Then Johnny noticed it. And then we all began to see it. A strange sheen in her eyes. A knowing smirk on her face. Something was just not right with that child. She was not a little girl anymore. She was something else. Something monstrous and hideous and evil was lurking behind the angelic mask of a child."

CHAPTER 36

I was squeezing Matthew's hand so tightly that it was turning white. I couldn't take my eyes off Carter. He looked so earnest that I knew he believed everything he was saying to be true. Based on what Jane had said earlier—Mercy was dead, and then she wasn't—I knew she believed it, too.

I didn't know what I believed. I could tell Matthew was feeling the same way.

The only thing I knew for sure was that I needed to hear the rest of the story. I'd reserve judgment until then.

"Go on, Carter," I urged him. "We're listening."

He lifted his glass to his lips with shaking hands, swallowed, and cleared his throat. "It started with animals," he whispered. "Thomas would find them in the yard, in the garden. Even on the patio. Squirrels, birds, chipmunks. Even the odd duck or two."

My whole body went cold. "You'd find them dead?" I choked out the words, not quite believing I was saying them.

He nodded, lifting a hand to his forehead and rubbing his brow. "We had no idea what was going on at first," he said. "But then I saw it myself, child. One afternoon, I was in the carriage house and, through the window, I saw Mercy in the yard. She lured a chipmunk to her with a handful of peanuts and then, quick as a wink, grabbed it and snapped its neck. And then she laughed. She dropped its poor little body, turned around, and saw me looking at her through the window. And she laughed again, locking eyes with me. I'll tell you, it gave me a chill."

I snuggled closer to Matthew.

"And then the accidents started happening," he went on. "Workmen would be on the roof and their ladders would go missing, stranding them there. Knives would be buried, blade side up, in the dirt to cut the hands of the gardeners. Tires on the cars would be slashed."

"She was trying to intentionally hurt people?" Matthew asked. "What did you—or more appropriately, her parents—do about it?"

Carter nodded. "Mr. Alban saw it right away, he knew. But Mrs. Charity wasn't having any of it. She was blind to what was going on, and nobody could make her see. But then Mercy tried to drown her sister in the lake, almost taking Johnny with them in the bargain."

He dabbed at his brow with a handkerchief. "We heard it, all of us. Fate's terrified screams, Johnny's shouting. The splashing. We ran to the lakeshore, me from the carriage house, Thomas from the gardens in back, Jane and her mother, along with Mr. and Mrs. Alban from the house, and we found Mercy holding her sister underwater, with Johnny trying everything he could to stop it. She turned on him, then, pushing him under . . ." He shook his head, remembering. "It took all of us to get her off of them. She was just a child, but it was like she had otherworldly strength."

I unfolded myself from the couch to grab the scotch decanter and refilled Carter's glass. "Then what happened?" I asked as I poured.

"Later that day, once Fate had been tended to and Johnny

had calmed down, I heard them arguing about it, Mr. and Mrs. Alban. He wanted to send Mercy away. Initially, she would hear none of it. But she couldn't deny that the girl had tried to hurt her other two children. She realized Mercy was dangerous and something had to be done.

"Soon enough, I was sent to collect the family doctor, who had been administering to the Albans for many years. He was sworn to secrecy—nobody was to know Mercy was alive. The world thought she was dead and buried, and by Mr. Alban's decree, it was going to stay that way. The doctor prescribed something for her, sedatives, I imagine. And Mr. Alban moved Fate and Johnny downstairs and locked Mercy away on the third floor. She was to live there, in captivity so to speak, away from everyone, until he and Mrs. Charity could agree on what to do."

"That's when he must have built the wing on the facility in Switzerland," I offered, shooting Matthew a look. "The doctor there told me it was built when Mercy was still a child."

Carter nodded.

"So what? She was locked in her rooms on the third floor for years?" I asked, shaking my head.

"She was," he said. "Charity tended to her, kept her company, fed her, and even, at night, took her outside. Mercy never interacted with anyone, except her mother, again. Or so we thought."

Another chill ran through me.

"Nobody knew that she had discovered the passageways. They had been locked, but she was able to unlock them. They became her world. She would creep about, watching us, watching her family, her sister especially."

"Wait a minute," I interrupted. "If nobody knew that, how do you know it?"

"I shouldn't say 'nobody.' There was one person who knew. Charity. When Charity discovered that Mercy had been using the passageways, she encouraged it. She was torn up about her child, you see, having to be locked away. It was guilt she felt because of her part in it. She knew her husband would send Mercy away if the child didn't remain sequestered and hidden, but even so, she wanted to give Mercy, evil as she was, some kind of life. And that's how the passageways became her world. Mercy began to live through her twin sister, imagining it was her out there in the main part of the house, doing whatever it was Fate was doing. Mercy became Fate's shadow."

I shivered and glanced at all four walls in the room. Was Mercy in the passageways right now, watching us? Did she have the nurse with her, or worse?

"Of course, nobody knew about this until much, much later," Carter went on. "And the household gradually returned to normal. Years passed. Fate met your mother at school, dear Adele, who brought so much light and love and laughter into this household. She became part of the family very quickly. Mrs. Charity especially took to her, and I think Fate looked upon her as the sister she no longer had. All of us began to exhale, believing the situation was handled for good. We didn't know something much, much worse was brewing."

CHAPTER 37

C arter, do you know for sure what happened to David Coleville that night?" Matthew asked.

Carter held up one hand, and in the firelight it cast a monstrous shadow on the wall behind him. "Back up, Vicar. You're getting ahead of yourself. There's part of the story you don't yet know." He paused to take a sip of scotch and leaned back in his chair. "I haven't talked about this in so many years, and yet I can remember every detail as though it were yesterday."

"Traumatic situations are like that," Matthew said, squeezing my hand. "Sometimes they don't recede." After a moment, he added, "Go on, Carter."

"We all thought Mercy had disappeared a full year before that ill-fated party happened."

"Disappeared? But—"

Just then, I heard a clattering in the entryway.

"Mom?" Amity appeared, dressed in a rain slicker.

"Honey!" I rushed to her side and wrapped her in my arms. "What are you doing here?"

She scowled at me. "What do you mean? We got a call at Heather's house that it was safe for me to come home. The police told Heather's mom you were expecting me."

The police hadn't even arrived yet, so obviously they hadn't called to tell Amity it was safe to come home. *Then who . . . ?* As that thought occurred to me, a sense of terror, the likes of which I had never known, took hold of me. The last thing I wanted was to have my daughter here. But she was standing right in front of me, smiling, and I didn't want to frighten her.

"Good, honey," I said to her, helping her out of her slicker and leading her into the living room, my hand firmly around her arm. The more people around my daughter at that moment, the better. "Carter is just telling us a story."

I settled Amity onto the sofa between Matthew and me as Carter went on. "Come to think of it, the journalist was here that summer also. The four of them, Johnny, Fate, David, and Adele, were thick as thieves, always playing croquet or sailing or just having drinks on the patio. I'd drive the four of them into town for movies or a night out." He smiled, thinking back. "It was then Mercy disappeared, just before the summer solstice party. Charity discovered she was gone, and as you can imagine, she raised quite the ruckus with her husband, but she had to do it quietly because, remember, nobody outside the family, not even Adele, knew Mercy even existed."

"My grandfather took her to the hospital in Switzerland, then, without anyone knowing."

Carter shook his head. "Back then, we, the staff, were not told anything, other than that she was gone and wasn't coming back. And frankly, we didn't care if she was dead, locked up, or if she simply went back to whatever evil had made her. All we knew was she was gone. And we were free of her."

I cut him off. "But . . . just a moment ago, you said you didn't realize 'something much, much worse' was brewing. That doesn't sound worse to me. That sounds like the solution."

"He hasn't gotten to the best part yet."

The voice was coming from behind us. Matthew and I snapped our heads around toward the archway and saw Mercy standing there, smiling, holding a ream of paper that I could only assume was the manuscript. "It's all in here. Haven't you read it, Grace?"

Matthew was on his feet in an instant, a look of terrible calm on his face. "Miss Alban! So nice to see you again."

She took a few steps into the room. "I asked Grace a question. Haven't you read it, my dear? You're the one who found it after all this time. Both of you." She smiled at Matthew.

Her stark lucidity, her complete control of herself, sent a shot of icy dread through my veins. She certainly was not the fanciful old woman I'd met at the funeral who thought she was at a party in 1956, nor the confused, rumpled lady dancing in circles around the girls. I wondered if the lack of her medication had caused that strange, deluded behavior, or if it was all an act, designed to shock and deceive.

"I knew he loved me," Mercy went on, coming closer still. The garish makeup she wore to the funeral was gone. Her hair was neatly pulled back, and she was wearing a simple blouse and slacks. She looked more like a fit, active seventy-year-old who had spent a lifetime exercising and eating right rather than someone who had languished in a drug-induced haze at a mental hospital for fifty years.

She set the manuscript on the table before us, and as she did so, I saw that she cradled a large kitchen knife, red with blood, in one hand.

"I knew he loved me," she said, smiling a radiant smile. "He titled this book for me. Why, it's all about me!"

"You were the girl in white," Matthew said, taking my hand

and leading me and Amity across the room, putting a table and a sofa of distance between us and Mercy. He nodded his head slightly to Carter, who made a show of refilling his drink but joined us.

"Of course I was, you silly man. Who else? The story frightened you; I know it did. You looked positively ashen when she was reading it to you."

"You were watching us," I said. "In the walls."

"As Carter just said, the passageways were my world," she said, shifting her focus to rest upon him. "My, haven't you gotten old. You were always so handsome."

And then she turned her attention to me. As she held my gaze, her face suddenly seemed very close to mine, and I became transfixed by her eyes—so dead, so lifeless, as though I were looking at a mannequin or into the eyes of a cobra hypnotizing its prey.

"Where is the nurse?" I said finally, my voice wavering.

"She didn't see me until it was too late." Mercy giggled. "It's so easy to catch people unaware. Lucky thing for the rain today, isn't it? You wouldn't want to have to clean up that much blood. Such a bother."

While Mercy was talking, I saw Matthew slip his phone off the table and hold it behind his back. I could only assume he was dialing 911, and I spoke up, so the police could hear what I was saying.

"So you're telling us that the nurse is dead?"

Mercy smiled. "Aren't we all, my dear?"

My stomach tightened as her grin widened, and as it did so, her face seemed to morph and change—her eyes glinted a bit too brightly, her mouth was contorted like an evil clown's. In that moment, I became convinced that everything Carter had said, the whole fantastical story, was true. This thing standing before me wasn't alive, not really.

"You killed the nurse, Mercy?" I repeated, for the police's benefit, hoping they were listening on the other end of the line. "Is that what you're saying to me?"

"I'm afraid it was necessary," she said, moving over to the sofa and sinking down onto the cushions, crossing her legs. "I'm not going back there. Now that I'm off those ridiculous medications, I can see clearly. It's no fun there. No passageways, no people to spy on. Nothing to do. No, I'm staying right here. This is my home, after all."

"And Jane?" I said, a bit louder than I had intended. "Jane Jameson? Did you try to kill her, too?"

Mercy shook her head at me and laughed. "Who else, silly girl? I hardly think Carter here would have done it. He's loved her his whole life. Isn't that right, Carter?"

I turned to him in time to see his face go ashen white, and then redden. "That's okay, Carter." I smiled at him. "We all love her." A tear escaped one of his eyes and he brushed it away with his hand.

"She intended to put me back on those horrible, mind-numbing medications," Mercy said. "That just wouldn't do. Not at all."

A thought ran through my mind and took the breath out of me. "You just confessed to one murder and an attempted murder," I said. "Why are you telling us all of this?"

"Why, to scare the life out of you, my dear." She smiled at me, standing up and grasping the knife. "I find it's always better to have my victims filled with terror and dread. It's easier for me that way, invoking that kind of evil. Don't you see, you silly girl, that I become much more powerful with those kinds of emotions swirling around me? I hardly have to do a thing! Just like poor Adele. She took one look at me and dropped dead."

She laughed then, a terrible throaty laugh, and I could feel Amity shaking next to me.

"You were here the day my mother died?"

"Of course I was," she sneered. "This is my home. Where else would I be?"

"I thought you were with Harris until the day of the funeral."

"As it turns out, that little fool wasn't the best babysitter."

"Where did she die?" I asked her, my voice splintering. "They searched and searched but didn't find her, until suddenly she was on the bench in the garden."

"I was playing a little game with Jane." Mercy raised her eyebrows. "Adele dropped dead when she saw me, but I took her into the tunnels that lead into the false basement until they had thoroughly searched the grounds. Then I laid her out in the garden. Jane's face went absolutely white when she saw her. Alabaster!"

"Were you the one in the false basement? The one who broke into the house and went through my things? Why would you do that?"

"You are terribly slow, Grace," Mercy said. "You're not getting the theme. Let me spell it out for you, dear. Were you afraid?"

I could feel my legs trembling. If she had done it all simply to evoke fear in us, it was working.

She stood up, casting a long shadow on the opposite wall. It was then that I noticed her shadow wasn't alone. I squinted to get a better look, and there, dancing on the wall alongside it, were four other shadows, moving closer to hers. I smelled lake water and my mother's perfume, and I heard my brothers' laughter so loud and raucous that I was sure everyone else could hear it, too. Their presence wrapped around me like a shield, and as it did, a sense of calmness passed over me. My family was here. And something else, too. It felt like the very house was standing with me. I wasn't afraid anymore.

I took Matthew's hand and I realized he was holding Mercy's gaze and praying, soft and low, the words of a familiar prayer I had grown up with. His face was as serene as a lamb's.

"You have lost, Mercy," I said to her as coolly and calmly as I could manage. "We are not afraid of you."

She moved toward us then, her eyes blazing, speaking words I didn't understand, ancient-sounding, primal words. She seemed to rise up, gaining strength and power from whatever dark spell she was chanting.

"You all are going to be dead within very short order," she shouted, raising her hand. "You will disappear just like they all disappear!"

CHAPTER 38

Freeze!" A voice boomed through the room from the entry-way. "Police!"

I turned around to see the officers slowly walking into the room, guns drawn, and exhaled deeply. I let down my guard just for a moment, turned away just for a second—we all must have. Because as quickly as that, Mercy was gone. It only took an instant for me to realize Amity was with her. That evil monster had my daughter.

Before the police could stop me, I rushed into the open passageway door.

In the darkness, I could see nothing beyond the dusty, spidery tapestry on the walls, but I thundered down the inky passageway all the same.

"Amity!" I shouted. "Amity, call out to me! I'm coming!"

I stopped, listening closely, trying to figure out which way they went, but heard nothing, only my own words echoing down the seemingly empty tunnels.

And then a singsong verse permeated the silence. "*The witch in the wood comes out to play . . .*"

My stomach tightened. "Mercy, you're not frightening me!" I shouted. "Honey, I'm coming for you!"

I ran at full speed, just making out Matthew's voice, calling my name, faint, in the background. But all I could think about was Amity.

My old senses of these tunnels shifted into high gear—I didn't need a flashlight, I didn't need any electricity—I knew where I was going on instinct. I was sure Mercy felt the same; this was her world, her lair. Twisting and turning we went, me shouting the whole time—"I'm here! I'm following you!"—until I was sure we were making our way toward the false basement room. The police would have no idea which way to go and would be far behind. It was up to me.

I crashed through the door to the secret room and flipped on the light to find Mercy standing near the sofa, the knife with which she had tried to kill Jane at my daughter's throat.

Mercy was smiling a serene and staid smile, while Amity's face was filled with fear.

"Amity," I said to her quietly, calmly. "Look at me. Don't be afraid. She feeds on fear."

"*Come devil, come imp, come monstrous thing / That hides underground in the day,*" Mercy sang, the knife twirling in slow circles at my daughter's throat.

"Mom!" Amity whispered. I held her gaze. On the wall behind her and behind Mercy, I also saw shadows.

"*Come alive this night and give them a fright / When the wood witch comes out to play.*"

Whether it was my family there to support me or some other, darker force, something overtook me at that moment and I rushed forward with as much hate and anger and determination as I had ever had. All these emotions fueled me as I planted my hands around Mercy's throat and fell on her. The knife clattered to the ground as I heard her head hit the floor with a thud. I squeezed hard.

"Run, Amity!" I shouted. "Get back upstairs!"

"*Come devil, come imp, come monstrous thing / That hides underground in the day,*" Mercy coughed and sputtered, her eyes becoming fiery red. I didn't care. No matter what evil lay within her, I would not let her hurt my daughter.

"You're the only monstrous thing here tonight, Mercy," I growled, my grip tightening on her throat, my arms growing strong with the support of generations before me. "This ends now."

I saw the twinkling, the laughter in her eyes. "You're right, Grace," she sang. "It does."

And then I felt myself rising up and crashing down onto the floor, Mercy on top of me. Now it was her hands around my throat, and I was powerless to stop whatever was going to happen. I could feel them tighten, more and more.

"How did you think you would ever get the best of me?" She laughed, and her grip loosened, just a bit. Through a cloud, I saw the knife raised in her other hand. I could feel I was losing consciousness, falling prey to the lack of oxygen she was forcing on me.

"No, you don't!" I heard my daughter's voice, far away in the distance, and saw Mercy fall to the side. Amity shoved her with all her might. There was a clattering, then, and scuffling for the knife. I grabbed for it and got the blade, its edge cutting into my hand. I didn't care. I turned it around and grasped the handle and slashed upward, connecting with something soft.

Mercy's face was a mix of disbelief and humor. "You can't kill me, my dear," she whispered.

I pulled back and, with all of my might, plunged the blade deeply into her chest. "I think I just did."

CHAPTER 39

We answered the police's questions as we sat in the parlor. The 911 operator had heard everything, via Matthew's cell phone call, and he and the officers had found their way to the basement room just as I had stabbed Mercy. Another squad was outside searching for the nurse's body, which they found later in the garden.

I held Amity in my arms and stroked her hair. She was crying softly and shaking, and I tried to comfort her but I felt much the same way, as though I was shivering deep within my core.

"You were very brave down there, honey," I said to her. "You saved my life."

She managed a smile as we sat together on the sofa. "You told me to run, but I just couldn't leave you. Why did she do that, Mom? What is she?"

My daughter's eyes were searching mine for answers I couldn't give her. "I don't know," I said finally. "But it's over now. She's gone, and she's not coming back."

Soon the coroner arrived, and they took Mercy's body away.

"I'm the next of kin," I told them. "When you've done the autopsy, I'd like her to be cremated as soon as possible." I knew it was probably silly, but I did not want Mercy buried on this property or anywhere near the house.

When they had all left, and it was just the four of us in the parlor, I turned to Carter.

"You recognized her, that day when you were driving us to the funeral, didn't you?" I asked him, remembering his reaction when we almost ran her down.

He nodded and sipped the last of his drink. "I did, child. I did. And now that it seems to have stopped raining, I'm going to head down to the carriage house," he said, getting to his feet and smoothing his suit coat. "I could use some dinner and my own bed."

"I know the feeling." I smiled at him and stretched, realizing I could do with a little food myself. "It's been a long day."

After he had gone, Matthew, Amity, and I retreated to the kitchen. They both hopped onto stools at the high table. I opened a beer for Matthew and had just stuck my head inside the refrigerator when something Carter had said replayed in my mind.

"He said there was something worse," I said, poking my head around the fridge door to look at Matthew. He wrinkled his nose at me.

"When Carter was telling the story," I said. "He said there was something worse to tell, but he didn't get a chance to tell it because Mercy interrupted us."

"That's right," Matthew said, putting his elbow on the table and resting his chin in his palm. "But to tell you the truth, I really don't want to know what it is. Carter's down in the carriage house. Mercy's dead, she can't hurt anyone anymore. You and your daughter are safe. It's over. And I think I've had enough of the supernatural for one day. I'm sure Carter believes his story is true, but for God's sake . . ." He let out a deep sigh. "Can't we just leave it? For today, at least?"

I thought I detected the urge to run in Matthew's eyes. I wouldn't have blamed him if he did. "You've got it," I said, and pulled some cold chicken, lettuce, and an avocado out of the fridge with a weak smile. "How about a sandwich?"

I LAY AWAKE THAT NIGHT, with Amity next to me in the big bed, and Matthew—who didn't feel right leaving us alone in the house—sleeping in the guest room down the hall.

Mercy had answered some of my questions—notably about my mother's death and the identity of our intruder—and I knew I should be satisfied with that. But what Carter had said was nagging at me. What was the "much, much worse"? And did it have anything to do with Coleville's death the next summer? I was so deeply ensnared in this mystery, I just couldn't let it go. I punched my pillow and turned on my side, thinking that I would talk to Carter about it the next day.

But then my eyes shot open. I didn't have to wait until the next day. Mercy had said: "He hasn't gotten to the best part yet." And then she referred to the manuscript, saying: "It's all in there."

I slipped out of bed and stole into my mother's study, where I had returned the manuscript earlier. I flipped on the reading lamp and put the pages on my lap, and a shudder went through me when I saw the red smudges Mercy's bloody fingers had left on it. I shook the image of her out of my mind and began to read.

Chapter Seven

The next morning, I made my way down to the dining room for breakfast, having every intention of telling my hosts that I'd have to take my leave. I had already made up a story—my father would need me back in Boston. But I didn't get a chance to tell them anything, because the dining room was empty when I reached it.

I walked from there to the study to the living room, wondering where in the world my hosts could possibly be. This wasn't like them, creatures of habit that they were.

Perhaps they were on the patio? I looked out the living room window—there was Lily, standing alone, dabbing at her eyes with a handkerchief. I pushed open the French doors and was at her side in an instant.

"What is it?" I asked her. "What's the matter?"

She looked at me with wide eyes. "Oh, Mickey, thank goodness!" she said, smiling warmly and touching my arm. "I'm so glad to see you up and around. We were all getting quite worried about you."

Whatever was she talking about? "Up and around?" I asked her, looking at my watch. "Am I late for breakfast?"

She smiled again, that beautiful, warm smile. "About four days late," she said, gently. "You were down with a terrible fever. The doctor has been here. I could've killed Flynn for that ridiculous prank, plunging you into the lake like that. I was terrified you had caught your death."

My head swam. I had lost four days?

"I don't understand," I began. "I—"

"So there you are, Rip Van Winkle!" I turned to see

Flynn running up the patio steps, his eyes shining. "Back in the land of the living!" He encircled me in a great hug. "I was so afraid for you, my dear friend," he whispered into my ear, his voice wavering.

He pulled back and looked at me, and I could see his eyes brimming with tears.

"Mother! Father!" he called out in the direction of the garden. "He's awake! Mickey is awake!"

I went through the motions of breakfast with everyone but couldn't quite grasp what they were saying to me. Four days lost? But . . . how? The last I knew, I had spent a fitful, sleepless night in my room after a frightening encounter on the lakeshore. Was everything I experienced some dark and feverish dream brought about by illness? A hallucination, then? It was the only explanation that made sense, and yet it felt wrong somehow.

Lily and Flynn and his parents chattered away, filling me in on the happenings of the past four days. But Pru was notably silent. She stared across the table at me with a strange glint in her eyes that I hadn't before seen.

Any comments she would make were harsher than her usual, flirty banter, picking at both Lily and Flynn in a way that was decidedly unlike her. Finally, Flynn spoke up.

"Whatever is the matter with you, Pru?" he asked. "You're positively gloomy, and you've been this way for days. And here we are with something to celebrate—Mickey's recovery. Lighten up, will you?"

She turned to me then, and in her face I saw something ghoulishly familiar. "I am sorry." She smiled, but as she did so, her eyes didn't light up the way they usually did. "I was just so worried about Michael. I guess I'm overwhelmed with relief that he's all right."

We dropped the subject then, but I noticed Lily and Flynn exchange a glance that told me more was going on than met the eye.

After breakfast, I planned to do some writing in the garden, so I hurried up to my room to get my writing pad and pencil. I found Prudence waiting for me, sitting on my bed, when I opened the door. She rose and was at my side in a moment, draping her arms around my neck.

"Alone at last," she whispered into my ear, and kissed me, forcefully and hard. I pushed her away.

"Prudence," I started, fishing my handkerchief out of my pocket and wiping my mouth with it. "This is hardly appropriate."

She laughed and moved closer, backing me against the wall. "I couldn't care less about that." She smiled. "I know how you feel about me, Michael. We have a connection. I'm wondering what you'd like to do about that."

"I-I'm sorry," I stammered. "But—"

"Don't be silly," she said. "You must realize that if you marry me, all of this will be yours."

"Listen to me, Prudence," I said to her. "I'm flattered by your attention, I truly am. You're a wonderful girl and any man would be lucky to have you. But my heart belongs to another. I think you know that."

She batted her eyelashes at me. "We'll see," she said, kissing my cheek. And then she took her leave of me, closing the door behind her.

Later, I happened to walk into the garden where Flynn and Lily were talking in low tones, their heads together.

"Oh!" Flynn said a little too loudly. "Mickey boy! I didn't see you there."

Lily's eyes were brimming with tears. She tried to brush them away with her sleeve, but I took her hand in mine.

"This is the second time I've seen you crying today," I said to her, glancing at Flynn. "Something's going on. Please take me into your confidence, both of you. Maybe I can help."

Flynn sighed. "It's Pru," he said, turning Lily. "I think he should know." She nodded quickly in response. "She hasn't been herself for days."

"I noticed at breakfast she was rather snappish," I offered. "Is that what you mean?"

"That and more," Lily said. "It's as though she has developed a kind of hatred for us, all of us, over-night."

"I had an unusual encounter with her earlier," I confessed, but I wasn't about to let on what it was.

I locked eyes with Flynn, and I could tell we were both thinking the same thing. This had something to do with the girl in white. Just then, I heard giggling from behind us, and we turned to find Prudence there, holding a croquet mallet and smiling.

"Anyone up for a game?" she asked, slowly swinging the mallet. "I'm dying to have some fun."

"A little bedtime reading?" It was Matthew, poking his head around the door. "I couldn't sleep and was about to head downstairs to get something to read when I saw the light under your door."

"I couldn't sleep, either." I smiled.

He eyed the manuscript in my lap. "You're looking for answers."

I shrugged my shoulders. "Guilty as charged. What Carter said earlier was really nagging at me. 'Something much, much worse.' I couldn't sleep until I knew what it was."

"Did you find what you were looking for?" he asked, yawning and running a hand through his hair. He looked exhausted.

I put the manuscript down and kissed his cheek. "You bet I did." I turned off the light and led him back into his bedroom. The answers to this mystery could wait.

CHAPTER 40

The next week went by in a blur. Jane came home from the hospital, moving more slowly than I'd ever seen her move, but on the mend and doing fine, her husband hovering around her like a mother bear. I had to wrestle her apron from her hands more than once and tell her in no uncertain terms that Amity and I were going to be waiting on her for the next few weeks until she was fully back on her feet, and finally, she grudgingly accepted our help.

After talking it over with Amity, we agreed to put the house on Whidbey up for sale and move back to Alban House permanently. We'd travel back there later in the summer to box up our things and let a realtor deal with the rest. I think Heather's friendship sealed the deal for my daughter, and for that, I was grateful, even though Matthew's description rang in my ears— the girl from down the lane and the girl from the manor house. It sounded chillingly like my mother and Fate, and that's one bit of history I didn't want to repeat.

The decision to stay in town led me to call the university and make an appointment to start preparations for the David Coleville Retreat for Writers and Artists. If we hurried with a call for applications, we could have the retreat up and running by the following June. It felt like the right thing to do, fulfilling my mother's vision. I knew she'd be happy about it, and likely was. But there was one more stone I needed to turn, one more piece of the puzzle I needed to solve, before I could dive into that project headfirst.

And that was how I came to be sitting at the patio table one balmy July evening with Jane, Mr. Jameson, Carter, and Matthew. Amity had helped me prepare dinner for everyone— chicken on the grill; red potatoes roasted with rosemary and onions; a crisp salad with goat cheese and balsamic vinaigrette dressing; and warm French bread, right out of the oven. But then I sent her out for a pizza with Heather. My daughter had heard about and seen enough of Mercy for several lifetimes.

When Heather's parents had pulled out of the driveway with Amity waving to us from the backseat, I filled everyone's wineglasses and cleared my throat.

"This dinner is to thank all of you for your service to my family over the years and to celebrate your continued service now that I'm coming back to live at Alban House," I said, raising my glass and nodding to Jane, Mr. Jameson, and Carter. "You have helped this family through both everyday life and unimaginable trials. One thing from you, among many, that we've always counted on is your discretion. And that's not going to change. Except for tonight."

I saw Jane eye her husband, and he squeezed her hand. "Before I go ahead with the retreat, I need to know what happened here at Alban House the night David Coleville died. If we're going to be honoring this man's memory, I want to do him the justice of at least knowing how he died. I think all of you know more than you're saying." I looked from each person to the next. "Now is the time to tell this story, just as my mother was going to do on the day she died."

I thought about Harris, and part of me wished he were here with us tonight, but I didn't quite know how to explain the Mercy part of the puzzle to him. My daughter and I had fought this monstrous woman for our lives, and I wasn't about to tell him the full extent of what had happened. He might be family, but he was still a stranger who had stirred up all of this, and he was going to speak to my mother the day she died. I still didn't completely trust him.

"Carter," I went on, "something you said the other night stuck with me. You said that despite all the strange and terrible things Mercy did as a child, there was something even worse that you hadn't told us. You said it happened the summer before Coleville died. That's when Mercy burst into the room, laughing and agreeing with you. She said it was all in the manuscript and asked if I'd read it. Now I have, and I've got a theory about what the 'something much, much worse' might be. But I'd like to hear from you all, who were here at the time, before I tell you what I think it is."

Turning to Jane and her husband, Carter nodded and cleared his throat. "She's right," he said to them. "It's time this comes out. We've lived with it for far too long. Frankly, I just don't want to carry the burden of it anymore."

Jane locked eyes with me. In them, I saw resignation mixed with loyalty. "All right," she said, her voice wavering. "Your mother was indeed going to speak of this to the journalist the day she died. As a way of honoring her memory, I'll speak of it now."

A sip of wine cooled my throat as I slipped my hand into Matthew's and settled back to hear Jane's tale. With the candles flickering, the lake lapping softly on the shoreline, and the sunset bathing the patio in a purplish hue, she began.

"It was the first year the writer was here," she said. "I had initially been afraid to have someone outside of the family come and stay for the whole summer, but Charity convinced me that young Adele was here often enough and none the wiser about Mercy. I had been worried that a writer's imagination would be sparked, that he'd discover her, but as it turned out, he was much too interested in Adele to see anything beyond her beauty and charm." Jane chuckled, remembering. "We could have been hiding an elephant between the walls and he wouldn't have noticed."

I stole a glance at Matthew—we both knew that wasn't quite the case. His imagination had indeed been sparked by what he saw and heard at Alban House that summer.

"But midway through the season . . ." Jane hesitated and twisted the napkin in her lap.

"Go on, dear," Mr. Jameson said to her. "It all right now. She's full and truly dead and gone."

"She went missing," Jane said finally. "Mercy. It was Charity who discovered her gone. She rallied the staff and called her husband and children in, too, and told us what she knew—Mercy was gone."

She closed her eyes for a moment before continuing. "Remember, now, the world outside of this household thought Mercy was dead and had been for years. And we had the writer in our midst, so your grandfather couldn't call the police or conduct a massive search. We had to pretend like nothing was wrong. But he had people, shall we say. And those people searched for Mercy for the rest of the summer—the house, the grounds, the lake, even the town. They checked the airline's logs, train logs. But they turned up nothing.

"We all believed—the family and all the staff—that Mercy had fled her confinement, so to speak; that she tired of living like a prisoner here in Alban House and decided to strike out on her own. Until—"

She shot a look at her husband. Taking a sip of the whiskey I had poured for him, he finished her thought. "Until I discovered the bones."

Matthew put an arm around my shoulder as we waited for Mr. Jameson to go on. "It was during the late spring of the next year, once the ground had thawed. I was digging up a new section of earth near the cemetery—Mrs. Charity had wanted a garden planted there to honor the Alban dead—when I came upon the skeleton. Someone had dug a shallow grave and covered it with not only dirt but driftwood and other debris."

He dabbed at his eyes with his napkin. "Of course, the body was completely decomposed. Mercy had gone missing almost a year before. But the white dress she wore was still intact. There was no doubting who it was."

Jane put a hand on her husband's shoulder and took up where he left off. "Mrs. Charity was inconsolable, as you might imagine. But in a way, deep down, I think she was also relieved. Mr. Alban certainly was. The staff definitely was. Mercy was gone, that evil was gone from our household. We didn't ask any questions about who might have put her into that grave—I always suspected Mr. Alban but I never said a word about it. We had a private family funeral, laid the bones to rest in the crypt, and were just glad that the horrible time in this family's history was over.

"By that time, Mrs. Charity had learned her lesson about black magic, and there was no talk of a repeat performance of what had happened ten years prior," Jane went on. "I never heard her ever speak of witchcraft again. It was over. And finally, thankfully, everything returned to normal in this household. But as you know, that wasn't the end of it."

Jane swallowed hard and went on. "You can't blame us for not seeing it. We wanted so to believe that the evil had gone, we wanted so to go back to the way things used to be."

"What didn't you see, Jane?" Matthew asked, giving me a look. "I'm not following."

"You didn't read the rest of the manuscript with me," I jumped in. "I think I know. Coleville saw it, too, the first summer he was here. It wasn't Mercy in that grave." I turned to Jane. "Isn't that right?"

Jane's face went ashen. "I had a hunch. But when the doctor told us Mercy Alban had been in his facility for the past fifty years, I put two and two together," she said, nodding. "But that's the first time."

"Coleville was writing about what really went on here at Alban House that summer, and he described how worried everyone was about 'Prudence's' behavior," I explained. Turning to Jane, I went on, "Coleville changed the names of the family, but his cast of characters was clearly my dad, Fate, my mother, himself, and my grandparents. He wrote about how Fate—Prudence, he calls her in the book—suddenly didn't seem herself. Her actions were strange and unlike her."

I paused to catch my breath a moment. "I think that's because it wasn't her. I think Mercy killed Fate and took her place because she was tired of being shuttered up on the third floor. She had been watching everyone for so long and wanted to join in. So she did. That's the 'something much, much worse' you were talking about that night, Carter, isn't it?"

Everyone stared at me. Nobody spoke. Finally, Carter said: "That's exactly the conclusion I came to, my dear, when I learned it was Mercy who had come back to us and not her sister." He sighed. "You must understand. Back then, we wanted to believe all was well. We took it on face value and didn't question anything. But your writer was absolutely right about Fate's behavior. It was off, strange, unlike her. All the staff remarked on it and whispered about it. But we came to the conclusion that it was the result of losing her sister, that was the reason she wasn't quite herself."

"In the manuscript, Coleville talks about losing four days after having an encounter with the girl in white on the lakeshore," I prodded. "When he came out of it, that's when he noticed 'Prudence's' behavior as being different. Did that really happen? Was he down with a fever?"

Jane nodded. "That he was. But I noticed . . ." She looked at her husband, who reached over and patted her hand.

"It's all right, dear," he said. "It's time the truth came out."

"What did you notice, Jane?" I asked her.

"Down on the lakeshore," she said, shaking her head and shuddering. "One night, the night before he went down with a fever, he was dancing and chanting around the fire ring with a girl who I presumed was Fate. Wild, they were. It seemed evil and wrong, what they were doing. I can't explain why, but it made me afraid, watching them. I closed my window and pulled the drapes shut. But later on . . ."

My stomach tightened into a knot. "What happened then?"

"Later on, I looked again. I had a ghastly feeling that it was Mercy out there, not her sister. I wanted to make sure. The fire was out, there was no more dancing, but I could have sworn I saw someone in the garden. I was just a girl myself, so I didn't say anything to anybody. And then when Mercy went missing the next day, I felt that was the end of it. We could rest easy."

"And you didn't check on Mercy that night?" I asked.

Jane shook her head. "That was not my place. It was Mrs. Charity who took care of Mercy."

I shivered, deep inside, as I looked from Jane to Carter to Mr. Jameson. "Do you think that Mercy had Coleville under some sort of, I don't know, spell or something, and together they killed Fate?"

Jane returned my gaze, and I saw her squeeze her husband's hand. She nodded, almost imperceptibly. "Aye," she whispered. "I think we finally know the truth. Considering all that has gone on within the past few weeks, I think that's exactly what happened."

After a moment, I continued. "And the next summer?" I asked, looking at Jane.

"Mr. Coleville was coming back to marry Adele, that was no secret," Jane began. "As I've already told you, Adele and Charity were buzzing for months about it. Miss Fate, though, she didn't really join in. She was not a part of this happiness. In fact, she was not a part of much of anything during that time. We on the staff suspected she might be in love with Mr. Coleville herself."

"If the manuscript is any indication, she certainly was," I said.

"He arrived shortly before the summer solstice party," Jane said, "and apparently it all came to a head that night, although, as I have told you, I was up in the house helping my mother, so I did not see the turn of events. What I'm fairly sure of, however, is that his death was not a suicide."

Carter cleared his throat. "It wasn't. I saw the whole thing from the carriage house."

I stared at him. "You witnessed what happened?"

"I did, indeed," he said, dabbing at his brow. "I saw Mr. Coleville and your mother sitting on the bench in the garden. They were kissing and cooing, like any couple would be on the eve of their wedding, when she appeared. Miss Fate—although we all know that it wasn't Fate at all. It was Mercy. She was shouting and yelling and shoved Adele away from Coleville, and that's when I saw the gun in her hand. She aimed it at your mother and fired, as quickly as that, but Coleville had moved between them. He took the bullet for her and fell. It all happened in an instant. Your mother began screaming and dropped to the ground, and Mercy aimed again at her, and I opened my door and ran toward them both, but that's when Johnny and Mr. Alban wrestled Mercy to the ground and got the gun out of her hand.

"Things happened very quickly after that," he continued. "I saw Mr. Alban hurrying his daughter out of there, through the gardens, and into the tunnels that lead to the house. I never saw her again until she showed up the day of your mother's funeral. Johnny and I led your mother into the carriage house—she was completely distraught—and he stayed with her there all night long. Never left her side. He loved her, even then."

Jane nodded. "That was our Johnny," she said, smiling at me. "About that time, I was instructed to usher everyone else out of the house. The party was over and it was time to go. Only when everyone was gone did your grandfather call the police and tell them about the suicide. That was the official line, and that's what we were told to believe.

"And that night, straightaway, your grandfather left Alban House with his daughter," she said.

And that was it. The mystery of David Coleville's death solved. He died saving my mother and his unborn child. Now, perhaps, both of them could rest in peace.

WE FINISHED OUR DINNER and lingered over dessert and coffee, and were talking of the past, when Harris Peters walked up onto the patio, carrying a bouquet of flowers.

"Hello, everyone," he said, smiling shyly. "I hope I'm not interrupting anything."

I held my hands out for the flowers but he passed me by and instead handed them to Jane. "I do hope you're feeling better, Mrs. Jameson."

"That I am, lad." She smiled up at him. "That I am."

Matthew looked just as confused as I felt. Something was clearly going on between Jane and Harris, but I had no idea what it was.

She took a long sniff of the flowers. "The lad came to visit me in hospital."

"We had quite a nice chat," Harris said as he pulled out a chair and sank into it.

"Okay," I said. "Now you've both lost me."

"It has to do with what we were talking about the other night at the bar," Harris began. "I gather from Jane that it's all true."

I scowled at her. "Can you shed some light on this?"

"You were wondering about why your mother and father

would've gotten married so quickly after David Coleville's death," Jane began. "You suspected correctly. She was with child. She and your father had been thick as thieves all their lives, he in love with her all the while, so they married. But your mother—she wasn't at all herself. She was in a deep depression and had been since the moment Coleville took his last breath. We have medications for that now, but back then there was nothing anyone could do. And when the baby was born, it became even worse. She didn't get out of bed for weeks, she wouldn't look at the baby, and, worse, she would not even acknowledge there was a baby. She insisted he didn't exist."

"Postpartum depression?" I offered.

"Aye, that, combined with losing the love of her life. She was not coping, not at all. The doctor had her sedated for much of the time." She smiled sadly at Harris. "It wasn't your fault, lad. She was out of her mind."

He nodded and held my gaze. The expression on his face was heartbreaking—a wistfulness for what might have been and a sadness for what was.

"And that's what led your father and his father to make the decision," Jane went on. "We put the baby up for adoption. Your mother truly didn't seem to realize a baby had been born and was now gone."

"And the payments?" I asked.

"After some months of tender, loving care from your father and a team of doctors, she finally came back to herself. When she realized what had happened, she was frantic," Jane went on, turning to Harris. "She was desperate to get you back. But the adoption was sealed. We had no way of knowing where you were or whether you were even still in the state. But, as I said,

Mr. Alban had people, and by that time, Johnny had people, and he helped your mother look for you. It took six years, but we finally found you. Right here in the same town."

Jane put a tissue to her eyes and turned to me. "She couldn't imagine the cruelty of taking him away from the only home he had ever known. It's not like he was a baby. He was a six-year-old who loved his parents more than anything. We were strangers to him. It well and truly broke her heart, but Adele couldn't rip him from his adoptive mother's arms. She loved him too much to do that to the child."

She put a hand on Harris's shoulder. "So a representative of the Alban family met with your parents, explained the situation, and let them know an envelope would be arriving in the mail once each month. They never told your parents who the benefactor was. And that was that."

A tear trickled down Harris's cheek. "And that was that."

Jane turned to me. "Your mother grieved for years, for the man she had lost and the child she had lost. But time has a way of easing those burdens, as much as they can be. Several years passed, your mother and father grew closer and closer, and soon you came along. And then the twins. It ws a time of such happiness here at Alban House."

"And, you told him all of this in the hospital, Jane?" I asked.

"Aye," She nodded. "As soon as I took one look at him at the reception after the funeral, I knew who he was. He is the spitting image of his father."

"But you didn't say anything," I said.

"I wasn't sure what to do," Jane admitted. "Things were happening so fast, and he was so angry at the reception."

"When he called here to make an appointment to see my—our—mother, didn't you know then?" I asked Jane.

She shook her head. "I never knew the lad's name. Remember, I was just the housekeeper. I didn't get all the details." She turned to Harris. "But, of course, your mother knew your name when I told her you had been calling. She didn't let on to me, but I think that's why she agreed to meet with you. She felt the time had come."

Harris's lower lip was trembling, and I could tell he was holding back the floodgates. I moved to him and threw my arms around him, and we wept together, for the mother he never knew and the mother I'd never forget.

When we had both dried our eyes, I took him by the hand, nodding to Matthew to follow us. "Come on, Harris," I said. "We've got something of your father's for you."

CHAPTER 41

Six Months Later
Alban House

Lights twinkled on the ten-foot-tall Christmas tree that stood in the parlor, filled to the brim with my family's ornaments, some from many generations before, others from my own childhood, and still others accumulated by Amity and me over the years. She, Matthew, and I had decorated the tree together, Christmas music softly playing, spiced eggnog in a tureen on the sideboard, a fire blazing in the fireplace. I couldn't remember a time when I was so deliriously happy.

After Amity had gone to bed, Matthew and I sat together on the sofa in the darkened room, watching the fire.

"It came today." He smiled at me. "I was waiting until now to show it to you." He opened the drawer on the end table, pulled out a small hardcover book, and handed it to me.

THE HAUNTING OF WHITEHALL MANOR

David Coleville

Foreword by Harris Peters

Months earlier, Harris and I had held a press conference at Alban House to announce the creation of the David Coleville Retreat for Artists and Writers, which we planned to run together. We also announced the discovery of a lost manuscript by Coleville himself.

It caused as much of a furor as we thought it would—the literary world was knocked on its collective ear and produced expert upon expert who examined the manuscript and concluded that it was indeed written by Coleville.

What would become of the manuscript itself remained to be seen. If we sold it at auction, it could bring millions of dollars. But I was leaving that up to Harris, and he seemed to want to keep something of his father's all to himself, for the moment at least. I also left it up to him to tell the world, or not, about his parentage. Although it involved my family, this was really his business, not mine. He chose to keep that to himself as well, for the time being.

I opened the book for the first time. "In the foreword, Harris tells the world the truth about Coleville's death," I said to Matthew, my eyes scanning the page.

"Do you still feel okay about that?" he asked, putting an arm around my shoulders.

"I do," I said. "The man died saving my mother. If he hadn't given his life for her, I wouldn't be here right now."

"I knew I liked the guy for some reason."

I opened the book to the first chapter, marveling at the look of the words on the printed page.

"You know, we never did go back and read this entire story," I said. "We always said we'd find some time to read it from beginning to end and learn how they fell in love."

"That's right," Matthew said, leaning back and setting his feet on the ottoman.

"What do you say, Reverend?" I grinned at him. "In the mood for a good ghost story?"

"Why not?"

So with snow falling, the tree lights twinkling, and the spirits of my family swirling around us, I took a deep breath and began to read.

Amity curled up on her bed, holding the volume in her hands, a large book with an embossed leather cover, its pages brittle and yellowed. She kept it hidden in her suitcase, not wanting her mother to know about it. Not yet.

Amity supposed that was because she knew she had gone against her mother's wishes when she found it and couldn't quite find the words to tell her how it had all occurred. She had discovered the book because she couldn't keep a secret as good as the existence of secret passageways from Heather. She just *had* to tell her. So one day, while her mother was off with Reverend Parker—she was *always* with Reverend Parker—Amity swore her friend to secrecy, popped open the panel door in her room, and led Heather into the darkness.

They didn't get far. There it was, sitting just inside the passageways, in front of her door. Amity couldn't believe she hadn't seen it before, but it was there now, plain as day.

"What's that?" Heather had asked.

Amity squinted at the book. "I have no idea." She bent down and picked it up, and as soon as she touched its leather surface, a trickle of electricity ran through her hands. "Whoa," she said, locking eyes with her friend. "This is weird."

She and Heather abandoned their expedition in the passageways and went back into the light of Amity's room and sat down on the bed, the book open between them. Amity carefully turned page after yellowing page to find strangely scrawled words in a language she didn't understand among illustrations of herbs and weeds and plants and powders. They saw pentagrams and candles and rings and other strange-looking symbols they didn't recognize.

The girls didn't know it then, but as they looked through the book, something strange and monstrous seeped out, rising from the pages just as it was intended to rise, just as it had risen time and time before. It swirled around the girls and nestled into their hair and their eyes and their noses, a faintly smoky scent of lavender and lilac and grass and fire. And soon, before they even realized what was happening, the symbols on the page transformed into something they knew, something familiar.

And that was how Amity and her friend began to read the spell book her great-great-grandmother had written in the old country, all those years ago.

SHE SAT ON HER BED, running her fingers along the book's embossed cover. As she did so, a strange little tune tinkled through her head. Amity knew she had heard it somewhere before but couldn't think where.

"*The witch in the wood comes out to play,*" she sang to herself.

At this, she could have sworn she heard a loud sigh coming from inside her room, all around her, as though the walls themselves were exhaling.

ACKNOWLEDGMENTS

One of the things I love best about writing is the surprise fac-
tor, when something occurs to me out of the blue while I'm
tapping away at the keyboard. It happened several times during
the writing of this book, including when I was crafting the scene
in which Grace is sitting in the library on a rainy day trying to
think of a way to coax her daughter into spending some time
with her. The idea of passageways hadn't even entered my mind
before that chapter, and it just came to me, as though Grace herself had whispered it into my ear. Later that evening, I was at
dinner with some friends who asked about how my next book
was coming along. "I think the house has secret passageways," I
told them. Their delighted reactions made me want to hurry
home to find out exactly where those passageways led and what
was lurking inside of them.

So, first of all, I thank my friends and my family for being
interested enough to ask about what I'm writing and for inspir-
ing me to come up with twists and turns I hadn't seen coming.
And speaking of friends and family, I owe a big debt of gratitude
to Janet Lyso and her daughter and son-in-law, Melinda and
Paul Smithson. After I had settled on the character of Matthew
being a Lutheran minister, I realized that I had no idea how a
minister might react when confronted with all of the strange
and otherworldly things that were swirling around Alban

House. Paul (a former man of the cloth himself), Jan, and Melinda gave me some excellent insights that really helped in the development of Matthew's character. To any Lutherans out there who take issue with something Matthew says or does when confronted with the supernatural: These are my mistakes, not theirs, and are certainly unintentional.

Thank you to all of the readers who came to see me at speaking engagements, invited me to attend their book clubs, or simply wrote to tell me how much they enjoyed my first book, *The Tale of Halcyon Crane.* It truly was awe-inspiring for a first-time author to show up at a bookstore, library, or book club to find the room filled to the brim with people, all with copies of my book in their laps. I'm grateful beyond measure and I hope to see you all again this year.

An enormous thank-you to all of the bookstore owners, booksellers, librarians, and readers, including the Midwest Booksellers Association, the Independent Booksellers Association of America, the Great Lakes Booksellers Association, and the Friends of the St. Paul Public Library for supporting and promoting my work. It means the world to me.

To all the authors I've met during the past two years, especially my colleagues from Minnesota, thank you for being so warm and welcoming to the new girl on the block. I'm honored by your friendship.

As always, my never-ending gratitude goes to my friend and agent, Jennifer Weltz, for helping me work out sticky plot points, for making me laugh during every conversation, and for being my most ardent champion. I don't know where I'd be without you but it certainly wouldn't be where I am, living my lifelong dream. Thanks, too, to everyone at the Jean Naggar Literary

Agency—you all are completely delightful to work with and I wish I lived closer to the city so I could take you out for cocktails. Repeatedly.

To my fantastic editor Elisabeth Dyssegaard—I am thrilled beyond measure to be working with you. Thank you for loving the story of the Albans as much as I do. Your masterful editing made the tale so much better told. Speaking of editing, thank you to the copy editors at Hyperion. I'm sure if you never see another ellipsis followed by "My words trailed off," it will be too soon.

To my son, Ben, thank you for making me the proudest mother on the planet because of the achingly fine young man you have become.

And finally, to Steve. Without your support and love, none of this would be possible. It means everything . . . of course it does!

When Grace Alban returns home after twenty years because her mother has died unexpectedly, she expects her visit to be fraught with sadness, some guilt, and a resurgence of memories from a childhood spent within the vast, ornate, and imposing family home.

What she doesn't expect, and yet finds, is a complex family mystery that undermines everything she knew to be true about her famous and eccentric family—a mystery that includes secrets, conspiracy, the occult, and murder. Her discovery not only threatens the way she remembers her mother, father, and grandparents, it threatens the very lives of Grace and her teenage daughter, Amity. Someone—or something—is moving within the walls of the old family home, through the secret passageways Grace used to play in as a child. That someone or something is watching them, and it doesn't like what it sees.

As Grace attempts to piece together a new version of her family's history with the assistance of her handsome clergyman neighbor, and reconcile each piece of new information with what she grew up believing, she's forced, too, to protect her home and loved ones from whatever evil lurks within the walls of the estate—be it friend, foe, or even, most surprisingly, family.

DISCUSSION QUESTIONS

1. When you were reading the novel, how many times did you think you'd "figured it out," but then have to change or qualify your assumptions about the Alban family mystery? Who did you originally think killed (or scared to death) Adele? Who did you suspect killed David Coleville? How many times did you have to change your opinion, and what were some of the early conclusions you came to about the characters and the plot of the novel?

2. Discuss Grace's relationship with her daughter, Amity. In what ways does it elude the "mom versus teenage daughter" stereotype?

Does it change, strengthen, or weaken during the course of the novel? What kind of insight does their relationship offer us? (Also, compare Grace's relationship with Amity to her relationship with her own mother, Adele.)

3. Grace comes from a family of prestige and privilege and money— discuss why she is nonetheless a sympathetic character in the novel and worthy of our sympathy. Note the particular difficulties or struggles in her life: the boating accident with her brothers, her father's suicide, her divorce, her growing alienation from her daughter. How do these plot points make her a character worthy of our attention and affection? Did any aspect of her character surprise you?

4. On a related note, is there any part of Mercy's storyline that makes us feel some sympathy for her—even though she is guilty of murdering at least three people by the book's end, one of whom is her own sister, and has a cunning, cold, and deliberately cruel persona? What, if anything about her personal history (i.e., being sequestered to the hospital in Switzerland) may have earned her some pity? Is she a less dynamic character because of her evil nature? Does this work well within the book, or would you have liked to have seen her good side (if there was one) at least once in the story?

5. How much did the setting of the novel contribute to the tone and suspense of the book? To this end, discuss the secret passageways in the house, the nearby lake, and the third floor where no one feels comfortable residing, and the ways in which these settings helped establish a mood and/or create suspense in the novel.

6. Consider Grace and Matthew's burgeoning romance throughout the novel, and discuss its function within the mystery story. Did it provide a welcome distraction or break from the drama of the mystery? Did it serve to help you understand any aspect of Grace's character? Was there any significance, in terms of symbolism or plot development, to Matthew's occupation (that of a clergyman)?

7. Similarly, discuss the significance, if any, of the names of the women in the Alban family: Grace, Amity (which means friendship or harmony), Mercy, Fate, and Charity. What kind of irony exists within the book because of these names? Are the names symbolic? What additional meaning or insight do the names of the women bring to the novel and its characters?

8. Did you like the way that Wendy Webb wrote and included entire chapters from David Coleville's lost, last novel? Did you like the parallel story? What did it add in terms of plot development and the tone of the novel? Discuss the ways in which those passages could have been used to a greater or lesser extent—and what they could have revealed to the reader that the original storyline, narrated by Grace, could not.

9. Most of the mysteries in the novel become reconciled or are explained by the end of the book, but others—Mercy's "reanimation" by her mother and grandmother, or Johnny's ghostly visit to Grace and Amity, for instance—are not explained as easily. Discuss how appealing you find this particular kind of novel—one that mixes the more realistic and gritty mystery novel with the gothic and supernatural romance. What does the novel gain by employing the elements of two different genres? What, if anything, does it lose?

10. By the end of the novel, Grace discovers that Jane and her husband, Mr. Jameson, as well as the chauffeur, Carter, all knew more about the day David Coleville died (and the Alban family) than they'd admitted to previously. Discuss your reaction when you read their confessions to Grace in Chapter 40, and in particular to Jane's confirmation that Harris was Adele and David's child. Was the ending of the book satisfying, or did it feel too neat? In the mystery novels you read, do you prefer to know everything by the story's end, or do you like to have a few unanswered questions remaining?

Q: The epilogue to *The Fate of Mercy Alban* suggests that the Alban family is not entirely safe and/or finally at peace. Do you intend to write a sequel to this book that focuses on Amity and her discovery of her great-great-grandmother's book of spells? As this is your second novel, have you considered publishing novels within a series? What do you like (or not like) about the idea of writing a sequence of related or interconnected mystery novels?

A: So far, I've written standalone novels, but they all follow the same basic themes. Family secrets and mysteries, a touch of the paranormal—ghosts floating around every corner or witches perched on the family tree; a big, spooky house where lots of skeletons lurk; a strong heroine who is plunged into a life-altering mystery; and a great guy who supports her as she navigates it all. So whether I write a sequel or a standalone, it will follow those themes.

Q: Before you began publishing novels you spent many years as a journalist in the Twin Cities of Minneapolis–Saint Paul. What did the profession of journalism teach you about writing and research that has been useful to you as an author of fiction?

A: Mainly, the discipline of the craft. I'm still a journalist when I'm not writing novels, and that means I write every day of my life. I've heard some authors say how difficult the writing process is, but for me, I've been writing every day for twenty-plus years, so it comes as naturally to me as breathing. That's the upside. The downside is that writing a magazine article is very different from writing novel. As a journalist, you tell a story. This happened, then this, then that, and, ultimately, this. As a novelist, you must show it. You can't simply say *Grace is angry*; you must show the reader she's angry. It took a long time for me to learn how to do that because I'd been a journalist for so long.

Q: Who are your own favorite authors, writers of mystery and otherwise? What have you learned about writing from reading other novels? Who do you read for inspiration?

A: I have lots of favorite authors. I love M. J. Rose, Stephanie Pintoff, Katherine Howe, Sarah Waters, S. J. Bolton, Steve Berry, Dan Brown. My favorite mystery series is by Louise Penny, who writes the Armand Gamache novels set in a small town in Quebec.

Q: Do you see yourself continuing to write mystery novels, or do you think you'll attempt a different genre? What do you find appealing about the *act* of writing a mystery novel? In what ways is it rewarding, and in what ways is it frustrating?

A: A very wise woman—my agent—once told me to think long and hard about the type of books I wanted to write, because if the first one was a success, I could be writing in the same genre for my whole career. I did think about it quite a lot, because I read and love all types of novels—whodunits, police crime stories, thrillers, women's fiction, historicals, young adult fantasy—but I settled on gothic suspense because that's where my real passion lies. And now that I have two successful novels under my belt, I feel I owe it to my readers to give them what they expect when they purchase one of my books. As a reader, I'd be very disappointed to pick up a new book by Jodi Picoult and find that it's a bodice-ripping romance, or dive into a new Fanny Flagg and find that it's horror. I never want to disappoint a reader. Not that novelists have to remain forever shackled to the genre of their first book, but personally, I just don't want to stray too terribly far away. That said, I'd love to write a series mystery someday about a small town and the strange and eerie things that go on there, so we'll see what the future brings.

Q: Are you working on a new novel? What is it about? When should we expect to see it in bookstores?

A: I am indeed! It's the story of a woman who takes a job as a companion for a mysterious and rather eccentric novelist whom the entire world thinks is dead, set at Havenwood, an enormous, ancient mansion in the middle of the wilderness. As our heroine delves into the mystery of why this novelist dropped out of sight and stopped writing, she finds strange and unsettling connections to her own family tree and wonders why she was really brought to Havenwood. It should come out next year. Stay tuned!
